GIRL BETRAYED

DANA GRAY FBI MYSTERY THRILLER
BOOK FOUR

C. J. CROSS

LIQUID MIND PUBLISHING

Liquid Mind Publishing
This is a work of fiction. All characters, names, places and events are the product of the author's imagination or used fictitiously.

ALSO BY C. J. CROSS

DANA GRAY MYSTERIES

Girl Left Behind

Girl on the Hill

Girl in the Grave

Girl Betrayed

Stay up to date with C.J. Cross's new releases and download her **free** Dana Gray Prequel, *Girl Awakened* by heading to the link:

PROLOGUE

IT'S FINALLY HAPPENING. I'VE WAITED SO LONG. ALL THE PLANNING, THE agony, the longing. It will be worth it. I can taste the sweet freedom just beyond my reach. It will be so liberating.

I've locked up this desire, this loss, for far too long. I tried to fight it. It's no use. I must do it.

It's the only way to make it stop.

I feel like an imposter in this skin. I've stretched it too far already. It hurts. It hurts all the time.

It will hurt until I make the hurt stop.

I pull up my hood. Let this black shroud be my armor. It's a poor substitute for a disguise but it will do. Disguising my identity is easy when my identity is a disguise. But soon I can shed this skin. Soon I can be myself.

Soon it will stop.

My victim walks toward me. He approaches with a smile. He shouldn't trust me, but he does. They always do. There's no time left. I grip the hilt of my blade, let the old steel calm me. It's time to end this madness.

Time to make it stop.

1

THE SUN-BLEACHED DOLLAR BILLS BILLOWED LIKE BOAT FLAGS IN THE humid breeze generated by the clusters of rusted fans. Dust clung to them like a second skin, dulling the metallic buzz until it was absorbed by the daily sounds of the busy marina. Sail lines clanked, buoys squeaked, seabirds squawked.

It was a soundtrack that normally soothed Jake Shepard, but he found his gaze restless. He systematically scanned the beach-clad patrons seeking shelter from the blazing Florida sun under the colorful umbrellas and sagging sun sails.

The crunch of pebbles beneath their feet as they stomped out a rhythm to the one-man band crooning Southern blues on stage was unnerving. It shouldn't be. Schooner's Wharf was the one place Jake could escape it all. Where he could blend into the leather-skinned locals crowding the old Key West dive bar.

It was easy to disappear among the clutter.

Stickers, coasters, and patches from every branch of military and police were stapled into the hurricane petrified wood.

Here you were everyone and no one.

Here Jake could pretend he didn't live his life looking over his shoulder.

At least that's how it'd been every other time he'd visited.

But something was off this time.

The creak of a saloon door had him looking toward the restrooms. That's when he saw her walking toward him, her dark hair unbound, sun-kissed freckles dappling her cheeks: Dana Gray.

Her grin widened as she walked in his direction. As usual, the mere sight of her distracted him to the point of carelessness. And that was when she was in her usual stuffy librarian attire.

Here, in a red bikini and white sundress that left little to the imagination, Dana was a vision. One that demanded all of his attention. So much so that the flash of gun metal surprised him.

It was almost indecipherable among the dull propellers and aged bronze ship paraphernalia. But Jake had been trained to spot it. Though this time, the loud echo of gunfire told him he was too late.

JAKE WOKE WITH A START, his hand automatically reaching out for Dana even though he knew she wouldn't be there. It didn't escape him that it was his own damn fault he was waking up from another nightmare alone.

Wiping the sweat from his forehead, he sat up letting the regret settle over him as he absorbed the scene around him. Another day in his cramped childhood bedroom.

Another day waking from the same dream-turned-nightmare.

Another day without Dana.

Jake exhaled heavily as he replayed his last conversation with Dana over again.

"Jake, I'll come with you."

"I appreciate the offer, Dana, but I can take care of this myself."

"I know you can, but I'm offering to be there anyway."

"It's not the right time, besides, you need to be here for Claire."

"We have plenty of time before Claire needs us. This is important, Jake. It's your family."

He knew precisely how highly Dana regarded family which was exactly why he didn't want her here. When he'd responded, he'd purposely let the frustration creep into his voice, so she'd know he was done negotiating. *"Dana, it's not the right time."*

He was beginning to wonder if it ever would be.

After their graveside kiss it seemed they'd finally gotten their timing right. So right in fact they'd ended up at his place, stripping each other bare as they pinballed down his hallway like a couple of horny teens. But their passion had been swiftly interrupted by a phone call from Wade.

Jake couldn't help wondering what would've happened if he hadn't answered. If they'd spent the night together, would he have truly let Dana in? Would she be here with him now, sitting beside him on the stars and stripes sheets still adorning his childhood bed? Or better yet, would he have made good on his promise to take her to the Keys, where they could be sitting at Schooner's, sipping cold beer between salty kisses?

The nightmare he kept waking from told him he'd made the right call. If life had taught Jake Shepard one thing, it was that a world where he got what he wanted didn't exist. Bringing Dana here would only have accelerated the end of something that might never be, no matter how much he wanted it.

2

DANA WAS JOLTED UPRIGHT BY THE RINGING OF HER PHONE. SHE TRIED to quell her disappointment when it wasn't Jake's number on the screen. Just another weather alert warning of freezing rain. Spring in D.C. was never dull.

She silenced the alert, but her distress over Jake was still loud and clear. He'd promised to call her when he'd left for the airport but that was almost a week ago.

Carefully, Dana closed the delicate pages of the mid-fifteenth century Venetian vampirism manuscript she'd been deciphering. She removed her white gloves and cringed at her chewed nails. Her nervous habit had resurfaced thanks to Jake's disappearance and now she was too distracted to concentrate on her work.

She looked around her empty office and tried not to take offense at the cavernous silence that echoed back at her.

Normally, she preferred the solitude the Smithsonian offered. But she'd grown so accustomed to having Claire and Jake fill the space, that without them, her normally structured world was off kilter.

She didn't know what to think of the radio silence between Jake and herself, but she was beginning to worry. He hadn't returned any of her calls or texts. She knew his uncle would never call Jake home if whatever was going on wasn't serious, especially after what Jake had just been through.

After the Vega case, Jake deserved a break. They both did.

Dana had even let herself envision the Key West vacation Jake suggested shortly before he'd pressed her against the wall outside his bedroom and kissed her breath away. Instead, Jake had gotten devastating news about his mother.

Dana didn't know much about the woman. Jake wasn't big on sharing information, but parts of their personal lives had inadvertently bled into the three intense FBI cases they'd worked together. Parts that had introduced Dana to Jake's Uncle Wade, and cemented Jake as someone she could rely on.

That's why the silence was so disturbing. Even during the worst of their cases, Jake always checked in with Dana. She didn't want to intrude on what was possibly a delicate family crisis, but if the worst had happened, she didn't want Jake to think she didn't care.

She never would've survived finding out the truth about her parents or being betrayed by her best friend without Jake. He'd been there for her, and she wanted to return the favor.

That is, if he wants me to.

Dana tried to silence her doubts. She thought of herself as a confident woman, but she also couldn't help wondering if Jake regretted their passionate interlude. It had been leading to what was sure to be a night to remember before Wade called. But maybe Jake had welcomed the interruption. It would be understandable if he'd just gotten carried away, swept up in the emotions after everything they'd been through.

Did the time away make him see things differently?

See her differently?

For once, Dana thought she and Jake were finally on the same page.

But maybe not.

Maybe ignoring her calls was his way of letting her down easy.

She'd be lying if she said the rejection wouldn't hurt, but maybe it would be the smart move.

She and Jake ... they were completely implausible. As cliché as the jock and the geek living happily ever after. Yet, she couldn't stop her mind from reliving those few minutes of blissful passion every time she closed her eyes.

Jake's stubbled jawline, rough against the delicate skin of her neck as he kissed his way down her throat to her chest, stripping away layers of clothes as he went. Heat zapped through her like an electric current as she remembered the feel of him against her.

Blushing despite being alone, Dana stood, forcing the vivid memory away. She shoved her glasses into her hair and stretched. Her back popped and her stomach growled. She frowned when she looked at her watch. It wasn't unusual for Dana to work late, but the uneasy feeling that now accompanied her late nights was new and unnerving.

She despised weakness, but this fresh fear that slithered into her gut during D.C.'s nocturnal hours was something she didn't know how to remedy. Neither home nor office felt safe to Dana. And with Jake and Claire both out of reach, it was too easy for Dana to let her mind wander to more sinister matters.

Given her field of expertise it wasn't that uncommon for Dana to seek answers in the darkness. It's where she lived most of her life. But her experience with Jake had only made her relationship with death more up-close and personal. And their last case had even drawn her intern into the line of fire.

Dana reminded herself that Claire was safe at one of D.C.'s best rehab facilities. As for Jake, she knew he was more than capable of taking care of himself. It was a trait Dana admired, and one she strived for in her own life. Yet if her liaisons with the FBI taught Dana anything, it was that occasionally, it was nice to have the right people in your corner.

She just hoped Jake knew she was in his.

3

"Christ, just when you think you've seen it all." Officer Hartwell shook his head, giving the crime scene a wide berth. He told himself it was so he didn't contaminate the scene, but in all honesty, he didn't want to get any closer than he had to. Pulling a handkerchief from his pocket he covered his mouth and nose, trying to block out the smoke. The DCFD response had been swift and overwhelming, easily containing the fire from destroying the entire building. However, Hartwell wasn't in a hurry to breathe in the ash filled air and fumes from the still smoldering wreckage.

Thankfully, the fire hadn't reached the corpse he now stood over.

"So, this is normal?" Officer Lennox questioned.

Hartwell shrugged at his new partner. "This is D.C. I'm not sure normal is a vocab word here."

Each case Hartwell worked made it harder to remember why he'd joined the Metro Police to begin with. If his green around the gills partner was looking for reassurance or handholding, his assignment would be short. But that was a good thing. Better to know if Lennox was cut out for MCVU sooner than later.

Hartwell was new to the specialized department himself. His first case with the Major Case Victims Unit was the now infamous Card Killer case; a task force cluster fuck that had ended and catapulted careers. He'd been lumped with the latter; finding himself appointed as head of MCVU.

It wasn't a title he'd ever hoped to achieve.

When Hartwell joined the force, it was to help protect and serve his community. He had no aspirations of calling the shots or leading a team, yet here he was doing both. His wife's voice echoed in his head. "Not wanting the job makes you perfect for it."

Hartwell knew power hungry people were the least equipped to handle power. He might be right for the role, but it still made him uncomfortable. Just as uncomfortable as the strange murder weapon lying next to the mangled corpse of the prominent politician.

Two Metro PD officers approached. "What do you make of this?" the older officer asked, nodding to the weapon.

"Colombo over here thinks it's a machete," the younger officer mocked. "I told him it's a karambit. Had one just like it when I was in Afghanistan."

"It's neither," Hartwell grumbled, kneeling to get a closer look.

"Then what is it?" Lennox asked, peering over his shoulder.

"It's a sickle," Hartwell answered, his stomach churning as he remembered the last place he'd seen one.

All three officers stared at Hartwell, a mix of disbelief and dread on their faces.

"A sickle? Like some Grim Reaper shit?" Lennox asked.

Hartwell stood and checked his watch. There was no chance of catching the game now. Thanks to the mutilated body of Congressman Norton Hayes and a medieval weapon, his night, no make that nights, were no longer his own. Sighing, he stomped off toward his car.

"Are you sure it's a sickle?" Lennox asked, jogging to catch up.

"Yep." Hartwell didn't feel the need to elaborate. He did his best not to think about the Card Killer case, but the twisted tarot card images were seared into his memory. A skeleton welding an ancient, curved blade wasn't something easily forgotten. So yeah, he was sure.

"That's a bold choice for a murder weapon." Lennox continued. "What do you think it means?"

"No, idea, but I know someone who will have a few thoughts." Hartwell pulled out his phone. "It looks like we'll be calling the Witch Doctor."

4

"ADAM?"

"No, Mom. It's me, Jake."

"Jake?"

"Yes. Jake, your son."

"You look just like my husband, Adam. You must be an airman, too. You pilots all have that look," she said, pride brimming in her watery blue eyes.

She looked so much older than her years. Her thinning brown hair was greasy and streaked with silver. It fell in limp strands over her boney shoulders. Jake tamped down the anger her protruding bones and sallow skin evoked.

He knew it wasn't Wade's fault.

Jake's mother had been an empty shell of a woman ever since his father walked out on them years ago. Wade had done his best, for both of them.

Jake swallowed his resentment and tried again. "Mom, I'm here to see you. I'm your son."

She vehemently shook her head. "No. No. I don't have a son. Not yet anyway. We're expecting." Her hands moved to caress her flat stomach and for a moment she paused, caught between two worlds.

That was always the hardest part for Jake, and if he was honest, it's why he seldom visited. It was easier to send money and communicate through Wade, than acknowledge the woman who gave birth to him was lost, caught somewhere between the past and the present.

Conjuring patience, Jake tried again. "Yes, you do. His name is Jacob Miller Shepard. He lives in Washington D.C. He's an FBI agent who protects people, and he came here because you need protection."

She looked confused. "I have Adam to protect me."

"No, Mom. You don't. He hasn't protected you or me or anyone in a long time. Wade is the one here taking care of you every day."

"Wade." It was reassuring to hear the inkling of recognition in her voice.

"Yes, Wade, your brother. And I'm Jake."

"Jake?" She tried the name on for size, seeming not to accept or reject it this time. "And you want to protect me?"

Hoping he was finally getting through to her he slowly nodded. "Yes."

"From what?"

Jake fought the emotion crowding his throat. "From yourself."

"I don't understand."

Jake let his gaze fall to the fresh white bandages on her wrists, the dried blood still beneath her fingernails. "Mom, you tried to hurt yourself."

She began to tremble. "No. No ... I wouldn't do that. Not to Adam. Not to our baby."

"But you did. Wade found you in the bathroom. Do you remember what you tried to do?"

She didn't respond and Jake hated himself for pushing her, but he needed to break through to her so she'd agree to be admitted and get the help she desperately needed. "Mom, you smashed a mirror and used a piece of it to slit your wrists."

She looked down, shock making her papery skin paler as she seemed to notice the bandages for the first time. "No! No! NO!" Her voice rose to a wail of indecipherable shrieks as she clawed at the bandages.

Jake was instantly on his feet ready to restrain her, but the moment he touched her she went feral, clawing at him like her life depended on it. The bedroom door burst open, and Wade rushed in carrying a small portable cassette deck. The twang of Peggy Lee blared over his mother's howling as Wade pushed his way into the room.

Jake watched in awe as the music instantly interrupted Helen's tantrum. Wade set the cassette deck down on the rickety bedside table and took his sister in his arms, rocking her in a slow two-step until she laid her head on his shoulder.

She went catatonic as Wade crooned along with the lyrics. *"Yes, it's a good day from morning 'til night. A good day from morning 'til night."*

When the song was over Wade gently helped her into the twin-sized bed in the corner and pulled the crocheted brown and pink quilt up to her chin. He placed a kiss on his sister's forehead as she closed her eyes and then motioned to Jake it was time to go.

Following his uncle out of the room, Jake looked back over his shoulder at his mother in the sliver of golden light cast by the closing door. It was like glimpsing a stranger.

5

DANA STOOD IN FRONT OF HER TELEVISION, SOMETHING SHE RARELY DID. But when the FBI's Assistant Director tells you to do something, the best course of action is to listen the first time.

"Turn on the news," was all Remi Jenkins said in that commanding tone of hers.

Dana had answered the phone on the first ring, worried it was something to do with Jake, but this was much worse.

She read the words scrolling across the news broadcast ticker at the bottom of the screen, but her mind rejected them: *Brutal murder at renowned rehab clinic. Whereabouts of patients unknown as fire rages on.*

"Claire?" The question came out in a breathless gasp.

"She's among the missing," Jenkins answered.

Claire was missing. Dana's chest tightened as panic began to rise. Instinct forced her logical mind to intervene before she spiraled down a dark path. "Missing is good. Missing means she could be alive," Dana said, more to herself than Jenkins. "I need to call her parents."

"Next of kin have already been notified," Jenkins assured.

"And Jake?"

"Left him a message," was all Jenkins offered.

So, Jake hadn't answered a call from Jenkins either?

Remi Jenkins was more than Jake's direct superior. She was a friend—family even. The fact that he'd ignored her call raised almost as many alarms as the fear-mongering news team invading Dana's television.

Pushing all thoughts of Jake away, Dana shifted her sole focus to Claire. "I should reach out to Claire's parents personally."

Their already estranged relationship had fractured further when Claire admitted her struggles with addiction, but Dana refused to believe the girl's parents had completely given up on their daughter. They lived on the west coast and hadn't seen her in years, but surely, they'd be there for her in a time like this.

Dana held the phone to her ear, her attention transfixed on the smoke billowing from the building behind the news crew.

Jenkins spoke again. "Claire's not the only reason I called. "

"What do you mean?"

"I can't get into it over the phone. How fast can you get to the lab?"

"The lab?" Dana hated sounding like a confused echo, but she was at a loss, her inquisitive mind reeling with too many questions.

"The FBI forensics lab. Your presence has been requested."

"By who?"

"Dr. Raynard. He asked for you by name. I assumed you were acquainted."

They were. Dana would never forget her first meeting with the man everyone in the FBI referred to as the Alchemist. "I don't understand. What does this have to do with Claire?"

"Don't know. Maybe nothing. Maybe everything. Won't know till you get here."

"But—"

Jenkins cut her off. "I can't say more. Just get here, Gray."

The line went dead, ending Dana's objections. She should've expected it. Jenkins didn't tolerate nonsense; a trait Dana appreciated. And right now, nothing seemed to make sense.

Snapping into action, Dana dressed quickly and grabbed her purse and phone on her way to the door, intending to get some answers.

6

WADE LOOKED LIKE A KETTLE ABOUT TO BOIL WHEN HE FINALLY FACED
Jake. "This isn't one of your suspect interrogations, Jacob! She's your
mother!"

"I know that."

"It sure as hell didn't seem that way."

Jake rubbed the tension from his jaw and took a breath trying to
collect his thoughts, but really, what was there to say?

Wade paced the length of the kitchen looking as frustrated as Jake
felt. "What the hell were you thinking, Jake?"

"I was thinking, she needs help! More help than either of us can
give her."

"We do just fine here."

"Wade! She tried to slit her wrists! She needs professional help. I
thought that's why you called me out here."

"I called you because you're the only one who can get her what
she needs."

"And what's that?"

"Your father."

Jake pinched the bridge of his nose. "We talked about this."

"No, I talked about it. And every time I bring it up you shut me down."

"Because he's the last thing she needs!" Jake yelled, unable to leash his temper any longer.

Reaching out to his father was also the last thing he was willing to do. Not that it would even work. He had no idea where the low life was.

No one did.

Jake's father had a lifetime to seek him out, yet he never had. But selfish people were predictable that way. They only thought of themselves.

Jake's phone vibrated on the kitchen counter. Dana's name glowed on the screen again, distracting him. Jake felt Wade's gaze on him as he strode across the kitchen to silence the call.

"You can get that," Wade objected.

"Don't need to."

All at once the fight went out of Wade. His lanky limbs seemed to give out as he sank onto the spindly chair at the small kitchen table. The ancient wood groaned, sounding almost as weary as Wade looked. His uncle stared up at him. "Jake, you gotta stop pushing people away."

"I'm not." Not wanting to find his father wasn't the same thing as not inviting Dana into his family drama.

"Pulling away isn't any kinder than pushing her away."

"I'm trying to put out one fire at a time," Jake muttered, slipping the phone into his pocket.

"Yeah, well take it from me, some flames need to be fanned or they flicker out on their own."

"What's that supposed to mean?"

"It means life only gives ya so many chances at happiness, kid. And even a blind man can see that woman makes you happy. Ignoring that is a mistake."

Jake reached up and pulled two glasses from the worn pine cabinets, pouring himself and his uncle each a generous amount of bourbon, neat, the way Wade had taught Jake to drink it.

Carrying the glasses over to the tiny table, Jake sat down, joining his uncle. "I'm not ignoring her, Wade. I know what's at stake when it comes to Dana."

Frankly, the way Jake felt about Dana scared the hell out of him, especially after spending the last few days with his mother.

Helen Shepard was a shattered woman, living proof of how foolish and destructive a misguided heart could be. But Jake was done letting fear keep him from living his life to the fullest. Dana was it for him. It was something he'd known for a long time, but he was just now willing to admit it.

That's why he'd come out here. If he wanted any chance at a future, he needed to start fixing his past. He wanted to set things right with Wade and his mother so he could go back to D.C., back to Dana, with no distractions. She deserved nothing less.

"I hope you do, Jake. If I've learned anything from your father's absence over the years, it's that sometimes leaving does more harm than good."

"Do you really believe that?"

Wade shrugged. "Don't get me wrong. I was never a fan of your father, or the way he treated your mother. Helen could've done better. But I could sing that song umpteen times and it ain't gonna make a difference. The heart is a stubborn muscle, and I just can't watch her slowly wither away pining for him anymore." Wade shook his head, running a hand through his thick salt and pepper hair. "I thought I could help her get past it." He took a slow sip of his bourbon. "I guess his hooks ran deeper than I knew."

"Then I don't get it," Jake argued. "Why do you want me to drag him back here?"

"Because if she's not over him after all this time, I don't think she'll ever be."

"So? He didn't deserve her then and he sure as hell doesn't now."

"You're right, but it's not about him. You'd be doing this for your mother. She wants closure, and she deserves it."

"Why now?" Jake asked.

Wade finished his drink and set it on the table with a heaviness Jake hadn't seen in his uncle before. "Because we're out of time, Jake. And I can't deny her dying wish."

"Wade—"

Jake's uncle cut him off. "No! She's my baby sister. I've known her for her entire life. In fact, I've sacrificed having much of a life of my own to be here and make sure she's cared for. So when I tell you it's time, you damn sure better take me at my word." Wade exhaled slowly, regaining his composure. "You know I'd do anything for your mother, but I know when she's given up. What she did to herself ... it was no accident. She'll do it again."

"We can get her professional help."

Wade shook his head. "She's been through all that, Jake. The hospitals, the medications, they don't work for her. Being here in this house, with familiar surroundings, it's the only thing that calms her soul. I'm not gonna force her away from her sanctuary at the end. I've gotten her this far. I'll get her the rest of the way. But I can't do that and track down your father at the same time. That part's up to you."

Every ounce of hatred Jake held for his father flooded his veins. The man had abused him and his mother before abandoning them, giving Jake every right to despise him. But still, Wade's words hit their mark.

Jake had come home to help, and this might be the only way he could.

"Jake," Wade pleaded. "She doesn't have the means to find him herself. If it's what she wants, it's the least we can do."

Feeling his phone vibrate in his pocket signaling yet another unanswered voicemail, Jake stood from the table. "I've gotta get back to D.C."

"And your father?" Wade asked.

"I'll look into it, but I'm not making any promises."

7

Dana made it to the FBI forensics lab a little after eleven. It was a nondescript-looking building on 8th Street near the Bureau's headquarters. The interior was sparse and industrial with three black plastic chairs in the waiting room. Scarred beige walls added to the austere atmosphere as Dana made her way down the cold hallway to the only room with a light on at this hour.

She'd been expecting Jenkins, but she was surprised to find Officer Hartwell when she was buzzed through the swinging steel doors. He was accompanied by a uniformed officer she didn't know.

"Thank you for coming, Dr. Gray," Hartwell said. "This is Officer Lennox."

The young officer extended his hand, and Dana shook it, but her attention was on Hartwell. "I was told Dr. Raynard requested me."

"I did." Dr. Felix Raynard practically danced into the room carrying an evidence tray with the reverence of the Mad Hatter. "But the request came from the top," he said, giving a jaunty bow to Hartwell.

"I wanted to go through the proper channels," Hartwell clarified.

"Relax," Jenkins said. "This isn't an inquisition. We're all on the same team."

Dr. Raynard grinned, adjusting his thick round glasses. "Ah, it's always so good to get the band back together, isn't it?"

Dana had forgotten how quirky the brilliant doctor could be. Though his brilliance overshadowed his peculiarities, it seemed he enjoyed playing the part of his moniker.

Known proudly as the Alchemist to those who sought his talents in forensic specialties, Felix Raynard had a reputation of being a genius recluse who dwelled in the FBI's forensic lab.

His job wasn't that different from Dana's. They both cataloged death. Though she preferred her ancient victims to the Alchemist's barely cold ones.

Studying his unkempt appearance, and the way the large gray opti-visor atop his head made his frizzy white hair stick out every which way, Dana had to admit the Alchemist seemed even more eccentric than the last time they crossed paths.

She smoothed down her stray curls, briefly wondering if her own nickname conjured the same unconventional image among others in the Bureau. *The Witch Doctor and the Alchemist. We're certainly a peculiar pair.*

"Wait." Raynard's gaze bounced around the room. "Where's Agent Shepard?"

That's what I'd like to know. Dana ignored the question, her attention on the evidence tray. "Is that why I'm here?"

Hartwell stepped up. "Yes. This was found at a murder scene."

Dana looked at Jenkins. "Claire's rehab center?"

Jenkins and Hartwell exchanged glances, making Dana's blood boil. She hated the bureaucratic dance between different justice departments. "If this has to do with Claire, I can save you some time and agree to consult on this case, no matter whose jurisdiction it lands in."

Jenkins raised an eyebrow, signaling the ball was in Hartwell's court. The officer sighed and gave a nod. "The weapon was found at the Passages Rehabilitation Center crime scene tonight. We believe it's the murder weapon."

"Who was murdered?" Dana asked.

Again, Jenkins and Hartwell shared a glance. It seemed like

Hartwell was about to answer but Jenkins cut him off. "The victim's identity is not being disclosed at this time."

"Then why am I here?" Dana asked.

Jenkins spoke up. "Hartwell believes we need your expertise on the weapon."

"A weapon like this is chosen for a reason," Hartwell replied.

Fighting her frustration, Dana donned a pair of exam gloves and approached the blade. She'd only agreed to help because of Claire, but now that she was here, the familiar tug of intrigue took hold. "May I?" she asked.

"It'd be my pleasure to embark on another expedition with you," Dr. Raynard quipped. Already gloved, he carefully opened the evidence bag and gently extracted the weapon, setting it on the gleaming silver exam table.

"Is it really a sickle?" Lennox asked.

Dana shook her head. "Common misconception. What you have here is a scythe."

"There's a difference?" Hartwell asked.

Dana nodded. "Quite a large one, historically speaking. A sickle has a more circular blade, a short handle and can be used with one hand, traditionally to reap wheat. A scythe's blade is flatter, more like a raven's beak. Its origin predates the sickle. It's a long-handled tool that requires the use of two hands. Wielded by the Grim Reaper, the scythe is synonymous with death. Many cultures believe the Grim Reaper to be ordained by God and put on earth to do his bidding. *Vita est morte est vita.*"

"Life is death is life," the Alchemist translated.

"That's correct," Dana replied. "Though seeing the phrase inscribed on the blade itself is rare, and something I'd need to research further."

"A noble weapon with a noble history," the Alchemist revered.

"There's nothing noble about how it was used," Hartwell muttered. "You said longhandled. This one's only about a foot long."

Dana nodded, pointing to the jagged end of the wooden handle. "It's been snapped off here. Possibly on impact. Was the rest of it recovered at the scene?"

Hartwell shook his head but jotted down a note. "Not yet, but DCFD is still on scene containing the fire. I'll circle back when it's safe and see if I can recover it."

"Why the scythe?" Lennox asked. "I mean for the Grim Reaper."

"It's an apt tool for harvesting," Dana replied. "The scythe has always been meant for reaping, whether souls or crops. Each feeds its own end. It really just depends on who's wielding it. How was the blade used?"

"Haven't gotten the official ME report back yet, but if I had to guess COD..." Hartwell drew a line across his throat. "First cut was through the jugular. Quick and clean."

Dana nodded. "That's the traditional way a Reaper is taught to glean."

This time it was Jenkins who spoke up. "Glean?"

The Alchemist piped up. "Extracting a vessel of its soul."

"Exactly. Gleaning is a Reaper's word for killing," Dana explained. "They don't kill unnecessarily, they glean, or cull to rid the world of sinners."

"You're talking about Grim Reapers like they're real," Lennox said.

"Because they are. Or were," Dana amended. "There have been numerous accounts of religious culture adopting the lore and legends of Grim Reapers."

"Great, so we've got a killer who thinks he's some sort of Grim Reaper doing God's work," Hartwell grumbled.

"That's one possibility," Dana replied. "But I'd prefer to fully examine all the evidence before labeling this a religious killing."

Lennox huffed a laugh. "Too bad. A lunatic in a hooded black robe wielding a scythe would be easy to find."

"Actually, you might be right," Dana replied, her gaze pinning Lennox. "If someone went to the trouble of using this particular weapon in this particular way, they might also dress the part. The garb of Death, or the black mourning robe, dates back to the early fifteenth century and is believed to have been chosen to resemble the dark robes of the priests or monks who officiated at the death bed. But I wouldn't presume the murderer is a lunatic. Traditionally, Reapers follow scripture, not lunar cycles."

Mercifully Lennox was stunned silent, so Hartwell spoke up. "Thank you for your help, Dr. Gray," he said, snapping his notebook shut.

The gesture reminded Dana so much of Jake that for a moment she found herself looking for him in the small crowd gathered around the exam table.

No matter how much Dana wished Jake would appear, she knew this time she was on her own. Unwilling to leave without answers, she spoke up as the group began to separate. "Is there anything else you can tell me about the case? About Claire?"

"I'll get you up to speed," Jenkins interrupted, steering Dana out of the lab.

DANA'S TEMPER flared as she digested Jenkins' recap of how the case was being handled. She did her best to remember she was speaking to a high-ranking member of the FBI, not just a woman she'd fought alongside in the trenches. "Jenkins, are you really going to let some high-profile politician get this whole case brushed under the rug?"

"No one's brushing anything anywhere. But this case is complicated. The identities of patients at Passages Rehabilitation Center are confidential. Especially this politician's. It isn't public knowledge that he was there, and his death makes this a matter of National Security."

Dana didn't follow D.C.'s political drama the way most in the city did, but she understood enough to realize any political involvement would make things more difficult. "So, this wasn't random, you think the victim was targeted?"

"I'm not making any assumptions, Gray, but there's no telling where this case is going to land."

"I don't care where it lands. I care about Claire. She's out there, scared and alone."

"There's no evidence to indicate she's alone. Other patients are missing. They could be sheltering together."

"Or they could be ..." Dana couldn't even bring herself to say it. Thinking it was terrifying enough. *Dead. Claire could be dead.*

Dana closed her eyes and pulled in a steadying breath, repeating her mantra.

One step at a time.

That's how she'd get through this.

It's how she'd solved her last three cases; it's how she'd find Claire.

Opening her eyes, Dana readjusted her glasses. Conjuring confidence, she let her mind brush against each of the facts she'd already learned. There were few besides the murder weapon.

The only sliver of solace was that this was most likely politically motivated. The fact that it happened at the rehab facility where Claire was could be merely coincidental—though Dana had her own beliefs about coincidences.

They didn't exist in science, and she'd yet to see them exist in her life.

Dana heard Jake's words in her head. *Prepare for the worst, hope for the best.*

She wanted him here so badly it physically hurt. But she knew whatever he was dealing with in Nevada must be important if he wasn't calling her back. Especially after her last voicemail.

"Jenkins, I can't sit around and do nothing. Let me help," Dana pleaded. "I know Claire. I know her habits, how she thinks, where she might go."

"As I've said, Metro PD and our agents are canvassing the areas nearest the facility. You've assisted with identifying the murder weapon. Now the best way you can help is to go home." Dana started to interrupt but Jenkins cut her off. "You're right, you know. The first place Claire would go is most likely somewhere familiar. Somewhere she feels safe, like your home. She could be there waiting for you as we speak."

Dana knew Jenkins was placating her, but she couldn't argue the logic. "Claire would call me."

"Patients at the rehab facility aren't allowed to have cell phones," Jenkins replied. "If Claire left in a hurry, she doesn't have a way to contact you. Go home, Dana. Wait for her there. If I hear anything I'll call you. But right now, the best thing you can do is let us do our jobs."

8

THE MOMENT THE WHEELS TOUCHED TARMAC JAKE WAS ON HIS FEET. HE didn't believe in abusing the badge, but he wasn't waiting a second longer to deboard his flight. He discreetly flipped his FBI shield at the flight attendant and was promptly escorted to the exit.

Jake jogged down the gangway, his phone to his ear. "Come on, Dana. Pick up."

With each unanswered ring, he gained speed, as if that would be enough to make up for his neglect.

When Jake left Nevada, he'd planned a much different homecoming. He'd even let himself imagine picking up a bottle of champagne, maybe some flowers. Instead, he was racing against the clock, hoping he wasn't too late. *Again.*

He'd made it all the way to the airport without listening to his voicemails. He didn't want anything to change his mind. Not work, not Dana's insistence on getting the timing right. He was going home to her, and he planned on telling her he wanted to be with her, come hell or high water.

But the damn notifications on his phone kept taunting him.

Once he boarded and found his seat, he caved. Skipping over the message from Jenkins, Jake listened to the voicemails from Dana first.

He was grateful he was in the air by the time he got around to her most recent one. Hearing about the incident at Claire's rehab clinic made him want to jump from the plane to get home faster.

Trying to remain rational, Jake swiped his credit card so he could access the plane's Wi-Fi. He checked the D.C. news first, but the reporter's words couldn't penetrate the loop in his mind. He kept hearing Dana's terrified voice over and over. "Claire's missing, Jake. If something's happened to her ... I know you'd be here if you could. Jake, I-I ..." She paused. "Just call me, okay? Please."

The fear in her voice tore Jake in two. He should've been there for Dana. For Claire, too. Christ! If anything happened to them while he was away, he'd never forgive himself.

Jake managed to focus long enough to listen to Jenkins' voicemail. He replied to both Dana and Jenkins via text but got no response. The little checkmark next to each sent text assured him the messages were going through, but it did nothing to calm Jake's nerves.

He'd hoped to get answers once he was on the ground but both Jenkins' and Dana's calls went to voicemail.

Anger and fear reached a boiling point as Jake peeled out of the airport parking garage. Instinct and training allowed him to navigate the slick D.C. roads at breakneck speeds.

He tried Jenkins again. This time she answered. "Shep, I can't talk right now. Like I told Dana, I'll call if I have any new information regarding Claire."

"You spoke to Dana? Where is she?"

"I sent her home. Are you back in D.C.?"

"Just landed. What do you mean you sent her home? Where was she?"

"Glad you're back, Shep. You should check on Dana. She'll fill you in. I told her to wait at home in case Claire shows up there, but she had that look in her eyes."

Jake knew it well. Dana was headstrong and had a history of doing whatever she thought was necessary to get answers, especially if it involved someone she loved. It was something Jake adored about the woman. But it also drove him crazy. "I'm headed to her place right now."

"Good. And Shep, a word of advice, stay away from this case."

"Jenks, you know I can't do that if it involves Claire."

"You'd better hope it doesn't."

"What aren't you telling me?"

"I'd say more if I could, but this is turning into a National Security nightmare. I've gotta go."

Jake swore under his breath. If this was a National Security case, Jenkins was right, Jake didn't want to be anywhere near it. The National Security Council would be involved, and that meant the White House and the unyielding force that came with it.

Even more desperate to get to Dana before she entangled herself in something beyond even her brilliant means, Jake accelerated onto the George Mason Memorial Bridge.

In reality, it took less than ten minutes to reach Dana's door, but to Jake, the drive seemed to take an eternity. He slammed the SUV in park and raced up her front steps, his chest tightening as he banged on her front door.

"Dana!"

Jake's heart pounded as hard as his fists, but there was no answer. The silence left his mind free to run away with sinister scenarios.

Was Dana inside and injured, or worse?

Or had she rushed off to do something heroic and dangerous to find Claire?

Jake was just pulling out his phone to call Dana again when he saw a beam of light flash through Dana's curtains. Slipping the phone back into his pocket he pressed himself against the stone column of the brownstone's porch and waited. Once again, the light beam flickered to life, this time it stayed on, bobbing through the house casting a wake of shadows in the unmistakable arc of a flashlight.

Someone was inside.

Someone who wasn't Dana.

9

DANA DROVE THROUGH THE WET WINDING STREETS OF HER Georgetown neighborhood. They were empty this time of night. The lack of traffic gave her ample time to settle into her feelings.

She couldn't remember the last time she'd been scolded like a child.

Dana hadn't expected Jenkins to be so cold. Not to her, not on a case that involved Claire. Dana had always thought Jenkins' affection for Jake extended to her as well. Had she misinterpreted their relationship? Or was this case more involved than Dana had been led to believe?

Thanks to her vast knowledge of occult history and ritualistic artifacts, it wasn't unusual for Dana to be called in to consult on peculiar cases. It's how she'd met Jake and Jenkins. But she'd never been kicked off a case before it even started. Then again, she'd never worked a case without Jake.

Dana hated the unwelcome feeling settling over her. She'd gotten the cold shoulder most of her life, but the cases she'd worked with Jake changed that. Or at least she thought they had.

Her time with the FBI created the ideal notion that she was part of something—*a team, a family*. Had it all been an illusion? A creation to fill the void of loneliness she'd taught herself not to acknowledge?

Reaching the western edge of her neighborhood, Dana parked on her quiet street and walked the deserted sidewalk to her home. She felt insignificant. Especially against the insurmountable task of finding Claire on her own. Only her stubborn nature allowed her to push back against the thought, chasing self-doubt away.

Instead, Dana listened to her inner voice. *You've made it this far on your own. Keep going.*

Squaring her shoulders, Dana reminded herself it was her intuition and persistence that solved three of the biggest FBI cases in a decade. She put a drug lord away, stopped a sadistic secret society, unmasked a serial killer, and solved her parents' cold case. She could find Claire.

With renewed confidence, Dana strode up her steps, stopping short when she saw shattered glass. The right sidelight window next to her front door was smashed.

Heart racing, Dana knew she had two choices. Fight or flight.

She made her decision almost instantly as she crept forward, reaching for the door handle. It spun easily.

Claire! Dana's heart soared, hoping her intern had broken the glass in order to find shelter inside. Still, Dana knew she needed to exercise caution as she entered her home.

Again, she heard Jake's voice in her mind. *Prepare for the worst. Hope for the best.*

She *was* prepared.

After Fuller and Vega, Dana was done feeling helpless. If anyone came for her again, she vowed to be ready. And she was.

Dana's breath caught as her pulse quickened, but she forced herself to think clearly. Without hesitation, she pulled the small snub nose handgun from her purse and entered her home. She held the gun steady, with both hands, the way Jake had taught her.

She moved slowly, her stance steady, deliberate, as she made her way through the foyer, avoiding the scattered shards of glass covering her Persian rug.

Dana soundlessly covered the black and white tiled hall that led to her kitchen. Steeling her nerves, she pulled in a breath as she braced herself and rounded the corner, weapon drawn. A shadowed mass stepped into the room the same time she did.

"Freeze!" Dana shouted.

The same word was echoed back to her, followed by, "FBI! Lower your weapon!"

Dana blinked in disbelief. Her eyes adjusted to the dark enough to make out the unmistakable face she hadn't been expecting.

10

STUNNED, JAKE STARED AT DANA OVER THE BARREL OF HIS SIG SAUER. She held her own weapon trained on him like a pro.

Since when did Dana have a gun?

"Jake?" Her voice snapped him from his trance.

He holstered his weapon, crossing the room in a few quick strides only stopping when his chest struck the nose of Dana's Ruger Max .380. "You gonna keep aiming that thing at me?"

As if just remembering she was holding a weapon, Dana expertly switched on the safety and tucked the gun into her waistband before throwing her arms around Jake. "What are you doing here?" she asked into his neck as he crushed her against him.

"I got your messages," he said, unwilling to let her go just yet.

"I'm sorry," Dana whispered, her voice muffled against him. "I didn't mean to pull you away from your family, but Claire..."

Unease rolled through Dana in a tremor and Jake tightened his hold. "Claire's family, too."

"I didn't know what else to do." Dana pulled back and looked up at Jake, her bright brown eyes filled with concern. "I can't get anything out of Jenkins. Did she tell you what's going on?"

Jake shook his head. "She was tight-lipped. National Security issues."

Dana threw her hands up and paced away from him. "I wish people would stop saying that like it's an excuse! A prominent politician was murdered with a scythe. That's not going to stay secret for long. Jenkins should just read us in so we can help!"

"Did you say *scythe*?"

Dana stopped pacing and faced Jake, her mind elsewhere. "Why are you bleeding?"

Rolling up his sleeve, Jake reexamined the gash on his forearm. It was superficial, but a bleeder. Adrenaline does that. Shrugging off the pain, he grabbed a kitchen towel and applied pressure. "It's nothing. I cut myself breaking in. By the way, I noticed you didn't install that security system yet. And when did you get a gun?"

Baffled, Dana blinked. "After our last case."

"Please tell me you have a permit to carry."

"Of course. Now why did you break into my house?"

Jake hesitated, not sure if telling her he'd seen someone in her home was the best idea at the moment, but Dana knew him too well.

"What aren't you telling me, Jake?"

"I got your voicemail on my flight back and came straight here after talking to Jenkins. I was banging on your front door when I saw someone inside with a flashlight."

Dana paled. "What?"

"I swept all the rooms, but they were gone by the time I got in."

Taking a step back, Dana sagged against the kitchen counter. She pushed her glasses into her thick brown hair, giving Jake a glimpse at the weariness she normally masked. "I thought this was behind us."

He was across the kitchen again, pulling her back into his arms. "Hey, it is."

Dana pulled back. "You don't know that. Someone was in my house. Claire is missing. It's starting all over again."

"This isn't Vega or Fuller," Jake said. "We put those monsters to rest."

"Then who?"

"I don't know. But we're gonna figure it out just like we always do, okay?"

She didn't look convinced, but this time, Dana didn't resist when Jake pulled her into his arms. She clung to him, finally releasing the stress she'd been carrying. Guilt tightened his chest knowing his disappearing act had added to it.

Rage shrieked inside his veins at the thought of anyone hurting Dana. The fact that it was him ... it was too much to bear.

Holding her tighter was the only way to quiet his demons.

Jake surrendered, burying his face in Dana's soft brown hair. Inhaling her soothing floral scent instantly brought him back to their intimate moment in his apartment.

Jake wanted more of those moments. More of her.

With Dana in his arms a foreign feeling settled over him. *Home.*

To some it might not mean much, but to Jake Shepard it was everything.

He was used to fitting his life into his rucksack, moving from mission to mission, never settling, never connecting. A man with a country, with a conscience, yes. But never a man with a home.

Dana changed all of that.

He hadn't wanted her to. But it happened all the same.

Jake lived his life by a code. He'd been called to protect and serve his country above all else. He saw things in black and white, following policy and procedure to the letter. First in the Army and now the FBI. He still believed in his calling. But Dana had introduced shades of gray into his black and white world changing it forever.

Somehow when he wasn't looking, she'd shifted the order of things.

Now, no matter what the cost, he knew he would protect and serve her above all else.

It made him feel even more foolish for leaving her behind when he went to Nevada. That place was a house, but never a home. It wasn't his mother's fault. It wasn't even Wade's. But Jake needed to stop letting his past rule his life. Instead, he wanted to focus on the woman in his arms and building a future with her.

Leaning back, so he could look into those gorgeous brown eyes,

37

Jake gently tipped Dana's chin up. "I'm sorry I left. But I'm back now and I'm not going anywhere, okay?"

She gave a weak nod, but that wasn't good enough. Jake needed her to know he meant it this time. Plain and simple, he was done biding his time. He was choosing her.

The moonlight lapped at the milk-white skin of her neck, making Jake's tongue ache to trace its path. He preferred actions over words, but Jake knew one word could get his point across better than anything. "Dana, I came back for you. I won't walk away again. I promise."

11

DANA KNEW FEW THINGS FOR CERTAIN. THE EARTH WAS ROUND. DEATH was inevitable. And Jake Shepard didn't do promises.

Yet here he was, standing in front of her, looking devilishly handsome, making promises—*to her.*

She didn't know what to do with it.

Luckily, Jake did. He tucked a strand of hair behind her ear, his blue eyes sparkling as he cupped her cheeks. "Tell me that's what you want."

Too shocked to speak, Dana nodded.

It was all the confirmation Jake needed. He pressed his lips to hers, kissing her breathless again. He tasted like cinnamon, like safety, like home—*like hers.*

For one blissful moment she let herself get swept away. But too quickly it was over.

Ever cognizant of danger, Jake pulled back. "Get your things. We'll stay at my place tonight."

"But Claire might come here."

"What part of someone was in your house did you not understand?"

Without Jake's lips clouding her ability to think, Dana's mind cleared, and her stubbornness returned. "I understand it perfectly, but I'm not leaving this house if there's even the slightest chance Claire is coming here. And you should go to your place in case she goes there."

"Dana, I'm not leaving you here alone."

"It's not up to you."

"The hell it isn't."

She crossed her arms tightly over her chest. "Call in a favor and have an agent babysit me if you have to, but I'm staying here."

"You don't call the Feds for a B and E. I need to report this to Metro."

"Fine, but no lights or sirens. That will frighten Claire."

Jake's only response was his crooked smirk which was as sexy as it was patronizing.

"Why are you smirking at me, Shepard?"

"No reason, Doc."

"Don't give me that. If I'm missing something I want to know."

"You're not missing anything. I was merely thinking how sexy you look when you're bossy."

"I'm not being bossy. Bossy would be telling you to board up the hole you smashed in my front window."

"Fine. I'll call Metro, *and* fix the window, but only if you go pack a bag, because we're going to my place the minute the ink is dry on the police report, which will be..." Jake glanced at his watch and sighed. "Shit, it'll be morning by then." Jake rubbed the thick stubble making his jawline even more irresistible. "Well, the good news is that gives Claire plenty of time to show up if she's headed this way."

Dana wasn't ready to give in, but Jake sauntered closer with that dazzling smile he only used on rare occasions. "Come on, Doc." He pinned her against the counter. "You got me to compromise. Take the win."

With Jake's lips against her neck, it certainly felt like a victory.

"Fine," she conceded, melting into his kiss. "You call. I'll pack."

DANA WAS JUST PULLING her leather duffle out of the hall closet when the whirl of blue and red lights cut through her home. The sinister colors bounced off every surface, slicing through the false sense of calm she'd allowed herself while cataloging her mental packing list. Dana reminded herself to breathe as her mind instantly recalled each macabre crime scene she'd witnessed.

Jogging back toward the front door, Dana caught Jake's eye. His expression matched hers. Something wasn't right.

The cops shouldn't be here yet. It was too fast.

Dana didn't know what that meant, but it couldn't be good.

Jake put down the broom, abandoning his attempt to clean up the broken glass in the foyer. Dana rushed toward him, but he held out a hand to stop her just as someone rapped on her front door. She halted in her tracks and they shared an entire conversation exchanged in a look.

The rapport she and Jake built working their last few cases was tested in moments like these. It wasn't easy for Dana to trust. But Jake had earned it, so she stayed where she was, grateful she could remain hidden while her view of the dining room window gave the perfect vantage point to her front porch.

All the warmth in Dana's body leached away when she spotted the silhouette of the officer solemnly waiting on the other side of her front door. The sight was as welcome as a crow or raven. The symbology was the same. An uninvited police officer was the modern world's messenger of bad tidings.

Dana steeled herself as Jake unclipped his holster snap before opening the door a crack.

The officer's voice reached Dana. "Hello, I'm Officer Drake. I'm looking for Dr. Dana Gray. Is this her home?"

"Can I see some identification?" Jake asked.

A swath of tense silence stretched on before Jake was satisfied with the officer's credentials. He spoke without opening the door an inch further. "This is Dr. Gray's home. What is this regarding?"

Careful to remain out of sight, Dana crept closer. She watched as the officer took a step back and motioned to his squad car before answering. "We picked up a suspicious person wandering this neighborhood, disoriented, no ID, basically catatonic. Normally, we'd have just brought her in, but she fit a new BOLO. When I called it in, we were instructed to bring her to this address."

The moment Dana saw the slight frame emerge from the squad car she was moving. "Claire!"

Jake tried to hold her back, but Dana pushed past him and the surprised officer on her porch. She was down the steps and pounding sidewalk before anyone could stop her. A second police officer escorted the girl Dana would recognize anywhere. "Claire!" she shouted again.

The girl's head didn't move, her gaze fixed on the ground, but Dana was sure her eyes didn't deceive her. She ran faster, calling to her intern again. "Claire! Claire!"

Still no response.

Finally reaching Claire, Dana threw her arms around her, but the girl didn't move. It was like clutching an under-stuffed rag doll. Dana grasped Claire's thin shoulders, holding her at arm's length. The girl's black hair hung in her face. Dana brushed it away to reveal pupils so dilated that the clear blue of Claire's irises were almost not existent— a sure sign of shock.

A tidal wave of anger crashed over Dana. "What did you do to her?" she accused the officer.

"I think it's better if we talk inside," the officer suggested.

12

"I DON'T UNDERSTAND," DANA PROBED WHEN OFFICER DRAKE FINISHED conveying his account of events.

It put Jake on edge that even Dana's brilliant mind wasn't comprehending Claire's behavior. He pulled his gaze from the drained officers to study Claire again.

She sat on Dana's antique couch, narrow shoulders slumped, shrouded in an orange chenille blanket. Claire's damp black hair hung in front of her face. With the two officers flanking her, the scene looked like some bizarre advertisement for a horror movie.

"I don't know what else to tell you, ma'am," Officer Drake replied. "You know as much as we do."

"And you expect me to believe she was like this when you found her?" Dana demanded.

"Yes," Officer Drake replied, annoyance edging his voice now. "Like I told you, we found the suspect nearby, wandering and disoriented."

"Suspect!" Dana interjected. "And just what is she suspected of?"

"She was acting possessed," the younger officer replied. He'd been quiet up until that point and from the disapproving glare

Officer Drake sent his way, Jake got the feeling he'd been instructed not to offer his opinion.

Officer Drake cleared his throat and directed his attention to Dana. "Ma'am, we brought Miss Townsend to you as we were instructed to."

"And you still haven't told me *who* instructed you to bring her to my address, especially if you didn't know who she was, because according to you, she had no identification."

Officer Drake's lips pressed into a thin line. Jake admired Dana's protectiveness when it came to Claire, but her line of questioning was wearing the senior officer down. Jake reached for Dana's hand, taking control of the situation before she got herself a free ride in the squad car parked outside.

"All that matters is that Claire is safe," Jake cut in. Ignoring the indignation in Dana's simmering brown eyes, he stood up and extended a hand to the weary officers. "Thank you for bringing her home and for taking the incident report about the break in, but it's been a long night. We'll take it from here."

The officers stood, but the younger one looked to his superior, who made no move to shake Jake's extended hand. "We were told to wait here," Officer Drake responded.

"Until when?" Dana asked.

"Until we got here." Everyone in the room turned to face the duo who'd just strolled into Dana's home like they owned the place.

"Jenks?" It was Jake's turn to look confused. "What are you doing here?"

Officer Hartwell stood beside the FBI's Assistant Director. Backlit by the ambient light of the foyer, they cut a menacing profile in Dana's normally inviting home.

Hartwell nodded to the officers. "Drake, Bryant, wait for me outside." The officers took their cue and Hartwell turned his attention back to them. "Dr. Gray, twice in one night. Sorry to interrupt your evening again."

"Again?" Jake questioned, garnering Hartwell's attention.

"Agent Shepard, I wasn't aware you'd be here." Hartwell turned to Jenkins. "I thought we had an understanding."

"We do," Jenkins replied.

"This doesn't feel like a tight circle," Hartwell grumbled.

"It's tight if I say it's tight," Jenkins snapped with finality.

"Feels more like a three-ring circus," Hartwell muttered just loud enough to be overheard.

"Does someone want to tell me what the hell is going on?" Jake asked, taking a step toward Hartwell. The two had buried the hatchet since getting acquainted with each other's fists during their last case, but Hartwell's tone was bordering on disrespectful, and that wasn't something Jake was about to tolerate.

"Why don't you follow up with your officers," Jenkins recommended, stepping between the two men to diffuse the tension. "I'll get Shepard and Gray briefed."

"Fine," Hartwell conceded. "But for the record, I'm not keen on bringing them on board."

Jake waited until Hartwell was outside before advancing on Jenkins. Keeping his voice low, he gestured toward Claire who still sat in a catatonic state on Dana's couch. "Please tell me you can explain what we're dealing with here."

Jenkins looked defeated as she shook her head. "The best I can do is direct you to someone who's offered to help."

"And who's that?" Jake asked.

"Dr. Roman Dvita has reached out. He's the psychologist from the clinic who's been treating Claire. He's advised us to refer any of his patients who've been affected by tonight's events to continue with his care."

Jake scoffed. "Now hardly seems like the time to be drumming up business."

Jenkins gave him a look that said he was missing something. With a slight nod of her head, she signaled for Jake to follow her out of the room, but he was done taking orders. "Enough with the secrecy. Just say it, Jenks."

Jenkins let the weight of her steely gaze move pointedly from Jake to Dana, but he held his ground. "Whatever it is, she needs to be read in on it, too."

Accepting Jake's decision, Jenkins walked forward and handed

Dana a photo. "Dr. Dvita made it clear that you have more than one friend in common. And if tonight's incident is any indication, they both might be in danger."

When Dana's eyes settled on the photograph, she looked like she'd been slapped. "Meredith and Claire?" The names came out like a sob. "What does this mean?"

"I suggest you call Dr. Dvita," was the only answer Jenkins gave before heading toward the door.

A million scenarios whirred in Jake's mind after looking at the photo of the two women. They'd been captured in an animated discussion, with a third party. The man's face was turned away from the camera, but Jake's gut told him he had something to do with this.

There was no love lost between Jake and Meredith, but if this mystery man hurt Claire, Jake would go to the ends of the earth to make him pay. Dana looked like she was going to collapse, but Jake needed answers.

Jumping into action, Jake led Dana to the couch and sat her next to Claire. "Stay with her, I'll be right back."

Jogging, Jake caught up with Jenkins just as Hartwell and the Metro officers were pulling away. "Jenks, what the hell? You drop a bomb like that and just walk out?"

"Jake, if you think that's the bomb, you've got another thing coming."

"What does that mean?"

"I don't know how else to say it. Stay away from this case, Shep. And if you care about Gray, you'll keep her out of it, too."

"How? I don't even know what the hell's going on."

"And it's better that way."

"Jenks, ya gotta give me something. I get a phone call from Dana saying someone was murdered at Claire's torched rehab facility and that she's missing. I show up here and find someone breaking into Dana's house and then Claire shows up looking like the walking dead. Now you give me a photo of Claire and Meredith, who's not supposed to have the freedom to make social calls by the way, and I'm supposed to just ignore all that?"

"You're supposed to be on vacation, Shep. So be on vacation.

Maybe take Gray and the Townsend girl with you. But make sure she follows up with her doctor and gets the care she needs."

"Jenks—"

"Jake," she stepped closer to him, her voice softening just enough to let her Louisiana accent through. "Wade filled me in. I'm sorry for what you're going through with your mom 'n 'em."

"If that's why you're keeping me off this ..."

"It's not, I just need you to keep your distance and trust me on this one."

Jake knew when arguing was useless, so he nodded, shoved his numb hands into his pockets and watched Jenkins drive away into the frigid night.

BACK INSIDE, Jake turned his attention to the most important women in his life. Both sat on the couch, draped under the warmth of an orange blanket. What he wouldn't do to crawl under there with them and sleep for a day straight. Or maybe longer.

His gaze washed over Claire, picking up the imperceptible differences that only surfaced when reunited with someone after a long period of time apart.

Claire was the same, yet different. It wasn't the weight she'd lost, the slightly darker circles under her eyes or the emptiness in her gaze ... but something below the surface he couldn't quite put his finger on.

He was suddenly reminded of his mother. Jake hated drawing that parallel and hoped he was just projecting his own fears into the current situation—the very thing the FBI had trained him not to do.

For a fleeting moment, Jake wondered if his lifestyle was finally catching up to him. He'd been running from one thing to another since the day his father walked out on him. First it was the Army, then the FBI, but none of it seemed to make a difference. He still felt that unfathomable void no matter what he did, except for now, in the quiet moments when he was with Dana and Claire.

All he wanted to do was to keep them safe and make the

moments they had together stretch long enough to carve out some normalcy. It was something he'd never craved before and that scared him because it meant he had something to lose.

Dana caught him staring and the crease between her brows deepened with worry. Shifting the blanket so it was only covering Claire, she stood up and joined him in the kitchen.

13

THEY BOTH LEANED ON THE KITCHEN ISLAND, MUGS OF STEAMING coffee in their hands. Jake stared into his mug, but Dana kept her eyes fixed on Claire, wishing she'd had a bag of decaf in her freezer instead of the high-octane blend now caffeinating her bloodstream.

Truthfully, Dana preferred tea, but she could tell Jake was running on empty, so she brewed a pot of the stale beans she'd found shoved behind the vanilla ice cream in her freezer. It only made her feel more on edge after they discussed what Jenkins said.

"It doesn't make sense," Dana muttered again. "What was Meredith doing at Claire's clinic?"

"Could she have been transferred?" Jake asked.

Dana shook her head. "I would've been notified."

"When was the last time you saw Meredith?"

Guilt stabbed Dana. She'd been keeping herself busy with work to avoid worrying about Jake, and Meredith paid the price. "Two weeks."

"We'll call over there first thing in the morning."

Dana nodded, but something else was bothering her. "The police said Claire was acting possessed, but she's been nothing but catatonic since she got here."

Jake shrugged. "It was just an interpretation. Possessed, catatonic, does it matter?"

"Yes. That's the thing, Jake. Catatonic states disrupt a person's awareness of the world around them. If Claire was like this when she left the clinic, she never would've found her way to my neighborhood."

"What are you saying? You think she was fine when she left, and she saw something that put her into this state on her way here?"

"I think there's more to the story than the officers told us," Dana insisted.

"Maybe so, but we're not getting to the bottom of it tonight. Let Claire sleep off the shock and see how she is in the morning."

"Jake, this is more than shock or PTSD."

He scrubbed a hand over his tired features. "We've been down this road with her before. If it's more, we'll get through it. I'm sure we'll hear from Dr. Dvita tomorrow. Until then the best thing for all of us is rest so we can come at this clear-headed."

Dana knew he was right, but patience felt impossible with so much restless energy coursing through her. The coffee was definitely a mistake. Dana set her mug down and drummed her fingers on the black soapstone of her kitchen island, her mind flipping through endless occult accounts of catatonic cases she'd studied over the years, but Jake refused to let her spiral.

"Hey," he spoke softly, his warm touch distracting her as he clasped her fidgeting fingers. "We've got this."

She bit her bottom lip to stop herself from arguing, nodding instead.

Jake's thumb freed her pinned lip, a wry grin gracing his face. "Not good enough. Let me hear you say it."

Dana rolled her eyes. "Jake ... I'm not a child."

But he doubled down. Taking both her hands and pulling her toward him, he squatted until he was eye-level. "Say it, Doc. We've got this."

It felt impossibly foolish to give in to his childish pep-talk, but when Jake devoted the entirety of his focus on Dana, he was irresistible. She caved. "Fine. We got this."

"Nah, you can do better, Doc. We've got this!"

"We've got this!" she echoed with more gusto this time. "Are you happy?" she asked, grinning despite her best efforts.

"Almost," he whispered. Jake pulled her closer, those stormy blue eyes drawing her in. "I meant what I said before, Gray. I'm back now. We're in this together. For as long as you'll have me. Promise."

The number of words in the world was infinite, and Dana knew more than most, yet she'd never imagined a single one could hold so much power over her.

Promise.

Each time Jake uttered the word, it pierced her soul, supplanting all doubt and apprehension.

Dana let herself get lost in the moment, reveling in the exquisite sharpness of what Jake made her feel when he kissed her.

He hadn't kept up with his shaving in Nevada, and the roughness of his stubble burned as he hungrily nipped a path down her neck. She'd been surprised by his new unkempt look, but she liked it. Even more surprising was how good it felt to have his coarseness against her skin.

Jake moved with calculated accuracy. His fingers didn't fumble, his hands didn't shake. He handled her body like he'd already conquered it. With one swift move he lifted her onto the counter and kissed her so deeply she wrapped her legs around him and moaned into his mouth.

Jake stilled, his fingers frozen midway through deftly unbuttoning her blouse. Dana pulled back; her eyes wide as she realized how carried away they'd gotten. Jake gripped the counter on either side of her hips and let his head drop to her shoulder while she tried to catch her breath. Finally, she whispered his name. "Jake ... we can't."

"I know," he said calmly. Then he lifted his head. There was a barely contained wildness caged behind his blue eyes when he gazed at her. Jake stared at her a moment longer before untangling himself and helping her off the counter. "Guess we still haven't gotten the timing right just yet," he teased.

"We will," she promised.

"I know." He placed a soft kiss on her forehead. "Get some sleep. I'll stay up and keep watch."

"Jake, don't take this the wrong way," she said, caressing his prickly cheek. "You look like you haven't slept in a week. I'll stay up with Claire. Besides, I'm not sure how much sleep I'll get after what we almost did," she joked, buttoning her blouse.

"Oh yeah?" he teased, not even trying to hide his flirtatious smirk. "You were into it? I couldn't tell."

"Shut up and get some shut eye. That's an order."

He grabbed her around the waist and pulled her into his arms. "That's not fair. You know I can't resist when you talk bossy to me, Doc."

Feeling lighter than air, Dana reached up and looped her arms around his neck. "Then you're in luck because you know I like to be in charge."

"Sign me up." After another passionate kiss Jake turned serious. "For real though. You're crazy if you think I'm going to sleep after someone tried to break in here."

"Jake, you need sleep, too."

"And I'll get it, but not until I'm sure you and Claire are safe."

"We took care of ourselves just fine before you crashed into our lives."

"I know that. But I'm here now. You don't have to do everything alone."

Dana looked down to disguise the sting the word still possessed. *Alone.* It's something she'd always been, something she'd always planned to be. But now, here was Jake, offering her true partnership. It was almost too much to wrap her mind around. "Speaking of doing things alone," she hedged. "Do you want to tell me about Nevada?"

Jake sighed deeply. "It's a long story."

"I'm the curator of the world's largest occult library, Jake. Long stories are kind of my thing," Dana murmured, hoping to lighten the mood.

Jake pulled her in closer, dropping a kiss on top of her head as he wrapped his arms tightly around her. "Alright, I'll make you a deal. You get some sleep now, and I'll wake you for the AM shift as soon as the sun rises, and after we've both gotten some sleep, I'll tell you all about Nevada."

Relenting, Dana agreed. She released Jake and poured him another cup of coffee, escaping from the kitchen while she still had the willpower to do so.

Pulling herself away from him after so many promises wasn't easy. But there would be time for them later.

Right now, Claire needed her.

Dana checked on her protégé one last time before retreating to her bedroom. The girl was still sitting on the sofa, looking impossibly small under the large chenille blanket, but at least her eyes were closed. She finally looked comfortable, her head slumped to the side against the rich leather.

Macabre images danced in the recesses of Dana's mind. She'd seen too many corpses posed the very same way. The steady rise and fall of Claire's chest was the only thing that chased Dana's dark thoughts away—*for now.*

She knew they would return. They always did. Relentlessly haunting her dreams.

14

Jake woke like he always did, bolting upright at the slightest unusual sound. This morning it was the creaking of an unfamiliar door. He reached for his gun on the nightstand before his feet even hit the floor, but Dana's shocked expression sobered him, reminding him where he was.

"Sorry," he muttered, setting the weapon down and wiping the sleep from his face. "Force of habit."

"I didn't mean to startle you."

"You didn't. This is the Army's doing," Jake said, standing to stretch his back. With hands over his head, he twisted from side to side letting his spine pop, crack, and settle back into place as best it could. After so many years sleeping on the ground and hauling 90-pound rucksacks around the desert, there was only so much he could expect from his abused joints.

Dana still stood apprehensively in the doorway, mug of coffee in hand. It was an enticing vision in the early morning light, and his stomach growled, prodding him for another fix.

He glanced at his watch and grimaced.

"I wanted to let you sleep longer, but I heard back from Dr. Dvita," Dana said sheepishly.

"Don't apologize," he said, sauntering over to her, wondering if she had any idea how gorgeous she looked in her oversized Georgetown sweatshirt. Jake loved the way Dana looked in the morning, her hair wild, lips and nose rosy from the Earl Gray tea she'd no doubt been drinking while reading some fascinatingly old tome.

Jake, on the other hand, looked worse for wear. Sleeping in his clothes only added to his bedraggled appearance. But he'd been so tired when Dana relieved his watch, he was out the moment his head hit the pillow.

"Thanks," he said, gratefully taking the coffee she offered. He took a long sip, savoring the way the warmth spread through him. Then he set the mug down and pulled Dana into his arms, holding her tightly just because he could. He kissed the top of her head before letting her go.

Dana grinned up at him. "What was that for?"

"'Cause I can. And because I know you were probably standing outside my door for at least twenty minutes wondering if you should let me sleep longer."

Dana cocked her head, hand on hip. "You think you know me that well, huh?"

"Yep. Plus, the coffee temperature gave you away." Jake grinned. "Next time nuke it if you don't want me to know how long you've been standing out there."

"Always the detective."

"Uh, it's Special Agent, ma'am."

Smirking, she tried to swipe the mug back, but Jake was faster. "I didn't say I wouldn't drink it," he teased. After another sip he asked, "How's Claire?"

"Still asleep."

"Any news on Meredith?"

"I have a call in to the hospital but haven't heard back."

"What about Dr. Dvita? Can he see Claire today?"

"Yes. Actually, he offered to come here."

"When?"

Dana bit her lip. "In twenty minutes."

"Damn, Gray." Jake shook his head, amused. "Give a guy a little more warning next time."

"I'm sorry. I wanted to let you get some sleep."

"It's fine. I just need a quick shower."

Ever prepared, Jake had a go-bag in the back of his SUV with everything he'd need to switch back into FBI mode. He downed his coffee and headed outside to grab it, first checking the patch job he'd done on Dana's front door.

He'd repaired it last night while the girls slept. The spare plywood he'd found in the basement was fine in a pinch, but he planned to head to the hardware store to get a permanent solution right after he finished installing the security system Dana still hadn't unboxed.

When he came back inside Dana was toasting bagels. The aroma made his stomach growl, reminding him he hadn't eaten since Nevada. He made a detour through the kitchen and snagged an everything bagel on his way to the bathroom, kissing Dana on the head as she swatted at him.

"Towels are in the hall closet," she called after him. "Don't leave them on the floor."

"Yes, dear," he answered around a mouthful of bagel, certain he'd never tasted anything so delicious. But Dana could've served him sawdust and he would've loved it. He'd missed this—the push and pull of their banter. When they were apart, he was like a one-sided coin; flat, heavy, inept.

But now, reunited with his other half, new life had been breathed back into Jake. And he was ready to take on whatever the day threw at him.

15

"MORNING."

Dana jumped at the sound of Claire's voice, nearly dropping the tub of cream cheese she was holding. "Claire! You're awake!" Dana shut the fridge and rushed over to Claire. She was about to throw her arms around the girl but stopped herself. Claire had strict boundaries when it came to personal space and Dana didn't want to overwhelm her. "How are you feeling?"

"Fine. Hungry. Got anything besides bagels?" Claire asked, stepping around Dana to pour herself a cup of coffee. She added creamer with a heavy hand then plopped down in one of the squeaky swiveling barstools at the kitchen island.

Dana blinked, taken aback by Claire's nonchalance. She took a tentative step closer. "What do you remember about last night?"

Claire took a sip of coffee, put it down on the counter and stared into it, perplexity filling her delicate features. She pushed her glasses back up her nose. "The last thing I remember is being in bed at the clinic." She looked at Dana. "Wait! How did I get here?"

Immediately, Dana regretted questioning Claire. She should've waited for Dr. Dvita. Dana was weighing how much to tell Claire about the events of last night when a loud clatter made both women jump.

"Is someone here?" Claire asked, her eyes filling with fear.

A string of profanity drifted toward the kitchen from down the hall, followed by heavy footsteps. Dana hurried to reassure Claire. "It's just Jake."

"What's Jake doing here?"

As if conjured from her dreams, he appeared in Dana's kitchen, shirtless and clutching two halves of what had once been a singular mask. "Please tell me this is a replica," Jake begged.

"It's not," Dana answered, rushing to retrieve the priceless Luba mask.

"Shit! I knocked it over when I was getting dressed."

Claire stood, the barstool screeching in protest at the sudden movement. "Oh my God! You and Sergeant McSexy? What the hell did I miss?"

Jake seemed to notice Claire for the first time. "Elvira! You're awake."

"And you're half naked," she shot back.

Jake had started toward Claire, but paused, realizing she was right. He tightened the towel around his waist, his skin still glistening from his shower.

"What's going on?" Claire asked, looking from Jake to Dana. "Are you guys ... together?"

Dana froze—a deer caught in high-beams. "No ... we're ... he ..." She stammered until Jake interrupted.

"I came over last night after Dana told me what happened at the clinic. We just wanted to make sure you're okay, Claire."

"I'm fine, but why does everyone keep harping on last night?"

Jake's brow furrowed. "Do you not remember what happened?"

Dana finally found her voice and jumped in. "We were just discussing that, Jake. Why don't you get dressed? Dr. Dvita will be here any minute."

"What?" Claire looked like a cornered animal. "Dr. Dvita's coming here? Why?"

The doorbell chimed and Claire backed away instinctively. "I don't want to see him," she whispered.

If Jake had been wearing clothes, Dana was convinced they would've been incinerated from the rage radiating off him. "Claire, did he do something to you?"

"Jake!" Dana hissed. "Get dressed and let me handle this."

"Not a chance in hell." He faced Claire. "Tell me right now, Claire. If that scumbag laid a hand on you, I need to know."

She was visibly trembling, but she shook her head. "No, it's not like that. I just ... I don't want to face the things he makes me face. Not in front of you and Dana."

"Jake." Dana spoke gently, placing a hand on his arm. "Take a breath, get dressed and trust me to handle this."

He locked eyes with her for a moment. Sensing her sincerity, he nodded and strode down the hall to her bedroom. The doorbell chimed again, and Dana reached for Claire's hand. "Do you trust me?"

The girl nodded.

"Then follow my lead."

DANA ANSWERED the door without removing the chain. Through the slivered opening she viewed the frail figure darkening her door. A short man with thinning gray hair and dark eyes peered back at her from behind wire-framed glasses. He blinked rapidly, like his eyes weren't used to daylight. A stiff breeze picked up, and the man sunk into the raised collar of his thick navy blue peacoat.

Dana pushed his vampiric likeness from her mind. "Can I help you?"

"Hello, Dr. Gray? I'm Dr. Dvita. We spoke on the phone."

"Can you show me some identification, please?"

The man blinked again, but then started unbuttoning his coat. He pulled out his wallet, passing the whole thing through the opening in Dana's front door. The wallet looked as old as the man himself. Dana gently handled the leather, searching the folds until she was satisfied it was none other than Dr. Roman Dvita standing on her front porch.

Taking a deep breath, Dana had one more thing to ask. "I was given a photograph from you last night. Who's in it?"

"Three of my patients. Two of whom you're acquainted with. Nancy and Laura. Err.. sorry, we use the names of Presidents and First Ladies at Passages to protect identities, but you know them as Claire Townsend and Meredith Kincaid."

"And who's the third person?"

"Another patient of mine."

"Who took the photo and why send it to me?"

"I took the photo. And I sent it to you because I believe these women are in danger."

"What makes you think that?"

"Because the man in that photo is dead, and I'm worried the others will be targeted next."

Dana stifled her shock, then passed the wallet back through the door and looked to Claire for permission to let Dr. Dvita in. The girl nodded from her spot near the dining room window where she'd been watching the exchange.

Dana let her hand brush over the cold steel of the weapon tucked in the back waistband of her jeans one more time before she unhooked the chain and invited the cold stranger inside.

16

JAKE SAT ON THE CROWDED COUCH NEXT TO CLAIRE, WITH DANA flanking her other side. The girl fidgeted between them while Dr. Dvita droned on.

No wonder Claire didn't like him. Some therapist! Weren't the patients supposed to do the talking? How could someone share their inner demons with this guy if they couldn't get a word in edgewise?

Dr. Dvita continued his lecture. "In my experience it's not uncommon for patients with fragile constitutions like Nancy's to repress unpleasant recollections. The incident from last night may have triggered something she's unwilling or unable to face. It's why I thought Nancy might benefit from meeting with another patient I'd been successfully rehabilitating."

"Meredith?" Dana murmured.

"Yes. Meredith Kincaid. She goes by Laura at Passages. I've been quite pleased with how she's been navigating her rehabilitation. And though she and Nancy suffered different past traumas, their post-traumatic symptoms were similar enough that I'd hoped they would benefit from sharing their struggles and triumphs."

"Did it help?" Dana asked.

Dr. Dvita looked pointedly at Claire. "At first, I thought so."

"At first? How many times did they meet?" Jake asked, his blood already boiling at the thought of Meredith freely roaming D.C. after nearly toppling Capitol Hill with the cult she'd killed for.

"Three times," Dr. Dvita admitted. "But I soon realized another influence might be subjugating their progress."

Jake hated the stuffy psycho-babble Dvita spouted. "English, please," he muttered. "And can we stop with all the code names? We all know who you're talking about."

"It's fine," Claire said when Dr. Dvita looked for her approval.

"Another patient I was treating interjected his beliefs into the equation, and I found it counterproductive."

"The man from the photograph," Dana said, handing Jake the photo.

Claire sucked in a breath when the image passed under her line of sight. She closed her eyes and held her breath.

Dr. Dvita directed his attention to Claire. "We spoke about this, Claire. It's what we were working on at the clinic, yes?"

Claire nodded.

"Do you remember the coping mechanisms I gave you?"

She nodded again.

"Shall we try them?" the doctor pressed.

Claire took three short breaths and released one long one. She repeated the sequence three more times until she opened her eyes, her breathing returning to normal.

"Good," Dvita praised. "Now why do you think that photo provoked that reaction?"

She shrugged. "I don't know."

"I think you do know. You need to stop repressing reality. You're in a safe space. You can recall your memories, no matter how traumatic."

Claire flinched and Jake had enough. "If she says she doesn't remember, she doesn't remember."

"Jake," Dana warned. "That's not helping."

He leaned forward. "Well pushing her to relive something she's not ready to isn't helping either."

Dr. Dvita intervened. "Your over-protective coddling is misguided, Agent Shepard. Claire is stronger than you give her credit for."

Jake glared at the tiny man. "Which is it? She's fragile or strong? You can't have it both ways."

"Actually, humans are remarkable that way. We have the capacity to be many things simultaneously."

"Listen, Doc. You may have a bunch of letters after your name but that doesn't give you the right to walk into my house and push the people I care about around."

The foolish little man sat there unfazed. "I was under the impression that this was Dr. Gray's home."

Jake stood, not even making it a step toward the man before Dana was in his path.

"Okay! Let's all take a breath. Everyone here has Claire's best interest in mind, right?"

Both men nodded and Jake relented, taking his seat again at the behest of Dana's glower.

"Why don't we let Claire tell us what she can handle at the moment," Dana suggested.

"She looked at the photo," Jake argued. "She doesn't remember what happened last night."

Claire swallowed. "But maybe I can."

"You don't have to do this," Jake replied.

"I know. But I want to know what happened."

Dr. Dvita spoke. "Right now, all we know is that there was a fire at Passages last night and one of my patients was murdered."

"Who?" Claire asked.

"I think it's best if we don't supplant images in your mind. Let them come to you naturally," he replied.

"But you think I know who did it?"

"Only you can answer that question."

"Okay," Claire sat straighter. "Let's begin."

17

—————

IT'S FUN TO LET THEM IN. TO LET THEM THINK THEY UNDERSTAND ME. But they don't. How can they when they can't even see me? I've always existed. Right here in plain sight. But not everyone can see me. Only those very few special ones. And oh how I make them feel special, feel chosen. I tell them everything they need to hear. It's how I draw them in. Deeper and deeper. Until they drown and I'm invisible once again.

But first I have to let them in.

Let them in so I can get out.

18

AT FIRST DANA DIDN'T TASTE THE BLOOD. SHE WAS SPELLBOUND BY Claire's hypnosis. She'd never witnessed one in person before. It seemed so simple, his voice the pendulum that lowered her into oblivion. He counted backwards.

"10."

"9."

"8."

"7."

"6."

"5."

"4."

"3."

"2."

"1."

And all at once the change occurred.

The labored breathing, the rapid eye movement, body tremors and muscle spasms. It was like watching a silent war.

All the while, Dana was fighting her own internal battle. Her heart ached as she watched her friend wrestle demons only she could see. The only thing keeping her rooted was Jake. He held her hand in a vice-like grip, tethering her to his side.

Even though Dr. Dvita had assured them of his experience and that Claire wouldn't be suffering physical harm, Dana knew watching Claire struggle was tearing Jake apart inside. His pulse pounded out a distress signal against her palm, but she could do nothing but stand by, silently chewing her nails until she drew blood.

Jake noticed it first. He pulled a handkerchief from inside his jacket and pressed it to her fingers. The crimson stain bled defiantly through the white fibers. The familiar queasiness that always accompanied Dana's encounters with blood made her lightheaded.

But Jake squeezed her hand tighter, his voice an anchor. "Focus on Claire."

Dana did. And that's when it happened.

All at once, Claire went still.

"Hello," Dr. Dvita said, his words deliberately soft. "Welcome back."

"It's good to be back." The voice hit Dana like a punch in the gut. It came from Claire, but it didn't belong to her.

"It's been a while since we spoke," Dr. Dvita prompted. "Can you fill me in on what you've been up to?"

Claire laughed. "Wouldn't you like to know?"

"I would," Dvita continued. "I'm particularly interested in what happened last night. After we spoke, where did you go?"

"Where I always go."

"To the garden to write in your journal?"

"Yep."

"Did you speak to anyone in the garden?"

"Yep."

"Feel like sharing?"

Something impish slipped into the voice coming from Claire. "I'd rather you guess."

"Okay. Did you meet with Laura?"

"Ding! Ding!"

Dana's stomach dropped hearing Meredith was at Passages. Was this one of the three times Dr. Dvita had mentioned or something he was unaware of? Sensing her panic, Jake squeezed reassurance into her hand.

"Did you meet with anyone else?" Dvita asked Claire.

"You tell me."

"How about Taft?"

"Ding! Ding! Right again."

"What did you talk about?"

"The usual. Death, taxes, world domination."

"Did you speak to anyone else?"

"This game is boring."

Taking that as a no, Dr. Dvita changed his questioning. "Where did you go after the garden?"

"Well, it was Wednesday so I peed in a cup and collected my lollipop."

"Did you really get a lollipop?"

"No, I got chocolate pudding."

"I thought you didn't like pudding."

"I don't. But Max does."

"Ah, that's right." Dvita continued leading Claire. "How is Maximilian?"

"He doesn't like that name. I told you that."

"Right. Sorry. Maximilian is a peculiar name though."

"He's a peculiar guy."

"He is," Dvita agreed. "Would you consider him a friend?"

Claire twitched, her hands balling into fists for a fleeting moment before she relaxed and replied with that detached voice. "He's just an orderly."

"I see. Well, I don't mean for this news to alarm you, but since you aren't friends perhaps you won't be concerned."

Again, Claire twitched, though infinitesimally this time. "What news?"

"Last night, Passages caught fire, and someone was killed. Do you know what happened?"

Claire twitched so violently Jake dragged Dana across the room to get to her. But Dr. Dvita held up his hand to stop them from inter-rupting. Just as suddenly as the convulsions started, they stopped.

And this time, when Claire spoke, it was in her own voice, and it was full of fear. "I told him not to go," she whispered. "I told him it would make him look guilty."

"Who, Claire?"

"Max."

"He was with you last night?"

"Yes. He said he heard something and came to get me and Betty out."

"Max kept you safe from the fire, didn't he?"

"Yes. He keeps everyone safe. I told him to stay with me, but he went back in to help the others."

"Why did they need help?"

"The Reaper." Claire's words were so quiet, Dana thought she'd misheard, but Dr. Dvita had heard it too.

"The Reaper," he repeated. "Who is the Reaper?"

"He comes for the wicked. He came for Taft, didn't he?"

"Yes," Dvita confirmed.

A single sob escaped Claire.

"Do you know who the Reaper is?

Claire shook her head. "I can't say."

"You can't say, or you don't know?" Dvita pressed.

Her head shook from side to side so vigorously her black hair covered her face, blurring out her features.

"That's enough," Jake bellowed. He shook Dana off and pushed his way into the room. "Bring her out of it now, or I will."

19

CLAIRE BLINKED UP AT THE THREE CONCERNED FACES STARING BACK AT her. For a moment she felt the calm that came right before truly waking. But then as always, reality slammed back into place, evaporating the escape of dreams.

"I remember," she said. "I remember what happened."

"Tell us," Dr. Dvita encouraged.

"Don't push her," Jake barked.

"I'm merely doing my job, Agent Shepard," Dr. Dvita replied.

But Jake refused to back down. "Yeah, well all I see is someone who's being bullied and pushed beyond her limits."

"It sounds like something you're familiar with, Agent Shepard. But I'll warn you, it does no good to deflect your own suppressed trauma onto others."

Jake looked like a kettle about to whistle. Claire wanted to hug him for jumping to her defense. Her Secret Agent Man. Always there to protect her. If she could retreat into the safety of his arms she would, but it hurt too much.

"Jake," she called, stopping his advance on Dr. Dvita. "It's okay. I need him to push me."

Looking wounded, Jake exhaled, but returned to his seat.

Claire had never been good at letting people in. And this was why. She couldn't turn her empathy off. She absorbed the injured expression on Jake's face like a cloud of toxic fumes. It hurt her tenfold, and she'd yet to find the proper release.

Maybe her parents were right. She was damaged; destined to spread her darkness to everyone around her. The words Claire overheard her mother speak all those years ago returned as if she was there in the room. *"There's something wrong with her. The way darkness infects her. It isn't right. If we're not careful, she'll infect us, too."*

They'd been right to cut her out of their lives. And if Claire really cared about Jake and Dana, she'd do the same. But letting go was so hard.

Look at what she'd already cost them. Her weakness had nearly gotten them both killed in the Card Killer case. But here they were, still by her side. Still trying to help. She didn't deserve it.

Dana crossed the room and sat on the couch beside Claire. "Can I get you some tea? Or do you want to lie down in the guest room?"

Her friend and mentor reached for her hand, but Claire pulled away. It killed her to do so, but if she let Dana in now, she'd never be strong enough to make things right.

"It's okay," Claire said. "I don't need to rest. I remember what happened last night. I want to get it out while it's still clear."

Jake sat down across from her, his ever-present little notepad already in hand. "Start from the beginning."

20

JAKE PUT HIS PEN DOWN AND SHOOK OUT HIS HAND CRAMP.

Claire had recounted the night with alarming detail, right down to the moment she saw the whirling red and blue police lights.

"It's my trigger," the girl said sheepishly. "The police lights. They remind me of Sadie and the Grave."

"It's nothing to be ashamed of," Dana replied, clutching her teacup like it was the glue holding her together.

Jake knew the feeling. He wanted to finish his report and send Dr. Doom packing so he could wrap Claire and Dana in his protection and keep the wickedness of the world away. God knew they'd experienced more than their share. But since that wasn't going to happen, he cleared his throat and did what he could to ease Claire's worries.

"You did good, Claire. I'll pass this description on to the police."

"You think it'll help?"

"Height, build, clothes, weapon ... it's a slam dunk, kid."

"But I didn't see the killer's face. I don't know who it was."

"It's more than we had before and enough to start putting together a suspect list," Jake assured.

Claire turned back to Dvita. "And you're sure Max is the only one who's still missing from the center?"

"Yes. Everyone's been accounted for except for him."

"It doesn't make sense. He wouldn't just leave. Something must've happened to him."

"There's no need to jump to conclusions," Dvita replied.

"I know him, Dr. Dvita. Passages is more than just a job to him. It's his home." She turned to Jake. "You can help the police look for him, right?"

"Your safety is my only involvement in this case, Claire."

"Jake, he needs our help. Max is the only reason more people weren't killed last night."

"That's not exactly true," Jake muttered.

"What do you mean?"

The alarm in Claire's eyes gutted Jake, but he knew better than to keep things from her. The doctor had been right about one thing. Claire was stronger than Jake gave her credit for and that stopped now. "Like I said, I'm not working this case, but based on the victim's political history it's possible this was a targeted strike."

Tears filled Claire's eyes. "I still can't believe he's gone. Who would want to hurt Congressman Hayes?"

"Claire," Dvita warned. "I'd prefer you continue to keep my patients' identities private."

But it was too late. The cat was out of the bag and Jake was choking on it. He'd been sucking down his third cup of coffee of the day when Claire uttered the name. It shot through him like a ghost from his past leaving a chill in its wake.

Regaining his composure Jake put his coffee down. "Hold on. Did you just say Congressman Hayes? As in Norton Hayes?"

Claire looked confused. "Yeah. Do you know him?"

Outrage turned Jake's voice to gravel. "He's the victim?"

"This isn't public knowledge," Dvita warned, but Jake had stopped listening.

He was already out the front door, his phone pressed to his ear. He swore when it went to voicemail.

Waiting for the beep only exacerbated his temper. "I can't believe this is how I found out the piece of shit responsible for Ramirez and *MY ENTIRE TEAM* is dead! If you think I'm standing down on this, you're out of your mind, Jenkins. Find a way to read me in and do it now, because I'm on my way to the morgue. I want to see that bastard on ice with my own two eyes."

Jake was already in his SUV, engine roaring to life on Dana's sleepy street when she appeared on the sidewalk. Arms crossed, she locked eyes with him, challenging him to leave.

Swearing, Jake punched the steering wheel. It hadn't even been 24 hours since he'd made her a promise and here he was running off again without telling her why.

She deserved better.

He'd told her they were in this together, and that meant letting her in—all the way this time.

Jake left the engine running and exited his vehicle. Meeting Dana on the sidewalk he took her hands.

"Jake, what's going on?"

"Norton Hayes wasn't always a Congressman, Dana. He used to work for the Department of Defense, and long story short, he's the one who sent my Special Ops team on that mission in Ghazni."

"Jake ... I know how much guilt you feel about that, but no one could've predicted that outcome."

"That's just it, Dana. I did and Hayes didn't care. As usual, his personal agenda took priority."

"What do you mean?"

"It's too much to get into now, but he was given a report explicitly stating the area was too volatile to infiltrate without more time to do proper recon. Hayes sent us in anyway and he never had to answer for that."

"Jake, the man's dead. Isn't that answer enough?"

"You know better than to think cutting the head off one snake ends this."

"So, what are you going to do?"

"Make sure another head doesn't grow back by getting put on this case. Because if I know anything about guys like Norton Hayes, it's that they never act on their own. If he was doing something shady enough to get himself killed, I need to find out who else is involved so I can see them coming if they have Claire in their sights."

"Do you really think that will happen?"

"I don't know, but I'm not taking any chances. The last two people we know he was seen with were Claire and Meredith. I'm not letting him put anyone else I care about in the crosshairs, Dana. The best way for me to do that is to get on this case."

"Okay, I get it, but I know you saw what happened in there with Claire," Dana said, gesturing back toward her house. "I'm concerned about her. Can't we trust Jenkins to take the lead for now?"

"Jenkins isn't going to want me involved in this case because she'll think I can't see past my history with Hayes."

"Can you?"

"If it means protecting you and Claire, you're damn right I can."

"Okay, do what you need to, but Jake, don't even think about keeping me in the dark on this. I need to know you're going to tell me what you find, even if it's not what I want to hear."

"Roger that."

Dana gave him a tiny salute, and he couldn't stop himself from pulling her into a quick embrace. "Hold down the fort. I'll be back as soon as I can."

21

Dana stood outside gazing after Jake's taillights, her fingers still pressed to her lips where he'd dropped a kiss before racing off to play hero.

His lack of fear was something she both admired and despised. She knew he was right. They needed answers and since he knew the deceased Congressman, he was the best one to get them. But that didn't stop Dana from wishing he could've stayed to help her deal with Claire.

The reality was, Claire needed help.

For the first time, it was clear to Dana that her intern wasn't getting better. In fact, by the light of day, Dana could see how much worse she looked.

The girl had always been thin and pale, but there was a gauntness to her now that Dana hadn't seen even when Claire was battling her addiction.

That coupled with the disturbing hypnosis session she'd just witnessed left Dana reeling. Through her field of expertise, she'd come across numerous accounts of demonic possession, identity disorders and dissociative delusions. Moments ago, she'd witnessed Claire exhibit traits of each.

Dana had a feeling what she saw was merely scratching the surface when it came to the inner turmoil her friend was battling, and that terrified her.

Being out of her depth wasn't a common occurrence for Dana. But she'd never let that stop her from pursuing the truth.

In her field, something that often appeared dark and sinister was simply misunderstood. It was Dana's job to peel back layers until she could shine light into the darkness and discover the truth.

Dana told herself to apply that same theory to Claire's situation. She didn't know exactly how to help Claire, but that wasn't going to stop her from trying.

Taking a deep breath, Dana turned back toward her house ready to start peeling back the layers.

"WHERE'S CLAIRE?" Dana asked, looking around her empty living room. Only Dr. Dvita remained where she'd left him.

"She said she was feeling tired and wanted to lie down," he replied.

Dana eyed him suspiciously and started down the hall to check for herself.

"You don't trust me?" he called after her.

"I don't trust anyone," Dana replied.

She knocked gently on her guest room door before entering. "Claire? Are you okay?"

The girl lay on her side, facing away from Dana. "Yeah. Just tired. Do you mind if I just take a few minutes?"

"Take all the time you need," Dana said, quietly shutting the door.

She returned to the living room and took a seat in the leather wingback chair opposite Dr. Dvita. "You're very good with her," he commented. "It's easy to see why she respects and admires you so deeply as a mentor and friend."

Dana smiled. "She said that?"

"Yes. It's very clear that you and Agent Shepard play a central role in her desire for rehabilitation." Dr. Dvita steepled his fingers as if weighing his next words. "Tell me, how long have you and Agent Shepard been in an intimate relationship?"

"What?" The question caught Dana completely off guard. "We're not."

"Ah, so it's new, then?"

"What it is, is none of your business."

"I disagree. Anything that adversely affects my patient is most certainly my business."

"I'm sorry, but my personal life is just that, Dr. Dvita."

"Maybe so, but Claire is a very perceptive individual. And since it appears she's staying here with both you and Agent Shepard, your personal life is an influence on her whether you'd like it to be or not." He adjusted his glasses and blinked in that unsettling way of his. "A word of advice, whatever's going on between you and Agent Shepard should be put on hold if you care about Claire's recovery."

"Of course I care, but what does our relationship have to do with it?"

"I'm aware of your credentials, Dr. Gray. You're an educated woman. You know what Claire exhibited while under hypnosis is far beyond the norm."

"What are you saying?"

"In my time with Claire it's become evident that she struggles with multiple identities, existing in various planes. The strongest one, and the one we want to help her cling to, is that of your trusted colleague and friend. She knows where she stands in that existence, with you as her mentor and Agent Shepard as her protector. If those roles change and she no longer recognizes where she fits, she may feel she doesn't belong and lose grip on this reality altogether."

"Dr. Dvita, with all due respect, I know what Claire exhibited today was unusual, but I've worked with her for years. She's never displayed signs of multiple personalities before."

"Often that's how mental health conditions occur. They're not there until they are."

"Right, but last year I wasn't there for Claire. She got mixed up with drugs and the wrong people. Isn't it likely that trauma is causing her confusion? There are a plethora of cases where subjects revert to past or imaginary identities as a protective coping mechanism."

"Absolutely. DID is usually caused by past trauma. But the issue isn't identifying the trauma. It's treating the symptoms."

"DID?" Dana sat back, letting her shock set in.

"DID is shorthand for dissociative identity disorder," Dr. Dvita explained.

"I know what it stands for," Dana snapped. "I don't agree with the diagnosis."

"You don't have to agree with me, Dr. Gray. But it's my professional opinion that Claire needs to continue seeking psychiatric guidance to keep her episodes from worsening. At the moment, she is under my care, and I'd like that to continue." He paused, his dark eyes evaluating Dana. "But if you'd rather a second opinion, I can make the necessary referrals."

Dana stared at the man, trying to decipher if he was driven by an ulterior motive. It was times like these when she missed Jake. He was much better at reading people than she was.

"You've shared your diagnosis with Claire?" Dana asked.

"I haven't," he answered. "I'm only sharing it with you because Claire authorized you and Agent Shepard on her medical release forms. You're both listed as her emergency contacts."

Dana ignored the pang of emotions crowding her chest. "Why haven't you shared your opinion with Claire?"

"In my experience labeling a disorder such as this can exacerbate the symptoms."

Dana nodded. She was familiar with the phenomenon: interpersonal expectancy effect, more commonly known as a self-fulfilling prophecy; whereby initially unfounded expectations led to the fulfillment of those expectations.

Believing you will do poorly on an exam and then failing the test, was a typical example. Letting one's beliefs influence their behavior and performances, contributing to the expected outcome could be harmful. Especially if the person's expected behavior serves to bring about destructive mental health issues.

"Do you believe Claire can still advocate for herself?" Dana asked.

"Yes. Her triggers can be managed, and she only exhibits dissociative identities while under hypnosis."

"Then why don't we let Claire decide if she wants to continue seeing you."

"I'm comfortable with that, so long as you agree to help her continue treatment elsewhere in the event she chooses not to stay with me."

Dana agreed. "So where do we go from here?"

"I'd like to see Claire again tomorrow. Due to the fire, we'll be unable to return to Passages for quite some time. While the police continue their investigation, I've arranged a space at St. Ann's. I'll be holding group meetings there twice a week for all my patients who've been displaced by these unfortunate events."

Dr. Dvita took a business card out of his wallet and scribbled an address and time on the back before handing it to Dana. "I think Claire would benefit from being able to discuss the events that took place at Passages with peers who understand what she's truly going through."

"I'll make sure to pass the invitation to Claire."

"Thank you." Dr. Dvita stood and shook Dana's hand. He was halfway to the door when Dana thought of something.

"What about Meredith?"

He turned to face her. "What about Miss Kincaid?"

"You said you thought Claire could benefit from seeing how far Meredith had come in her recovery, but you said something changed your mind."

"Not something, someone." Dr. Dvita released a long exhale. "I don't want to speak ill of the dead, but I'm glad Congressman Hayes is no longer spreading his poison in the world."

"What do you mean?"

"Do you know what the term *primary* refers to in my profession, Dr. Gray?"

"Yes, the influencer."

"Correct. Congressman Hayes was one of the most gifted influencers I've ever come across. The trouble was, he didn't use his persuasion for good."

"Why was he at Passages?"

"I wish I could say more, but deceased or not, he's still my patient and protected under privileged confidentiality."

"Do you think he was trying to influence Claire?"

"I'm not sure, but I'd like to find out. It's why I'd like to continue seeing her."

"And Meredith? Did he try to influence her?"

"You'd have to ask her."

"I will," Dana challenged.

"I'm sure you will." He turned to leave but Dana wasn't finished with her questions.

"One more thing. Do you think it's odd Claire is so concerned with Max?"

He gave a tired smile. "I wouldn't use the term odd. It's quite common for patients like Claire to get attached to the people who treat them kindly. In Claire's case I would find it *odd* if she didn't seek out someone to connect with."

"I'm glad she made a friend there."

But Dr. Dvita was quick to dash Dana's relief. "I don't know that Max is the kind of friend Claire should have. It's my understanding they bonded over the similarities of their troubled pasts."

"Troubled? Is he someone we should be worried about?"

"Isn't there always something to worry about, Dr. Gray?"

Dana watched Dr. Dvita walk out her front door, leaving her with the chill from the brisk morning and his parting words.

22

Green case folders fanned across the lackluster steel counter, each one encapsulating the end of a life. Jake didn't bother glancing at them. He'd already found what he'd come for. Dana was right. His trip to the morgue didn't make him feel better.

Seeing the cold slab of flesh didn't make Jake feel anything at all.

He didn't know what he'd expected.

Absolution from his guilt?

Satisfaction that Norton Hayes was no longer breathing?

Whatever Jake had been hoping to find eluded him.

But still, he stood before the open drawer unable to pull himself away. The temperature-controlled unit hissed its protest, spilling chilled air into the cavernous space. Jake couldn't tear his gaze away from the mangled corpse of the man who'd taken so much from him.

The brutal lacerations across Hayes' throat should've evoked some kind of emotion from Jake, but they didn't.

Maybe it'd finally happened. The job had fully desensitized him.

Jake was contemplating his profession when the peaceful inner sanctuary of the D.C. Medical Examiner's office was rudely interrupted.

"Shepard! Do you have any idea the shitstorm you just caused me?"

"Hi Jenks, I see you got my message."

"Don't give me that attitude! I just got pulled out of a meeting with the DOJ so I could talk down the Chief ME who was convinced '*my guy*' was making threats."

Jake waved off her accusation. "I wouldn't call them threats. More like stern suggestions."

"Shep, this isn't a joke. I told you to back off this case loud and clear. I need you to hear me."

Jake dropped his nonchalant act. "No, I need *you* to hear *me*. I know you think I can't handle this case because Hayes is the reason my team came home in pine boxes, but I would've hoped I've proven myself to you over the years."

"Yes, Jake. Threatening your way into the morgue to feed your sadistic vendetta against Hayes has given me the utmost faith that you can *handle* this."

"I needed to see for myself."

"Jake. I get it. I have my demons, too. I'm sorry you weren't the one who got to slay this dragon, but it doesn't matter. Nothing is going to bring back the men you lost. I know you know that, and the only thing you're proving right now is that I was right to keep you out of this in the first place."

Jake laughed. "If you think I'm going to back off now that this bastard has tangled Claire and Dana in his web of self-serving bull-shit you haven't been paying attention."

"No, Jake. You're the one not paying attention. I've told you from the beginning that this one is out of our league. Today that was made official."

"What are you talking about?"

"Why do you think I was meeting with the DOJ?"

"They're taking over?"

"Of course they are."

Jake scratched his head, pacing away from Jenkins as he digested the news. "The only reason the Department of Justice would get involved is if they suspected this goes higher up than just some congressional misconduct." He stopped pacing. "Why was Hayes in rehab?"

"Jake, the man's dead. Let him rest in peace."

"He's a public official. There's no way his murder doesn't get press. If there's dirt to find, it'll come out."

Jenkins sighed in defeat. "Hayes was in for substance abuse."

Jake's temper spiked, his first thought of his fallen comrades. "Drugs? How far back does it go? Because if that's why he made that call in Ghazni—"

"Jake, don't go dredging up the past. It's only gonna make those families relive their losses again. It's time to let it go."

"I tried to let it go, but I watched Hayes get away with murder, and then get rewarded with a cushy Congressional office. I'm tired of watching politicians build their careers on the backs of good men and women they view as disposable."

"This goes higher than Congress. Hayes was on the short list for the VP ticket. They planned to announce it when he got out of rehab."

"What? They were going to put him in the White House?"

Jenkins shrugged. "Word is he was willing to back POTUS's agenda."

"Is that all it takes? Hayes would back anything if it served his personal agenda. And I'll tell you one thing, I'm gonna find out what it was, because my gut tells me it's why he's lying in the morgue."

"You can give your gut a rest, Jake. You're not getting assigned to this case."

"Assignment or not, it's still my job to serve this country." Jake jabbed a finger at Hayes's corpse. "That's why I'm gonna make sure this spineless prick's agendas die with him."

Jenkins sank down onto the cold metal stool with a heavy sigh. "I know you're not gonna let this go, so let's hear it. I know you've cooked up a theory already."

"Jenks, think about it. There's no way Hayes was qualified to run for Vice President. That means he has something on someone powerful enough to make that happen. To anyone who didn't want him in office, his death may look like dodging a bullet, but what I'm worried about is the bullets left in the chamber."

"Jake if you dig into this, I'm telling you, one of those bullets is gonna have your name on it."

"What aren't you telling me?"

"Hayes was at Passages for more than just substance abuse. He was caught with a minor."

"What the—"

Jenkins held her hands up and rushed to finish her explanation before Jake could fully fly off the handle. "The girl was a 17-year-old junkie and says the whole thing was consensual."

"That doesn't make it okay!" Jake punched the closest thing to him, denting the metal cooler. He held onto the pain stinging his knuckles, but it wasn't enough to quiet the rage roaring through him. "He's lucky he's already dead, because if I find out that son of a bitch even looked at Claire wrong ..."

"Jake, I've got no love for the man, or the way Hayes ran the DOD when he was there, but you can't go around crying scandal about a decorated Veteran and Congressman who was almost decapitated by someone playing Grim Reaper. Everything I told you is off the record, and it needs to stay that way."

"I'm not looking to smear his name, Jenks. I just want to make sure whatever got him killed isn't gonna roll down hill and land on Claire or Dana, or even Meredith for that matter."

The cool exterior Jenkins always exuded slipped. "Did you find out what she has to do with this?"

"She and Claire share the same therapist. He apparently thought they could learn from each other, so he hosted a few group sessions for them at Passages."

"Jesus. Has anyone checked that woman's room for a Grim Reaper costume?"

Jake knew Jenkins was only half serious, but it was refreshing to find someone who shared his sentiment when it came to Meredith Kincaid. Dana was too blinded by guilt to see that the woman who she'd once considered a friend might be beyond saving.

"Now do you see why I need to be a part of this investigation?" he asked.

"Jake, you're under the misguided notion that I have any say in this matter. I told you, it's out of my hands."

"Then I'll offer my services to the Department of Justice."

"The hell you will. You're still on leave after your last case, and if you even think about throwing your hat in the ring with the DOJ I'll tell them you're not mentally fit to return to duty."

"Jenks—"

"Don't Jenks me! It's not gonna happen. Even if you could manage to talk your way into this, they'll boot you the second they find out your history with Hayes."

"Then tell me what to do, Jenks! Because the star witness in this case is Claire, and I'm not throwing her in a room with the DOJ if I don't have a seat at the table."

Jake watched his mentor's face pale. "Claire witnessed the murder?"

"Yes," he pulled his notebook from his pocket. "She repressed it, but her therapist helped her remember and I got it all right here."

"Jake, if you don't hand that over, it's obstruction of justice."

"You think I don't know that? It's why I'm trying to cement myself in the investigation."

She shook her head. "It's too late. Metro has 24 hours to turn the investigation over to DOJ. Hartwell's overseeing the evidence transfer. You need to give him Claire's witness account."

"In exchange for what?" Jake demanded.

"Good faith."

Jake fumed. "That's not enough."

"It's gonna have to be this time, Jake. I worked this thing with Hartwell from ground zero. You know everything we do. DOJ has got this buttoned up tighter than a gnat's ass." Jenkins stepped between Jake and Hayes's lifeless body, silently sliding the drawer back into the refrigerated core and shutting the locker. "Jake, it's time to let this go."

"And do what?"

"I don't know. Get back to having a life?"

"Is that what you'd do?"

Jenkins gave him her patented *don't test me* glare. She used it on him so much in his youth that he and Wade coined it 'the look'. "No, Jake. I don't have a life to get back to because I never knew when to stop putting the job first."

Jake cocked an eyebrow in her direction. "You realize you're asking me to do something you couldn't."

"Okay, you don't wanna go home to Dana and Claire, fine, but I'm pretty sure there's something else that should be higher on your priority list than picking a fight with a dead man. And from what I hear, you don't have a lot of time to make good on your word to your uncle."

"Wade told you?"

"Of course, Wade told me. That man never met a thought he didn't share."

Jake smirked. "He sure loves the sound of his own voice, doesn't he?"

This time it was Jenkins who grinned. "Don't I know it. He tells me everything. Even the things I don't wanna know."

"Do you think I should do it?"

"What I think isn't relevant."

It was Jake's turn to give Jenkins 'the look.' "Since when?"

"Fine. I get your reservations. After what your father put you through, I'd have them, too. But this isn't about us. If Wade says this is what Helen needs, trust him."

Jake threaded his hands behind his head and exhaled, suddenly drained. "It's that simple?"

"It can be."

Resigned, Jake followed Jenkins out of the morgue. The midday sun stung his eyes. He'd gotten used to the shadowy depths that entombed D.C.'s deceased. It made him think of Dana and her library. He'd always thought it was creepy, but he'd recently seen the appeal.

Things that were already dead, couldn't hurt you. And right now, that was all he wanted. To stop everyone he loved from hurting.

Claire, Dana, his mother, Wade, Jenkins.

Not finding a way onto this case made him feel like he was failing them.

Maybe Jenkins was right. If he had to let Hayes go, he could still do right by his mother and Wade. He just needed to find a way to protect Claire and Dana at the same time.

Jenkins turned to face Jake when they reached the parking lot, but he was the one who spoke first. "We've been through it haven't we, Jenks?"

"Sure have."

"I don't think I've ever told you how much it's meant to me that you've always had my back."

"Any time, soldier."

"That's not what I mean, and you know it."

In a rare show of affection, she put a hand on his arm. "Jake, if I've helped shape your life in any way, the privilege has been all mine. But promise me one thing. If you've learned anything from me, I hope you don't repeat my mistakes. Life is short. Don't wait too long to start it."

23

AT FIRST, I WAS WORRIED THEY WERE ON TO ME. THERE'S ONLY SO much I can control.

The political fallout wasn't part of the plan, but I can see now that it should be. It's working perfectly. Even better than I could've planned.

The connection to Agent Shepard is a brilliant twist. One that should keep him off my back.

It's why I chose to kill him first.

It was harder than I thought to do it. He struggled. I hadn't expected that. He knew what was at stake. He should've been prepared.

But now that I've started, I can't stop.

A few more days.

A few more kills.

Then I'll be free.

24

DANA MANAGED TO OCCUPY HERSELF FOR EXACTLY FORTY-FIVE MINUTES after Dr. Dvita left. Her kitchen was spotless, and she'd successfully returned her bathroom to order after Jake's hasty shower, but more importantly, she'd given Claire her space.

It was killing Dana not to go in and check on the girl, but she'd made herself wait what she deemed the appropriate amount of time. Not too long as to appear she didn't care, but not too soon to show her worry. Though a glance in the mirror told Dana her face would instantly betray her concern.

Her glasses made her already doe-like eyes seem bigger than they were. And right now, they were two fathomless pits of worry. Deciding to switch to contacts, she pulled her hair back into a messy bun and washed her face. Hoping she now exuded an air of effortless ease, she took a deep breath and padded down the hall to knock on her guest bedroom door.

It turned out Dana's primping was unnecessary. Because when Claire didn't answer, Dana burst into the room like a tornado of panic.

Claire was in the room, but Dana's relief at finding her there was short-lived. The girl sat on the edge of the tidy bed, her slight frame facing the window.

With Claire's back to Dana, she had no idea if the girl was in another catatonic trance.

Dana whispered her name, hoping not to startle her. "Claire?"

Claire turned around. "Oh, sorry. Were you calling me? I must've been lost in thought."

"No, it's okay. I just knocked. I was going to make some lunch. Would you like to join me?"

"Sure. I'll be out in a minute."

Dana stood awkwardly in the bedroom, caught between being desperate to stay, yet eager to leave. She hated this new clumsiness between them. Dana missed the easy bond she and Claire had always shared.

From their first encounter, Dana felt they were kindred spirits. The approximate ten-year age difference had never really been a factor. They'd always been able to relate as colleagues, women, and friends.

But ever since returning from her book tour last year, Dana found their relationship strained.

It worsened when Dana was forced to lie to Claire during her last FBI case, and further still when she recommended Claire be admitted to rehab.

It didn't seem to matter that everything Dana had done was in Claire's best interest. Somehow, their relationship had been altered, and Dana feared there was no going back. She'd gone from mentor and friend to caretaker and pseudo-parent.

Dana felt equipped for neither. But sadly, Claire had no one else. A fact made evident by the lack of interest her parents continued to show. They'd yet to return any of the phone calls or messages Dana left for them last night.

It made Dana even more desperate to connect with Claire. She hated thinking they'd be forever stuck in this limbo. She wanted her friend back.

Letting herself find hope in Dr. Dvita's words had been a mistake.

Claire may have described Dana as a mentor and friend, but actions were louder than words.

Hesitant to push Claire beyond her comfort level, Dana began backing out of the bedroom. "Feel free to help yourself to any of my clothes. I'll be in the kitchen."

Claire's voice stopped her. "Dana. I'm sorry if I scared you."

"You don't have to apologize."

"I do." Claire walked slowly around the bed to face Dana. "I don't know what it looks like when I'm under hypnotherapy, but I can remember how it feels. And if it looks half that bad, then I'm sorry you had to see it."

Dana took a tentative step closer. "Claire, are you comfortable continuing to see Dr. Dvita, because I can help you find someone else."

"Dr. Dvita is fine."

"Are you sure? When I first told you he was coming here you acted like you were afraid of him."

She nodded. "It's hard to explain. Like I said, I don't exactly remember what I'm going through when I'm under hypnosis, but my body does. I have this involuntary response every time I see him. Like fight or flight. I want to run, but I know I need to stay and fight if I'm going to get better. Does that make sense?"

Dana absorbed Claire's description. "It does. I just want you to know that if at any point you don't like Dr. Dvita's approach or his treatment becomes too much for you, we can look for someone new."

"Thanks, but I'd rather stick with him. I feel like I'm making progress, and if I start with a new doctor I'll be starting over again." Claire sank down onto the bed, sitting again, like she no longer possessed the strength to stand. "I've been in a dark tunnel for so long. I just want to be on the other side already."

"You'll get there, Claire."

"Sometimes I'm not so sure."

Dana's heart went out to the girl. Without thinking, she went to sit on the bed next to her, but Claire flinched away the moment Dana touched her. "Sorry," Dana muttered, retreating to the door to give the girl some space. "I'll be in the kitchen."

Dana busied herself chopping vegetables, but it left her mind idle enough to ponder if Claire really would get better. It'd been months since she nearly OD'd and, in some ways, Claire seemed worse than ever.

After admitting Claire to rehab, Dana spent countless nights reading about the lasting effects of heroin use. She wished she could stop her analytical mind from recalling them, but the facts resurfaced unbidden.

Changes in the physical structure and physiology of the brain were the most concerning.

Deterioration of the brain's white matter.

Irreversible imbalances in decision-making abilities.

Irregular behavior and responses to stressful situations.

Then there was insomnia, memory loss, depression, and antisocial personality disorders.

Today, Dana had seen Claire exhibit almost every single symptom.

Claire had always been guarded with her personal space, especially when it came to physical touch. But over the years, she'd seen the girl blossom socially. Especially when it came to Dana and Jake. But in the short time she'd been at rehab, Claire had gone from hugging Dana to flinching away from her touch again.

It fit within the parameters of Dr. Dvita's diagnosis, but there was something immensely sad about being unable to comfort her friend.

25

JAKE BLEW INTO THE METRO PD PRECINCT LOOKING WINDSWEPT. THE biting spring weather couldn't seem to shake winter's grasp. An image of palm trees and sun setting over the clear blue sea flashed into his mind.

Maybe Jenkins wasn't wrong about the whole vacation idea.

Pushing his daydreams away, Jake focused on why he was here.

He passed his credentials to the officer behind the bulletproof glass and was buzzed in without any fanfare. Hartwell was easy enough to find thanks to his shiny new office.

"Nice digs," Jake greeted.

Hartwell was already shaking his head. "Shepard, I don't need flak from you right now. I've already got my hands full."

"What if I told you I was here to help?"

"I'd call bullshit."

Jake slapped his notebook down on Hartwell's cluttered desk. "If you're calling eyewitness accounts bullshit these days things must be going pretty well at Metro."

Hartwell stopped shuffling papers and grabbed the notebook, his eyes scanning Jake's notes. "Male, six-foot, small build, black hoodie, scythe." Hartwell's eyes snapped up to meet Jake's. "The witness used this word, scythe?"

"Yes."

Hartwell still had his finger hovering over the word scythe. "Is this legit?"

"I took the statement myself."

"I can't get you on the case, Shepard."

"I know. That's not why I'm here."

"Then how 'bout you stop wasting my time and tell me what you want."

"Claire Townsend is the witness."

"That poor girl witnessed this mess?" He shook his head. "First the nightmare with the Card Killer and now this? Talk about tough luck."

"That's why I've gotta ask, is there any way you can get me access to the case files before you have to transfer everything to DOJ?"

"I'm sorry. I wish I could help, but DOJ is on my ass and I'm not looking to make any enemies over there."

"I get it." Jake took a seat in front of Hartwell's desk and eyed the stack of case folders. "But what do you say you step out to make copies of my witness account and I'll just wait here?"

Hartwell laughed. "Do I look like I was born yesterday? I don't think so."

"Hartwell, do me this solid and I'll owe you one."

"Yeah, a lot of good that'll do me when I get a pink slip for missing evidence."

"Nothing's gonna go missing. Stand here and watch me if you have to," Jake argued. "Hartwell, Claire's like a kid sister to me. I have to know I did everything in my power to make sure nothing was missed that could put her in danger."

Hartwell stood and crossed his arms. "Are you saying you don't think I can do my job?"

"I think it's been established that we're both good at our jobs," Jake rebutted, holding Hartwell's stare.

"Fine." He picked up his desk phone and dialed an extension.

Jake couldn't hear the voice on the other end, but Hartwell's message was clear. "I need you in my office," was all he said before hanging up.

Jake was momentarily wondering if he was about to get a police escort out of the building. But when a fresh-faced officer poked his head in, Jake regained his composure. He had about a hundred pounds on the officer, leaving him confident he could still walk out with his dignity.

"Lennox, I need you to make one copy of each of these pages. Go directly to the copier and directly back, and if you show anyone else what's on these pages, I'll assign you to the drunk tank for the rest of your career."

"Got it," Lennox said, taking the notebook and hurrying away.

Hartwell opened the folders on his desk. "You've got till he gets back."

Jake grinned. "That's all I need."

26

CLAIRE CAME INTO THE KITCHEN WEARING DANA'S CLOTHES. THE oversized black sweater and leggings only made the girl's slim frame look even smaller. Dana wanted to say something flattering, but she'd never been the flattering type.

Instead, she offered, "I can take you to pick up your things from storage tomorrow if you'd like."

"Thanks," Claire replied, taking a seat at the kitchen island.

Dana placed a piping hot bowl of butternut bisque in front of Claire. "Speaking of tomorrow, Dr. Dvita said he's having a group meeting at St. Ann's if you're interested. He's opened it to all his patients from Passages."

"Yes. I'd like that."

Dana served herself a bowl of soup and took a seat next to Claire. She stirred her spoon, wondering how best to start a conversation about Claire's rehab. She didn't want to come off as prying, but she wanted Claire to know she could talk to her. Dana blew on her soup, wishing she'd had more time with her own mother, so she'd be better equipped to handle difficult discussions.

Dana was only thirteen when she lost her parents. Their memories faded with each year that passed. She was determined not to let that happen with Claire.

Her friend was right here in front of her, and Dana was going to fight to hold on to their memories, so they'd have a chance at making more.

"Anyone particular you're hoping to see at St. Ann's tomorrow?" she asked.

Claire shrugged.

"Do you think Max will be there?"

Claire's gaze slid to meet Dana's. "Why do you say it like that?"

"Like what?" Dana asked.

"Like you think I know something I'm not saying?"

Dana put her spoon down. "I don't think that."

Suspicion crept into Claire's voice. "What did Dr. Dvita say to you?"

"We discussed the importance of continuing your treatment, especially after what you just witnessed."

She huffed a bitter laugh. "Let me guess, you think it made me more damaged than I already am?"

"No one thinks you're damaged, Claire."

"You do. It's why you're lying to me right now. I despise liars. I thought you did, too. That's why I wanted to work for you. To shed light on the darkness. Isn't that what you always say? Or was that a lie, too?"

"Claire ... I ..." Dana stammered, at a loss for words.

She'd been so shocked by Claire's sudden mood swing that she hadn't even heard Jake come in, but his booming voice preceded him. "There's my favorite girls." He strode over to Dana and Claire and gave their shoulders a squeeze. "What's for lunch? I'm starved."

Claire shoved back from the counter and stood. "I'm not hungry," she muttered before stomping down the hall and slamming her bedroom door.

Jake raised his eyebrows. "What was that all about?"

Dana slumped in her seat; her appetite gone as well. "I don't know what's going on with her, but it's not good."

Jake picked up Claire's spoon and started shoveling the barely touched soup into his mouth. "Let me guess?" he muttered around a spoonful. "Dr. Doom filled your head with a bunch of nonsense psychobabble that's got ya second guessing our girl."

"Jake, he might be right."

It was Jake's turn to push back from the counter. "You're kidding, right? He's known her for all of a few weeks. This is Claire we're talking about. The girl who's saved our asses more than once. Hell, Dana, we're the reason she even needs help. If it wasn't for our cases, she wouldn't have been dragged through hell and back."

"You think I don't know that?" Dana whispered. "I regret every moment of her involvement, but I can't change the past. And the truth is, after what she's been through, we might need to accept that she might not be the same person we knew."

"That sounds an awful lot like what I said to you about Meredith. Do you remember what you said to me?" Jake reached over and took her hand. "You said, we don't give up on the people we love. We don't give up on family."

Dana had to bite her lip to keep her tears at bay. She pulled her hand from Jake's and stood. She paced over to the window, crossing her arms tight enough to hold herself together. "What if I was wrong?"

Jake moved behind her and pulled her into his arms. "Hey." He turned her to face him and gently hooked a finger under her chin, lifting it until she met his eyes. "You're not wrong. And whatever this is with Claire, we're going to fight through it together, okay?"

Dana gave a feeble nod.

"Now," Jake said. "Tell me exactly what Dr. Doom said to mess with that beautiful mind of yours."

The alarm on Dana's watch buzzed, saving her from answering. Silencing it, she reached for Jake's hand. "I will. I promise, but it's not something we can discuss with Claire in earshot. Besides, I have an appointment to go see Meredith, and I don't want to be late."

Jake squeezed her hand. "Okay, I'll hold down the fort and work on chasing down some of my old DOJ contacts."

"The DOJ is handling the case now?"

Jake nodded, scrubbing a hand over his stubble. "I just came from talking to Hartwell. He gave me a peek at the crime scene evidence. Right now, they don't have any solid leads. He said he'll do his best to feed me any new leads, but there might not be any now that DOJ's taking over."

"And did you see Congressman Hayes?"

"What's left of him." Jake sighed. "You were right. I don't feel any better, but I'm not in the mood for an 'I told you so.'"

"I wasn't going to say that." Dana hated that he thought she would. "I understand the need for closure after loss."

Jake's eyes softened. "I know you do."

"We can talk more when I get back."

"Okay but do something for me."

"What's that?"

"Try to focus on what we have going for us. Claire is safe. She's here with us." He took a step closer. "Things can go back to normal. We just need to give it some time."

Dana wanted more than anything to believe that, but normal had never been her reality. She studied death for a living, and Jake ran headlong after it. With those parameters, normal seemed impossible. And so did all hope of them finally getting their timing right.

She wanted to be with Jake, but if it would put Claire's mental health in jeopardy, she'd have to lock her heart away again. It was something she was used to by now, but the fleeting glimpses at what she and Jake could have been was like teasing a death row inmate with a pardon.

"We've got this, Dana. One step at a time."

Dana met Jake's gaze, his bright blue eyes steady and reassuring. "One step at a time," she answered.

"Now go get some answers from Meredith."

When Jake pulled her in for a kiss, she let him, stretching up on her toes to savor every moment, knowing this kiss would have to be their last for a while.

Dana turned to go, but Jake pulled her back.

"When you get back, let's do movie night. Claire can pick the movie. I'll make the popcorn. You pick up the takeout."

She nodded and forced a smile before leaving the warmth of her home and heading out into the windswept day.

27

JAKE STOOD AT THE WINDOW WATCHING DANA DRIVE OFF. SEEING HER near tears was more than enough to rattle him. She was a strong woman—always reminding him of a desert flower; wild and beautiful, and deceptively strong. Somehow managing to survive despite the inhospitable environment. He told himself she'd survive this, too.

She had to.

He was so close to having everything he'd never let himself want. With his fantasy within reach he wasn't about to let some headshrinker take it all away. Jake knew he wasn't wrong about Claire. She was still the girl they knew. He just needed to find a way to help her find her way back. It wouldn't be easy considering the most recent horrors she'd witnessed, but he wasn't in the habit of giving up on people who'd saved his life.

Without much of a plan, he found himself knocking on Claire's door. "Claire, can I come in?"

The lock tumbled and the door creaked open enough for him to see the pale shadow of the girl he considered family. Stuffing his hands in his pockets, Jake weighed his options. He'd never been much for coddling, so he approached the situation the only way he knew how—head on.

"I may not have a bunch of letters after my name, but I don't need to in order to see what's right in front of me." He pushed the door open fully and looked straight into Claire's ice-blue eyes. "Claire, whatever this is you're going through, I know you're strong enough to handle it."

She looked down, picking at the hem of her too-long sleeves. "What if I'm not?"

"Then you lean on me. I've got your back, kid."

She glanced up at him, eyes full of pain. "I heard what you said about Hayes. How can you hate him and not hate me?"

"What do you mean? You're nothing like Hayes."

"But I am. We both made mistakes, and we were both working on making amends for them in rehab."

"I don't know what he said to you about his *mistakes*, but you're nothing like him."

"You may not want to see it, but he wasn't that different from me. And just like me, he was trying to get better, trying to change."

"People like him don't change."

"If you believe that, then you must believe I can't change either."

"That's not what I'm saying, Claire. Why is what I think of him so important anyway?"

"Because! Hayes was like me. He understood what I was going through. He was showing me what kind of life I could have if I could finally silence these demons, because he'd done it before. But if after all he did to try to fix things, if people like you just end up hating him anyway, even after he's gone, what's it all for?"

Jake exhaled slowly, trying to gather his thoughts. "Claire, I'm trying to see this from your perspective, but you have to know you are nothing like Hayes. Time and time again he put himself and his agendas first and his selfish aspirations got people killed. People I cared about. I don't know how to forgive that. Not when Hayes is the only reason they died."

Claire cocked her head to the side, her voice suddenly an icy whisper. "But I'm the reason people die, too."

Jake instantly regretted his choice of words. "Claire, Sadie's death was not your fault. What happened to her was tragic, but she made her own choices. We all do."

He hadn't meant to bring it up, but of course Claire's thoughts would go to her friend. Watching someone die tends to cement itself in your DNA. And yet again, Claire had watched another person die right in front of her last night. Hayes may have been getting help, but the fact that his death had inadvertently made things more difficult for Claire only made Jake hate the man even more.

Claire crossed her arms. "I guess we'll have to agree to disagree."

Sighing, Jake started to retreat from her room, then paused, turning back to face her. "I know this might be a long shot, but do you think we can put our differences aside long enough to work together on something?"

"Depends what it is," Claire replied.

"I've decided to find my father."

28

St. Elizabeth's federal psychiatric facility wasn't known for its inviting atmosphere, but these days, Dana felt more at home there than anywhere else in D.C. The pale ivory walls and spotless white linoleum tile floor welcomed her like a familiar friend. Even the sterile scent of lemony-fresh cleaner put Dana at ease.

Here everything was as it should be. Neat, orderly, safe. The clang of the magnetic locks closing behind her drove home the security measures of the psychiatric facility. No one was getting out without notice, or more importantly ... no one was getting in.

Ever since seeing Meredith's face in the photograph with Claire and Congressman Hayes, Dana hadn't been able to shake the feeling that her friend was in danger. She knew it was irrational. Dana had to hand over her credentials and two forms of identification just to get buzzed past the front desk. But her time with Jake and the FBI had taught her to trust her gut.

It's why she was here.

That and Dana couldn't ignore the guilt nagging her for letting the time between her visits with Meredith stretch longer than it should.

After quickly signing in with the nurse on Meredith's floor and surrendering her handbag and cell phone, Dana walked through her second metal detector of the day and submitted to a pat down before being escorted to room 241.

Relief whooshed through Dana's lungs when she glimpsed Meredith sitting in her bed, a book propped open on her knees. The nurse punched in a code on the keypad and the door buzzed open. Meredith looked up, grinning the moment she saw Dana. "I didn't know you were coming today. It's been a while."

"I know. I'm sorry about that."

Meredith dogeared a page and shut her book. "You don't need to apologize. I've been keeping busy."

"So, I've heard."

Meredith's grin faltered. "What's wrong?"

"How do you know something's wrong?"

"Because I know you, Dana. It's been weeks since you've visited and now you show up unannounced looking like you've seen a ghost."

"When I saw this, I thought I had." Dana fished a photograph out of her pocket and handed it to Meredith. "When were you going to tell me about your outings?"

"Whenever you deemed me important enough to visit again," Meredith shot back.

"Please tell me this wasn't to get my attention."

Meredith's gaze lit with amusement. "You know, I almost forgot how narcissistic you are. But in a way, I guess you're right. This was about you."

"How do you mean?"

"I agreed to meet with Claire because I know she means something to you, and Dr. Dvita thought I might be able to get through to her but ..."

"But what?"

Meredith sighed. "Listen, I know you live your life serving the dark, but only in the light can healing begin. And that girl—well I don't think there's an ounce of light left inside her."

Dana jabbed at the book on Meredith's bed. Its self-help title befitting the rest of the collection stacked neatly on the simple desk

C. J. CROSS

in the corner. "Oh, and I supposed you're an expert in psychology now?"

"What's wrong with trying to understand where I went wrong?"

Dana fought the urge to pace, rubbing her temples instead. "I'm sorry. There's nothing wrong with it. I just don't appreciate you passing judgment on Claire."

"Why not? It takes crazy to know crazy."

"Mere ..." Dana warned.

"No. I told Dr. Dvita and now I'm telling you. Something is deeply wrong with that girl, and she's spreading it to everyone around her at that rehab center. I told him I wasn't going back there. The best thing they can do is get her out of there before she and her little friends get carried away."

"What do you mean?"

"I sat it on one of their group sessions the last time I was at Passages. Claire was going on about how scared she is, feeling surrounded by death. I went to go talk to her after the session, but she and her friends were laughing, carrying on about visions of black robes and scythes, like it was all some big joke to them."

Dana's scalp prickled with fear. "What did you say?"

"Black robes and scythes. I heard them talking about it plain as day."

"Who?"

"I don't know, there were four of them. They all go by these ridiculous code names. The only ones I know for sure are Claire and Congressman Hayes. He goes by Taft, but I recognized him from my time on the Hill. He's a total prick, by the way. Definitely not a good crowd she's running with. The orderly seemed nice enough, but the red-haired little thing is a sociopath."

"Did you tell Dr. Dvita all of this?"

Meredith shrugged. "Mostly. I wanted to make it clear I was done helping."

"But did you tell him what you heard Claire say? Specifically, about the scythe?"

"No, I don't think so."

Dana scratched her head, unable to stop herself from pacing the length of the tiny room. "That doesn't make sense," she muttered to herself, but Meredith interrupted her thoughts.

"It doesn't have to make sense to be true."

Dana stopped in her tracks, whirling on her friend. "Mere, try to remember! What exactly did you tell Dr. Dvita you heard?"

"I don't know. What's the big deal?"

"Congressman Hayes is dead. Someone slit his throat with a scythe."

Meredith blinked in disbelief. "What? When?"

Dana held up the photo again. "Shortly after this photo of you and Claire was taken with him."

The color drained from Meredith's face. "What are you saying? You think I'm in danger?"

"I don't know. I was brought in to help identify the murder weapon, but I'm not officially working this case."

"What about Jake?"

"He doesn't have any more information than I do at the moment. The whole thing is being kept tight-lipped due to political ramifications."

"Dana, if I'm in trouble, I need to know I'm being protected."

Seeing her visible distress, Dana sat down on Meredith's bed, taking her friend's hands. "I didn't come here to frighten you. There's no reason to believe you're in danger."

"Dana, I know what I heard. Claire said the word scythe and then a Congressman was murdered with one. That's not a coincidence. If she thinks I can implicate her and her friends they're going to try to tie up loose ends."

"You're sure you heard her say that?"

Meredith's eyes were pleading. "I know I'm in a psych ward, but I know what I heard, Dana. I wouldn't make something like this up. Especially not when things are starting to look up for me."

"What do you mean?"

"My sister's been by to visit. Abby even said she's willing to bring my niece by soon. And she's going to live stream her wedding so I can be a part of it. Plus, she's helped me get a new lawyer, who says if I keep cooperating, I can possibly get my sentence reduced and get out of here before the end of time. I'm not going to do anything to screw that up."

Warmth filled Dana's chest, momentarily driving away the chill Meredith's revelation filled her with. "I'm so happy to hear Abby's back in your life."

"Me too," Meredith whispered through a teary smile. "Dana, I know Claire is your friend. But I was your friend once, too."

"You still are, Mere. That's why I'm here. I told you I'm not giving up on you and I meant it."

"Then promise me you'll be careful around Claire. If there's one thing I know, it's when someone isn't in control of themselves. She reminds me of myself, or at least how I was before I got help."

"Claire's getting help, too. I'm taking her to see Dr. Dvita tomorrow."

Meredith's eyes lit up. "He records all his sessions. Ask him to see his footage of Claire. Then you can see for yourself. There's a darkness inside her, and we should all be afraid of what happens if it's found a way out."

29

Jake sat at Dana's kitchen island, watching Claire through tendrils of steam from his coffee. She was perched on the barstool next to him, her fingers swiftly dancing over the keyboard. A curtain of black hair surrounded the boney shoulders protruding from the wide neck of the oversized black sweater she wore, and every few minutes her staccato of typing was interrupted just long enough for her to push her cat eye glasses back up her button nose.

All wide-eyes and lanky limbs hunched over a keyboard—Claire was a scene straight out of an anime comic, but Jake couldn't help thinking this was the most alive he'd seen the girl he'd affectionately nicknamed Elvira.

He also couldn't help thinking that Dana was wrong for buying into Dr. Dvita's assessment.

Claire wasn't the damaged, fragile girl Dvita was peddling. If anything, Jake thought she was doing remarkably well after all she'd gone through. He'd seen cases like this before, where doctors prolonged treatment just to keep collecting a check. But he'd be damned if he'd let that happen to Claire.

"So, what else do you need from me?" Jake asked.

Claire gave him a sideways glance. "Um, patience would be nice.

We just started looking, and since you don't have anything besides a name and birthdate it's not exactly a lot to go on, but you knew that already. I mean, finding people is like your thing, right?"

He huffed a laugh. "Yeah, in the middle of a war zone maybe, but this isn't like tracking a terrorist. I'm looking for a civilian. Besides, you're the research genius. I thought you might have some tricks up your sleeve."

"What do you think I've been doing? Playing D & D?"

He arched a brow. "I'm not even going to pretend I know what that means."

Claire smirked. "Some Secret Agent Man." She turned her attention back to the laptop to continue typing.

"Do you think Dana'd be into helping us with this project?" Jake asked.

"Are you kidding? She's a professional researcher. She lives for this stuff. Plus, it's for you. Putting you first is her favorite hobby."

Before Jake could ask what Claire meant by that, she was turning the laptop toward him. "This website is probably your best bet for tracking someone down who doesn't want to be found."

Jake blinked at the dark web portal staring back at him. "How do you know about a site like this?"

"Research genius, remember?" she teased.

Jake took a sip of his coffee and skimmed the website. Everything and anything was available for purchase. In his line of work he knew black market hubs like this existed, but it was alarming how easily Claire had been able to gain access.

"Do you use sites like this often at the Smithsonian?"

"How do you think Dr. Gray and I satisfy our taste for vampire blood?" Claire mocked.

"Very funny, Elvira."

She grinned. "Occult artifacts aren't exactly lining the shelves of an Amazon warehouse. Sites like these are the best resource for tracking down things that shouldn't exist. Spell kits, sacred bones, moon stones, ritualistic tools. Most of them are hoaxes, but every once in a while, we find a genuine artifact."

"Like that mask I broke?" Jake asked. "Think we could find another one on here?"

Claire laughed. "No, that was a one of a kind artifact from the African Kazanzi. It was worn during voodoo funerals to keep death away from the living. It was on loan from a museum in New Orleans."

Jake cringed. "What was it doing in Dana's house?"

"Her work on tracing the origin of vampirism is highly sought after. She'd just managed to link the original Venetian vampiric cult to one that appeared in early eighteenth-century New Orleans when I started working for her. The museum loaned her the mask to help prove her research along with a grant to continue researching her theory in New Orleans, but she never went."

"What stopped her?"

Claire's clear blue eyes bore straight into him before she answered. "You did."

"What?"

"You barged into her office with a case folder and dragged us into a world with different kinds of monsters than the ones we study."

There was no accusation in Claire's voice, but Jake felt it all the same. "Claire, I never wanted this life for either of you. If I knew what would come of all of this, I never would've set foot in the Smithsonian."

She gave him a tight smile. "Yes you would. It's what you do. Actually, it's what we all do, I guess. We bring light to the darkness in the world."

Jake nodded, knowing she was right. He talked a good game, but he'd been given a direct order to bring Dana onto that FBI case with Cramer. Of course, he hadn't known his former boss's motive at the time, but back then Jake wasn't one to disobey orders. And even though he wished he could've spared Dana and Claire the pain being thrust into his life had caused them, he didn't know how to reconcile the fact that he'd do it all again, if it meant having them in his life. The alternative was too damn depressing.

The only thing he could do now was try to make amends.

"Well, technically, I'm still on leave, and it looks like you've got some free time. Maybe it's time to take that trip to New Orleans."

Claire perked up. "Really?"

"Yeah, why not? I've got an old Army buddy who lives there. We could reconnect while you and Dana do your thing."

"I would love that."

"Yeah?" A ghost of a smile played on Jake's lips. "Me too. It'd be nice to get things back to normal."

Claire gave him a heavy dose of side eye. "You're calling vampire research normal now?"

"Okay, so maybe not normal, but normal enough for a couple of occult librarians," he snarked.

Claire frowned. "I'm not actually a librarian. I should be, but after dropping out of my PhD program and getting fired, I'm not really sure where I stand."

"Dana said she'd have you back when you're ready. And school will be there when you're ready, too."

"But what if I'm never ready?" Claire asked, her mood suddenly somber.

"Hey, you will be. We're gonna get through this. Me and Dana are here to help you. And if you don't think Dr. Dvita is the right fit, we'll find you someone else or no one else if you think that's better."

"No, I want to keep seeing Dr. Dvita. He's helping me face my addiction and learn how to cope with my trauma."

"You sure? 'Cause he didn't exude a whole lot of bedside manner from what I saw. With Passages shut down it might not hurt to get a second opinion."

Claire gave him a knowing look. "You mean while you do a background check on Dvita?"

He held his hands up to convey innocence. "No one said anything about that."

"You forget I'm on your laptop, Secret Agent Man. You should really wipe your search history more often."

Jake pulled the FBI issued laptop away from her. "Hey, can you blame me? I look out for the people I love. That includes you."

Claire blinked her big blue eyes like Jake had just told her the earth was flat. "You love me?"

"Of course. You and Dana are family."

Claire looked down, her cheeks blushing. "Earlier, when you came running into the kitchen in a towel, I kinda got the feeling you and Dana were more than just family."

"Would that be so bad?"

She shrugged. "I don't know. I kinda like things the way they are."

Sensing Claire was less than receptive to the conversation, Jake changed the subject. "Well, I guess we've got enough on our plates as they are. Speaking of plates, I'm starving. Wanna place a to-go order for Dana to pick up?"

Claire brightened. "Thaiphoon?"

"You know it!"

30

TWO YELLOW SMILEY FACES GRINNED BACK AT DANA AS SHE HEFTED THE bags of takeout into her arms. But even piping hot dumplings from her favorite Thai restaurant couldn't erase the chill Meredith's words had left her with. *There's a darkness inside her, and we should all be afraid of what happens if it's found a way out.*

There was no denying Claire wasn't herself, but what Meredith was suggesting was worse than anything Dana could've predicted. Of course, Meredith wasn't the most reliable source, but if what she said was true, it meant either Claire had predicted the Congressman's murder or had some hand in it.

Dana wasn't willing to accept either.

She didn't know what to believe, but as she walked up the dark sidewalk to her house, she knew she needed to find her poker face. The two people waiting for her inside knew her better than anyone else and she didn't want to give anything away until she had a chance to process this information and check the facts.

Tomorrow she'd take Claire to St. Ann's and speak to Dr. Dvita. If she could get access to the tapes of Claire's sessions like Meredith suggested she could form her own conclusions.

Dana's feet felt like lead as she trudged up her front steps. "I just need to get through tonight," she reminded herself.

———————

THE NORMALLY DELICIOUS coconut curry soup tasted like sawdust in Dana's mouth. Washing it down with copious amounts of wine didn't help either. But what could she expect with Claire settled calmly between her and Jake on her living room sofa?

To an outsider, the scene looked perfectly mundane, cozy even. And maybe it was. Maybe Dana was reading entirely too much into things. The girl sitting cross-legged next to her was her friend and colleague, not a cold-blooded killer.

Though Dana knew better than most, wishing something untrue, didn't make it so.

Pushing her unease away, she did her best to pretend it was just like old times. Her, Jake and Claire, watching cheesy movies.

Tonight's selection was *Interview with a Vampire.*

Oblivious to Dana's inner turmoil, Jake extended his arm across the back of the sofa. For an instant, he let his thumb subtly stroke the back of Dana's neck. The fire it ignited within her was instant and all consuming. She flinched away, playing it off like she was reaching for more dumplings, but the bag was long empty.

"You snooze, you lose," Claire teased.

"Want me to make some more popcorn?" Jake offered.

Dana shook her head. "No, thanks." She was having enough trouble keeping what she'd already eaten down. She forced her attention back to the screen and focused on Louis and Lestat's doomed existence.

When the last scene of *Interview with a Vampire* finally graced the screen of her television, Dana breathed a sigh of relief.

Claire leaned forward and grabbed the remote off the coffee table. "Anne Rice is a genius."

"If she approved the makeup and wardrobe, I strongly disagree," Jake teased.

"You're missing the point," Claire argued.

"Which is?"

"Life is death is life."

Jake huffed a laugh. "Well, that's morbid." His voice was still light as he continued to rag on the costumes and special effects, but Dana had stopped listening. Her attention was fixed solely on Claire.

The way the girl had spoken jarred something loose in Dana's memory. *Life is death is life...* Dana had translated that concept a thousand times, in dozens of different languages. But it all came back to a single origin—that of the Grim Reaper and it was on the blade that killed Hayes.

Suddenly, all the oxygen in the room evaporated. Dana couldn't catch her breath as panic clawed its way up her throat making it impossible to breathe. This wasn't a coincidence she could ignore.

First Meredith's accusation and now this quote. If there was a Grim Reaper play book, Claire was practically reciting it.

Dana needed to talk to Jake, but first she needed to collect herself. "I've got some work to catch up on," she said, starting to excuse herself.

"Now?" Jake objected. "It's late."

"No rest for the weary," Dana replied halfheartedly.

Jake was on his feet now, moving to intercept her route to her office. "Come on, Doc. We're finally all back together. Let's make the most of this time. We could play cards, or watch another movie—"

"Or you could tell her about New Orleans and your dad," Claire interrupted.

Jake cut a glare across the room that could've shut down a firing squad, but Dana ignored it, her eyebrows raised in question. "New Orleans and your dad?"

Now it was Jake's turn to backpedal. "You're right. It is late."

"Too late for you to drive home," Claire interjected. "You should stay here tonight."

"She's right," Dana agreed. "I'll be up working, you can take my room," she offered, quickly adding, "just for tonight."

Jake guffawed. "I'm not kicking you out of your bedroom."

"You won't be. Like I said, I planned to get some work done, so I'll be in my home office. There's a couch in there. I usually end up sleeping there when I'm in the middle of a research project anyway."

"What are you working on?" Claire asked. "Anything I can help with?"

Dana shook her head. "I'm just tying up some loose ends."

Claire shrugged through a yawn. "Well, you know where to find me if you need help."

Dana watched her disappear into the kitchen with the popcorn bowl and the last of the takeout containers.

"Dana," Jake started. "I can just stay on the couch."

The idea was laughable. Jake's giant frame took up most of her antique sofa when he was sitting. Sleeping there wouldn't be good for his back, or her beloved piece of vintage furniture. "It's not a big deal, Jake. It's one night. Just take my room. It's not like we're making it a habit."

A hint of a smile tugged at the corner of his lips. "It wouldn't be the worst habit, would it?" he asked, his voice sultry and low.

There was a sudden clatter in the kitchen and Claire swore. "Sorry. I-I just dropped a plate."

Dana took a step back from Jake, her glare instantly shutting down his flirtation before she turned to march toward the kitchen.

"You okay?" Dana asked, rushing to help Claire who was dumping chipped pieces of ceramic into the trash.

"Yeah. Sorry, it just slipped. I'm really sorry."

"Claire, it's okay. It's just a bowl. I'm not worried about it." But Claire's eyes were already welling with tears. "Hey, what's wrong?"

Claire shook her head, flinching away from Dana when she tried to reach for her. "Nothing. I'm just tired. I'm gonna go to bed."

Dana watched Claire flee the kitchen, ducking past Jake on her way down the hall, slamming her door shut. He stood there, a look of bewilderment on his face. "What was that all about?"

Dana crossed her arms, jaw muscles ticking. "I have work to do. If you're staying, there's fresh towels in the linen closet. Try not to break any other irreplaceable artifacts this time."

Then she breezed past him and slammed her own door.

31

Jake had been watching the red digits tick by one by one for over an hour. If he could speed time by sheer willpower, the digital alarm clock next to Dana's bed would've melted by now. After seeing steam come out her ears, he knew better than to make the short trip down the hall to her office. He'd learned rushing the stubborn woman never helped. She'd come talk to him when she was ready. But in the meantime, he was going stir crazy.

He'd just finished changing the alarm clock to military time when there was a light knock on the bedroom door. "You awake?"

Like he could sleep. "Yeah."

Dana hurried through the door, instantly filling the air with a nervous energy that had Jake on his feet. "What's wrong?"

Instead of answering, she grabbed his hand and dragged him into her bathroom. When she locked the door behind him and turned on the shower, his hope soared. But as soon as Dana began speaking in a rushed urgent whisper, he knew her mind was somewhere else entirely.

Tamping down his disappointment, he pulled his mind out of the gutter and focused on the information spewing from Dana's gorgeous mouth. "Whoa, slow down. What are you talking about?"

"Claire," she whispered. "After everything Dr. Dvita and Meredith said and what I just researched tonight, I'm worried. I think she's involved in the Congressman's murder."

"Okay. Start from the beginning."

So, she did.

Jake gave himself a moment to digest everything Dana had just unloaded on him. It was a lot to unpack. From Dvita's snap diagnosis to Meredith's unfounded accusations, he could see how Dana would make connections after diving down a rabbit hole of psychiatric episodes and Grim Reaper legends all night, but this was Claire they were talking about.

"Dana, I'm hearing you, but I just spent all day with her and I've gotta say, I disagree. I didn't see anything out of the ordinary considering what she's been through."

"What does that mean?" Dana pushed.

"It means she's been through a lot. She just needs time."

"What if it's more than that?"

"It's not."

"You can't possibly know that."

"No, you're right, but my gut's telling me it's true. And beyond that, since when do you make assumptions?"

Dana frowned. "You're right. That's why I'm going to ask Dr. Dvita for access to Claire's therapy sessions. Mere said he records them. Maybe it'll give me the proof I'm looking for."

"Do you hear yourself? You've already convicted her in your mind."

"That's not true. I want this to be a complete misunderstanding, but right now I can't explain how that's possible. Claire is the only witness to the murder; she was talking about it before it happened, and she just recited the inscription on the murder weapon. That information hasn't been made public."

Jake had to admit it looked bad, but he'd seen evidence stacked to perfection crumble in too many cases to lose hope. "Dana, all you have is conjecture. There were no prints on the weapon, no DNA to run through CODIS. If Claire witnessed the murder, maybe she was close enough to see the inscription on the blade."

"Then why didn't she say so when she was under hypnosis?"

"I don't know. Eyewitnesses sometimes repress traumatic details that they can only recall later with time to process the shock."

"Yes, but that's the point of hypnosis. It's a safe space to revisit traumatic memories."

"Well, I guess you've made up your mind. Shall I go get the handcuffs?"

"Jake, I'm being serious!"

"I know you are, and frankly, it's scaring the hell out of me."

"I hate this, but we have to consider the possibility that she's involved in this somehow."

"Yeah, well it'd be nice if you put an equal amount of energy into proving that she's not. I mean, have you even thought about the logistics of it? Claire's what, a hundred pounds soaking wet? Hayes is built like a gorilla. He'd have no problem overpowering someone like her."

"His attacker had a scythe. That tends to even the playing field, Jake!"

"It doesn't make any sense. Claire liked the guy."

"What do you mean?"

"She told me so today. She said they were the same and was all bent out of shape because I could forgive her and not him because they both killed people."

"She said that?"

He sighed, nodding. "It makes me sick that she's still blaming herself for Sadie."

Dana bit her thumbnail, lost in her tumultuous thoughts. Jake hated seeing her so distraught. He took a step closer, rescuing her hand from her nervous habit. "Look, right now, we don't have a lot to go on. You know I'm all for action, but in this case, I think we're going to have to sit tight and see what shakes loose. It's only been twenty-four hours. Things might look different tomorrow and all this worrying will have been for nothing."

"Hartwell didn't have any updates since you last spoke?"

Jake shook his head. "And I don't expect much now that DOJ took over. I put some calls into my contacts over there. I got a guy keeping his ears to the ground for me, but I know how they operate. By the time they give up any information this case will be cold."

Dana pressed her palms to her eyes. "Another cold case. Perfect."

"Hey, we're not working this case. And until we are, I say we let it go."

"And do what? I can't just sit around here staring at the walls with these kinds of thoughts running loose in my head. I need a distraction."

"I've got a few ideas." Jake caught Dana around the waist and pulled her closer, but she stiffened in his arms.

"I was thinking more along the lines of what Claire meant when she brought up New Orleans and your father."

Nothing could kill the mood faster for Jake than the mention of his father. His desire was dowsed like a flame in an ice bath.

32

Dana hadn't meant to wield the question like a weapon, but she could see it wounded Jake just the same. The heat blossoming between them instantly dissipated, replaced with a palpable tension. Hoping to ease it, Dana placed a hand on Jake's chest, letting it rest over the dog tags he wore beneath his shirt.

It was no secret he wore them. When they'd first met, Jake carried three names close to his heart. He'd since let go of Ramirez, but two silver tags remained. She knew one was in honor of Wade Shepard, the man who'd raised Jake, but Dana had long wondered about the third tag.

She'd glimpsed the worn silver letters enough times to suss out his name and had all but confirmed its significance to Jake.

Adam Miller.

Father to Jake Miller Shepard.

"Is that why you went to Nevada?" Dana questioned. "To see your father?"

Agitation radiated from Jake's exhale. He pushed off the wall and away from Dana. She'd expected him to end the conversation and leave the room like he always did when things got too personal, but instead he leaned over her bathroom sink and stared at his reflection in the mirror. She caught his eye in his reflection but made no move to rush him.

Finally, he scrubbed a hand over his tired features and turned to face her. Leaning against the counter he folded his arms over his broad chest. "I went to Nevada because I thought my mother needed me. Turns out my father's the only one she wants."

"So, you're looking for him?"

"Wade thinks it's what's best, so yeah, I guess I am."

"And Claire's helping you?"

"At first I thought it'd be a good distraction for her, but she's scary good at finding things on the black market."

Dana couldn't keep the pride from her voice. "She's always been a brilliant researcher. Is that what she meant by New Orleans? Did you find ties to your father there?"

Jake huffed a soft laugh. "No, that was me trying to make up for crashing into your lives and throwing everything off course."

"What do you mean?"

"Claire told me about New Orleans and the research invitation you passed up to work with me and the FBI. I thought maybe now would be a good time to follow up on that. The three of us getting out of town might not be the worst idea considering."

Dana hated the guilt lacing Jake's voice. She stepped closer, reaching a hand up to caress the thick stubble that was threatening to become a full-blown beard. "Jake, you don't have anything to make up for. I don't regret working with you. I'm glad you're in my life."

"Me too. But I regret the pain it's caused you." His hand automatically found the scar on her shoulder where his bullet had torn through. Whenever he touched her there, she felt something other than pain and scar tissue. A piece of him had been knitted to her the day he shot her and whenever he was close to her like this, she could feel him underneath her skin.

The possession of his touch took hold of her, and she let him pull her closer, until his lips pressed against her scar. He kissed a path from her shoulder to her throat before she managed to tear herself away.

"Jake," she panted. "We can't do this right now."

He pushed off the counter closing the distance she'd put between them until her back was against the wall. "Why not?" he asked, blue eyes dark with desire.

"There's something else I need to tell you."

Unable to find a way to sugar-coat Dr. Dvita's warning, Dana blurted it out before she lost her nerve. When she was done, Jake's pulse was visibly pounding with indignation. "So let me get this straight, I'm supposed to take some guy's word that pursuing any sort of romantic relationship with you is going to send Claire off the deep end?"

Dana threw her hands up. "You make it sound ridiculous when you say it like that."

"Dana, it *is* ridiculous. This guy doesn't get to just show up and dictate our lives."

"He's not *some guy*. He's a licensed professional. And he's spent a lot more time with Claire than we have in the past few weeks."

"Fine, then we change that. I'll move in here so we can both spend as much time with her as possible."

"I don't think that's the best idea."

"Why not?"

Dana crossed her arms. "You know why."

Jake smirked. "Listen, I know I'm irresistible, but I can control myself if you can."

"Jake, this is serious. You saw how she reacted when you said you were going to make staying here a habit."

"That was a joke. And she dropped a dish. That's not exactly straight jacket material."

"You can't make jokes like that. We're supposed to be creating a stable environment for her where she feels like she belongs."

Jake grimaced, grabbing the back of his neck.

"What is it?" Dana asked.

"Probably nothing, but she did mention that she wanted things to stay the same when it came to you and me."

"What? Why did you bring that up?"

"I don't know! Maybe because I'm trying to figure out how this works. Me, you, Claire, your Grim Reaper murder conspiracy."

"Do you have to make it sound so ridiculous?"

"You can't have it both ways, Dana. You think Claire's part of this, or you think she needs our protection."

"I don't have all the answers. All I know is that I don't want to do anything to jeopardize Claire's mental health by sending her the wrong message about us."

A bitter huff escaped as Jake shook his head, pacing away from Dana. "Well, she'd have to be a damn mind reader to intercept whatever the hell message you're trying to send me."

"Jake, I'm not doing this to hurt you."

When he turned back there was anger storming in his blue eyes. "I know that. But sometimes I need to know where I stand. It's been two years, Dana, and I still feel like I'm standing in that graveyard waiting for an answer to my question."

What about us?

Dana could hear his words. The question Jake asked her standing near Cramer's grave loomed between them like a headstone.

She knew her answer. She'd known it for a long time. But admitting what was in her heart didn't come easy. "Jake, you know how I feel about you."

"No, actually, I don't. I'm the one who came here making declarations. I said I'm as in this as you want me to be, but you haven't given me an answer."

"What almost happened in your hallway, in my kitchen, whenever we're this close ... isn't that answer enough?"

"No. It's not. Screw timing and putting things on pause. I want to be with you. But I need to know that's what you want too."

"I'm afraid to say what I want out loud."

"Why?"

"Because I've lost everyone I've ever loved, Jake. And if I lost you ..." She exhaled and swiped angrily at the tears threatening her eyes. "I won't put how I feel out into the universe just to have it taken away."

"That's not going to happen."

"You can't guarantee that. Claire, our jobs, there's so many reasons this might not work."

"Yeah, but there's one big reason why it might." Jake moved closer, circling his arms around her waist, and gazed down into her eyes. "Dana, do you want to be with me?"

More than anything! The words clawed at her throat desperate to get out, but Dana forced herself to swallow them down. She blinked back her tears and stared directly into Jake's all-consuming blue eyes, willing him to understand her. "When I give you my answer, I want it to be with no strings, no pause buttons, no one weighing in but us." She pressed her hand to his chest, letting his warmth steady her. "Jake, I know it's a lot to ask, but I think this is worth the wait."

He closed his eyes and bowed his head, letting his forehead rest against hers. He inhaled deeply, like he was breathing in strength. When he opened his eyes, his calm had returned. "I *know* this is worth the wait." He tucked a strand of hair behind her ear, that cocky grin of his returning. "And, sweetheart, the universe doesn't decide if we work, we do. And as long as we both want the same thing; I can wait as long as it takes."

33

JAKE WIPED THE SWEAT FROM HIS BROW AS HE JOGGED UP DANA'S FRONT steps. He was winded after his run, but he'd needed an outlet to expel his pent-up energy after spending last night pretending it didn't kill him to sit in Dana's bedroom doing nothing but talking.

Concocting a plan to deal with Claire was necessary, but after getting Dana as close as she'd ever been to admitting her feelings, it wasn't exactly the homecoming Jake had envisioned when he'd first hopped off his flight from Nevada. He certainly wouldn't have predicted their first sleepless night together would've been so PG.

Well, there had been that *one* NC17 moment at the end.

Jake forced himself not to think about how good Dana tasted in that stolen moment last night. She'd told him good night and made it as far as the bedroom door before turning back and pinning him with those big brown eyes of hers. Jake didn't know who crossed the room first, but Dana was in his arms, kissing him like she'd rather drown than come up for air.

When she finally pulled away, she grinned. "I figured I'd give you something to make the wait worthwhile." Then she sauntered out the door ensuring Jake wouldn't get a lick of sleep.

One minute the woman was shutting him down, the next she was curling his toes. Jake didn't know when she'd be ready to hit the un-pause button, but he was sure as hell of one thing. Dana Gray was going to be the ride of his life.

He stopped his mind from wandering, knowing he'd need to tack on another mile to his already strenuous morning routine if he didn't. He reminded himself Dana could've shut him down completely last night when he put her on the spot, so he was willing to take the win for the moment.

When he opened Dana's door he couldn't help grinning at the warm scene. The inviting aroma of coffee filled the air as Dana and Claire poured over a laptop at her kitchen counter. Claire wore Dana's oversized Ghostbusters tee, her black hair plaited in two perfect braids, cat eye glasses perched on her nose. Dana was still in her clothes from last night, her wild mane of brown hair piled on top of her head, betraying her night had been at least as sleepless as Jake's. She yawned, then took a sip from her favorite turquoise teacup as she looked over Claire's shoulder.

Jake wanted to walk up behind her and wrap his arms around her, sexy bed head and all. But even from where he stood in the foyer, just being there, knowing the two people he cared about most in the world were safe and happy ... it was enough to keep a man idling on pause forever.

"Morning," Jake said, joining the happy scene in the kitchen.

"Morning," Dana greeted, color creeping into her cheeks.

"I hear we're stuck with you," Claire teased when Jake pulled up a chair.

He raised his eyebrows and took a swig from his water bottle. "Says who?"

"I filled her in on our idea," Dana added.

"Oh yeah? And you're okay with that?" Jake asked.

Claire nodded. "It makes sense. It'll make it easier for us to work together and compare notes on your father."

Jake tried not to flinch at the nonchalant way Claire referenced the man who haunted his past. Changing the subject, he picked up where his conversation with Dana left off last night. "I'd still be more comfortable if I wasn't kicking you out of your bedroom. I can stay in the office."

"We've been over this," she argued. "I'll be at the Smithsonian during the day and will need my home office to work on our research at night. Besides, I'm pretty sure my bed is the only piece of furniture big enough to accommodate you."

"When are you going to sleep?" Jake pressed.

"Vampires don't need sleep," Claire teased. "We come alive at night."

"Oh yeah? I don't see you giving up your bedroom, Princess."

Claire smirked. "Not gonna happen, Secret Agent Man. I do have some ground rules for sharing our space though," she added.

Dana and Jake exchanged a worried glance, but Claire didn't seem to notice. "You have to shower after you run. You smell like a locker room!"

"What, this?" Jake lifted his arm and threatened to smother Claire in his sweaty armpit.

She squealed and rushed to hide behind Dana.

"I second that motion," Dana added. "And no walking around the house half naked," she amended. "This is my home, not the FBI locker room."

"What do you think we do at the FBI? Catch bad guys then sit around naked in the sauna talking about it?"

Claire perked up. "You have a sauna?"

Jake shook his head. "No, Elvira. I was being sarcastic. Don't you have a meeting to get ready for?"

She glanced at the clock, eyes widening. "Shoot!" Then she rushed toward her room to change.

Jake shared a look with Dana. "That went well."

"Yeah, Claire's been, well, Claire all morning."

"See. Can we agree yesterday's worries might've been an over-reaction?"

"We'll see how things go with Dr. Dvita today."

Jake nodded. "Okay. Keep me posted."

"You still going to the Bureau?"

"Yeah. I may be on leave, but if I keep showing up at HQ, maybe

Jenkins will get the hint. Plus, I'll have better luck catching wind of any new leads on this Reaper business if I stay in the mix of things."

"Okay, be careful."

"Always am," he said with a wink.

They both stood there awkwardly for a moment, torn between how to part considering the new unspoken bond between them.

Jake was first to break the standoff. "I want to kiss you so bad right now," he murmured.

Dana grinned smugly. "I know." Then she whispered. "Me too."

Jake leaned in but Dana shoved him away. "Claire's right. You need to shower ASAP."

Laughing, Jake headed down the hall toward Dana's bathroom, all too happy to follow orders for a change.

34

CLAIRE WATCHED DANA TAP HER CRACKED CUTICLES AGAINST THE steering wheel impatiently as they made slow progress in D.C.'s morning commuter traffic. Her mentor's fingers were always the first to pay the price when she was stressed. Claire had a sneaking suspicion Jake was the reason the nervous habit had returned. It was kind of cute the way they thought they were being sneaky. But anyone with eyes could see how into each other they were.

Watching them in the kitchen this morning had been like witnessing two teenagers trying to keep their PDA under wraps in the classroom. Claire might not have been part of the popular crowd in school, but she was an excellent observer, and she could spot a secret from miles away.

She had to admit, it bothered her a little. Not that they were together. She didn't care about that. But it was a little insulting that they felt they needed to hide whatever they were to each other from her.

Did they think she was so emotionally fragile that she wouldn't be able to be happy for them just because her own life was surrounded by sorrow?

Dana slammed on the brakes, punching the horn at the car that had just swerved into her lane.

"Picked up some of Jake's habits I see," Claire teased.

"What?"

She gestured to the bumper-to-bumper traffic. "Road rage is usually his thing."

"Oh ... right," Dana replied, immediately fretting at her thumbnail again.

Claire fought a smirk. It was kind of fun watching the perfect Dr. Dana Gray squirm. But she didn't want to torture her mentor. They'd been through a lot in the past two years. Claire's addiction and entanglement in the Card Killer case had strained their relationship, but in the end, Dana had stood by Claire. She was the one who always showed up. Not her parents.

Claire knew they'd been called after the incident at Passages, but she wasn't holding her breath for them to contact her. They'd made it clear they'd washed their hands of their "death-obsessed" daughter long ago. The truth was, Dana and Jake were all she had.

And if they had each other now, she'd try to be happy for them. She was about to say so when Dana pulled into an unfamiliar parking lot.

"We're here," she announced, parking in front of a towering limestone cathedral.

With St. Ann's looming in front of Claire, all thoughts of her friends' budding relationship faded away. Claire's skin prickled with nervous excitement the way it always did before her group therapy sessions. The prospect of better understanding herself was thrilling to Claire. And she especially enjoyed knowing she wasn't alone when it came to disturbing thoughts.

Some of the things the others shared were horrible and haunting, but they gave her hope that she could climb her way back out of the crippling depression and addiction that had almost swallowed her whole.

"You ready?" Dana asked.

She nodded and opened the passenger door, leaning into the blustery morning air.

Inside, Claire searched the crowd for familiar faces. A sudden pang hit her square in the chest when she realized she was looking for a face that wouldn't be there.

Congressman Hayes had been someone who'd given more hope than anyone else. She'd seen the darkness inside him. It reached out to hers like a twin flame. They hadn't spent too much time together, but he was someone who'd truly seen her and hadn't looked away.

She'd known that their acquaintance would be brief, but still, she was unprepared for the pain of parting this way.

Continuing to observe the group of people milling about the cavernous rectory attached to the church, Claire's unease grew when she realized there was another missing face in this crowd.

Max, where are you?

He was the real reason Claire had been eager to show up today, but he was nowhere to be found. She was straining to see over the group when she spotted a wave of blood red hair streaking toward her. "Betty!"

35

Dana watched the red-haired girl Claire spoke to in hushed tones with unbiased curiosity. There was something intimate about the way they leaned into one another while they whispered that sparked her interest. Especially since Claire had been so stringent with her personal space with Dana and Jake.

Just then Dr. Dvita walked over to her.

"Who's that girl Claire is speaking with?" Dana asked.

"She goes by Betty."

"Claire mentioned her when she was under hypnosis. She was with her and Max the night Hayes was killed."

"That's right."

"Has anyone questioned her?"

"Yes, of course. The police did, and I spoke to her as well."

"And?"

"She said she didn't see anything."

"You believe her?" Dana asked.

"Are you suggesting I shouldn't?"

"No. But I'd like to sit in on your group session today if that's okay."

"That's highly unusual, Dr. Gray. Group sessions aren't open to outsiders."

"I understand. But I'm here in a professional capacity."

Dvita blinked rapidly. "I wasn't aware you'd been assigned to the investigation."

"Officially, I haven't, but given my area of expertise, I might be able to offer valuable input."

"Forgive me, Dr. Gray, but I'm afraid your expertise has no merit here. Allowing you to sit in would violate the safety and sanctity I offer my patients."

Dana was dumbfounded. "Dr. Dvita, one of your patients was brutally murdered with an occult artifact. There is no one else in this city who has more expertise in that field. If someone here can shed light on what happened, we are duty bound to make that happen."

Dvita cocked his head. "Careful, Dr. Gray. You sound more like that FBI agent you spend so much time with than the Smithsonian's renowned archivist."

"Look, I came here for Claire. You're the one who implored me to continue her therapy."

"Yes, and that's precisely what I'm doing, Dr. Gray. This is a therapy session, not an interrogation. My patients need to feel safe to share what they went through. Badgering them like suspects will do more harm than good. They've been through enough of that already when they were questioned by the police."

"I understand. I don't need to say a word. If I can just observe—"

"Dr. Gray, I think it's best if you stick to your job and let me do mine."

He started to turn away, but Dana was desperate to get what she'd come for. "Can I at least see the tapes of Claire's sessions?"

Dr. Dvita turned back to face her, his expression stony. "You spoke to Meredith Kincaid."

He hadn't posed it as a question, but Dana couldn't stop herself from asking. "Why do you say that?"

His smile held no warmth. "You might understand death, Dr. Gray, but I understand the human mind."

"Then you should know mine isn't easily swayed. I'd like to see Claire's tapes."

"Then I suggest you come back with a warrant."

"What if Claire wants to show them to me?"

He shrugged. "Then I'd have to recommend she reconsider."

"I don't get it. Yesterday you hypnotized Claire in front of me and were more than willing to share details about her recovery. What's changed?"

"Nothing has changed, Dr. Gray. I'm looking out for the well-being of my patients. And I wouldn't be doing my job if I surrendered private sessions that could easily be misinterpreted by the untrained observer. Psychiatry is a complex field. Having to explain that only proves my point." He extended his arm, pointing to the exit. "Leave the expertise to the experts."

36

CLAIRE CLUNG TO BETTY, LETTING THE GIRL'S OVERPOWERING PERFUME settle around her like a cloak. With her eyes shut tight, Claire let herself imagine they were still at Passages and none of this had happened. When she opened her eyes, Hayes would be there with that *'you can trust me'* smile, while Max watched on stoically from the corner.

Max ... God, she missed him. She hated thinking of him out there alone.

Betty pulled away, breaking Claire's imaginary bubble. "Claire, tell me the rumors aren't true. Do the police really think you witnessed the murder?"

Claire flinched. "Who told you that?"

"Lincoln told me. I ran into him at the precinct. My interview was after his. I guess he overheard some cops talking about you witnessing it."

Claire swore, her eyes darting around the room until she found Lincoln. The stoner was standing with two men in dark suits that screamed security detail, and they probably were, considering his popstar parents. "Lincoln has a big mouth," Claire muttered.

"What did you tell the cops?" Betty pressed.

"The truth."

Betty scrutinized her. "Then why do you look so worried?"

"Why don't you? Hayes is dead, Max is missing, and I think Meredith might be a problem."

"Meredith?" A spark of concern flashed across Betty's bright green eyes. "I thought that issue was taken care of."

"Me too."

Meredith had been a thorn in Claire's side from the very beginning. She'd almost lost Dana and Jake because of her. There was no way Claire was going to be the reason the deceitful woman wormed her way back into their lives. That's why Claire had gone to Hayes immediately after Dvita first brought Meredith to Passages.

He'd known exactly how to handle Meredith.

Everything had been working perfectly until ... it wasn't.

Claire closed her eyes again, sucking in a deep breath.

She missed Hayes. If he were here, he'd know what to do. He had a naturally devious mind. One Claire craved. Ironically, she was a genius in her own right, but only because she possessed an eidetic memory. The gift enabled her to recall and recite anything and everything. But she'd come to regard it as a curse. One that forced her to remember things she'd prefer to forget.

Sadie, Fuller, the Grave and everything she'd seen there—even now, the memories flipped through her head like a morbid scrapbook, haunting her even while she was awake. That paired with the crippling depression, courtesy of her parents' rejection, had made her a prime candidate for addiction.

Claire wasn't blameless. She knew she'd played a part in everything that happened. And that's why she'd been trying so hard at Passages. She'd met Betty and Max and Hayes. They made her feel less alone. With them, she'd finally found what she'd been searching for. But now ...

Three loud claps echoed through the room making Claire jump. Dr. Dvita's voice rang out. "Group, let's gather."

Betty gripped Claire's hand tightly, her gaze fearful. "Find me after," she whispered. "We need to find Max and make sure he doesn't talk."

"He's not going to say anything," Claire said, trying to reassure her friend.

But Betty shook her head. "I'm not willing to take that risk, and you shouldn't either." Then she turned her back on Claire and went to join the group.

37

"I'm telling you, Jake, it was like Jekyll and Hyde. He practically threw me out of there after mentioning Meredith. Something's off."

Jake clutched his phone to his ear. "You brought up Meredith?"

"No, Dvita did, but that's not the point. I wasn't trying to dispute his competence. I mean we witnessed him break through to Claire on a level I didn't know existed, but he was so defensive today. He told me I'd need a warrant if I want to see Claire's tapes. I think he's hiding something."

Jake pinched the bridge of his nose. He'd been excited when he saw Dana's name on his caller ID. He'd take any excuse to ignore the mountain of paperwork that had piled up on his desk in his absence, but Dana hadn't taken a breath in nearly ten minutes.

"Dana, last night you thought Claire was the D.C. Reaper. Now you're telling me it's Dvita?"

"The D.C. Reaper? Did the story break?"

"Not yet, but I got a heads up that the Post has it. NSA issued a gag order, but based on the buzz at HQ, it's only a matter of time before somebody runs with it."

"Is Claire implicated?"

"Right now, you know as much as I do, which is pretty much nothing."

"What about Jenkins?"

"I don't know. I'm trying to avoid her considering she hasn't cleared me from leave yet. She'd be pissed if she heard I was still sniffing around this."

"What else have you learned?"

"Not much. Mostly that I'm not the only one with no love for Hayes. Maybe this was him getting what he deserved. With any luck the DOJ will prove this was an isolated event. The best we can hope for is Claire witnessing it was just collateral damage. If that's the case, we'll get her the help she needs to move on."

"I don't think it's that simple, Jake. I think Dvita knows something he's not telling us about what happened to Hayes. Either that or he's covering up something even deeper. He was a completely different person today. I don't know how else to explain it."

"Dana, I mean this in the best way, but when you're trying to prove a theory, you're like a dog with a bone. It can rub some people the wrong way."

"So, you're saying it's my fault his personality did a 180?"

"I don't know, Gray. The guy spends his life studying nut jobs. It's bound to rub off." Jake regretted the words the moment they were out of his mouth, but the sharp intake of breath on the other end of the line told him Dana had taken his comment to heart.

"And I spend my life studying death. What does that make me?"

"Dana. You know I didn't mean it like that." He exhaled his frustration. "Forgive me if I'm being short. Being back here, dredging up questions about Hayes, it's got me on edge, but I didn't mean to take it out on you."

"It's fine."

But the tightness in her voice told him it was anything but. "Hey, why don't I pick up lunch and meet you both at the Smithsonian when you're done?"

"That's not a good idea. After what happened with Sadie there, I worry being back would be a difficult reminder for Claire."

"Okay, then why don't you both come here. We can order in."

Her voice pitched with surprise. "To the J. Edgar Hoover Building?"

Jake didn't know why she was saying it like that. Dana had been to his office dozens of times when they were working a case. "Yeah. Why not? I'll leave visitor badges downstairs."

"You're not even supposed to be there. How are you going to get us in?"

Jake sighed. "Dana, I've worked here a long time. Can you give me some credit?"

"I don't know if it's a good idea to bring Claire somewhere people are talking about what happened to Hayes."

"What else are you going to do? Go home and put her under house arrest? She's not a child, you can't babysit her forever."

"I know that, Jake."

He couldn't ignore the strain in her voice. "Hey, I know you're just trying to protect Claire. That's what I want, too. We're on the same team, Dana."

"I know. She's just been through so much and I don't know how to help her. I hate feeling useless."

Jake avoided looking at the folders of cold cases stacked on his desk. He knew the feeling of helplessness all too well. "We've gotta keep the faith. It hasn't even been 48 hours."

"You always say the first 48 hours are the most important."

Of course Dana's beautiful mind would conjure up Jake's words to use against him. But she wasn't wrong. Statistically, the likelihood of finding new evidence in cases like these plummeted after the 48-hour window closed. He'd be lying if he said he hadn't been fighting his own impulses as he watched the clock the past day and a half.

"I just wish there was something more we could do."

Jake knew the familiar drive all too well. The hum of his senses honing in on details that didn't quite fit. The thrill of finding that needle in a haystack. Some of his most vital leads started out as hunches, and when those hunches led to cold hard evidence, well, there was nothing quite like chasing that high.

It's part of what kept him at the Bureau this long. Jake was good at his job. He possessed instincts that couldn't be taught, instincts that

solved cases and saved lives. But he'd seen those same instincts in
Dana. She viewed the world differently than anyone he'd ever met,
and her endless intellect in all things dark and otherworldly made
her a natural. That's why telling her to ignore this hunch felt wrong,
even if he was doing it for the right reasons.

"Sometimes part of this job is knowing when it's out of your
hands," Jake said. "We have to trust the DOJ will get the job done. In
the meantime, I need to shift my focus to keeping my word to Wade."

"Have you had any luck?"

"You mean tracking down a ghost?" Jake huffed a bitter laugh.
"Not exactly."

Jake hadn't even started, choosing to procrastinate with backlogs
and paperwork rather than opening the wound that searching for his
father would inflict.

Claire and Dana helped with a preliminary search, but he'd
known it wouldn't result in any real leads. If Adam Miller was that
easy to find, Jake would've tracked the deadbeat down years ago to
give him a piece of his mind.

"Jake." Dana's voice pulled him from his spiraling thoughts.
"You're right. We're a team. Leave the visitor passes. We'll be at your
office as soon as Claire's finished here."

38

THEY ALL SAT THERE. SO SIMPLE. SO EASY TO MANIPULATE. SO MANY lambs to sacrifice.

I tried to warn them.

I gave them ample time to save themselves.

But they can't see what's right in front of them.

They can't see me.

All of them are fit for slaughter, but I know who's next.

I will carry out my orders. But sometimes I like to imagine I don't have any. That I can do as I please.

Soon. I remind myself that soon, I will be free.

Soon, my life will truly be mine to live. The way it always should've been.

For now, I watch. I wait. And I grin in the face of this hallowed ground that the foolish lambs think protects them.

39

A FAINT HINT OF INCENSE HUNG IN THE STALE AIR OF THE RECTORY. With their eyes closed, Claire could study the group freely. There were fourteen of them, all dutifully doing their meditative breathing, just as Dr. Dvita instructed. Claire tried, but the air was heavy with judgment.

She didn't like meeting at St. Ann's. The rectory wasn't in the church, but it might as well have been. It was a building next door, connected by a narrow breezeway of stained glass windows. Flyers for community events and AA meetings made a colorful collage on the cork board next to the giant crucifix affixed to the wall.

It was all a bit too B-horror movie for Claire. As she looked around the room, she expected someone to start speaking in tongues or burst into flames.

Her eyes kept falling to the two men missing from the group. Hayes and Max. Though he was an orderly and not a patient, Max had always been invited to participate in the group sessions at Passages. It was at one such session that he and Claire bonded.

She normally hated group sessions. Everyone spent way too much time droning on about themselves and their 'problems.' Most of the patients at Passages were socialites, celebrities or political types who needed a time out from the real world. It was a holiday where they could dry out from their habit of choice, only to return to it and the cushy life that awaited them at their leisure.

But it was Max who made her realize not everyone was like that. There were a few who'd come to Passages as a last resort. And even fewer who came involuntarily.

Max was one of them. They'd connected instantly. Two lost souls. Perhaps even soulmates. The ache that existed in his absence was overwhelming. She needed him to be okay. He was her only way through this.

Claire's mind wandered back to her conversation with Betty. They had much more to discuss, but Dr. Dvita was in a hurry to get started.

"Thank you all for being here today. The work we do is important. We can't let outside influences, no matter how tragic, stray us from our mission. Progress through passage."

The group recited Dvita's mantra. "Through rites of passage we evolve."

"That's right," he praised. "We must leave our dependance behind in order to transform into our highest selves."

"Mistakes can be mended, challenges can cultivate," the group parroted.

It was these cult-like mantras that made the group sessions at Passages so intolerable to Claire. Luckily, they were voluntary, so she rarely went.

But it was one such session where she'd first met Max. He was someone who found strength in numbers, explaining it was comforting for him to be in a group setting. She expressed how uncomfortable sharing to a room full of strangers felt. That's when he'd come up with the perfect compromise. A smaller group of their choosing. It's how they came to meet with Betty and Hayes. After that, their little circle was inseparable.

It was almost strange how simple their friendship had started, especially when Claire thought about how complex it was now.

The mention of Max pulled her attention back to Dr. Dvita. "Let us keep Taft and Max in our thoughts."

Claire didn't like the way Dr. Dvita lumped Max with Hayes, like he too was dead. And she hated that everyone here referred to Hayes as Taft. Max was the only one at the center who didn't go by the ridiculous presidential or first lady moniker. But why would he? People without identities didn't need to conceal them.

"What happened at Passages is a tragedy," Dvita continued, "but it would be an even bigger tragedy to let the progress of many be erased by the actions of a few. I encourage you to keep your focus centered on the horizon, with your goals in sight. Know that my door is always open if there is anything you want to discuss regarding this terrible matter we've all endured. Considering the situation, Passages will remain closed until further notice."

A murmur of discontent rumbled through the crowd.

"But ... but, I will continue to conduct group sessions here and will be available for individual sessions as needed. There will be a flyer on the board with the dates and times of the group sessions, along with my availability for additional sessions. I encourage you to sign up after class if you have anything you would like to discuss pertaining to Taft."

An older man in a yellow sweater raised his hand. "Do you know who killed him?"

Dr. Dvita studied him momentarily before answering. "Right now, the investigation is on-going. That's why it's so important for us to have these discussions. It's possible that we may have information that could help the police."

Betty spoke up. "We've already been questioned by the police."

"Yes, but I think everyone here knows how things can get locked in our subconscious. Sometimes the tiniest details make all the difference. That's why I'm acting as a liaison to the investigation. If you think of anything, please come to me first."

Half a dozen hands shot up.

"Privately," Dr. Dvita amended.

All but one hand went down. Dr. Dvita addressed the same man in the yellow sweater. "Yes, Carter."

"Will we get in trouble?"

"No," Dr. Dvita answered. "The police have assured me they're not looking for anything other than cooperation."

Another hand went up: Lincoln. "Some people are saying what happened to Taft is karma. Do you believe that?"

"Ah, you pose an interesting question." Dvita circled to address the group. "Lincoln is suggesting the idea that the universe returns what we give it, in that Taft got what was coming to him."

"Like vigilante justice?" another patient asked.

"Yes! Like Batman," someone yelled.

"Max liked Batman," another interjected.

After that the conversation swung like a pendulum of speculation and accusations.

"Do you think it was Max?"

"Why else would he be missing?"

"Maybe he's dead, too."

"Or he was the killer."

An ache began to form in Claire's jaw. She didn't know how much more of this she could sit through. It felt like she was witnessing the precipice of something that would end with pitchforks and an angry mob.

Claire caught Betty's eye across the room. She was right. They needed to find Max. And they needed to do it on their own.

40

DANA STOOD OUTSIDE ST. ANN'S, ARMS CROSSED PROTECTIVELY against the chilled spring air. While some places in the country were already enjoying the joyous season of rebirth, D.C. was still hidden under a blanket of frost as winter roared its final breaths.

She could've waited in the car where she'd be safe from the elements, but she wanted Claire to know she was here for her. Especially after the frosty welcome Dr. Dvita had exhibited earlier.

Mercifully, the rectory doors groaned open, and people began to filter out. Dana spotted Claire, still inside, speaking urgently to the girl with the unnaturally red hair again. Not wanting to interrupt, Dana hung back and observed.

When Claire finally exited the building, Dana greeted her. "Hey, how'd it go?"

Claire scrutinized her like she was weighing her response. "As good as could be expected, I guess."

Dana waited to press her further until they were back in the warmth of her car. "Who's the girl you were talking to? A friend?"

"What?" Claire asked, visibly distracted.

"The girl with the red hair. I saw you two talking. Is she the one you were telling us about when Dr. Dvita came over?"

"Oh, um, yeah. That's Kylie, er Betty. I'm not sure what to call her now that we're not at Passages."

Dana nodded. "I can imagine. You've been through so much, Claire. I'm glad you have Dr. Dvita, and Betty, but I want you to know that I'm someone you can confide in too if you need help making sense of things."

Claire crossed her arms, angling her body toward Dana. "I've been interrogated by the police, my psychiatrist, and today I had to listen to a bunch of rehab patients spew vigilante justice for the last hour. If there's something you want to ask me, just ask it already."

Dana merged into traffic, keeping her attention on the road. "I'm sorry. I'm not trying to interrogate you. I'm just scared. I want to help, but I don't know how." Dana reached across the car, her palm extended.

Claire hesitated, but finally took it. "I'm scared, too," she whispered. "And I'm not mad at you for being suspicious. I would be too if the situation was reversed."

"Then let me in and we can tackle this together."

"What do you want to know?" Claire asked.

"Everything."

Claire took a deep breath, exhaling it with the weight of the world. "Then I think you better pull over."

DANA WAS STILL busy digesting Claire's play-by-play from the St. Ann's session. She was trying to keep everyone straight and the code names weren't helping. There was Max, Lincoln (aka Cash), Betty (aka Kylie), and Taft (aka Hayes). Instinct made her want to have Jake run background checks on all of them, but she knew that would just launch another lecture about staying out of the way and letting the DOJ do their job.

Claire spoke up. "Do you think you could help me look for Max? I'm really worried about him being out on his own. He's never left Passages before."

"Never?"

"No. His mother was a patient there. She was pregnant when she was admitted, and she had him there."

Dana blinked. "I need more details."

"She died due to complications during delivery. Max had no one else so Dr. Dvita took him into his care so he wouldn't become a ward of the state. He's been at Passages ever since, which is why I'm so worried about him. He's out here on his own for the first time and no one else seems to care."

Dana drummed her fingers on the steering wheel, lost in thought. "I think we should talk to Jake. This is his area of expertise."

"Finding people is his superpower," Claire agreed. "But I know he has his hands full searching for his father."

"I guess that just means we'll have to divide and conquer," Dana said, starting the engine.

"Where are we going?" Claire asked.

"Jake invited us for lunch."

Claire perked up. "Really? That's perfect. There's this new Thai restaurant Betty told me about that I've been dying to try."

"Actually..." Dana filled Claire in on Jake's invitation to help him with his research. "Unless you're uncomfortable going to the FBI headquarters."

"No, why would that bother me?"

Dana kept her eyes on the road. "It's an intimidating place."

Claire gave her a dubious smirk. "We work in a dark underground bunker surrounded by death. I think I can handle a stuffy office building."

The comment was so quintessentially Claire, it made Dana's shoulders sag with relief. She'd missed her friend and colleague. Even the slightest glimpse of her old witty banter filled Dana with renewed hope. She knew they still had a long road ahead of them to rebuild the bonds that had been severed, but today, Claire had given her an inch, and Dana was willing to make up the mile.

She was just about to put the car in drive when Claire spoke. "Can we please go to my storage unit first? I'm tired of wearing clothes that are three decades too old for me."

Dana ignored the jab at her fashion sense or lack thereof. "First stop, Capitol City Storage."

41

THE STORAGE CENTER WAS ONLY A FEW MILES FROM ST. ANN'S AND mercifully, traffic was moving now that rush hour was over. Dana pulled up to the gate and punched in the code: Claire's birth date.

They drove through the quiet parking lot and pulled up to her unit.

This was the first time Claire was seeing it.

Dana and Jake packed up her belongings when she was in rehab. She stared at the small blue door. It was strangely depressing realizing her life could fit in a five-by-five space.

Dr. Dvita's words came to her unbidden. *Depression takes what you let it.*

Claire pushed back against her crushing thoughts and got out of the car. When she saw Dana following, she stopped her. "You don't need to come in with me."

"I know. But I'd like to."

Claire shook her head. "Dana, trust goes both ways. Let's start here."

42

Jake tried not to smirk as he watched Claire tear into her fourth dumpling with ravenous abandon. It felt like old times having Dana back in his office. Claire joining them was an added bonus. As was the gem of a Thai restaurant she'd found. The spicy basil chicken certainly elevated his mood and possibly his blood pressure.

"Where did you hear about this place?" Jake asked, grabbing another piece of spicy chicken with his chopsticks despite the perspiration gathering on his brow.

"My friend, Betty, from Passages told me about it," Claire answered.

"How'd it go today?" Jake asked around a mouthful of food.

Claire and Dana exchanged a look before Claire answered. "It was fine, but something came up that I was wondering if you'd help me with."

"Oh yeah? Lay it on me." Jake welcomed the distraction considering the abysmal day he'd been having hitting dead ends trying to locate his father.

"Max didn't show up at St. Ann's today. No one has seen or heard from him since Hayes died." Claire wrung her hands. "We got really close at Passages. I know he doesn't have anyone in his life, and Max isn't the sort of person who does well on his own. I'm worried something happened to him and I was thinking since finding people is your superpower, maybe you'd help me look for him?"

The comment deflated Jake. He knew Claire meant it as a compliment, but it was a reminder of how much Wade and his mother were counting on him to find someone too.

He knew if he dug far enough, he'd find answers, because Claire was right; finding people was what he did. The trouble was, sometimes how he found them did more harm than good.

Jake knew that however this thing with his father turned out, he and Wade would deal with it. But if he looked into this kid Max and the outcome wasn't the one Claire was hoping for, she might not be able to cope.

He didn't want to let her down, but he didn't want to cause her unnecessary pain either.

Jake proceeded cautiously. "I appreciate your confidence in me, but it might be misguided."

"What do you mean?" she asked.

Exhaling, Jake set his meal down and threaded his hands behind his head. Jake looked back at the stack of folders on his desk. Corporate espionage, homegrown terrorism, human trafficking—he never thought he'd feel this way, but he'd take tracking down a Grim Reaper and a scared kid over any of them.

"I hope this Max guy isn't wrapped up in the Hayes investigation, because we're gonna have to sit this one out and let the DOJ do their thing."

Claire looked crestfallen. "No one is looking for a rehab runaway. If they are it's only to pin Hayes's death on him."

"Why do you say that?"

"You should've heard the way everyone was talking about Max today. They've all but convicted him. It's like they don't even care that he's the reason we all got out before the fire got too bad." Claire swiped at a tear. "He didn't do anything wrong. They just want to blame him because he's different, but I'm not going to let that happen."

Jake glanced at Dana. This was starting to feel like the Sadie situation all over again. Claire hadn't trusted him to help then. He didn't want to make the same mistake twice.

He pulled out his notepad and flipped to a new page. "Different how?"

Claire perked up. "You'll help me find him?"

"Unofficially," he warned. "Now tell me what you know."

When Claire finished her lengthy description, Jake snapped his notebook shut. "I'll make sure this gets into the right hands."

"Wait, you're not going to look for him?"

"Claire, I can't, and neither can you. If the DOJ catches us poking around, things could get a whole lot worse."

"How? We didn't do anything wrong."

"A US Congressman was murdered. The DOJ is out for blood, they don't necessarily care whose. In cases like these it's guilt by association and the whole party goes down. That's why I'm doing everything I can to keep you as far away from their investigation as possible."

Claire crossed her arms, her frustration clear.

"I know you're worried about your friend, but I need you to trust me. I've got some contacts who can look into Max discreetly." Jake stood up and walked over to his desk. He came back after rummaging around in his drawers. "Here, I know you lost yours in the fire," he said, handing Claire a burner. "I've got the number. If I hear anything, I promise, you'll be my first call."

Claire powered on the phone. "Can I call Betty in case she's heard anything about Max?"

"Yeah. You can use conference room B down the hall if you want some privacy."

"Thanks."

Claire left the room and Dana stood, ready to follow, but Jake stopped her. "Let's give her a minute."

"I don't think that's the best idea. Betty might not be the best influence based on what I saw at St. Ann's today."

"I took the necessary precautions," Jake said, holding up his phone. "That phone has an app that transmits location and conversations directly to me."

Dana's eyes widened. "Did you do that to my phone, too?"

He grinned and grabbed her hips, pulling her closer. "That would certainly make my life easier, wouldn't it?"

Dana leaned into his touch, letting her fingers glide over his cheek. "I didn't know you were going to shave."

Jake rubbed his smooth jawline. "The Bureau might actually be worse than the Army when it comes to keeping up appearances."

"That's a shame," she admitted. "I liked the beard."

"Roger that," Jake grinned, tipping her lips up to meet his.

"Jake ..." she pulled away. "We talked about this."

He exhaled, letting his forehead fall to Dana's momentarily while he collected himself. "Right. It's just been a day."

"Still nothing on your father?" she asked.

Jake shook his head. "It's like tracking a ghost."

"Well, now you're talking about my area of expertise," she offered. "Want some help?"

"Thanks, but I've got some calls into my old contacts. It's a Hail Mary, but that's where I'm at right now."

Dana slipped her hand into his. "Don't lose hope."

"I think I needed to hear that." He squeezed her hand. "Thank you for being here. It means more than you know."

Whatever Dana was about to say was cut short when Jenkins burst through Jake's office door, Claire by her side.

43

FURY ROLLED OFF ASSISTANT DIRECTOR REMI JENKINS LIKE A THUNDER cloud. Dana wisely stepped back from Jake, knowing keeping her mouth shut was the best move.

Jenkins hauled Claire into the room by her arm, shoving her into the nearest chair and slamming the door closed behind her before addressing the room.

"Are you kidding me? Why on earth would you think bringing her here was a good idea?"

Jenkin's accusatory finger was pointed at Claire, but her anger was directed solely at Jake, who immediately went on the defensive. "I know I'm not officially off leave, but I needed somewhere to work a special project, and Claire and Dana are helping."

"Does this look like a recreation center to you, Shepard? This is the goddamned FBI!"

"I know where we are, Jenks."

"The fact that you brought her here says you don't have a clue!" Jenkins waved her cell phone in Jake's face. "Do you have any idea the position you've put me in?"

Jake took the phone, his outrage suddenly morphing into shock when he read what was on the screen.

Curiosity had Dana edging closer. "What's going on?" she asked, trying to see Jenkins' phone.

Jenkins ignored her question, her fury still fixed on Jake. "Did I or did I not give you a direct order to stay out of this Hayes situation?"

"Jenkins, I can explain."

"I'd rather you didn't." She snatched her phone back. "The article spells it out perfectly."

Dana paled. "The Post ran the article? I thought there was a gag order?"

When Jenkins turned on Dana, she regretted opening her mouth. "You knew about this, too?" A bitter smile spread across her face. "I don't know why I'm surprised. Where there's trouble, there's Dana Gray." Jenkins strode so close to Dana she could see the woman's fillings. "I know you're used to Jake bringing the calvary in to save the day, but your presence here has just made that impossible."

"Dana has nothing to do with this," Jake interjected, shoving his way between the two women.

Jenkins glowered at him. "Like hell she doesn't. Ever since you started working with her you've thrown policy and procedure out the window. The law isn't flexible, Shepard. And this time you've gone too far."

"Hold on. I hate Hayes, but I'm not gonna let him jeopardize my career. I heard what you said to me at the morgue."

"Apparently not." She held up her phone again, reading from the article Dana couldn't see. "Witness tampering, obstruction of justice, unauthorized disclosure of classified information and that's just the tip of the iceberg now that Homeland and the NSA are involved! I can't protect you, Jake. If they say so, you're gone. And I won't even know where to begin looking. Did you even think about what that will do to the people you've got depending on you? Are you really this reckless?"

"Jenkins—"

"No." She held out her hand. "Badge and gun, now."

"What?"

"You're suspended." She shook her head, face flush with anger. "Never thought this would be my last act as Assistant Director."

Jake paled. Jenkins was being suspended, too? That couldn't be! "No, Jenks. This is a temporary misunderstanding," he argued. "We'll sort this out."

"*We* won't do anything. If you come to your senses, I'll be in Nevada. Unlike you, I don't betray family."

44

JAKE EXHALED SOME OF HIS TENSION FROM THE PASSENGER SEAT WHEN Dana drove them out of the Bureau's parking lot. Surrendering his government vehicle had been almost as humiliating as losing his badge and weapon. But he was counting himself lucky that security hadn't escorted him directly into NSA custody.

Claire was in the back seat, eyes wide, spewing an endless stream of questions that Jake couldn't answer. "I don't understand what just happened. Did Jenkins lose her job? And why did she suspend you?"

"I tried to keep your name out of the witness report," Jake answered. "So much for Hartwell having my back," he muttered to himself.

Jake was planning to call the backstabbing Metro officer and rip him a new one, despite the good it would do now. He continued to scroll through the article the Post had issued:

... some speculate Agent Shepard's abuse of power was prompted by his alleged relationship with Dr. Dana Gray and known associate Claire Townsend, who's recently been hospitalized for a drug overdose. Townsend, only witness to murdered Congressman Norton Hayes, was seeking psychiatric care at Passages Rehabilitation Center when the death occurred.

Allegedly Agent Shepard's decision, concealing the case's only witness,

161

has thwarted progress in apprehending Hayes's assassin. Disregard for protocol call in this case has called Shepard's integrity into question. The Department of Justice is calling for the FBI to reevaluate all cases involving Agent Shepard. Repercussions could jeopardize major arrests, overturning countless cases, including the prominent D.C. Card Killer, and the Romeo & Juliet murders, where Shepard's direct supervisor and mentor was implicated, spawning the question, how far back does the corruption go?

Jake closed the article; afraid he wouldn't be able to keep his temper in check if he read more of the slanderous accusations.

Dana spoke for the first time since security had escorted the three of them from his office. "The timing of this doesn't make any sense. Why now?"

"Now's as good a time as any when an appointed official has been brutally murdered and it looks like a federal agency is trying to cover it up."

"But why is this blowing up all of a sudden? Hayes was murdered almost two days ago."

"I made a lot of calls. I guess I ruffled the wrong feathers. Hayes isn't the only soldier-turned-official with skeletons in his closet."

Dana shook her head. "Jake, I saw the article. This attack seems more personal than that."

"You think someone is trying to shut me up?"

"I don't know yet. But something doesn't add up. I get how it looks bad for you, but what did Jenkins do to get suspended?"

Jake struggled to keep his cool when he really wanted to shove his fist through the dash of Dana's old Range Rover. But since he was now without a source of income, he refrained. "I used Jenkins' ID number to issue visitor passes for you and Claire today."

Dana glanced at him nervously. "So, it looks like she brought us there. For what?"

Jake shrugged. "Sheltering fugitives is an easy leap."

"But she didn't even know we were there."

"That will only make her look incompetent."

"Isn't that better than complicit?"

Claire spoke up. "This is all my fault. There has to be something we can do."

"Right now, we just need to go home, lay low, and cooperate with whoever comes knocking."

"Jake, I don't mean to be blunt, but maybe it's better if you go back to your place until this blows over."

He shook his head. "This isn't the sort of storm that passes quickly, and I don't like the idea of you two being alone."

"Jake, we'll be fine—"

"Gray, I need you to not fight me on this," he snapped. "Claire's been tied to the Reaper case, and you keep conveniently forgetting someone broke into your house two days ago. I'm staying with you and Claire. End of discussion."

45

DANA'S JAW TIGHTENED, BUT SHE REMAINED SILENT AS SHE DROVE THE rest of the way to her house. Jake hadn't spoken to her like that since their first case together. She'd thought their relationship had evolved to mutual respect, maybe even more, but here he was, back to barking orders like she was one of his soldiers.

As a renowned historian with multiple PhDs, she wasn't used to being verbally belittled. She understood the gravity of the situation Jake was facing, but the disrespect was still unacceptable. Though she wanted to address the issue, it was a battle for another time.

When Dana turned down her street, all thoughts narrowed to the problem ahead.

More than a dozen news vehicles were parked in front of her house, reporters milling about on her sidewalk. "Are you seeing this?" she asked, slowing down.

Jake swore, loudly.

"What do I do?" Dana asked.

"Keep driving," Jake ordered.

Dana turned to look at him. "Past my house?"

"Yes."

"To where?" she asked, trying to remain calm as she approached the chaotic scene.

"Give me a minute to think," Jake muttered.

Claire's voice was strained as she leaned toward the front seats. "What's going on?"

"Duck down." Jake commanded, doing the same as Dana drove past the news crews covering her home.

"Should we go to a hotel?" she asked when they were clear.

"No," Jake answered. "We don't want it to look like we're hiding. I'm sure reporters aren't the only ones with eyes on us. People who hole up in hotels have something to hide. I don't want to give this story any more traction."

"So, what's the play here?" Dana asked.

"Drive around the block and park down the street so they don't get a make on your vehicle. We'll cut through your neighbors and use your back door."

"I'm sure that's being staked out, too," she warned.

"I'm counting on it," Jake said. "Whoever orchestrated this needs to see we're not that easy to intimidate."

"Except we are," Claire replied, her voice nearly trembling.

Jake turned to face her. "You didn't do anything wrong. Remember that."

She nodded.

Dana parked down the street from her house, and Jake faced her and Claire. "Heads high, mouths shut," he ordered.

Nodding, they followed him, rushing through the gauntlet of reporters who'd anticipated their move.

46

Jake sat on the edge of Dana's desk, watching the crowd of reporters through her window. They churned under the streetlights like hungry insects. They were persistent, he'd give them that. He'd been watching them for at least an hour and not one news van had packed up to leave. He'd hoped the footage they got of them entering Dana's home would've been enough to get them to leave, but no such luck.

It had, however, earned him a phone call from his FBI appointed attorney instructing him to stay put or he would be considered an enemy of the state. Jake had to bite his tongue to keep from erupting on the man, but he knew that wouldn't help his case of glorified house arrest.

After spewing a few more infuriating catchphrases like 'hang tight' and 'this will blow over' his attorney ended the call, promising to find the source of the article so he could start proving it was nothing but slander.

Dana walked into her office. The sandwich she carried said peace offering, but the determined set of her jaw said otherwise. Jake knew that look. Dana had an agenda, and he wasn't going to like it.

Jake spoke first, figuring offense was the best defense. "I shouldn't have bit your head off in the car."

Dana set the white ceramic plate down in front of him. The smell of toasted bread and melted cheese made his mouth water—comfort food. But it wasn't the remedy he needed. He'd had a pit in his stomach since Jenkins wounded his pride. Stripping him of his badge and gun had been humiliating. But taking that frustration out on Dana was what he was most ashamed of.

Jake's eyes met Dana's. To anyone else her dark amber gaze was unreadable, but Jake could see the hurt she hid behind her impenetrable stare. He stood and rounded the desk to stand in front of her. "I mean it," he implored, stooping to eye level. "You didn't deserve that."

"I know. But now's not the time to have this discussion."

Jake bit down his response, unhappy to add another aspect of their relationship he had to put on hold. But it was a product of his own making. "Okay. What did you come in here to discuss?"

"Claire. She's been texting nonstop with a girl that goes by Betty from Passages. I was starting to tell you about her at your office. I'd feel better if you looked into her."

"Dana, we're basically under house arrest here. If having a friend as an outlet right now is helping Claire, I don't see the harm."

"The harm is we don't know anything about this girl or her involvement in what happened to Hayes."

"First it was Claire, then Dvita, now you think this Betty person is responsible for what happened to Hayes? Make up your mind, Dana."

"That's just it, Jake! I don't have enough evidence to. I don't understand why this doesn't bother you."

"It does, but in case you haven't noticed, I've got a few fires to put out at the moment and no clue how to do it. But if I don't figure it out, every case I've ever worked on is in jeopardy of being torn open and that means criminals are going to walk. Criminals like Vega."

Jake regretted his words the instant they were said, but instead of inciting the fear he'd expected, Dana's gaze narrowed with anger. "Jake, you once told me to focus on the immediate threat. You've spoken to your attorney, there's not much else you can do about your suspension, but the best way to fight these accusations and keep everyone behind bars who belongs there is to figure out who killed Hayes and why. Prove your innocence so you and Jenkins can go back to doing what you do best."

"And how exactly am I supposed to do that without a badge?"

"It's never stopped you before."

Jake flinched, recounting all the times he'd disobeyed direct orders or blurred the lines of the law for Dana. Jenkins was right, Dana Gray made him reckless, but he wouldn't change a thing. They'd hunted serial killers, dismantled drug rings, and infiltrated a human trafficking cult together. Without following Dana's gravely accurate intuition, more lives would've been lost.

Jake had taken a vow to protect and serve. As far as he was concerned, he'd done nothing but uphold it. "You're right," he said. "But this time is different. We don't have the FBI to fall back on. We're on our own."

"I'm okay with that," Dana replied.

Jake knew it wasn't a foreign concept for Dana. Orphaned as a child, she'd grown up with only herself to rely on. But for Jake, it was an unsettling notion. His father may have left, but he'd never been without family. Wade, his mother, Jenkins, the Army, the FBI.

Yes, he was a loner, but he was never truly alone.

But with Dana standing resolutely in front of him, he realized she was offering him an olive branch, an opportunity to find a way through this—together.

"What do you need me to do?"

47

Dana relayed her concerns about Claire's experience at St. Ann's along with the story Claire shared about Max and his upbringing. It had raised alarms for Dana. Two broken halves didn't make a whole. She knew that from her own struggles with trust and intimacy. But she worried Claire would be drawn to someone with the same abandonment issues.

Psychological abuse was sneaky that way. People often thought if no one beat you, you couldn't have scars. Dana knew that was far from true.

"It's the vigilante justice comment that worries me the most," Dana said. "I don't like to feed stereotypes, but there's substantial evidence to support a group of unstable individuals easily finding it reasonable to take matters into their own hands. We need to make sure that doesn't happen or at least limit Claire's exposure to it. And everything she told me about Max ... I can't say he's a good influence."

"Okay, let's start with finding out more about Max and Betty, and we can monitor their phone conversations to make sure nothing stands out, but Dana, we have to tread lightly with Claire. PTSD is isolating enough. I don't want her to feel like we're not in her corner."

"Jake, I think it's more complicated than PTSD."

"I think I have enough personal experience to recognize the signs."

"I'm not challenging your understanding. I'm just asking that you consider this goes deeper."

"Deeper how?"

"I was up all last night doing some research. I kept coming back to the comment the officer made the night they picked up Claire. Her behavior exhibited commonalities in possession, exorcisms, and poltergeist studies."

"Dana, I know your mind is conditioned to go there, but this isn't witchcraft. It's politics. I know in D.C. they can look like one and the same, but in this case, it's just Hayes being a thorn in my side to the very end. Claire's just another casualty of his self-serving vortex."

"Maybe so, but if I could cross reference my findings with Dr. Dvita's research it might give me some answers."

"Well, that's gonna be difficult unless you're shacking up with another guy who can get you a warrant."

Dana couldn't appreciate Jake's attempt at flirtation at the moment. Her mind was too deep down a rabbit hole of conjecture. She pushed past him, walking around to sit at her desk. "Do you think Hartwell would help us?"

Jake practically growled at the mention of his name. "Considering the reality TV nightmare parked out front is the parting gift from the last favor I asked, I'd say it's doubtful. Besides, the next time I talk to that prick, it's not going to be to ask a favor."

Dana opened her laptop and stared at the screen as it powered on. "Well, since we're stuck here, why don't we make the most of it and dig into researching Dvita?

Jake shook his head. "I think it's best if we put a hold on that for now. Everything I touch is currently under investigation. It's best I don't make things worse for Jenkins by ruffling more feathers. Besides, my attorney will have an aneurism if I don't heed his not too subtle 'stand down' orders."

"Okay, but there has to be something we can do to be productive."

An idle mind was the devil's workshop, and Dana needed a distraction. "What about looking into your father?"

48

CLAIRE TIPTOED AWAY FROM DANA'S OFFICE. THE PARANOIA THAT DREW her there only grew worse when she heard her name in the muffled conversation. The sudden vibration in her pocket made her jump. Unable to discern much from Jake and Dana's hushed tones, she was relieved by the excuse to tear herself away. Especially when she saw it was Betty calling.

"Claire? Where are you?"

"I'm still at Dana's. Why?"

"Can you get away? We really need to talk in person."

Claire peeked through the curtains at the dining room window. "The reporters are still here. I don't think I'm going anywhere for a while."

Betty's silence made Claire's skin crawl. "What's wrong? Is it Max?"

"No but he needs us more than ever. We're his only chance now, and we're running out of time."

"Why? What aren't you telling me?"

"I can't talk about it over the phone."

"Betty?"

But the line had already gone dead.

49

ANGER STABBED JAKE LIKE A SPEAR WHEN HE SAW THE NAME FLASHING across his caller ID. "You've got a lot of nerve calling me, Hartwell."

"Figured you'd blame me," Hartwell grumbled. "For what it's worth, I held up my end of things. Still am. Believe me or don't, but that's why I'm calling."

Jake waited while a familiar commotion crackled on Hartwell's end of the line. "You asked me to keep you in the loop." Hartwell exhaled. "I shouldn't even be sharing this ... but we found another body."

Jake had known what was coming before Hartwell managed to get the words out. Even before he heard the sirens in the background, years of training had told him what was coming. "Who?" was all Jake asked.

"No ID. John Doe, early twenties, same MO as Hayes."

"Where?"

"You with Dr. Gray?" Hartwell asked.

"Yeah. Drop a pin and we're on our way."

"Just Gray. If you set foot on scene, we've got orders to take you into custody."

Jake stiffened. "Orders. From who?"

"I'm not at liberty to say. In fact, this conversation never happened," Hartwell insisted. "Just send Dr. Gray." Then he hung up.

Jake still held the phone to his ear, listening to the deafening silence as Dana stared at him, questions dancing in her eyes. As soon as he put the phone down, she spoke. "It happened again, didn't it?"

Jake nodded. "Hartwell wants you on scene."

Dana was already moving toward the door. "Wait, just me?"

"Turns out my voluntary house arrest is more order than suggestion. He made it very clear he'd have no choice but to arrest me if I come anywhere near this."

"What? On whose orders?"

Jake stared at the news teams still surrounding Dana's house. "That's the question."

"Jake ... I don't have to go."

"No, you're our best shot at figuring out what's going on here. And Hartwell's right. If I go anywhere near this, it'll only jeopardize your findings."

"Jake, crime scenes are your thing. I'm much more comfortable analyzing after the fact."

"Don't sell yourself short, Gray. You're a damn good investigator. I wish I was gonna be out there with you, but you've got this." His hand went reflexively to his hip, the foreign absence of his firearm unsettling. "You have your gun?"

She nodded.

"Good. I need to know you'll use it if necessary."

"Jake, is there something you're not telling me?"

"No, but if I can't be with you, I need to know you'll protect yourself."

She grinned. "I was taught by the best."

He crossed the room. Stopping in front of Dana he pulled his dog tags from around his neck and pressed them into her hand. "Here." He didn't know what possessed him to do it. He wasn't superstitious. Perhaps Dana's beliefs were rubbing off on him, or maybe he just wanted to feel like a piece of him was with her.

"Jake, I'll be fine."

"I know," he muttered, before pulling Dana into his arms, rules be damned. He dropped a kiss atop her head. "Be careful," he warned, immediately annoyed at himself for being overbearing, but unable to stop himself, he added, "And if anything feels off, I mean anything, you call me immediately. I've got your back."

Dana laid her hands against his chest, gazing up at him. "I know you do."

Worry creased the space between her brow, but her gaze was determined, her lips tugging down at the corners. He could tell she was conflicted, fighting her own resolve not to kiss him. He pulled her closer, not doing a damn thing to help.

Dana tipped her chin up, her dark eyes drinking him in. But Claire's blood-curdling scream ensured Jake would never know what side of conflict Dana had been aiming to settle on.

Jake rushed into the living room, Dana behind him.

Claire stood in front of the television, news footage of Hartwell's crime scene filling the screen.

"You don't need to see this," Jake said, trying to take the remote from Claire, but she yanked it back.

"No, you don't understand. I know him."

"Max?" Dana asked, her voice full of apprehension.

Claire shook her head violently. "It's Lincoln."

50

Dana neared the police tape, wishing she'd be able to stay on this side of things. But Hartwell spotted her, immediately waving her over. She ducked under the yellow plastic tape delineating the crime scene in the parking lot of Montrose Park and joined Hartwell.

"Sorry it took me so long," she apologized. "Getting clear of the news coverage at my house wasn't easy."

"I hope Shepard conveyed that wasn't my doing."

Dana nodded; her lips pressed together in concern. "We've got a bigger problem."

"What's that?"

"Your John Doe ... Claire ID'd him."

Hartwell scratched his head in confusion after Dana finished relaying Claire's reaction to the news footage. "Cash Holloway? You're not serious?"

"I'm afraid so."

Even Dana knew Cash's celebrity parents. Theo and Zariah Holloway—rock royalty. The Cuban and Haitian born artists recently surprised the music world by putting down roots in D.C. where they were using their influence to lobby for civil rights.

"You're absolutely sure?"

176

"Yes. He was a patient at Passages with Claire. We both saw him today at St. Ann's. He's wearing the same thing," Dana said, gesturing to the jacket she could see peeking out from beneath the coroner's sheet.

Hartwell swore. "For once those vultures were helpful," he grumbled, glaring at the news cameras hovering just behind the police tape.

He pulled out his phone, punched in a number and spoke quietly to whomever was on the other end. "Get a message to the Holloways. I need a positive ID on a John Doe I'm sending to the morgue." He paused. "Yes, those Holloways. And do it discreetly."

Hanging up, Hartwell turned back to Dana. "Two bodies in 48 hours. This guy is out to prove something."

"The question is what?" Dana replied.

"I've preserved the scene for you. I'm hoping being here in person will give you a better picture of what we're dealing with."

"No fire this time?"

Hartwell shook his head. "I don't think we're dealing with an arsonist. The fire at the first scene was most likely a diversion. Our killer didn't need one out here."

"Were there any witnesses this time?"

Hartwell nodded. "About half a dozen. We took statements. They all add up to the same thing. Assailant in a black hoodie fleeing the scene on foot."

"Male?"

"There's some discrepancy there. We're still compiling statements."

"And the weapon?"

"Well, you're the expert. You tell me." Hartwell led the way into the fray of police officers, evidence techs, and first responders.

A thin mist of rain had begun to fall. The wet pavement danced with the reflection of police lights in the darkness. Dana stooped next to the sheet-draped figure to examine the large blade on the ground. The yellow evidence marker looked out of place next to the scythe. Like it was a movie prop rather than a murder weapon.

"The inscription is the same," she said, her gaze transfixed on the

Latin phrase etched into the blade. *Vita est morte est vita.* She looked up at Hartwell, who stood over her like a shadow. "Are you sure the scythe used on Hayes is still in evidence?"

"Had the same thought. Everything was transferred when DOJ took over. So, no, I can't be sure. I can put a call in, but then we run the risk of them taking this case, too."

"It's a risk worth taking," Dana replied. "Besides, they'll know soon enough thanks to the press."

Hartwell frowned but conceded. "I'll make the call."

"I'd like to compare the snath."

Hartwell frowned. "English, Dr. Gray."

"The wooden pole the blade is attached to. This one is intact. If DOJ still has the scythe from the first scene in evidence, we can take a sample from both cores and see if they're a match. Wood can be as telling as a fingerprint."

Hartwell scribbled something in his notebook, sparking Dana's familiar longing for Jake. It was strange to be at a scene without him, but she was more comfortable than she'd expected.

She didn't know if it was a particularly good thing. Death was her life, but the destruction of it, she didn't want that to be something she ever got used to.

Dana walked the crime scene, her mind consuming everything, not just the garish yellow evidence markers that dotted the landscape like morbid Easter eggs. A gust of wind nudged a nearby swing set to squeak out a sinister lullaby.

Careful to sidestep the blood spatter, Dana circled back around to the victim. She needed to face what lay beneath the sheet. The EMTs lingered, gurney and body bag ready, waiting for the signal Hartwell wouldn't give until Dana finished with the scene.

Jake would've already peered beneath the sheet. It's where he would've started, but Dana needed to summon her courage. Crouching down she nodded to the two officers guarding the body. They looked to Hartwell for confirmation and once his team filed in, blocking the news cameras enough to allow the victim some dignity, he gave the signal.

The officers lifted the sheet with a reverence that made Dana's chest tighten. Having seen the crime scene photos from Hayes, she thought she was prepared. But she was mistaken.

She exhaled, fighting her reflex to recoil from the gruesome remains.

No one deserved to die like this.

The young man—Cash Holloway—lay face up, eyes wide, mouth ajar with a scream that no one could hear. His throat was so brutally lacerated it looked like someone had come at him with a chain saw.

Dana tucked her nose into her elbow, her eyes tearing despite her efforts to block out the smell of death permeating the air. She closed her eyes, trying to fight her body's dizzying response to the sight of blood.

Breathe... It was Jake's voice that calmed her. She closed her eyes and clutched at the dog tags beneath her jacket. Finding her inner strength, she pushed through, cementing every last grisly image to memory.

51

I watch, admiring my work. I've drawn a bigger crowd this time, but I don't mind. They can't catch me. They have no idea where to look. I'm all around them, but they don't see me. They only see what I want them to see.

A violent, deranged killer. A Grim Reaper, turned loose on their precious city.

By the time they figure it out, it will be too late.

My only concern is her.

I knew this would draw her in. I made sure of it.

I got rid of him, too. Without him, she shines. She can do his job better. Better than any of them. FBI. Cops. They're no match for her.

I like watching her.

It's why I chose her.

She's not next. But her time is coming.

52

The D.C. Reaper strikes again. A second grisly attack unfolds at Montrose Park.

Jake flipped through the channels, but each station was running a different version of the same gruesome story. He stopped scrolling when a blurry image of Dana filled the screen. She knelt between two Metro PD officers next to a shrouded body. Taking voyeurism to the extreme, the footage was so magnified the image was blown out, but Jake stood transfixed as he watched Dana. He should be there, not her. This wasn't the life she'd chosen. But he'd dragged her into it anyway.

He'd been following orders. At least that's what he'd told himself at the time. But it was getting harder to justify. Jake used to believe in what he did, believe he was serving the greater good, even if that meant walking a fine line with the law. But he was no longer balancing on a precipice between justice and vengeance. He was in freefall, and this landslide was poised to drag everyone down with him.

Jake pressed the mute button before throwing the remote across the room. It hit the wall with a satisfying crack, landing in a heap of plastic and batteries.

Claire's bedroom door creaked open. She peered out at him. "What happened?"

"Nothing," he muttered, sinking onto Dana's uncomfortable couch.

Claire's gaze moved to the shattered remote. "Do they have a suspect?"

"No."

She joined him in the living room. "Jake, you just turned the remote to roadkill. What's going on?"

"I don't know! That's the problem. I'm stuck here, doing nothing. While Dana's out there with the Grim Reaper on the loose."

Claire's eyes widened. "Do you think she's in danger?"

Jake pushed his anger down when he heard the fear in her voice. "There's no reason to think that. I'm just pissed at being sidelined. Dana's not in any harm. She's surrounded by police. Besides, that woman is tough as nails. No one knows that better than us, huh?"

Claire's pale lips pulled into a weak smile. "Where is she right now?"

"Her last text said on her way to the morgue, with Hartwell."

Claire leaned against the couch. "I still can't believe Cash is dead. I just saw him today."

"How well did you know him?" Jake asked, unable to stop the FBI agent in him.

She shrugged. "As well as you can know someone you meet at rehab, I guess. He was kind of a jerk ... sorry ... I shouldn't say that about someone who was just decapitated."

Jake paused, his gaze studying Claire. "Decapitated? Where did you hear that?"

She fidgeted with her phone. "I was scanning the news coverage online."

"You can't believe that garbage. It's all click bait. We're living proof of that," he said, gesturing to the vans still parked outside with their spotlights aimed at the house.

Jake had selfishly hoped the new Reaper development would take the heat off him, but so far, he hadn't been that lucky. If there was one thing D.C. had an abundance of, it was overzealous news crews.

Claire's phone buzzed and Jake watched her open her messaging app, texting a quick reply. "Who was that?" he asked.

"Betty. I called her when I saw the news about Cash. I hope that's okay."

"As long as you're not sharing information about me or Dana, I don't have a problem with it."

"Do you think ..." Claire paused. "Would it be okay if Betty came over? I know this has been hard on her, too. She could bring us some take out from that Thai place we had earlier. Maybe take our mind off all of this for a bit," she added, glancing at the television.

"I don't think it's a good idea, Claire." Jake sighed when her shoulders sagged. "I'm sorry, but with the scrutiny we're under right now, it's not a good idea for anyone else to get pulled into the fray."

Claire continued to stare at the floor.

"Look, I know this is hard, but we need to lay low for a little while. But that doesn't mean we can't order take out."

Claire muttered, "Never mind. I'm not hungry," before disappearing back into her bedroom.

53

Claire locked her bedroom door behind her before calling Betty. She answered at the first ring. "Well?" Betty asked.

"You were right," Claire answered.

"I told you that you couldn't count on Mr. FBI."

It pained Claire to acknowledge that Betty was right, but they were past the point of arguing.

"Are you going to meet me or not?" Betty hissed.

"I'll be there."

"You're sure you can get away?"

"It won't be a problem," Claire answered.

"Good. Tell no one."

54

THE OVERHEADS BUZZED THE WAY ONLY FLUORESCENT LIGHTS COULD, intensifying the dull pounding in Dana's temples. She found herself at Hartwell's precinct, pouring over photographs of evidence from the Hayes murder. It was all that had been left behind after the case was taken from Metro.

Dana examined the scythe they'd collected from the park. She'd been over all thirty-one pieces of evidence they'd gathered with a fine-tooth comb but kept coming back to the same dilemma. "Without access to the original evidence there's no way to make definitive connections or rule out if this is a new blade, or the same one used on Hayes."

"We're lucky DOJ left us with this much," Hartwell grumbled, rubbing his bleary eyes before flipping to another page of photographs.

Hartwell wasn't the only one showing signs of fatigue. They'd been at this for over an hour. Dana took off her glasses and pinched the bridge of her nose. She longed to be back in her own lab, where the lights weren't so harsh and answers to all the questions bouncing around in her mind were at her fingertips.

She was sure her ancient tomes could shed light on the Reaper-like nature of these killings. But the odds of getting Hartwell to let her move the investigation out of the Metro police precinct to the bowels of the Smithsonian were nonexistent.

Again, she found herself missing Jake. Her partnership with him and the FBI had granted her certain liberties she now realized she'd taken for granted. Doing this on her own, and by the book, was much more difficult than she'd anticipated.

The red tape was endless. Hartwell shot down each of her suggestions, quoting the many policies they'd violate.

At her wits' end, Dana asked, "DOJ hasn't gotten back to you about access to the original evidence?"

"I'm not a damn genie, Dr. Gray. The DOJ isn't at my beck and call."

"Maybe I can offer some assistance."

Dana looked up to see the Alchemist walking into the room. "What are you doing here?" she asked, delighted to see a friendly face after being surrounded by so much frostiness.

He returned her grin. "Officer Hartwell thought you might like some assistance."

Dana looked at Hartwell, who crossed his arms. "What?" he asked. "I didn't say I was useless."

"Where shall we begin?" the Alchemist asked, pulling on a pair of latex gloves.

"I guess at the beginning," Dana suggested, feeling a renewed surge of energy.

"Well, I'll leave you to it," Hartwell said, heading back out the door the Alchemist had just come through.

Dana quickly brought Dr. Raynard up to speed regarding the crucial evidence in Cash Holloway's crime scene. Together they compared it to the Hayes scene. Location, weapon, time of day, gender, ethnicity, brutality, eyewitness descriptions.

Not much lined up. What did, was vague at best. And sadly, didn't require her expertise to amass. Resting her elbows on the table in defeat, Dana squeezed her eyes shut, willing herself to see some mystical missing link. Something only her particular skill set could explain. Without it, she had no hope of being officially assigned to the case.

No hope of keeping Claire safe.

No hope of helping clear Jake's name.

What am I missing?

Dana heard Jake's voice in her mind. *Find the intersect. Find the killer.*

The Alchemist spoke as though he had heard Jake, too. "I was sorry to hear about Agent Shepard. I always thought he was one of the good ones."

Dana bristled. "He *is* one of the good ones."

"The media seems to feel differently."

"Jake is a decorated hero. A piece of unfounded bad press shouldn't erase a lifetime of service. What happened to innocent until proven guilty?"

"Nothing would delight me more than to be proven wrong, Dr. Gray, but in my experience, in this town, accusations don't need to be true to do irreparable damage."

"And I'd wager to say it's acceptance of baseless speculation that does the real damage."

"Still, it would behoove you to keep your distance if you don't want to be dragged down with the ship."

"I'd rather sink at Shepard's side than be a coward controlled by the tides."

"Careful, Dr. Gray, blind loyalty is as dangerous as a scythe."

"There's nothing blind about me. We're done here."

Dana stormed out of the precinct, leaving the Alchemist to convey the line she'd drawn—an abyss, challenging all who'd attempt to cross.

55

It was all Claire could do not to abandon Jake mid-sentence, but that would make her look even more suspicious. She couldn't believe she'd slipped up. Mentioning the decapitation was a mistake. One Jake hadn't missed.

She'd seen the change. The slightest narrowing of his sharp blue gaze. The ever so slight tilt of his head, the way his voice tightened, choosing each word more carefully than before.

There were benefits to knowing someone as well as she knew Jake, and Claire hated that she was using it against him. But she knew she wouldn't have another chance.

That's why she hadn't wasted time. Why she didn't look back.

She'd simply pulled on a black sweatshirt and baseball hat before letting muscle memory guide her soundlessly out into the night. Now, miles away from the warmth and safety of Dana's home, Claire found herself wishing she'd had another alternative. But Betty was quick to remind her, they were out of options.

Claire looked at the clock on the wall of the coffee shop. It matched the time on her phone. Which confirmed that Betty was late. Claire took another sip of her coffee, but it did nothing to keep the chill from creeping up her spine. Something was wrong.

Betty knew the stakes, and still she'd insisted Claire meet her here. For her not to show up ... Claire didn't like to think about what could be preventing her friend from making this meeting.

"Where are you?" Claire pressed send on the message, willing a response to appear.

The silence that answered was deafening. Everything inside Claire was telling her to leave. But it was too late. By now, Jake would've discovered she was gone. She'd broken his trust. It couldn't be for nothing.

Claire finished her coffee, forcing herself to stay put. The only reason she'd come tonight was because of Max. If there was a chance she could help him, she would. She owed him that much. But as the minutes ticked by, she knew the window was closing.

Jake would send the calvary soon. Then Claire wouldn't be able to help anyone.

56

I WAIT AND I WATCH. I'M ALWAYS WATCHING. ALWAYS WAITING. BUT IT won't be much longer. She's in my sights now. This kill is so close I can almost taste it.

One kill closer to my revenge.

One kill closer to making them see me. The real me. Not just this skin which doesn't fit. I can't wait to take it off. I can't wait to be myself again. Reborn. Renewed. Rewarded.

I inhale deeply, tasting the frosty air as I remind myself to be patient.

I'm so close now.

One kill closer.

One kill closer to her.

57

ANGER ROLLED OFF DANA IN WAVES. SHE REPLAYED THE ALCHEMIST'S condescending words as she drove through the quiet neighborhood of Georgetown student housing. She could navigate these streets in her sleep, which only gave her irritation more time to simmer.

Dana regretted letting Raynard get to her. She left without even telling Hartwell where she was going, partly because she didn't exactly know. When she'd gotten in her car, she thought she was heading home, but with her mind elsewhere, she found she'd changed course, heading toward the Smithsonian.

Not too long ago, it would've seemed like the most natural thing in the world. But it had been a while since her office had felt like a sanctuary. She paused at the light on 10th and E street, wondering if she should follow whatever instinct led her this way, or turn back toward home. Toward the people who were counting on her.

As if sensing her dilemma, Jake's name flashed across Dana's caller ID. She accepted the incoming call despite knowing she didn't have the answers he was calling for.

"Hey," she answered.

"Just checking in," he greeted. "How's it going?"

"It's been a long night."

"Always are."

When she was silent, Jake said, "We'll get through it, Gray. Remember, one step at a time."

She sighed. "I know. But these steps don't seem to be leading anywhere."

"Wanna talk it through?" he offered.

"When I get home," she replied.

"When will that be?"

The light turned green, and Dana pulled a U-turn on the abandoned street. "On my way now."

"That's the best news I've heard all night."

Dana could hear Jake's smile through the phone, and it lightened her mood considerably.

"You hungry?" he asked. "I can whip something up."

She hadn't eaten, but the crime scene killed her appetite. "Thanks, but I don't think I can eat."

Jake's voice was gentle now. "Tell me what I can do."

"There's a bottle of Pinot in my pantry. Have it open when I get home?"

"Done."

Jake's voice filled the car, wrapping around Dana like a security blanket she didn't want to let go of. She wanted to be with him. The ache came on as sudden and ferociously as an earthquake, threatening to shake loose her grip on reality.

Putting whatever they were to each other on hold was the logical choice, but ignoring her feelings wasn't working. Dana was constantly oscillating between desire and denial. One minute she was pushing Jake away, the next she was imagining his arms around her.

It was infuriating, and it was affecting her ability to think clearly.

Their current living arrangement wasn't helping. Without time apart Dana was having trouble compartmentalizing the case. She knew Jake would want to know everything about the crime scene the moment she walked in the door.

Truthfully, there was no one's input she wanted more, but sharing the horrific details of Cash Holloway's murder would only make it harder for Jake to follow orders and stand down. She didn't know what to do—about the case, or her feelings.

"How's Claire?" she asked, wanting to change the subject.

Jake sighed. "She's in her room."

"All night?" Dana asked.

"Just since we had a difference of opinions."

"About?"

"She wanted to have Betty over. I told her it wasn't a good idea."

Dana frowned but didn't answer.

"What?" Jake asked. "Was that the wrong move?"

"No. I would've said the same."

"Then what's wrong?"

Dana hesitated to say it, but she couldn't fight her suspicion. "When's the last time you checked on her?"

"I'm trying to give her some space."

"Jake, I don't know if—" The flashing red and blue lights in Dana's rearview choked her words off mid-sentence.

"Dana?"

"Shit. I'm getting pulled over."

"What? By who?"

It was hard to see past the glare of lights, but Dana recognized the outline of the government vehicle. "I don't know. Black SUV. Unmarked. Jake, I have to go."

"No! Dana, listen to me. I'm going to hang up and call you back on a video call so you can screen record your interaction. Whatever you do, keep recording."

"Jake—" Dana tried to object, but he'd already disconnected. Seconds later his incoming video call lit up her phone. Dana glanced in her rearview. The driver was exiting his car. If she didn't answer now, she wouldn't have a chance to.

Dana hit the green phone icon and Jake's face filled the screen. "I'm here," he said. "Hit screen record." She complied with shaky fingers. "Tell me what's happening," Jake ordered.

"He's out of his car." The knock on her passenger side window made Dana jump. The man standing outside her car wore black cargo pants and a black flak jacket. The absence of insignia made her pulse quicken. "He's knocking on my window. What do I do?"

"Roll your window down an inch and ask for his identification."

She did.

The man wordlessly complied, shoving a bifold with a heavy silver badge against her window.

"Give me his name and Metro ID number?" Jake demanded.

Dana stared at it in disbelief.

"Dana? Can you hear me? What's his badge number?"

"He's not Metro PD," she whispered.

"Who's he with?"

The man outside her window returned the badge to his jacket and leaned down to peer directly at Dana. "Special Agent Matthew Spector. Homeland Security Investigations."

Jake swore but the agent ignored him, his gaze locked on Dana. "Dr. Gray, please disconnect your call and step outside the vehicle."

"Dana don't—" But she was already gone; her fearful eyes his parting gift.

58

THE SHRILLNESS OF CLAIRE'S RINGTONE ECHOED THROUGH THE EMPTY coffee shop earning her a scowl from the bored barista. The number read *unknown,* but Claire quickly answered anyway. Relief swept through her when she heard Betty's voice on the other end.

"Where are you?" Claire demanded. "I've been waiting here forever."

"I know," Betty answered. "I can see you."

Claire's head swiveled from side to side. The coffee shop remained as empty as ever.

"Stop," Betty ordered. "You look paranoid."

"That's because I am!" Claire snapped. "Where are you?"

"I'm sorry. I'm just being cautious. Come outside and take a left. Walk two blocks, then take another left. I'll meet you beneath the overpass."

"This is ridiculous. Why can't you just come here?"

"I'm watching to make sure you're not being followed."

"I'm not. I told you; Jake has no idea I snuck out. Or at least he didn't, but now that I've been sitting here for an eternity—"

"Claire! You know what's at stake. Just do it."

"No. I missed the memo where you were put in charge, but I'm done following blindly. If you have news just tell me."

"Not over the phone."

"Then come to the coffee shop."

The barista shot Claire a withering glare, probably hoping she'd just leave already so the girl could close up for the night.

"Just tell me one thing," Claire said. "Did you find him?"

"Meet me and find out." Then the line went dead.

Out of options Claire stood up, dropped a few bills on the table and walked back into the inky blackness of the frosty night.

Betty's directions were easy enough to follow. Left, two blocks, left again. As promised, they led to a sketchy looking overpass.

The traffic on the street above sounded like thunder rolling over-head as Claire slinked further into the shadows. She let her eyes adjust. Graffiti, cardboard boxes, soiled sleeping bags, crushed beer cans and broken bottles ... all the signs of a five-star transient hideout.

Claire wanted to call out for Betty or Max but kept quiet on the off chance they weren't the only ones hiding here.

This wasn't the kind of place she wanted to be caught trespassing.

The crunch of gravel behind her made her whirl around, but not in time. The scream died in her throat as strong arms circled around her, a large, gloved hand covering her mouth.

59

DANA USED HER KEY CARD TO ACCESS THE ELEVATOR, STEPPING ON WITH the silent Agent Spector by her side. She still wasn't sure bringing him here was a good idea, but when he'd asked if there was somewhere private where they could speak, the Smithsonian was the first place that came to mind.

Being on her home turf offered a modicum of comfortability. She'd yet to learn if her sense of security was false, but since Agent Spector hadn't offered any other information, she'd decided to take every advantage she could get.

Dana hated the worry she knew she was causing Jake. She'd seen the anguish in his eyes right before she'd disconnected their call. He was part of the reason she'd chosen to come to the Smithsonian. It was a place Jake would look for her if things with the mysterious Homeland Security agent went south.

The elevator doors rolled open, and Dana stepped out into the familiar library she called home. "My office is right this way," she offered.

Past stacks of dusty books and display cases of ancient bones, Agent Spector followed without pause. If he was affronted by the subject matter of sub level three, it didn't show.

Finally, they arrived at Dana's office. Agent Spector took a seat first, making himself comfortable in the leather chair in front of her desk. Out of habit, Dana took her own seat, behind the desk, like she was the one conducting this strange interview.

Agent Spector stared at her, an amused look on his weather worn face. At first Dana had thought they were around the same age, but upon closer inspection, she estimated he was a bit older, maybe late forties.

His tanned face held a boyish charm, and his physique was beyond impressive. It was the dusting of salt and pepper at his temples that gave him away. It spread through his short sandy brown hair like cream mixing into coffee.

Dana sat across from the quiet man, fidgeting with her ragged nails while she waited for him to speak. She understood the technique. He was waiting her out. Seeing if she'd get spooked and offer up some fact he didn't know he wanted.

She was determined not to fall for it, but in the end, he was more seasoned than her.

"You asked for somewhere to speak. I assumed that meant you had something to say," Dana pressed.

His grin was so sudden, Dana wondered if she'd imagined the flash of white teeth and dimples. It was a wonder he didn't deploy it more. His smile was full of a boyishness that made it hard for her to remember he was a federal agent with the power to lock her up and throw away the key.

"I have many things to say. But I'm more interested in your opinions."

"On what?"

"Cash Holloway."

"Are you taking that case from Metro, too?"

He nodded. "It seems so."

"What does that mean?"

"We received a call from Metro PD requesting joint evidence analysis."

Dana mentally kicked herself for insisting Hartwell make that call.

"Don't worry," Spector said. "You only expedited the inevitable. HSI has a TFO unit in route to seize the crime scene evidence as we speak."

"If you took the time to call me back, you might've saved yourself the trip," Dana said.

"We don't take matters of National Security lightly, Dr. Gray."

"That's just it. Cash Holloway's death proves we're most likely dealing with a serial killer, not a political terrorist."

"Cash Holloway's parents are public figures who are notoriously vocal about their political agenda. That makes it impossible to eliminate the possibility of a political threat," Spector argued.

"The only thing similar about the Hayes and Holloway murders is the weapon. This is serial. It should go to the FBI's Behavioral Analysis Unit, and you know it."

Spector grinned. "You've worked three FBI cases, Dr. Gray. That hardly makes you an expert."

She narrowed her eyes. "I've worked enough cases to know that if the alphabet soup of D.C. agencies stopped using red tape to measure their pissing matches, we'd get a lot more done."

"I agree."

"Yeah," Dana scoffed. "That's why you keep swooping in and taking all the evidence Metro collects."

"A second look never hurts. You should know that better than anyone."

"What do you mean by that?"

Spector nodded toward the library beyond the open door of her office. "Your books and artifacts have been examined by centuries of experts, but still, you find new occult discoveries every day."

"You know a lot about me."

"It's my job."

"Why did you pull me over? I know it wasn't because you're interested in my studies."

"I need a favor."

"From me?" Dana crossed her arms. "There are easier ways to ask."

He flashed that disarming grin again. "Meredith Kincaid. I'd like you to ask her to speak to me."

"About what?"

"The same things you spoke with her about on your last visit, I expect."

Dana briefly wondered if Meredith's room was bugged. Or maybe she was. Jake had acted like it was nothing to put spyware on Claire's phone. Surely Homeland Security wouldn't find it difficult to do the same.

Agent Spector interrupted her thoughts. "I'd like you to ask Miss Kincaid to cooperate."

"You're Homeland. Can't you make her?"

"My position allows certain liberties, yes. But I prefer not to employ them unless absolutely necessary."

Dana heard Jake's voice in her mind. *Gain before you give.* She wasn't granting a favor unless she could get one in return. The question was ... what to ask for?

"Why Meredith?" Dana asked, stalling.

"Her name has come up in our investigation. I'm just seeing if any dots connect."

"Dots as in Dr. Dvita?"

Spector's intense blue eyes bore into Dana's. "You have a keen sense of suspicion. I see why Agent Shepard liked working with you. Shame about him."

Dana gritted her teeth, wishing people would stop saying that in the past tense. "If I do this, what do I get in return?"

"I'll owe you a chit."

A favor from Homeland Security? It was a veritable get out of jail free card. Something to keep in her back pocket for a rainy day.

Trouble was, Dana wasn't much for rainy days.

She reached inside her shirt, her fingers tightening around the dog tags, knowing exactly what favor to cash in on.

60

CLAIRE'S HEART POUNDED AS HER FEET LEFT THE GROUND. THE BURLY arms around her nearly squeezed the life out of her. But she didn't care. She threw her arms around Max's neck in relief and squeezed back. "I was so worried about you," she squeaked. "Are you okay?"

Max set her gently back on her feet and nodded, kissing her with the ferocity she craved.

"Where have you been?"

He quickly signed his reply.

Claire shivered to think he'd been hiding in places like this since the fire. None of this was his fault, but he was the perfect scapegoat. Labeled as violent and non-verbal, the authorities wouldn't hesitate to blame Hayes' and now Cash's death on him. But they didn't understand Max. No one did but her.

Claire spoke as she signed. "It's okay. I'm here now. I'm going to take care of you."

Max leaned down, stroking a strand of hair from Claire's cheek as gently as if he was caressing a butterfly. She stood on her toes and kissed him again. His lips were cold, but they still spread a warmth through her that she couldn't explain. She wanted it to be like this forever. Just her and Max, together in a new life. One that they could still have. They just had to keep him hidden for a little while longer.

Betty's presence pulled Claire from Max's embrace. "I told you to stay hidden," Betty scolded.

Max ignored her, standing resolutely behind Claire. "What's the plan?" she asked.

"I was hoping you had one," Betty replied.

Claire took Max's hand. "He needs somewhere to hide."

"This was the best I could find on short notice," Betty said. "But I agree, we need something more permanent."

"I might have a place," Claire offered. She fished her keychain out of her pocket and pulled off the key to her storage unit. "It's not perfect, but it's safe and at least out of the cold."

"Where?"

Claire explained where her storage unit was. "I have some furniture and a few boxes of my things there. Fresh clothes, bedding. You'll be comfortable there," she said while signing to Max. "We can get you some food, too."

"I'll get the food and get Max settled," Betty interrupted, snatching the key. "You two can't be seen together."

"Why?"

"You're under house arrest with an FBI agent and a shrink. It should be obvious."

"Dr. Gray isn't a shrink. And I told you, they don't know anything."

"Yet," Betty clarified. "And we have a better chance of keeping it that way if we keep you and Max apart. We've come too far to go back now."

Claire knew Betty was right, but it didn't mean she liked it. She wanted to stay with Max, to finish what they started. They just had to wait a little bit longer. Soon it would all be over, and she'd finally have the life she deserved.

"We need to talk about Cash," Betty said, her tone rife with accusation.

"There's nothing to talk about. It's done."

"Have you spoken to Dvita?"

"No. Why would I?"

"You know why," Betty said. "Just stick to the plan."

"I am," Claire insisted.

Betty grabbed Max's hand from Claire's. "Come on. We need to go." But before leaving, Betty turned back to face Claire. "Don't come back to group," she warned. "Your friends are getting too close."

61

THE LAST THING JAKE SAW WAS THE FEAR ON DANA'S FACE, THEN THE video call disconnected. He couldn't get the image out of his head. Dana, with the shadow of a man hovering near her car window. His face was too blurred to make out, no matter how many times he rewatched the screen recording.

Jake already called Hartwell three times, and he was doing a great job of pacing a groove into Dana's hardwood, but otherwise, he was utterly useless, and it was killing him.

Jake hit redial again. And again, Dana's voicemail greeted him. Each syllable of her voice hammered him with paralyzing fear.

Jenkins had made it clear she was done assisting Jake in this matter. And with his FBI access suspended, the only search engine he had at his disposal was the old-fashioned public internet. A quick search of Matthew Spector had come up empty. But if the guy was really Homeland, that wasn't surprising.

Jake knew he could knock on Claire's door. The girl could have him on the dark web in a matter of minutes, but he didn't want to worry her. She'd already lost so many people she cared about. If something happened to Dana...

Jake shut down the thought, commanding his mind not to go there.

A few more minutes of fruitless web searches, unanswered phone calls and useless pacing and Jake found himself at Claire's bedroom door anyway. He knocked lightly. "Claire? I need your help."

When there was no response, he knocked louder. "Claire. It's important."

He turned the clear glass knob, but the door was locked. The solid oak of the antique door made kicking it in unappealing, but the old skeleton lock was another story. The simplistic mechanism was comprised of only two parts: lever and deadbolt. An Allen wrench would easily get the job done, but thankfully Jake didn't have to go that route. Dana displayed a collection of antique skeleton keys in one of the many ornate curio cabinets adorning the cluttered corners of her home.

Jake grabbed the ring of keys from the case and was back at Claire's door, clicking it open in a matter of seconds. But unlocking the door only unlocked more problems.

Claire was gone.

62

SCREW ORDERS. JAKE WAS DONE WAITING. IF THE FBI WANTED HIM handcuffed, they could come do it themselves. Until then, he was going to follow his gut, which right now told him to track down Dana and Claire.

He grabbed his jacket, calculating the time it would take to give the press the slip, get to the gun safe in his apartment and then begin his hunt. He was two paces from the front door, when he heard the lock tumble.

Jake's hand went to his hip instinctively, despite knowing his weapon wasn't there. He swore, retreating out of sight. It wasn't likely an armed assailant had sauntered up to the front door with the hoard of press outside, but old habits were hard to break. He crouched, ready to attack if need be.

The door swung open activating the security system. Warning beeps counted down to the alarm if the code wasn't entered in time. Jake heard the keypad being punched, then the telltale *beep-beep* of the system resetting.

"Jake?" Dana's voice reached him, luring him forward like a magnet.

Her eyes were full of questions when she saw him stalking toward her, but desperation overrode logic, and he pulled her into a fierce embrace.

Chest heaving, Jake inhaled her scent, letting her floral fragrance quiet his frayed nerves. She looked up at him and he forgot himself, capturing her lips with his.

For a moment, Dana was lost too, her arms around his neck, fingers raking through his hair. But all at once she pulled back, looking at him like she was truly seeing him for the first time.

"Were you going somewhere?" she accused, eyeing the FBI field jacket he'd donned shortly before she'd arrived.

It was useless to deny it. Jake could feel it coming. The moment his lips left Dana's he'd landed in an argument. Or maybe picked up where the last one ended. It was getting harder to tell. "I didn't know where you were," he answered defensively.

She crossed her arms. "So, you were going to disobey a direct order to drive around D.C. aimlessly?"

"If that's what it takes, yeah. I thought you were in danger!"

Dana's gaze softened but her arms remained crossed. "Jake, we have to break this cycle."

"Of you chasing down danger on your own? Yeah, I agree."

"I didn't chase anything. Hartwell called me to the crime scene, you know that. Just like you also know I'd rather not be there, especially without you."

"Yeah, well that's the situation we're in, isn't it?" he said, bitterly.

"Because you don't trust me to take care of myself."

"Trust has nothing to do with it! In the past two years you've been shot, kidnapped, and hospitalized. So, excuse me for worrying when you disappear in the middle of a phone call."

Dana exhaled slowly, the fight leaving with her breath. She closed the space between them, laying her hand on Jake's cheek. "I'm sorry I worried you. If the situation were reversed, I probably would've done the same thing."

Jake smirked. "Rushed after me and landed yourself in even more trouble?"

"Yes, but that's what I mean. We have to break this cycle. We have to trust in each other enough to know we can handle whatever situation we find ourselves in."

"Dana, I know you're right and I can 'yes ma'am' you all day long, but the bottom line is if you're in trouble, I'm going to do everything in my power to get you out of it. That's just how I'm wired."

It was her turn to fight a smile. "Like a stubborn soldier."

He pulled her closer, arms encircling her waist. "A stubborn soldier who's in love with you."

Dana's eyes widened. "Jake ..."

He held up a hand to stop her objection. "Can we table this argument? We have a bigger problem."

63

DANA HAD TROUBLE HEARING OVER THE WHOOSH OF HER OWN heartbeat. Jake had just dropped the L word and then changed the subject in the same breath. She blinked through the sensation of whiplash, trying to focus on what he was saying about Claire.

"Where is she?" Dana asked, struggling to regain her composure.

"I'm right here," Claire answered, walking into the room.

Jake whirled around. "Where the hell have you been?"

"I thought you said she was in her room?" Dana interjected.

"I was," Claire insisted, but something in Jake's intimidating stance suddenly made her change her tune. "I mean, I was, but I just had to get some air."

Dana looked from Claire to Jake. The bulging vein in his neck was hard to miss, and it was enough to make anyone spill their secrets. But all Claire offered was a meek apology. "I'm sorry. I didn't mean to worry you."

Jake stalked closer to Claire, his frame towering over her. She trembled in his presence, and rightly so. Dana had never seen Jake treat Claire with anything but kid gloves. But now, seeing him flip off his humanity and go full FBI interrogator on her raised an unexpected protectiveness in Dana.

She crossed the room to stand next to Claire in a show of solidarity. She didn't know what was going on between Claire and Jake, but whatever it was, she wanted everyone to remember they were on the same team.

"Hey," Dana interjected softly. "Whatever it is, we'll face it together."

Claire looked nervously at Jake, who gave an eventual nod.

"I'm sorry," she whispered again.

"That's been established," Jake muttered. "What hasn't been is your whereabouts. Start talking."

64

CLAIRE SAT ON DANA'S COUCH, HUGGING HER KNEES TO HER CHEST. Despite Jake's intimidating warning, she hadn't told him where she'd been or who she'd been with. Only that she'd slipped out for some air. "Sometimes I feel like I'm suffocating. I just need to get outside and breathe. I knew you'd tell me no," she said to Jake. "So, I went out the window."

Dana seemed appeased with Claire's half-truth, but it was harder to tell with Jake. He'd eventually given up his questioning and followed Dana to her office.

Claire told herself she'd kept the truth from them for their own protection. If her plan fell through, plausible deniability would be the only thing to protect Jake and Dana's careers. Despite what she had to do, she still cared about them.

At least that's what she told herself.

But fear had also been a motivator. The trouble was, Claire didn't know what she feared more. Jake's anger, Dana's disappointment, or what would happen if they found out the truth.

She watched Dana trying to console him through the gap in her office door. She'd no doubt left it open to keep an eye on Claire. But it also made it impossible for Claire to ignore the deepening intimacy between Jake and Dana.

The soft touches, the tense glances, the way they leaned into each other; it created an electrical charge that was uncomfortable to be around. Claire worried if she didn't pretend to be oblivious to their undeniable chemistry it would ensure front row seats to an explosion of affection.

She should feel guilty—she was likely one of the problems keeping them apart—but she didn't.

Her own problems were all that mattered now.

She was proud of herself for not caving under pressure. It was the first of many tests to come.

65

JAKE REACHED HIS LIMIT. THE WEIGHT OF THE DAY HAD TAKEN ITS TOLL. He'd lost his badge, been hung out to dry by the Bureau, sidelined from an investigation that was pulling Dana deeper and now Claire had lied to him.

He didn't believe her bullshit 'I needed air' story for a second.

Jake wished he could say his years of training made the lie easy to spot. But when it came to Claire, he was guilty of having a blind spot. One he never would've realized if it wasn't for the video surveillance he'd had installed along with the security system, unbeknownst to Dana and apparently Claire.

He'd checked the footage after he'd found her missing from her room. There was a clear shot of her bedroom window. It was never opened.

Jake glanced at Claire through the open door of Dana's office. She sat on the couch, the picture of remorse. As far as tells go, Claire didn't have any. She'd spun her lie expertly. The best thing he could do was continue to let her believe she'd gotten away with it. Confidence is what trips most people up.

The trouble was, Jake didn't want Claire to trip. He wanted to stop her before the fall.

There was only one reason people lied. And Jake intended to find out what Claire was hiding.

But he had to do it without involving Dana. She had enough on her plate without worrying more than she already did about Claire. Especially after her encounter with Agent Spector.

Jake wished he could say hearing Dana's recount of her conversation with the Homeland Security Agent had soothed his nerves, but it had done the opposite. "I'd be more comfortable with you working with him if I could access his CV."

"I'm not working with him," Dana amended. "He just wants me to get Meredith to cooperate."

Jake raised his eyebrows. "And you're willing to entrust Meredith to this unverified HSI Agent?"

"I don't really have a choice, do I? He's going to question her with or without my help. With it, this ends faster."

"Unless it's not a political strike."

"Now you're doubting it?" Dana asked.

Jake shrugged. "Your first instinct is usually the right one. This Holloway kid might have celebrity parents, but I don't see the connection between him and Hayes."

"Me neither. It doesn't help that I didn't get to walk the first crime scene. But from the photos, this one feels different. More violent. Almost like it's two different killers with the same MO."

"Okay, so if it's not political, what's the agenda? Who's behind it? The fact that no one has claimed responsibility, domestic or abroad makes me think you're right. This is serial."

Dana chewed her nails, lost in thought. She looked up at Jake. "Even if we're right, there's not much to go on. I have plenty of research to compile a profile based on Grim Reaper rituals, but Hartwell has no prints, no DNA, and Agent Spector won't give me access to the weapons, or any other shred of evidence. Without it, the haystack's too broad."

"The Alchemist examined Hayes with you, right? He photo catalogs every case he's ever worked on. I'm sure he'd give you access."

Dana sighed. "I'm afraid I burned that bridge."

The crease between Jake's brow deepened. "What do you mean?"

"Turns out our friend the Alchemist is as loyal as the media when it comes to gossip."

Jake couldn't contain his grin. "And let me guess, you gave him a piece of your mind?"

"I may have said I'd rather go down with the ship than change with the tides."

An actual laugh escaped him. "And that's why I love you."

"Yeah," Dana paused. "About that."

"What?"

"You can't suddenly say that word like it doesn't mean something."

"Who said it doesn't mean something?" Jake took her by the shoulders. "Dana, it means everything. After watching you get pulled out of your car by HSI tonight and being helpless to stop it ... After everything we've been through. It's all the more reason to say that word. I love you. I've made peace with that. One day, I hope you can, too."

———

DANA STOOD speechless in Jake's presence for the second time in less than an hour, trying to absorb his calm revelation. It was a complete departure from the way he normally went about things, and it was jarring. She was much more adept at handling his temper and misguided machismo. But this wasn't an argument. Jake had simply led her to a fork in the road and let her know what path he was choosing.

The rest was up to her.

"Keep researching your Reaper theory," he said calmly. "I'm going to go check on Claire."

Then he kissed her atop her head and walked out of the room.

66

IT'S FINALLY TIME. I'M DONE WAITING. DONE HIDING.

It's time to reap.

I don't want to, but I must take this next step. I promised I would. It is my destiny. I've been chosen. I've prepared. I can't stop now.

This is bigger than me. It was set in motion long ago. Now I have the honor of carrying out another step.

I'm so close to having it all. I can't let anything hold me back.

Not emotion.

Not affection.

Not all the superficiality of this world.

There will be a new world when I'm done.

It's time.

I tap her on the shoulder. She turns to face me. She even has the audacity to look impatient. I grin.

67

HARTWELL GLANCED AT HIS PHONE, SAW THE NAME ON THE SCREEN AND silenced it again. Eight missed calls. Jake Shepard was one persistent son of a bitch. But he would have to wait.

Cold bodies always took precedence over warm ones.

"This Grim Reaper must have one hell of a quota to meet," Lennox said, standing over the mutilated body at their newest crime scene. Hartwell hadn't even had time to take a shower between scenes. He could still smell the decay on him from Cash Holloway, and it was making him ornery.

"This isn't the time to crack jokes," Hartwell reprimanded.

Lennox looked down like a scolded dog. "Sorry, sir."

"Tell me what you see."

"Female, late twenties, COD exsanguination from throat laceration."

"You mean estimated COD," Hartwell corrected.

Lennox looked up at him expectantly. Teaching crime scene 101 to this kindergarten cop was not on his short list, but he did it anyway. Shoddy police work wasn't getting another case yanked from Metro on his watch.

"Every scene gets examined with fresh eyes, zero bias, regardless of how similar it looks to any other. Assumptions lead to mistakes. Now, go again," Hartwell ordered.

Lennox nodded, this time crouching for a closer look. "Female, mid-twenties, throat laceration, blunt force trauma to the skull and face, defensive wounds. Awaiting ME and tox screen to confirm COD."

Hartwell nodded his satisfaction. He knew Lennox's first assessment of the vic was correct. The sheer amount of blood loss meant she was alive when her throat was slit. But that was no excuse to get sloppy.

The possibility of copycat crimes was on the rise thanks to the news' morbid obsession with sharing every detail they could get their hands on, and then some. If this case did go serial, he knew the agency in charge would leak false breadcrumbs to help weed out tips from people just looking for their fifteen minutes of fame.

But in this case, as far as Hartwell could tell, this scene was the real deal.

Hartwell knelt near the murder weapon. There was no need for Dr. Gray this time. It was a scythe. He found himself uneasy with how comfortable he was becoming with the peculiar blade.

The same inscription adorned the bloody steel. *Vita est morte est vita.* The Latin riddle taunted him, as if to say death was inevitable and there was nothing he could do to stop it.

But he'd be damned if he didn't try.

Reexamining the scene, Hartwell focused on the differences.

The MO had changed slightly, the killer choosing a female victim for the first time. Also, she wasn't someone with political or celebrity status. The vic was most likely a runaway judging from the stamp on her hand—St. Jude's, a halfway house on 5th and Lex.

Hartwell had worked that beat as a new boot. He knew the area well and was still tied into a few of the key players on that block. He briefly wondered if that would be enough to retain jurisdiction over this case.

Another change was the aggressive brutality evident from the scene. The defensive wounds indicated the victim fought back. Had that spurred the unwarranted bludgeoning after her throat had been severed? Or was this murder personal?

Either way, it was clear the killer was escalating.

68

CLAIRE ANSWERED THE KNOCK AT HER BEDROOM DOOR, UNSURPRISED TO see Jake's hulking frame standing there. Like an overbearing guard dog, he hadn't left her alone for more than a few minutes since she'd come back to Dana's.

She glanced at the clock, annoyed at the hour. Suspicion was warranted, but this was ridiculous. She still needed to sleep.

"Jake, it's four in the morning."

"I know what time it is."

"Then why are you waking me up?"

"Press is gone."

His words erased the fog of sleep from her mind. "Did something happen? Another murder?"

He shrugged. "Maybe we're just old news. You still want air?" he asked, changing the subject.

Accusation hung between them, and Claire wasn't sure how to respond. She peered around him, to see Dana sitting at her desk, lamp light glowing in the predawn hours. It seemed no one had gotten any sleep.

"Maybe later," Claire finally answered, beginning to close the door but Jake's boot stopped her.

"We need to talk," he said, handing her a jacket. "I think it's best if we get some air."

They stood on Dana's back porch. It was smaller than the brownstone's ornate street facing facade with all its imposing stone and columns, but the narrow overhang sheltered Claire and Jake from the dampness that hung in the chill spring air.

There was no furniture on the back porch, just a few potted plants in need of attention. Claire leaned up against the house, arms wrapped tightly around the borrowed peacoat she wore. She had her own jacket in her room, but Jake hadn't offered her the chance to grab it.

He stood there silently watching her with his intimidating 'Special Agent' stare. He was waiting for her to talk first, but she wasn't going to. If he wanted to accuse her of something, he could, but she wasn't foolish enough to divulge information he was only guessing at.

Jake exhaled loudly, ending their silent stalemate. "You're going to make me ask, aren't you?"

"Ask what?"

"For the truth."

Claire did her best to calm her breathing, but it was hard with Jake looking at her like that. She'd seen him look at criminals that way. It hurt more than she liked to admit. "I don't know what you're talking about."

"Give it a rest, Claire. I know you didn't slip out the window for '*some air*,'" he said, his fingers making mocking air quotes.

"What do you want from me, Jake?"

"Let's start with the truth."

69

JAKE COULD DO THIS ALL DAY—HE HATED IT—BUT HE WOULD DO IT. *Had* to do it.

He considered Claire family, but the moment he caught her in a lie, something shifted. This was him giving her the chance to shift it back.

He was hoping like hell she'd just admit the truth so they could go back to the way they were meant to be—him, Dana, and Claire—on the right side of justice.

Jake wasn't sure what was going on with Claire, but he knew they needed to work together before this case tore them apart.

He hated being suspicious of her, especially after chastising Dana for the same thing. Granted he had proof Claire was keeping things from them, whereas Dana had just been buying into Dvita's propaganda. But that did little to assuage the sting of betrayal he felt staring into Claire's unblinking blue eyes.

The fact remained; she was hiding something. And it was Jake's duty to get to the bottom of it. "Tell me where you really went."

She didn't answer.

"Really, you're gonna plead the fifth?" He pulled out his phone.

"You know, I can just see for myself." It was true, but Jake hoped the threat would be enough.

As expected, Claire cracked, her icy exterior faltering the moment Jake pulled out his phone. "Did you tap my phone? That's illegal."

"It's my phone," Jake replied. "You just borrowed it."

Claire pulled her phone from her pocket, staring at it like it might bite her.

"Let's try this again. Where did you go and why?"

"I thought you already knew everything," she shot back defiantly.

Jake closed the distance between them. Towering over Claire he went into interrogation mode and didn't hold back. "What I know is that you snuck out after I told you not to, you lied about using the window, you went to a coffee shop in midtown to meet Betty. Then you walked a few blocks over, where you met, I'm going to guess, Max. Which means you know where he's hiding. How'd I do?"

Claire was trembling, back pressed against the wall as she stared up at him. "What is this, the Federal Bureau of Intimidation? You don't even have a badge. What right do you have to interrogate me?"

"You know what? You're right. Why don't I call Metro? They can send a whole team of badges over—"

"Wait! I-I know it looks bad but it's not what you think."

"And what do I think?"

"Max has nothing to do with these murders."

"That's not for you to decide."

"You don't understand. He's harmless, but no one's going to believe that. Max is nonverbal. I know sign language so I'm able to communicate with him. I'm all he has."

"You've already told me his sob story, but that doesn't give him a free pass. If he's done nothing wrong, he has nothing to fear."

"You don't get it," she shot back.

"Maybe not, but what I do know is the penalty for harboring a fugitive, and obstruction of justice, both of which you're in violation of."

"Jake, I can't turn him in. He has no one else. And I-I'm in love with him."

Jake paused, momentarily empathizing with Claire. Love was a powerful motivator. He didn't want to be a hypocrite. He was guilty of bending the law a time or two for Dana. But ultimately, he had no choice here. Pushing Claire to give Max up was the best move for all of them.

"If you don't turn him in, he truly will have no one else, because I'll have no choice but to hand over this evidence," he said, holding up his cell phone. "Tell me where he is, and I'll personally escort him into custody and make sure he gets a good lawyer."

Tears began to stream down Claire's cheeks as she shook her head back and forth inconsolably. "No. No, I won't do it."

"Claire, this isn't a negotiation. This is an opportunity. Help yourself, help Max, help me. I don't want to tell Dana you lied."

70

A DULL BUZZ RUSTLED DANA FROM HER RESEARCH. PREDICTABLY, IT took her a moment to draw herself from the pages of ancient history and back to the real world. For an instant, she had a strange flash of déjà vu as she tried to separate the Grim Reaper tale she'd been entwined in with that of the real Reaper terrorizing D.C. presently.

Again, the buzz jostled her awareness, drawing her attention to her phone.

Dana uncovered it from the mountain of paperwork crowding her desk, only to pause when she saw the name glowing on the screen. She answered, hoping her foreboding feelings were misguided.

"We've got another one." Hartwell said, quickly confirming Dana's fears.

"The Reaper?"

"Looks like it. Scythe found on scene matches the others, down to the inscription."

"Have you ID'd the victim?"

Hartwell grunted. "What's left of her."

"It was a woman?"

"Yeah. Name Kylie Marx mean anything to you?"

Dana's stomach dropped. "Does she have red hair?"

Hartwell paused. "Why?"

Dana squeezed her eyes shut, collecting her thoughts before they dragged her down the dark tunnel she'd been dancing around for days. "She was a patient at Passages."

Hartwell swore. "Seems our Reaper's got a particular pallet." He sighed deeply, making Dana wonder when he last slept. "I'll pass it up the pole to DOJ or HSI or whoever the hell is running this thing now."

"Hartwell, this isn't political. Surely, they'll see that now."

"That there's a serial killer playing Grim Reaper with a bunch of displaced rehab patients? Yeah, I sure as shit hope so. But I'm not holding my breath."

"What do you mean?"

"I've seen lesser agencies hold pissing matches over parking violations. I want this thing in the right hands more than anybody, but I don't get a say once it leaves my jurisdiction. The red tape alone is going to take months to weed through. Not to mention the chain of evidence nightmare. This thing has passed over more desks than a day-old donut."

"I don't think we have that kind of time," Dana warned. "I've been looking into Grim Reaper lore. I think I found a connection, and if I'm right, this is going to escalate and quickly."

"What aren't you telling me?"

She heard Jake's voice in her mind. *Facts first.* Right now, she didn't have any. Just a sinking feeling and a connection that was still out of reach. "It's barely a theory. I need access to the evidence to see if I'm on the right track."

"Don't we all," Hartwell grumbled.

"If this lands back on your desk, I want in."

"You'll be my first call, Dr. Gray."

Dana hung up the phone, dreading what she had to do. She glanced through the open door of her office to Claire's bedroom. The door was ajar, the house quiet. Too quiet.

She stood up and walked toward the kitchen. The coffee pot was still warm, but there was no sign of Jake or Claire. She was just reaching for her phone to call Jake when she heard voices on her back porch.

She poked her head out, shocked to find Claire and Jake in deep conversation. From the sharp edge to Jake's voice, she knew whatever they were discussing was serious. If it were any other news, she'd resist interrupting, but this couldn't wait.

"What's wrong?" Jake asked, taking in Dana's ashen face.

"Hartwell called." She looked from Claire to Jake. "I think we should go inside."

71

"THEY FOUND ANOTHER BODY."

Claire's knees buckled at Dana's words. "Max?"

Jake jumped on the offensive. "Why would you think that?"

"It's not Max," Dana said.

Claire clutched the barstool for support, waiting for Dana to continue. Her face betrayed her when she had bad news to deliver. The smile lines near her mouth always bunched, chin twitching with melancholy. "Just tell me," Claire begged.

"It's Kylie Marx."

Bile rose so suddenly, Claire barely made it to the kitchen sink before vomiting.

Dana held her hair back, while Jake looked on in concern.

Claire knew he would tell Dana everything now. He had to. The time for bargaining was over. She understood that, but it changed nothing, no matter how bad things looked now.

It was just Claire and Max now. The way it was always meant to be. If Jake wanted to launch a manhunt, he'd have to do it without her help.

She stood up. Squaring her shoulders, she wiped her mouth with

228

the back of her hand and looked directly at Jake. "I need to go lie down."

72

DANA CLOSED THE DOOR TO CLAIRE'S BEDROOM AND WALKED AIMLESSLY to her living room, sinking down on the couch.

"How is she?" Jake asked, walking into the room.

"The same," Dana replied.

Claire had gone catatonic the moment she lay down. Dana watched it happen. She'd helped the girl into her bed and watched the startling emptiness consume her eyes.

It was like flipping a light switch. One second Claire was there, the next she blinked out into oblivion.

That was three hours ago, and still there was no change. Dana checked on Claire every twenty minutes, feeling more and more helpless. She didn't know what to do. Calling Dr. Dvita was the obvious move, but she didn't trust the man. Her gut told her he was somehow wrapped up in all of this. She just didn't know how yet.

"I think you might be right," Jake admitted, taking a seat next to her. "This is more than PTSD."

Dana looked up, forgetting how drained she was the moment she heard the tone of Jake's voice. He knew something. Facing him, she asked, "What were you two talking about on the porch?"

Jake reached for his cell phone and opened an app. With a few clicks, the screen filled with images of her home. "I had cameras installed along with the security system. I didn't want to take any chances after the break in."

Dana looked at him, not at all surprised he'd gone to such lengths. Jake idled at overprotectiveness on a good day. After the past few days they'd had, she was amazed he hadn't started passing out ankle monitors. "I can see that," she replied, brushing past the privacy violation. "Why is it relevant to your conversation with Claire?"

Jake tapped a few more commands into the phone, pulled up a camera view of the back of her house and rewound the feed, pausing the image. "This is Claire's window." He pointed to the time stamp. "This is when she told us she snuck out for air."

He pressed play and Dana watched the video. The image never changed. Then, suddenly, there she was—Claire—darting across the backyard and out of view. Dana looked back at the closed window. It never opened. "She didn't go out the window?"

"No."

"Then how did she get out?"

"I don't know yet. But the bigger problem is where she went."

"Tell me," Dana said, knowing Jake had already figured it out from his tone.

He switched apps and pulled up a feed of text messages, handing Dana the phone so she could see for herself. She read the conversation that was obviously from the spyware on Claire's phone. The text thread was between Claire and Betty, and it had been going on since Jake gave Claire the phone.

Dana looked up when she'd finished reading through the messages. "She went looking for Max?"

Jake nodded. "And I think she found him."

"Why didn't you tell me about these messages earlier?"

"I wanted to see where they led."

"Sometimes it's better to prevent the problem, rather than solve it," she suggested.

"Sometimes, but in this case I was right. We needed to know if we could trust her, what she's hiding. Now we have the answer to both. The end justifies the means."

"Jake, we're supposed to be a team and you're still going off and doing stuff like this without telling me. You can't keep apologizing, then asking for forgiveness."

"I don't apologize, you know that. And I won't do it here. It got Claire to tell me more about her and Max. I ran a basic background check on him. I'll send you the info so you can share it with Hartwell. He can use facial recognition software to help find him."

Dana exhaled. She was too exhausted to go down this road again. She needed to reconcile that maybe she and Jake would never fully trust each other enough to get on the same page, but now wasn't the time. What little focus she had left needed to be dedicated to figuring out what was really going on with Claire before she ended up in the Reaper's sights.

"There's something I need to show you, too." Dana led Jake into her office and pulled up the last page she'd been researching on her laptop before Hartwell's phone call interrupted her.

"So far, we know the Reaper is targeting patients from Passages. And I think I found the connection." Dana pointed to the webpage she had open. It was an ancient Islamic legend of the Seven Sleepers and she quickly walked Jake through the crux of it.

"Seven young men in danger of religious persecution sealed themselves inside a cave. They were each given a blade to take their own life rather than renounce their faith. They fell into a deep slumber and miraculously woke centuries later. The tale grew in popularity and can be found throughout history in Greek, Syriac, Arabic, Persian and Latin, as evidence of resurrection.

"Since then, the names of the Seven Sleepers have been synonymous with immortality. They've been inscribed on all matters of talismans—amulets and seals, but most commonly, blades.

"In many occult practices, blades inscribed with the names of the Seven Sleepers were used for sacrificial rituals believed to bless the victim with immortality and ensure their resurrection."

"Okay," Jake drawled, rubbing his jaw. "And this ties into the D.C. Reaper case, how?"

"Here." Dana opened a second tab in her browser. "This is an illuminated manuscript depicting the origin of the Grim Reaper according to Christianity. It listed the names of the priests ordained with the order of *messorem animarum*, which translates to Reaper of Souls."

Jake's brow furrowed when he tore his gaze from the screen to meet Dana's. "You're saying these priests were given a license to kill?"

"These are the first known Grim Reapers in history." Dana had trouble keeping the excitement out of her voice. Though in her realm of study, this wasn't a field she'd ever delved into before. But if she was right, this discovery not only held historical value, but it might also be the key to unlocking the most current nightmare plaguing D.C.

"Look at the names," Dana said, using her cursor to highlight each one.

Martinian.
Dionisius.
John.
Constantine.
Malchus.
Serapion.
Maximian.

Jake's attention snagged the last name. "Max is the only name on that list."

"It's not the names of our victims." Dana split her screen to show both browsers. "The names of the first Grim Reapers, match the names of the Seven Sleepers."

Jake blinked, confusion and disbelief creasing his brow. "What are you saying?"

"Christians believed the myth of the Seven Sleepers was a mockery of their religion. One they refused to let grow. Believing time was meant to devour all things, they sent Reapers, their ordained agents of death, after them. They believed only the death of all Seven Sleepers could rid the world of sin and restore their beliefs. Each took on the name of one of the Seven Sleepers and hunted them down to cleanse the world of their unholy sins."

"So, some old priests went on a witch hunt to kill people with these unfortunate names to prove their religion was better?" Jake asked.

"That's one way of putting it," she replied. "But look at this." Dana opened another tab. "The priests carved phrases into their blades so that, as Reapers, they wouldn't have to see their own reflection in their blades when they killed."

"Let me guess. 'Life is death is life' was the phrase of choice?"

"Yes!" Dana exclaimed, elated that Jake was getting it. "I think this means there's going to be seven reapings."

He frowned. "Three murders already, that means four more patients are going to be targeted."

"Yes. But what I can't figure out is how we make sure Claire isn't one of them."

"I think we start by finding this Max person," Jake suggested.

Dana shook her head. "I think Dr. Dvita is the key. It was his DID research that led me to the Seven Sleepers."

She quickly ran through how the psychologist's lengthy research into a dissociative identity disorder known as Folie à deux—an uncommon psychiatric phenomenon where delusional ideas or behaviors are transferred from one to another or many others through hypnosis—brought Dana to the revelation of Seven Sleepers and the Grim Reapers.

Jake scratched his head. "I don't follow."

"The most famous case of Folie à deux involved a married couple who suffered a shared delusion derived from the Anatolian legend of the Seven Sleepers. The case resulted in the husband murdering his wife under the deluded pretense that she would be resurrected."

Dana paused to pull up another article. This one was a publication singing Dr. Dvita's praises for his research pertaining to Folie à deux. "He's spent a lifetime researching the cultural and religious implications of this disorder. He believed it could be controlled and even cured through hypnosis. Jake, what if he's taken it too far?"

He rubbed his face. "And what, subliminally brainwashed one of his patients into thinking they're a Grim Reaper so they can wreak havoc on the city?"

"We saw him hypnotize Claire and bring forth some other identity."

"Yeah, but what you're suggesting is a leap."

Dana crossed her arms. "Fine, let's hear your theory then?"

"I think Claire's wrapped up in feelings for this Max kid. He's bad news, but she can't see it. You should've heard her, Dana. She thinks she's in love with him and has made him out to be some sort of saint. She's hell bent on protecting him. And this," he pointed to Claire's closed bedroom door. "This is her coping mechanism. We can't keep letting her retreat and shut the world out."

"And we can't keep ignoring the signs of her Dissociative Identity diagnosis. Jake, I don't want this to be true either, but it all fits. And Dr. Dvita is behind it. I know it."

"Even if you're correct, right now all you have is a wobbly theory."

"I know, but it could be enough to get me the warrant I need to access Dvita's files."

Jake started to object, but Dana's phone interrupted. They both stared at the screen. Jake's expression told her they were sharing the same worry. *Was there another body already?*

The caller ID read unknown. "Put it on speaker," Jake instructed.

Dana complied, quickly answering. "This is Dr. Gray."

Agent Spector's voice filled the room. "You got what you wanted. We're handing this case back."

"What does that mean for Meredith?" Dana asked.

"We no longer need to speak to Miss Kincaid."

"Then I guess we're done here," Dana said, curtly.

"Almost."

73

JAKE EXPECTED THE COURTESY CALL. THE THIRD VICTIM HAD PROVEN the matter wasn't one of National Security. What he hadn't expected was the cryptic message Agent Spector offered before hanging up. *"Check your mailbox. I did what you asked. Now I'm the one owed a favor, Dr. Gray."*

Jake wanted to ask Dana what Spector meant, but she was already rushing toward the small copper box mounted next to her front door. Jake heard the tired hinges groan open then close as he followed Dana toward the door.

He met her in the foyer, where she held a yellow Post-it note in one hand, her other clutched something he couldn't see in her fist. "What is it?" Jake asked.

Dana looked at him, her eyes sparkling cautiously. "Hopefully, it's what you've been looking for."

She handed him the note and unfurled her fist.

Jake stared at the dog tag in her palm, then the ten-digit code printed neatly on the paper. He despised the emotion that tightened his chest. "Dana, what did you do?"

"Trusted my instincts," she replied.

Jake shook his head and tried to hand the note back. "I don't want it."

"What? Why not?"

"I heard Spector. Whatever this cost, it's not worth it."

"It didn't cost anything. I asked him to help, and he did."

"Trust me," Jake said, pressing the paper back into her hand. "This wasn't free."

74

"Jake!" Anger coursed through Dana as she watched him storm away from her. She followed him down the hall as he disappeared into her bedroom. She wasn't sure if he was sulking or packing but she was certain this conversation wasn't over.

She was moments from barging in after him when her phone rang again. This time it was Hartwell's name on her caller ID. "This is Dr. Gray."

"We're back on," he said, skipping formalities. "How soon can you be here?"

"Where? What happened?"

"FBI forensic lab. Just got word from the BAU. The D.C. Reaper case got bounced to them, and they've asked Metro for joint assistance. I got you on the team as an expert witness." Dana paused, staring at the closed door in front of her, then said, "Give me twenty."

"No, this is dangerous," Jake argued. "I'm not comfortable with you going alone."

"I don't have a choice," Dana replied.

"Yes, Dana, you do. You're the one with all the choices here. I'm suspended and that's my fault, but I signed up for this life. You didn't. I dragged you into it, and I regret it every day."

"You're wrong, Jake, I signed up for it, too. It was my choice to work with you on that first case. It was my choice to continue working with you. Everything that's happened to me, it's on me. I made the decisions that led me here. And this is me, choosing to sign back up, for us, for Claire, for whatever lies ahead. I need to know you can respect that."

Jake growled as he paced away from her. He looked like he wanted to punch something. Thankfully for the sake of all the irreplaceable antiques in Dana's home, he didn't. When he turned to face her, his pain was obvious, etched across his face like a scar.

"What am I supposed to do?" Jake implored. "Stay here and do nothing while you put yourself in harm's way, again?"

"You're supposed to trust me."

"I do. You know I do. That's not the issue here."

"Then what is?"

"If something happens to you ..." he threaded his hands behind his head and blew out a breath before sinking down to sit on her bed. Jake looked up at her, his blue eyes a storm of sorrow. "It's not supposed to be this way."

She moved close enough to stand in front of him. Jake let his arms circle around her waist, hanging his head to rest on her stomach. "I know," she whispered, running her fingers through his hair. "I can't promise you nothing will happen. You know that."

He looked up at her, his expression a mirror of misery.

"Each day we wake up with the knowledge that it might be our last. The challenge is pushing past that fear and finding a way to live anyway. What you've helped me learn is that it's a whole lot easier to do when you don't have to do it alone." Dana knelt down until their faces were level. "I don't want to do it alone anymore. I want to live this life with you, Jake. But I want a partner who will back me up, not fight me every step of the way."

He stroked her hair away from her face. "Dana, that's what I want, too. Tell me you believe that."

"I do," she whispered, letting her lips graze his.

Jake drew her in for a kiss she wished never had to end. But she tore herself away. "I have to go."

"And I have to stay," he said, morosely.

She dropped one more kiss to his lips. "Jake, Claire needs you more than I do right now. Protect her. You're the only one who can." Then she pulled the dog tags and Post-it note from her pocket and pressed them into his hand. "You may not agree with my methods, but this means something. Look into it ... for me."

75

JAKE WATCHED DANA WALK OUT THE DOOR, THE NOTE AND DOG TAGS heavy in his hand as he wondered, yet again, what his troubles had cost her.

He sat on her bed for a long time, fighting every instinct to chase after her. Of course, that's exactly what she'd asked him not to do. She'd finally answered his question, admitting what he'd hoped all along. She wanted to be with him, but she needed a partner, not the over-protective Alpha-hole he tended to be.

The way she'd claimed responsibility for her choices made him admire her even more—even if it did little to absolve him of his guilt. Her choices were her own, but Jake knew he had a role in bringing her down this dangerous path. He'd devoted his life to the philosophy: protect and serve. Accepting he couldn't do that for the woman he loved was intolerable.

Still, he knew Dana was right. Jake wanted to respect that, but he didn't know how to deal with being sidelined like this.

Normally, he would bury himself in work when his personal life got too complicated, but now even that wasn't an option. He stared down at the note, now crumpled next to him on the bed. It glared back, a yellow reminder, warning him to stop putting off the inevitable.

He'd call, but not until he was ready.

Jake slipped his dog tags around his neck, then stood, shoving the note in his pocket before walking down the hall to check on Claire. Right now, she was the only one he could help.

The door was ajar, just as he'd left it. He knocked before pushing his way into the room. Claire still lay on her side, staring into nothingness. Jake pulled up a chair and sat down, hoping she could sense his presence from whatever far corner of her mind she'd retreated to.

He regretted his earlier actions. She needed his support, not accusations. It wasn't clear what was going on with Claire, but if he was going to find out, he needed to gain her trust again.

Claire didn't trust easily. Jake had known that from the moment he'd met her. Like most individuals of immense intellect, she appeared shy and awkward at first, but Jake had pushed past that to the fiercely loyal, brilliant, hilarious girl beneath her many layers of gothic attire.

She'd let him in—as much as Claire let anyone in—and Jake hadn't taken that lightly. That's why this was so difficult. Seeing her like this now ... it was as if with a push of a button, that girl he'd known had been erased.

The parallels to Jake's mother were eerily similar.

She too was someone he couldn't hold on to no matter how hard he tried. Every time he reached for her in the abyss behind her eyes, she slipped further away. Jake was tired of watching the people he loved disappear right in front of him. His mother, Ramirez, countless others he'd served alongside ... he couldn't bear to lose Claire, too.

For a while longer he watched Claire. The steady rise and fall of her breathing tried to fool him into thinking she was just sleeping. But her eyes remained wide open—staring at him and at nothing all at once.

Standing, Jake walked over to the bed. He rested his hand on Claire's shoulder, expecting the flinch that normally came from unsolicited contact, but she remained completely still. If she was still in there, she was buried deep.

He suddenly wished he knew more about her—her family, child-hood, fears—anything to help him reach her. Jake knew the basics: only child, grew up on the west coast, estranged from her parents. In many ways, Claire and Dana had been cut from the same cloth. Both genius outsiders, trying to shine light into the darkness to make up for the lonely hand life had dealt them.

Neither woman liked talking about their pasts. But Jake couldn't fault them. He preferred to keep the past where it belonged, too. Speaking of, Jake reached into his pocket and pulled out his phone. It was time to make the call he'd been putting off.

Before he left the room, he gave Claire's shoulder one last squeeze. "I know you're still in there, Elvira. I'm not going anywhere, so you find your way back here, and we'll figure this out together."

76

DANA GLANCED IN HER REARVIEW THE ENTIRE DRIVE TO THE FBI forensic lab. She trusted Jake not to follow, but the media was a different story. The increase in Reaper hysteria had returned the news vans to her street. When she'd walked to her car, a reporter from one of the networks tried to approach.

"What can you tell us about the D.C. Reaper case being turned over to the FBI? Have you and Agent Shepard been assigned?"

She'd muttered "no comment" and hurried to her car. Halfway to the lab she thought she spotted the same news van from her street behind her, but she was being paranoid. News was big business in D.C. and most networks had multiple vans.

Still, she heard Jake's voice in her mind. *Stay on the hunt or become the prey.*

Dana had been there too many times. She may have chosen this path, but she was determined to do things differently, and that meant learning from her mistakes.

She turned onto 8th Street, showed her ID to the guard manning the gate, and pulled into the safety of the FBI's forensic lab lot. She turned off the car and sat there for a moment, watching the traffic roll by on the other side of the fence. Nothing suspicious, but she'd promised Jake she'd be careful, and she planned to do everything in her power to hold up her end of the bargain.

She called Hartwell from her car to let him know she'd arrived.

"Great. Meet me in the lobby. I'll walk you back," he said.

Inside, Dana took in the familiar beige walls and black chairs. The waiting room looked even more worn in the watery morning light filtering in through the glass doors. The reception area was still unmanned, but Hartwell pushed through the metal door, his arrival announced by the loud buzz of the lock disengaging. "Follow me," he said, waving her through. "Let's walk and talk."

Dana followed Hartwell down the chilly hallway, listening intently as he caught her up on the case. "SSA Richter's the Unit Chief in charge. He's seasoned, knows his way around cases like this, but isn't all that happy to have been dragged down here from Quantico."

"I thought you said they requested a joint effort?"

Hartwell nodded. "They did, but since the murders are local, they preferred to conduct the investigation on their own turf. Only thing that got them here was the crime scenes and you."

"Me? I can work anywhere," she objected.

"Let's not mention that," Hartwell warned. "I don't want to add commuting to Quantico to my day. Besides, Shepard would blow a gasket if I sent you to Quantico."

"Agent Shepard doesn't dictate where I work."

Hartwell raised his eyebrows. "Does he know that?"

Dana ignored the rhetorical question.

"He does know you're working this case, right?" Hartwell pressed.

"Yes."

Hartwell grunted, shaking his head. "I can't decide if that's a good thing or not."

"Why?"

"The last time I called you in, he blew up my phone like it was the Dr. Gray hotline."

"That's my fault. I got detained by Homeland Security after I left here."

Hartwell stopped short, looking her up and down with amusement. "Christ, you're both shit magnets!"

"What's that supposed to mean?"

"Nothing. Just tell Shepard to lay off the speed dial. I'm not your babysitter. I pulled strings to get you on this case because I've seen what you can do. You and the BAU are the best chance we have at catching this psycho. But this is happening in my city, so I'm making the rules, which includes running the investigation from here, so don't mention that you're willing to go to Quantico. I'm needed here. The department's overworked as it is, and this case is wearing me thin."

The deep purple bags under Hartwell's eyes were proof of that. He looked like he hadn't slept since the last time she'd seen him here. "Understood," Dana replied.

The answer seemed to suffice, because Hartwell led her into a busy room and began making introductions. "This is Dr. Dana Gray. She's our expert witness. I've worked with her on a case like this before. Her background in occult studies was paramount in identifying key evidence, so take what she says seriously, no matter how bizarre it sounds."

There were brief nods of acknowledgement before everyone returned to the work they'd been doing prior to Dana's interruption. She did her best to ignore the mocking murmurs of *Witch Doctor* that always followed her in the narrow-minded FBI circle.

This was always the part she found most difficult, integrating herself into an established unit. She never knew where she belonged, and her tendency to jump right in often rubbed people the wrong way.

Deciding to take a page from Jake's book, she took the temperature of the room. There were ten people examining a mountain of evidence from all three cases. Officer Lennox was a familiar face, and so was Dr. Raynard, but Dana didn't expect the world-renowned forensic scientist would be happy to see her after their last interaction. Opting to save that confrontation for later, she decided to start at the top.

Approaching Agent Richter, she asked, "Where would you like me to begin?"

He faced her with open assessment, scratching the salt and pepper stubble already showing on his freshly shaved face. "Dr. Gray, you come highly recommended. I hope you can live up to the hype."

"So do I," she answered. "I look forward to continuing my collaboration with the FBI. I'm familiar with standard policy and procedure thanks to my work with Agent Shepard, but if there's a particular way you prefer to operate, please let me know."

Agent Richter laughed. "You've worked with Jake Shepard? How is the one-man army?"

Dana smirked. "So, you know him then?"

"We go way back. If you're good enough for that blow hard I'm sure we'll get on just fine." He turned back to the folders spread out in front of him. "How familiar are you with the evidence?"

Dana informed him of the crime scenes and evidence she'd already examined. "Then you know we haven't got much to go on. No prints, no DNA, no fibers. Whoever this Unsub is, they're meticulous, organized, and know how to contain a scene."

"The weapons," Dana asked. "Have they been analyzed?"

Richter waved over another BAU agent. "This is Agent Walsh, our analysis and algorithms specialist." Dana shook the young man's hand.

"Show Dr. Gray the weapon analysis," Richter commanded.

Walsh obliged, pulling up the results and mirroring them onto the large smart board covering one wall of the exam room. "The weapons are identical. Steel iron alloy. A substance produced in massive quantities in fourteen different countries."

Dana frowned. "What about the snath?" She'd been about to explain the snath was the wooden handle attached to the scythe's blade, but Agent Walsh needed no explanation.

"All three snaths are also a match, constructed of American ash wood."

"That's something we can use," she suggested.

"Ash grows throughout the entire eastern US from New York to the Gulf of Mexico," Walsh explained. "The American Hardwood

Export Council is only required to catalog raw material distribution. Tracking manufacturing beyond that point is impossible."

With her hopes dashed, Dana expressed what evidence she wanted another look at.

Richter, nodded. "Have at it. Flag anything you want another set of eyes on. Agent Vaughn will add it to the board. I'd like to narrow our scope by finding patterns that intersect."

"Find the intersect, find the killer," Dana replied.

Richter grinned. "Looks like Shepard found a disciple."

"Or perhaps it's the other way around," she teased.

A mega-watt smile spread across Richter's face. "Oh, I'm gonna like working with you, Gray."

"I hope you feel that way after you hear my theory on the D.C. Reaper."

"Theory? As in you already have one?"

"Several actually."

Richter spread his arms toward the mountains of evidence in the room. "This isn't for show, you know. You might want to take a look first."

"I will, but if I'm right, I don't think we have time to waste."

Richter folded his arms like a father facing a petulant child. "Let's hear it."

77

Jake held the phone to his ear counting the rings. When the call finally connected, he didn't expect the voice on the other end.

"Shepard residence," a familiar twang greeted.

"Jenks? What's wrong? What are you doing at Wade's?"

"It's called friendship, Jacob. Look it up."

"Jenkins! Did something happen to my mother?"

The fear in his voice must've gotten through to her, because Remi Jenkins sighed, her tone softer when she answered. "No. She's fine, or as fine as can be expected all things considered. I just came out here to give Wade a hand since I've found myself with some unexpected free time."

Jake knew the jab was directed at him. And deservedly so. "How's Wade?"

"The man's a bona fide saint," Jenkins replied. "I honestly don't know how he does it. I've been here for 48 hours, and I'm exhausted just watching him."

"That's because he's Air Force. Still thinks he's flying solo. Doesn't let anyone pitch in," Jake teased.

Jenkins chuckled. "That's rich coming from you, G. I. Joe."

Jake's eyes crinkled as he grinned. He missed this. The banter he'd always shared with Jenkins. She was so much more than his boss. Remi Jenkins had many titles. His uncle's best friend. The woman who helped raise him. Role model. Mentor. Friend. And most importantly, family.

"Jenks ... I'm sorry." Jake sputtered the words, eager to spit out the foreign taste. What the hell was happening to him? He didn't do promises or apologies. Now in the span of a few days he'd done both.

"You've been a real ass, you know that?"

"I do," he admitted.

"Well, at least you can admit it."

"Thanks for being out there while I can't."

"Jake, you're the one who should be out here. I know you know that."

"I tried, Jenks. I was just making things worse."

"I don't believe that's true."

Jake exhaled, the heaviness returning to his chest. "We all have our strengths," he admitted. Wade was the saint. Remi their strength. Jake the soldier. He could serve them best by hunting down the only solution to this problem: his father.

"How's that going?" Jenkins asked, knowing what he meant in that unspoken way of hers.

"I've got a possible lead." But before she could respond, he added, "Don't get Wade's hopes up. It's early. There's still a lot to flush out."

"Well, if there's anyone who can get it done, it's you."

The sentiment and pressure of her statement churned in his gut. "Tell Wade I called."

"I will. I ..." she paused. "Your mother ..." she paused again, unable to find the words.

"Tell it to me straight, Jenks."

"I don't think she has much time left."

Jake swallowed hard. "Roger that," was all he could manage.

"Take care of yourself, Jake."

"You, too."

Jake hung up the phone and pulled the yellow Post-it note from his pocket. He'd waited long enough.

78

Dana stood at the smart board and gazed at the less than tasteful photo of a Grim Reaper. BAU Agent Walsh had taken liberties and added the photo to the box Dana labeled *Reaper* in her preliminary sketch.

Ignoring the tactless art, she focused on the row of seven boxes beneath. The first three were filled with morgue photos of each victim: Norton Hayes, Cash Holloway, Kylie Marx. The remaining four boxes contained only question marks.

"Based on the theory of the Seven Sleepers," she began.

"We're familiar with the legend," Agent Garcia interrupted. "Seven men sought refuge from religious persecution by hiding in a cave. They fell into a deep slumber and miraculously woke centuries later."

"Correct," Dana answered. "I believe we're dealing with an individual who is trying to recreate his own Seven Sleepers."

"To what end?" Hartwell asked.

"In our line of work, there's not always a rational explanation for irrational behavior," Agent Richter warned.

"In this case, I agree," Dana interjected. "I believe the Reaper is acting on the deluded notion that if he can complete seven murders with seven blessed blades, he'll be able to resurrect his victims, just as the Seven Sleepers were resurrected."

"The pattern so far has produced one victim every 24 hours," Agent Davis added. "Do we expect the pattern to continue or accelerate?"

"There's no indication that the pattern will deviate," Dana answered.

"The Unsub is detail driven," Richter added. "Numbers, patterns, repetition. It all matters."

"Agreed," Dana replied. "If the pattern continues, we can assume the D.C. Reaper has seven days to complete his seven harvests. That means we have four days to stop four more murders."

"Great," Hartwell grumbled. "Is this scythe-wielding psycho picking off people at random or do you have a guess at his targets?"

"His victims aren't random," Dana replied. "So far, all three victims were patients at Passages Rehab Center, treated by Dr. Dvita. I believe we should focus our efforts there."

"How many patients does he have?" Richter asked.

Walsh was on it, furiously typing away on his laptop. Specializing in analysis and algorithms, Dana had no doubt in the BAU agent's ability. In a matter of seconds, the smart board displayed a list of patients. There were hundreds.

Dana frowned. "Rule out deceased and reference only patients who were at Passages during the fire."

Walsh keyed in the parameters and the list shrunk. Eleven names stared back at them, but only one made Dana's heart sink.

She knew Claire's name would be there but seeing it on the murder board made it feel like a foregone conclusion.

"Eleven? That's a number we can work with," Hartwell said, sounding reenergized. "Hell, I'll put 'em in lock up for the next four days if it'll stop this thing."

"I'm afraid it's not that simple," Dana replied.

Hartwell crossed his arms. "Why not?"

"Interrupting the pattern could cause the Unsub to deviate from plans and cause unpredictability," Richter said, echoing Dana's thoughts exactly.

Hartwell's face reddened. "I know you're not suggesting we let this monster keep slashing innocent citizens."

"No," Richter answered. "But we have more factors to explore. We need to dial in every angle to get a clear picture of the Unsub's motives if we're going to stop them."

"That sounds like it's going to take time we don't have," Hartwell muttered.

"Trust the process," Richter answered.

Hartwell looked to Dana, who nodded her agreement. Shaking his head, he said, "Then let's get to it," before walking away to refill his coffee.

For the next two hours Dana and the BAU team explored every possible factor of the three known victims. Age, gender, religion, birthdate, family history, illness, hospitalizations, education. Nothing matched.

When they got to the presidential and first lady nicknames assigned at Passages, it spawned a lengthy debate about whether the Reaper was killing them in the order of Presidency, which then spiraled off into tangents of conspiracy theories involving everything from the Freemasons to Watergate to the Illuminati.

Dana led the discussion back to occult matters when they still hadn't managed to find any connecting threads. She hoped delving deeper into the Grim Reaper's modern-day interpretation would be able to shed light on something they were missing.

The BAU team eagerly debated the significance of the dark hooded cloak and wielding a scythe. They argued the minute religious differences between cultural messengers of Death. The Grim Reaper, angels, demons, ravens, crows and so on.

It made Dana miss Jake's skepticism. Anything she suggested, the BAU team ran with without question. It was making the spectrum broader instead of narrowing it down. She and Jake worked because he challenged her, and that forced Dana to reevaluate and reapply her knowledge to the present problem.

That's what she needed to do here, because Hartwell was right, time wasn't on their side.

Dana pulled Hartwell aside. "I know BAU still has a lot to sort through to build their profile, but I can't shake the feeling that Dr. Dvita is behind this. Do you know he told his patients that he's been acting as a police liaison during the investigation?"

"He isn't."

"I know. I think he was just trying to get everyone to go to him with information rather than the police. Something just feels off. I want a warrant so we can access his files, particularly his hypnosis recordings."

Hartwell shook his head. "You got anything besides your gut? Because that's not enough evidence to execute a warrant."

"No, but I know he's involved in this. I saw him hypnotize Claire. It was powerful."

"Powerful enough to persuade his patients to kill?" Richter asked, joining the discussion.

Dana swallowed the fear that statement evoked. "He's hosting a group meeting for all his patients from Passages at St. Ann's tomorrow. Come with me and see for yourself."

"By tomorrow we'll have another victim," Hartwell argued.

"All the murders have taken place under cover of darkness," Dana reminded him.

Hartwell scoffed. "Oh good, that's a comforting tip I can announce at the press conference. I can see the headlines now. D.C.'s afraid of the dark!"

"When is the press conference?" Dana asked.

"Today at noon," Hartwell confirmed.

"Maybe we can use it to our advantage," Richter suggested.

"You wanna drop some breadcrumbs?" Hartwell asked.

"Dvita's too smart for that," Dana argued.

The corner of Hartwell's mouth twitched into a lopsided smirk. "Only one way to find out."

"If we play it right, release a false profile, the Unsub might actually call the tip line to clear things up," Richter said. "We know he's smart, organized, a psychopath versus psychotic. He's the kind of killer who will inject himself into the investigation. Especially if he thinks we don't understand why he's killing."

"What if it's more than one Unsub?" Dana asked.

"There's not adequate evidence to prove that theory," Hartwell argued.

"And there's nothing to disprove it either," Richter said. "Go on, Dr. Gray."

"I don't have any hard evidence, but the scenes have all been completely different. One was outside a rehab facility. One in a park. One in a parking lot. And then there are the victims. Different race, ethnicity, gender. We'd never link them if it weren't for the murder weapon. And the brutality of the second victim's death is on a different level."

"I have to agree with Dr. Gray," the Alchemist interjected. "After examining the lacerations made on all three victims, it's my opinion they were inflicted by at least two separate individuals of varying heights."

Dana mouthed a silent 'thank you' to Raynard, accepting his olive branch.

Richter frowned. "You bring up valid points, but I have to tell you, the odds of cases like these leading to multiple unsubs are nearly nonexistent. Our profile points to a white male, mid 40s to 50s who's highly intelligent, professional and works alone."

"Actually," Walsh interrupted. "Raymond Fernandez and Martha Beck, known as the Lonely Hearts Killers, worked as a pair killing an estimated seventeen women in the 1940s. Or the Lethal Lovers; two nursing aids from Michigan who went on a killing spree at the hospital they worked at in 1987. Then there was the Podkopaevs, a Russian family of four who killed together in 2009. And how can we forget the Manson family—"

"Okay! Okay," Richter said, interrupting Agent Walsh's morbid monologue. "We get the point. But one key factor you're missing is that all except the Manson family were sexual deviants. There's been no evidence of sexual assault on any of these victims."

"That's our breadcrumb," Hartwell said. "We say our Unsub is a sexual deviant."

"Is agitating a highly dangerous murderer really the best idea?" Dana asked.

"We're out of better ones," Hartwell replied.

"Fine," Dana grumbled, "but while you're dropping breadcrumbs, I have another lead I'd like to follow."

"What's that?" Hartwell asked.

"Meredith Kincaid."

Hartwell's tired expression hardened. Dana could see he knew the name. Though he hadn't worked the Priory of Bones case, he'd certainly heard about it. Everyone in D.C. had.

The last thing Dana wanted to do was drag Meredith back into a criminal investigation, but she couldn't shake the feeling Mere might be able to shed light on Dvita's motives.

Unwilling to leave any stone unturned, she quickly explained Agent Spector's interest in Meredith.

"Already have her listed as a person of interest," Richter confirmed. "She's worth a visit."

"I'm worried the Reaper might target her."

"She's not on our list of potential targets," Richter said.

"I know, but Dvita's treated her. He even brought her to Passages to mentor Claire."

"What?" Hartwell's complexion soured. "Dvita took a convicted felon from the nuthouse on a field trip, and I'm just hearing about it now?"

"It's all in the files HSI sent over," Richter replied without batting an eye. "But Dr. Gray raises a fair point. We need to expand our parameters to include patients Dr. Dvita is currently treating outside of Passages." He strode over to Agent Walsh who quickly executed the command.

Dana watched the list of targets grow from eleven to more than sixty. Hartwell swore, crumbling his paper coffee cup before throwing it in the trash. "Any more good news for me to share at the press conference?" When no one in the room spoke up he kicked the trashcan. "That's what I thought. I need a shower. This suit was stale two crime scenes ago. Call me when you have something I can share with the press."

Dana watched Hartwell lumber out of the room, his frustration palpable. She too felt the pressure of the ticking clock. They'd been at this for hours. The more time they spent here, the less time they'd have to apprehend the Reaper before the next kill.

Without a definitive direction there was only one thing left to do. Dana rolled up her sleeves as she approached the nearest evidence table and began the daunting process of combing through it again.

79

I can't tear my eyes away from the clock. It moves so slowly, its incessant ticking wearing on my nerves. Everywhere I look, they scurry, worry and hurry. All trying to find me. But they never will.

Time may be moving slowly, but it is moving all the same. Just like grains of sand falling through an hourglass, what shall come is inevitable.

I tilt my head from side to side, stretching my skin. It prickles with my desire to see this through. To kill again.

Not yet, I remind myself.

I must follow the plan. It's all laid out so perfectly.

Now is the time to wait and watch.

Soon it shall be time to reap and sow.

80

THE TACKY PAPER STUCK TO JAKE'S PALM AS HE CRUMBLED THE NOTE IN his hand. He'd been staring at it long enough that he had the number memorized. The country code was France, but the rest was a mystery. One that would remain that way unless he worked up the nerve to dial the number.

This was ridiculous. It was just a phone call. Jake had been to Iraq, Afghanistan, and places people hadn't even heard of.

So why was making this call so terrifying?

You know why, his subconscious chided.

He did ... but admitting that was easier said than done.

The moment he made the call, he could no longer avoid the inevitable. He would find his father, or he wouldn't. Either way, he'd be failing his mother.

If he called and it turned out to be another dead end, then Jake was back to square one and his mother would be out of time, never getting the closure she deserved.

But if he called and managed to track down his father, the results could be even more disastrous. Jake might not be able to persuade him to come, or if he did, his father's presence might just make things harder for Jake's mother.

Jake cursed Dana for putting him in this position. She'd gone behind his back and now he was forced into a corner. Even if she'd done it for the right reason, she'd done exactly what he'd asked her not to. Just like he did to her time and time again.

He stared at the note, wondering if they'd ever truly be able to change their habits?

Jake checked the time, annoyed with himself for how long he'd been debating this.

"Screw it," he muttered. It was time to get this over with.

He punched the numbers into the phone and hit call. The phone rang repeatedly until finally, the mechanical click of an answering machine kicked in. Jake squeezed the phone tighter, pressing it to his ear as the voice on the other end filled the space between them.

"*Bonjour, vous êtes arrivé à la résidence Berger. laissez un message s'il vous plait*".

The language was foreign, but the voice ... Jake would know that voice anywhere.

It was the voice of a ghost.

One who haunted his dreams as a child and sometimes even now as an adult.

Jake hung up the phone, his father's voice cutting through him, a draft so cold it sliced bone deep.

81

Dana rushed in the front door, eager to discuss all she'd learned about the D.C. Reaper with Jake, sure he would have some keen insights she'd missed. But when she saw him, she stopped short.

He sat on her couch, shoulders hunched, elbows on knees, head in his large, scarred hands. His gaze was fixed on his cell phone, which sat unassumingly on the coffee table in front of him.

The scene was peculiar enough, but stranger still, Jake hadn't even looked up when Dana disarmed the security system. She took a tentative step toward him, then thought better of sneaking up on the ex-soldier with killer instincts.

She spoke, hesitantly. "Jake?"

When he looked up, the storm of pain in his eyes made Dana feel like she was being swept out to sea. She rushed to his side. "What's wrong? Is it Claire? Your mother?"

He shook his head and handed her the yellow Post-it note that had been crushed in his hand. "It's my father. I think I found him."

Her eyes widened. "You spoke to him?"

"Not exactly. Voicemail. It was in French, but it was his voice, Dana, I know it."

"Did you leave a message?"

He shook his head. "Didn't want to spook him. The country code is France. I need to trace the number, use it to get a last known, then go there."

"To France?"

"If that's where he is."

Dana resisted every selfish objection to ask him to stay. Jake was always there for her. It was her turn to repay the favor. She knew he needed to do this, and she'd asked for the space to prove herself. It was time she delivered.

"I'd go with you if I could," she said, reaching for his hand.

"I know. But Claire ..."

"And the case ..."

"Maybe it would be better if you came. Both of you. Out of D.C., somewhere safe."

She gave him a look. "Jake ..."

"Yeah, I know," he said. "But I had to ask."

"When are you leaving?"

"I don't know. As soon as I can get a trace and clear up this suspension situation."

"I'm sure it won't be long," she assured him.

"Yeah, but my lawyer will have to file an appeal." Jake rubbed the weariness from his face. "I don't want to think about the red tape involved. Tell me how it went with the BAU."

Dana sighed.

"That bad?"

"No, the team is great, it's just ... I never thought I'd miss working with a grumpy, skeptical soldier so much."

He laughed. "If that was your attempt at flattery, you've got some work to do, Gray."

"I'm serious. We work well because we're both so stubborn in our beliefs. Whenever those beliefs intersect in a case, we know we're on the right path. With the BAU, they take each lead like its law and immediately dissect every possible way it could fit within the case."

Jake smirked. "Like bending puzzle pieces."

"What?"

"Something me and Jenks used to say anytime the BAU got involved. They mean well, and they're good at what they do, but you're right, they'll bend an arrow to make a theory fit."

She flopped back on the couch. "Tell me about it."

"Who's on the team?" Jake asked.

Dana gave him the rundown.

"Richter's a good guy. We go way back."

"He said as much."

"You can trust him. The others, I'm not familiar with."

"Really? You're not all in some big FBI fraternity?"

"Our paths may have crossed on a case or two but it's not like we sit around trading case files over drinks. We deal with monsters at work. Makes ya not want to take the job home with ya. Know what I mean?"

She did and it sobered the light mood she'd been trying for, so she decided to ask the other question that had been nagging her all day. "How's Claire?"

"Same."

Dana hated the state of limbo that had taken over her home.

Her and Jake.

Claire.

This case.

She wanted it all to go back to the way it had been.

Good, familiar, comfortable.

She'd always been confident when it came to navigating her life. When she wasn't, she had her research in the bowels of the Smithsonian where she could hide from real life for a while. But ever since the Card Killer case, her life had been turned upside down. Putting Vega away was supposed to right things, but it hadn't. The physical scars may have healed, but returning to the life she'd known before didn't seem to be an option.

"She needs help," Dana said. "More than you and I can give her."

"I know," Jake replied.

"And if you're leaving ..."

His deep exhale signified that he'd already realized this but was out of ideas.

"She can't go back to Dvita," Dana warned. "He's involved in this Reaper business. I'm not sure how, but I plan to get to the bottom of it. Richter and I are going to St. Ann's tomorrow to sit in on his group therapy session. If we get lucky, we'll get a warrant out of it and can access the rest of his patient files from Passages."

"What else?" Jake asked.

"Honestly? Not much. Hartwell's giving a press conference at noon, but there's really not much to go on. The BAU came up with a profile, but he can't tell all of D.C. that we expect four more murders over the next four days."

"Suspect pool?" Jake asked.

"If you ask me, it's Dvita. But the BAU has a big fat question mark at the top of their Grim Reaper board."

"Targets?"

"Four more if the Seven Sleepers theory holds, but that hinges on Dvita being the Reaper. We narrowed his field of Passages patients down to eleven. But I still think Meredith factors in. And when I suggested that, the target field got flooded with all Dvita's other patients."

"What's Meredith got to do with this?"

"I don't know yet, but Spector's proven his hunches are good. Richter and I are going to see her tomorrow after Dvita's sessions."

Jake leaned back on the couch and stretched his long arms out, letting one rest on Dana's shoulders. "I wish I was in this one with you."

She leaned into him. "Me too."

"Here," Jake said, pulling his dog tags from his pocket and giving them back to Dana. "Hang onto these for me since I can't be out there with you."

Dana started to object, but Jake stopped her with a look. The dark storm clouds parted in his eyes as he said, "What you did for me, getting that number ... I should've said thank you. So let me say it now."

Dana let him drape the cool metal chain around her neck. She reached up and ran her fingers over the raised letters and braille. She knew how much the dog tags meant to Jake and what it meant that he kept giving them to her. Emotions too heavy for words overwhelmed her.

With nothing left to say, she drew her feet up onto the couch and leaned into Jake, happy just to be beside him sharing a stolen moment while they could.

82

FINGERS WRAPPED AROUND HER TRAVEL MUG, DANA SAT IN HER CAR, drinking her tea in the St. Ann's parking lot. So far Hartwell's bread-crumbs hadn't bore fruit, so she was following her own hunch about Dvita.

The weather was even more miserable today. A winter chill dug its icy claws into the fragile spring morning. Dana knew the war would be spring's, but with the frost covering the ground it was hard to imagine the emergence of fresh green shoots just around the corner.

She didn't know what she admired more. Spring's persistence, or winter's fortitude.

She would need both to get through today.

Richter showed up right on time, and they both ascended the stone stairs together. The tone inside the rectory was more somber than the last time Dana was there. Then again, the group was now permanently short two members.

Cash Holloway and Kylie Marx would never share with their peers again, but their presence was everywhere. Dana heard their names whispered on the lips of every cluster of patients she passed.

"Where's Dvita?" Richter asked.

Dana nodded to the nave, where most of the room was gathered. "There," she said. "He's always at the center of things."

"Typical narcissistic behavior," Richter replied.

"Not exactly an ideal characteristic for a therapist."

Richter raised an eyebrow. "We're here to observe, not judge."

"Right." Dana chewed on her thumbnail, missing Jake's sarcastic wit. He would've said something like, *He probably has commitment issues, too.* And Dana would've smiled inappropriately, and elbowed him in the side, which always soothed her nerves in times like these.

As though he could feel Dana's gaze on him, Dvita turned and looked directly at her. His demeanor quickly changed, his dark eyes narrowing as he excused himself from the group and marched toward them. "Dr. Gray, it's good to see you." But his voice said otherwise. He looked past her. "Where's Nancy?"

"Claire's not coming today," Dana replied.

"What? Why not? I imagine she's in a fragile state considering the news. She and Betty were quite close."

Richter spoke up, saving Dana from answering. "SSA Grant Richter, FBI."

Dvita looked at Richter's outstretched hand but didn't take it. "I'm sorry. This isn't an appropriate time for whatever this is. I'm about to conduct a private group session."

"That's why we're here," Dana replied.

Dvita glared at her. "You invited him?"

"We're only here to observe," Richter said, retracting his hand and attempting to calm Dvita's outrage, but he wasn't having it.

His bearded face reddened, cheeks puffing out like an angry blowfish as he stammered. "I-I'm afraid that's not possible."

"Are you stating you'd prefer to interfere with a federal investigation?" Richter questioned.

"What? No!" Dvita denied. "But this is not how I conduct business. If there are matters you'd like to discuss, I'll have to insist we do it in private, at my office."

Richter shook his head. "Not necessary. For the time being we're just here to observe."

"Am I part of a formal investigation?" Dvita demanded.

"Would you like to be?" Richter asked. "Because that can be arranged." He took a step closer to Dvita, dwarfing the little bearded man. "Or perhaps you'd prefer I inform your group that you're not interested in justice for their peers? That's why we're here."

Richter was good. Dana was enjoying watching Dvita squirm. His obstinate resistance erased any doubts she had. An innocent man wouldn't protest this much. Dvita was hiding something. She'd stake her career on it.

Now she just had to hope Richter felt the same way.

"Fine," Dvita muttered. "You can stay, but in an observational capacity only. I don't want any interruptions or interrogations. My patients have rights."

Richter nodded. "Understood."

***

DANA KEPT her hands in her pockets to keep from biting her nails during Dvita's lecture, because that's what it was. There was no group interaction at all. He stood in the middle of the circle of seated people, pompously preaching.

Opening by acknowledging the loss of "Lincoln" and "Betty," he then droned on about the importance of remaining steadfast in the face of grief to honor the fallen. Everything about his message was subliminally telling his patients to keep their mouths shut.

"Is it me or is he purposely not giving anyone a chance to speak?" Dana asked.

"It's not just you," Richter replied.

"I know this isn't my field of expertise, but I still think he's hiding something."

Richter frowned but pulled out his cell phone. "I think it's time we get that warrant."

83

"You're my attorney," Jake growled into his phone. "You've got to do something."

"Agent Shepard, I assure you I'm doing everything that needs to be done in this situation."

"Everything but tell me how long until my suspension is lifted," Jake snapped.

"OPR has already cleared you. The last step is NPO. I'm meeting with the FBI's Public Affairs specialist tomorrow."

"You're joking. Some bad PR is holding this up?"

"Agent Shepard, this made the national press. The FBI isn't in the habit of handing out second chances. We are aiming to keep our perception that way."

"You're aware there's someone cutting down D.C. citizens with a scythe on our streets and you're telling me the FBI would rather worry about their public image than have more able bodied agents trying to stop these murders?"

"I'm telling you to be patient."

Patient! The vein in Jake's neck threatened to pop. "I've been patient. It's been four days. I can't put my life on hold for much longer. Isn't there anything you can do to speed up the process?"

"The legal system has rules in place for a reason. Hold tight and let me do my job, Agent Shepard."

"Well do it already so I can get back to doing mine!" Jake disconnected the call and slammed the phone down on the table, his confidence in his FBI appointed attorney at an all-time low. The man sounded like he was in his nineties, and he probably had just as many open cases on his docket.

Jake needed to get his suspension and house arrest situation cleared up or it wouldn't matter if he made any progress on his trace.

He'd called the phone number multiple times, listening to the message over and over, like the voice would change somehow. But it didn't. Jake could no longer avoid the truth. His father recorded that message, and this was the closest Jake had ever come to finding him.

Checking the tracing program he'd set was still running, Jake walked back to Dana's bedroom and finished packing his bag. He'd hoped his attorney would've given him the green light already. When he did, Jake needed to be ready.

The groan of floorboards made him stiffen. When the door creaked open, he hadn't been expecting Claire. She stood there, clear-eyed and alert, her gaze landing on Jake's bag.

"Are you going somewhere?" she asked.

"Eventually."

"Oh." She looked down, picking at the hem of her black sweater. "It was nice while it lasted, I guess."

"What was nice?"

"You, me, Dana, all under the same roof. It felt ... normal."

"I'm not going anywhere yet," he assured Claire, steering her into the living room where he sat her down on the couch. Taking the chair across from her, he couldn't help staring.

"What?" Claire demanded. When Jake didn't answer, her paper-white skin paled even further. "Oh God! I did it again, didn't I? I fugued out!"

"Is that what the kids are calling it these days?" he teased, trying to ease some of the fear he saw in her eyes.

"How long?"

Jake shrugged. "Not as long as before. Long enough to scare me."

Claire buried her face in her hands. "Why does this keep happening?"

Jake moved to the couch and tried to take her hand, but she leapt away from him. "Sorry," she muttered, pacing now. "I just hate this, ya know? It's scary not being able to trust myself, my memory."

Jake hated to push her, but he needed to know. "What's the last thing you remember?"

She paused. "The back porch, with you ... and ... oh God! Betty!" Claire sank down onto the floor. Jake rushed to her side. "She's dead, isn't she?" Claire sobbed.

Nodding, Jake took a seat beside her.

"The Reaper?" Claire asked.

Jake nodded again.

Claire sniffed, wiping her eyes with her shirt sleeve. "When is this going to stop?"

"Dana is working with the BAU as we speak. They'll figure it out."

"No, not the Reaper. Me. I don't want to keep phasing out, reliving terrible moments every time I come to. It hurts too much."

"I know this is hard, Claire, but we'll figure it out."

"Will we?" she whispered, her voice broken. "How? Sending me to another program, another doctor? It's not working."

"I wish I had the answers, Claire. I don't. But I can tell you we're not giving up."

She laughed. "Your packed bag says otherwise."

"I'm not going anywhere right now."

He meant what he was saying, but Claire was right. Eventually Jake would have to leave if he wanted to track down his father. Sighing, he let his head fall back, reconsidering his plans. It was an impossible situation. How could he choose one family over another? Wade and his mother were blood, but Dana and Claire, they were something more. They were the family he chose.

84

DANA SAT IN THE PASSENGER SEAT OF RICHTER'S SUV, ANXIOUSLY waiting for Hartwell to arrive with backup. The request for a search warrant had been filed but Richter had warned Hartwell the lengthy process would take too long. Stating he had reason to believe waiting would place others in danger, and possibly allow Dvita time to destroy evidence, Hartwell had agreed to meet them with a team for rapid search and seizure.

That's how she found herself staking out Dvita's home office.

"Is this even legal?" Dana asked, adjusting the straps of her tactical vest.

"Exigent circumstances," Richter replied. "It's what we do when a suspect spooks," he explained. "And that man is the definition of spooked."

Dana had to agree. Dvita had abruptly ended his session when one of his patients asked if he knew who the Reaper would come after next. Feigning the beginnings of a migraine, he excused himself and rushed out of St. Ann's without another word.

Not following him wasn't an option. Dana rushed outside in time to see Dvita's blue Volvo peel out of the parking lot. The next thing she knew, she was climbing into Richter's SUV before he objected.

They'd been sitting outside the small red brick colonial on Klingle Street for less than five minutes, but it was more than enough time for doubt to begin to creep in. Dvita was smart, maybe too smart. "What if this is a trap?" Dana asked.

Richter cocked an eyebrow. "What makes you say that?"

"I don't know. I mean I was there; I saw everything you saw. He's definitely hiding something. But trying to keep everyone quiet, rushing out in the middle of his session ... it almost feels scripted."

"Like he wanted us to follow him here?"

"Maybe. What if he's drawing us away from the real killer?"

"Look, Gray. All you can do is trust your gut. It got you this far. And mine is saying the same thing. Dvita's our guy. He's the Reaper. He fits the profile. He knew each victim, is the right height and build to inflict the injuries. It's everything but the smoking gun."

"Which we'll find inside?"

"If we're lucky."

"What if we don't find anything?" Dana asked. "We said it's possible there's more than one killer. What if we can't prove it's him?"

"Then we keep looking."

Dana didn't know what answer she was looking for. If Dvita was the Reaper, then this would be over. But if he was the killer, then it also meant that Dana had blindly turned Claire over to a monster. And she didn't know how to rectify that.

Hartwell's voice crackled to life over the radio. "We're two clicks out."

"Roger that," Richter replied. "Eyes on Tango. Locked and loaded."

"10-4."

Richter looked at her as the screech of tires turned onto the street. "You don't have to go in."

"No. I want to."

"Alright. Let's see it through."

85

I LIKE WATCHING THEM CLOSE IN WITH THEIR SIRENS AND GUNS. THEY look like little toy soldiers waiting to be toppled.

I grin, knowing they can't stop me.

Let them come.

Let them find me.

Let them try to lock me away.

They can use all their powers, but they'll never compare to mine.

To whom I command.

I'm a force that can't be contained. Not by handcuffs or jail cells.

I'm the one in charge here.

It's amusing they don't know it yet.

But they will.

Let her come, too. She thinks she's so smart. Thinks she knows me.

She doesn't yet. But she will.

86

DANA'S PULSE POUNDED AS SHE WATCHED HARTWELL'S TEAM EXECUTE A knock and announce before busting down Dvita's front door.

The team of officers rushed inside, Hartwell and Richter following closely behind. Dana was one of the last to enter after the all-clear was given.

She entered the cop-filled study to see Dvita sitting calmly at his desk, hands raised above his head, a black jump drive clutched in his right fist. "Take him into custody," Richter ordered. "And read him his rights. We do this by the book, people. The D.C. Reaper isn't getting off on a technicality."

Dvita laughed. "The D.C. Reaper? You can't be serious!" He laughed again. "Honestly this is a huge misunderstanding. I'll cooperate any way I can, officers. All my files are on the jump drive I was holding. I rushed back here to get it ready for Agent Richter and Dr. Gray. You're welcome to it if you think it will help."

"You have the right to remain silent," Hartwell growled, getting in his face. "But by all means, keep talking, buddy. Nothing would make me happier than to nail your ass to the wall."

Dana hated the way Dvita smirked as Hartwell cuffed him.

Even after the police hauled him out to the waiting squad car, she couldn't get the image of him sitting calmly at his desk out of her mind.

He'd been waiting for them.

"Something's not right," she said, looking at the stack of files neatly piled in the center of his desk. The jump drive sat on top in an evidence bag. "He had it ready to hand over."

Richter rubbed the graying stubble on his jaw. "I agree. He doesn't answer the door, but then acts overly cooperative and gives up this flash drive."

Hartwell walked back into the office, visibly agitated. "That's because he's lawyered up." He threw a business card on the desk, displaying the name of one of the most prominent law firms in town. "He knows if he appears to be cooperating, a judge won't grant a search warrant. We'll only get access to files relevant to the case. Which means only what he sees fit to give us."

"What about the jump drive?" Dana asked.

"We have to turn it over to discovery."

"Then we request a warrant for immediate access to whatever's on it," Dana said.

"We'd need to be specific," Hartwell argued. "HIPAA doesn't mess around when it comes to protecting patients' privacy."

"We just need access to the files for his patients from Passages," Dana replied.

"That's more than we have the time or manpower to comb through," Richter warned.

"Then the eleven names the BAU came up with," she specified. "Start with Hayes, Holloway, and Marx. Then anything you can find on Claire Townsend and Max Durnin. He's the missing orderly at Passages. He and Claire may be romantically involved. They were both close to Kylie Marx."

"The only eyewitness is romantically involved with the only missing patient? Christ, Gray, anything else we need to know?"

She shook her head, regretting having kept the information private. "I didn't think Claire's personal life was relevant."

"Everything is relevant!" Hartwell shouted, pacing the room.

"You're right. I'm sorry," she apologized. "I think we should talk to Claire."

"We already tried that," Hartwell grumbled.

"That was right after Hayes was murdered. She's lost two more friends since then," Dana added.

"And you think that's going to suddenly jog her memory?" Hartwell shook his head. "Even if it does, we're not going to get reliable information from a psych patient."

"It's worth a shot. Maybe making Claire feel like she's part of this, helping in some way, will get her to open up about Max. If we can find him, we might find what we need to unlock this case."

Richter stepped in. "Couldn't hurt. Let's talk to Claire after we visit Miss Kincaid."

"What do you want me to do with Dvita?" Hartwell asked. "I can only hold him for twenty-four hours."

"Do it." Richter ordered. "If there's another death while he's in lockup, we know we've got the wrong guy."

87

DANA STOOD IN DVITA'S OFFICE WHILE RICHTER AND HIS TEAM photographed the scene. She was in the way, having to move every few seconds to avoid being in the shot. Dvita's lawyer had shown up making sure no one ventured to other areas of the house so her only option was to wait in the car or remain in the crowded office.

She decided to stay put. Something was keeping her there. She let her gaze rove over every inch of the office, waiting for some new discovery to jump out at her. Rows of pristine built-in shelves lined with books mocked her, their pages whispering the promise of secrets that just might be the answer, but she was unable to touch them.

Dvita's lawyer perched in the doorway like a hawk, waiting for someone to make a false move.

"Excuse me," Agent Garcia said, nodding to the portion of the room yet to be photographed.

Dana moved out of the way, stopping next to Dvita's desk. A hunter green ink blotter was the only color on the mahogany monstrosity. He'd even chosen a leather planner in the same reddish-brown hue as the tropical hardwood. She looked at the date staring back at her. It was off. The planner's pages lay open to a date two days past.

278

That seemed out of character for someone as meticulous as Dr. Dvita.

She glanced at the lawyer, whose attention was occupied by Agent Garcia. Dana quickly scanned the planner, reading the handwritten notes scrawled in Dvita's overindulgent cursive. Clients' names with appointment times dominated the page. Everything looked normal until she got to the small, shaded box at the bottom of the page labeled: Don't Forget. There were two things scribbled there. The word *Milk* and the number 241, which was circled twice.

She stared at the number, letting it rub against the shadowy recesses of her mind until all at once it clicked.

Meredith!

88

DANA GRIPPED HER SEATBELT AS RICHTER TORE THROUGH ANOTHER intersection, sirens blaring. If she was right, time was their enemy. But so was every car on the road with the way Richter was driving.

"We can't help anyone if we're dead!" Dana yelled as they narrowly swerved around the car in front of them.

"I still think you're wrong," Richter replied. "There's no way Dvita or anyone else can get to Meredith. She's in a secure psychiatric facility."

"Dvita's a doctor. He's treated her before and can easily get access."

"Well right now he's locked up. The only person he has access to for the next twenty-four hours is his attorney."

"He could've set this plan in motion already. It was written in his planner two days ago. I'm not taking any chances."

"Then I suggest you let me focus on the road, while you get a hold of someone over there."

Dana dialed St. Elizabeth's again. This time someone picked up. "Hello, this is Dr. Dana Gray, I need to be transferred to the floor nurse on two."

"Hold, please."

Dana bit her lip while the smooth jazz of the hold music filled the car. The juxtaposition of the slow instrumental sound and the speeding car was jarring. Dana felt like she'd been suddenly transported into an action movie. Particularly the scene right before the car careens off the road in a series of slow-motion flips and fireworks.

Finally, the music cut off and another voice filled the car. "Floor two, Avery speaking."

Dana sighed in relief. She knew Nurse Avery! The level-headed floor nurse was as old as St. Elizabeth's and had been on Meredith's floor since Dana first started visiting her. "Avery! It's Dana Gray. I need a favor."

"Dr. Gray? What can I do for you, baby?"

"I need you to check on Meredith Kincaid."

"What about her?"

"Is she in her room?"

"Sure was last I checked."

"When was that?" Dana asked.

"Just finished up rounds about five minutes ago."

"And Meredith was fine?"

"Yes, baby. What's going on?"

"Can you check again for me?"

Avery exhaled deeply. "Give me a moment."

The sound of jazz filled the car again, as Dana pictured Nurse Avery slowly waddling down the hall, her white Crocs squeaking on the linoleum.

A minute later, Avery's voice came back on the line. "She's there, baby. What's this about?"

"I need you to put Meredith in a different room."

"Swap rooms?"

"No. It's imperative that no one is in room 241."

"Dr. Gray, I'd love to help but we're pretty full up here on two, besides, moving patients from one room to another even on the same floor is considered a transfer, and I'm not authorized to do patient transfers."

Shit! Dana caught Richter's eye and he motioned for the phone.

"This is SSA Grant Richter, FBI; I'm authorizing this patient transfer. Meredith Kincaid needs to be moved out of room 241. It needs to be done ASAP. This is a matter of life and death."

"Agent Richter, I'd love to help, but moving patients isn't something we take lightly here. There's a mountain of paperwork. And even then, it's not that simple. We're dealing with patients, not inmates. They have peculiar proclivities and superstitions we have to accommodate. Some hate the number 13 or have to face West. Life is hard enough for 'em. It's my job to do what I can to make it easier. Which means not disrupting them by playing musical rooms."

"I understand," Richter replied, "But we have reason to believe Meredith Kincaid is in imminent danger. Failure to facilitate this request may result in the end of life. Are you prepared to accept responsibility for that?"

"Sir, I already told you. I can't move anyone without the proper authorization. Period."

"What if you don't have to move Meredith?" Dana interrupted.

Avery sucked her teeth, then said. "I'm listening."

Dana laid out her plan step by step. When Avery begrudgingly agreed, she hung up.

"Think it'll work?" Richter asked.

"It has to."

89

DANA KNEW SOMETHING WAS WRONG BEFORE THEY EVEN ARRIVED AT ST. Elizabeth's. The telltale glow of red and blue lights was visible in the distance, the sirens blaring her worst fears. "We're too late."

"You don't know that," Richter said, flashing his badge at the gate attendant when they finally reached St. Elizabeth's.

"Sorry, restricted access only," the man replied.

"I'm here on official FBI business," Richter stated.

The guard stepped back into his hut and made a call. A moment later he returned, lifting the gate, and waving them through. But they were stopped again when they tried to enter the hospital.

"What's going on?" Dana asked the grim-faced officer barring their entry.

"Lockdown protocol. No one in or out till we get the all clear."

She and Richter stepped back, waiting with the crowd of confused onlookers filling the parking lot.

"You're the sort who likes to say I told you so, aren't ya?" Richter muttered, when Dana caught his eye.

Dana shook her head. "I'd much rather say I'm wrong. Life just doesn't seem to work that way."

They stood in the parking lot watching the sun sink lower in the sky. An hour later, the doors whooshed open, and a gurney wheeled out. The sealed body bag confirmed Dana's fears. Heart in her throat she started toward the silent ambulance, when she heard her name being called.

Nurse Avery cut her way through the crowd, waving at Dana. The old woman was out of breath by the time she reached her.

"What happened?" Dana demanded.

"I did what you asked," Avery said, clutching her chest as the wind swept her chin length gray hair into her face. "I switched the room number plaques just like you said, but I told you, our floor was full. No empty beds."

Dana glanced back at the gurney being loaded into the silent ambulance as Richter joined them.

"Poor thing OD'd," Avery sobbed. "It's my fault."

"Let me guess," Richter said, "The body on the gurney was in room 241."

Avery nodded. "Yes, but it's not Meredith."

All the tension seemed to ease from Dana at once and she had to fight to stay on her feet. "Who is it?" she asked.

"Sharon Thompkins. She's a lifer. Been with us for more than twenty years."

"How did she die?" Richter asked.

"Took a lethal dose of Lorazepam."

"Is that even possible?" Dana asked.

Avery shrugged. "We do what we can, but sometimes patients stash their meds for this reason."

"Is it something you would've expected Sharon to do?" Dana pressed.

"No, never. She was stage 5. She didn't possess the mental capacity to do something like this."

90

THE SUN WAS A RED BALL OF FIRE COLLIDING WITH THE HORIZON BY THE
time Dana was back in Richter's SUV heading toward the city. She
wanted to call Jake and fill him in on everything that happened, but
she was preoccupied, her mind busy trying to piece together the frag-
ments of clues they'd gathered today.

Catching her chewing her nails again, Richter asked, "What's
bothering you?"

"What isn't?"

"I know we didn't stop the murder, but at least it wasn't Miss
Kincaid."

"But if the Reaper isn't Dvita, or there's more than one killer,
they'll know they failed here. I'm worried someone will still try to get
to Meredith."

"I know the MO was different here," Richter said. "But a life is a
life, isn't it? If Sharon's death was orchestrated by our killer, we have
to assume she is the fourth victim."

"I don't know," Dana muttered. "This case is so twisted I don't
know which way is up, only that we're always a step behind."

Richter smirked. "Welcome to the BAU."

Dana stewed on her thoughts for a moment longer, landing on

one looming question. "I still don't understand Meredith's role in all of this," she said.

"Neither do I," he replied. "But we'd better get to the bottom of it if she was important enough for someone to try and tie up loose ends."

"Someone? Don't you mean Dvita?"

Richter frowned. "I'm not so sure."

"You were the one who said trust your gut."

"I know, and now I need to take my own advice," Richter said. "Dvita's in lockup. There's no way he could've got to her."

"We discussed this. He could've already had this plan set in motion," Dana argued.

"Possibly, but it doesn't feel right. I guess we won't know until we talk to Meredith."

"Maybe not," Dana said, an idea forming that just might fast forward through all the red tape and get them the answers they needed. "How do you feel about hypnosis?"

AFTER GETTING RICHTER ON BOARD, Dana dialed Jake. His voice was the perfect salve for the chill and fatigue the day had gifted her.

"We're fine," he reassured her when she asked about him and Claire. "What's going on?"

Dana filled him in on the events of the day while Richter drove.

"Wow," Jake said when she'd finished.

"Yeah," Dana almost laughed. "That about sums it up. The important thing is Meredith is okay, but we're not getting in to see her today. St. Elizabeth's is still on lockdown. Richter and I are heading back to the house."

"For what?" Jake asked.

"I want to run something by you. It's about Claire."

Dana laid out her plan and was met with Jake's silence. "What do you think?" she pressed.

"I think it just might be crazy enough to work, but it has to be Claire's decision. She's been through enough. I'm not going to force her to do anything she doesn't want to. And the BAU and Hartwell have to sign off."

"They already have."

"Of course they have," he muttered.

"Jake, we don't have a lot of time. If we're wrong about Dvita, then the Reaper is still out there and someone else is going to die tonight. I'm just trying to make sure it's not Claire."

"I know, and that's the only reason I'm agreeing to this."

"Okay. I'll see you soon." She hung up the phone and looked at Richter. "He's in."

91

WITH THE STREET FINALLY FREE OF NEWS VANS JAKE DECIDED TO GET some air. Collar popped against the unseasonable chill, he took a seat in one of Dana's rocking chairs, trying to gather his thoughts. He sipped on another cup of coffee, having lost count of how many this made. They all tasted the same; bitter and agitating. He needed the caffeine, but it did nothing to quiet his concerns. Even adding a shot of bourbon didn't help. So, he added one more.

Jake had a lot on his mind—Dana, Claire, his mother, Wade, Jenkins, his father, his career. The endless wheel of worries tumbled inside him at all times. It was exhausting and it wouldn't stop until he came to a decision. *Where was he needed most?*

As much as he'd hassled his attorney, Jake knew his suspension would be resolved soon, which only added pressure to make up his mind.

He was still on the front porch wrestling with his thoughts when Richter pulled up. Seeing his old friend pulled a smile out of him. Jake stood, greeting Richter and Dana at the door.

"Richter, I would'a thought you'd be in the five-sided puzzle piece by now," Jake ribbed his old C.O.

Richter smirked. "They keep trying, but I keep tellin' 'em there's too many old bullet-catchers in the Bureau that need my attention."

"Hooah!" Jake bellowed as they clasped hands.

Richter echoed the Army sentiment and patted Jake on the back as Dana joined them.

"You didn't tell me you knew each other from the Army," she said, glancing between them.

"It was implied," Jake said with a wink.

Dana rolled her eyes at him as Richter nodded to Jake's coffee mug. "You got any of that for me?"

"Plenty," Jake said, opening the door for them. "Come on in."

Richter walked in first and Jake caught Dana's hand, holding her back. "Hey," he said, lowering his voice as she stared up at him. "You okay?"

He could see from the heaviness in her normally bright eyes that she wasn't, but she nodded anyway. Jake squeezed her hand, letting her know he was there, nonetheless. "Come on, it's freezing out here."

Inside they gathered in Dana's kitchen, Jake and Richter over coffee, Dana with a cup of freshly steeped mint tea. Jake watched the way she stared into the tendrils of steam, lost in thought as he and Richter reminisced about their Army days.

Jake studied the furrowed crease between Dana's eyebrows, resisting the sudden urge to kiss her there. He knew better than to interrupt when she was working through something, but he hated seeing the toll this case was taking on her.

Claire padded into the kitchen, her arrival a welcome interruption. "I thought I heard you," she said, grinning at Dana, but she froze when she saw Richter.

Dana jumped into action. "Claire, this is Agent Richter with the BAU. We've been working together on the Reaper case."

"Oh," was all Claire offered.

"Hello, Claire," Richter said, offering a kind smile. "It's a pleasure to meet you."

He extended his hand and Claire took a step back. Richter did the same and the room stilled to a strange standoff.

"Why are you here?" Claire finally asked.

Richter answered honestly. "To speak with you."

"About what?"

"The case we're working on. I'd like to ask for your help."

"Why me?"

Richter looked at Dana who nodded. "Because we think you're the only one who can get us the answers we need in time."

"In time for what?"

It was Dana who answered. "To stop the Reaper from killing the next victim tonight."

92

CLAIRE SAT IN THE LIVING ROOM, JAW SET TIGHT AS SHE NODDED AGAIN. "I want to do it," she insisted. Dana and Jake exchanged looks which only annoyed her further. "I said, I want to help," she repeated, enunciating each word.

"Maybe take some time and think about it," Jake recommended.

"I don't need time, and we don't have it, right?" Claire asked, turning her attention to Agent Richter.

It was obvious Dana and Jake had asked the BAU agent to take the lead in proposing this plan to stop the Reaper. Claire wasn't sure if it was Richter's calm demeanor that won her over or the fact that it was a neutral party asking rather than Dana or Jake.

Either way, she had difficulty denying the logic. Even with her help, they still might not find what they were looking for, but Claire didn't want to be the reason more people suffered. Especially Max. What she didn't understand was why Jake and Dana were suddenly fighting her when she finally agreed to cooperate.

Dana's voice interrupted Claire's thoughts. "We understand what we're asking is a lot—"

"No!" Claire erupted. "It's not. Not if it proves Max is innocent."

"Even if it means going under hypnosis again?" Dana clarified.

Claire nodded. "Yes, but ..."

"What is it?" Jake asked.

Claire fidgeted with her sleeves, pulling the hems past her fingers against the sudden chill. "I'll do the hypnosis, but you don't need it to find Max."

Jake leaned forward in his chair, but Richter spoke first. "Tell us how we can help him, Claire."

She winced, closing her eyes against the pain divulging the truth caused. "I hate betraying him."

"You're protecting him," Richter said. "That's admirable. But there comes a time where hiding him hurts him more than it helps."

"He didn't do anything wrong," Claire insisted, her voice cracking.

"The best way to prove that is to bring him in and clear his name." When Claire still didn't answer, Richter said, "The longer he stays in hiding the worse this looks for him."

She nodded. "Okay, I'll tell you, but only if Jake is the one to bring him in."

"I'm suspended," Jake started to argue, but Richter held a hand up.

"I'll make a few calls. See if I can't make that happen. Either way, I'll have to go with Jake. Is that okay?" Richter asked.

Claire hesitated, a single tear betraying her internal struggle. Finally, she nodded. "Max is at my storage unit. I met him and Betty two nights ago and gave them my key. I haven't heard from Max since."

Richter stood, phone already to his ear. He squeezed Claire's shoulder as he walked by her. "You're doing the right thing, Claire."

More tears slipped down her face, "Then why doesn't it feel like it?"

Jake was by her side. "I'll make sure he's treated fairly."

She looked up at him. "They deserve justice. Him and Betty both."

93

Dana sat with Claire, waiting for the FBI's hypnotherapist to arrive. It was a contact of Richter's. Jake trusted him, so that went a long way with Dana. Still, she spoke to the woman on the phone and verified her credentials, before sharing her home address.

Now all that was left to do was wait.

Claire sat on the couch, staring at her phone like it held all the answers to the world. She'd texted Max on Richter's orders, advising him to surrender to the agents that were on their way there to help him.

"Anything?" Dana asked, handing Claire a cup of tea.

Claire shook her head and Dana curled up on the chair opposite, her own mug of tea warming her hands. She savored the warmth as a shiver rippled through her remembering the last time she'd witnessed Claire undergo hypnosis.

Dana was still angry at herself for letting Dr. Dvita into her home. Even more than that, she hated that she'd been footing the bill that gave Dvita access to prey on Claire and his other patients.

She didn't need the hypnosis. She knew Dvita was behind this somehow. Hopefully Claire would give them the evidence they needed to prove it.

Glancing at the clock, Dana took a sip of tea, letting the warm mint reawaken her senses.

"You okay?" Claire asked.

Dana's gaze met hers. "I should be asking you that."

"I imagine your day was more stressful than mine."

Dana sighed. She couldn't get into it. It was all she could do to compartmentalize the day as it was. "I'm just grateful you're willing to help. I think you're the only one who can tell us why Dvita went after Meredith."

Claire asked, "Do you really think he's the Reaper?"

Dana nodded. "I can't prove it, but yeah, I've never been more sure."

She reiterated what she's seen in Dvita's planner, then the situation at St. Elizabeth's.

Claire clutched her teacup. "What if it's not there? Whatever you're looking for in my memories."

"You just need to describe your encounters with Meredith and Dvita. Whatever we're missing is either there, or it isn't."

"If it's there, the hypnotherapist will find it?"

"That's the plan." Dana paused, "Even if we don't find what we're looking for tonight, we can keep looking, together. I miss working with you, Claire."

"Me too."

"Maybe we can talk to Richter. Get him to let you assist me with my research on this case."

"Like old times." Claire grinned. "I'd like that."

Dana smiled, too.

Claire blinked her big blue eyes at Dana, suddenly emotional. "I can't tell you how much your tutelage has meant to me over the years. Without you I never would've made it this far."

Dana started to tell her that wasn't true, but the doorbell interrupted them.

94

Jake stood next to Richter, strapping his tactical vest on. He didn't feel completely himself without his Sig Sauer 9mm, but after nearly a week, the adrenalin was overdue. He'd been so blindsided by his suspension that he hadn't realized how much he needed this—being back out in the field doing his job. He missed it.

Time off between cases was rare, and Jake had too much of it lately. It gave him time to recognize his job was more than just the penance he'd signed up for after the Army.

He valued his career with the Bureau; being out on the streets, making a difference. Protect and serve—it was in his DNA. Wherever he went next, he needed to find a way to keep that purpose forefront.

Richter's radio crackled to life. "Alpha team ready," Hartwell announced.

"Roger that," Richter replied into his radio. He rechecked his weapon and looked at Jake. "You ready, soldier?"

"Hooah," Jake answered.

"Remember, you're here as a civilian."

"Don't remind me," Jake muttered.

"You're lucky you're here at all. The interim AD is not a fan of yours."

Another thing Jake didn't need to be reminded of. "Yeah, he's made that crystal clear."

Richter clamped a hand on Jake's shoulder and squeezed. "Put it out of your head."

"Working on it," he replied. Richter nodded and started to get out of the SUV, but Jake stopped him. "Thanks for going to bat for me. Means a lot."

"Anything for the One-oh-one. Now let's bring this kid in."

Jake grinned. "Roger that."

He followed the team in, trying to adjust to flanking the rear rather than being lead. It was as much of an adjustment as being without a weapon, but ultimately, Jake was glad to be part of the team again. The BAU agents took their positions with Hartwell and SWAT on either side of the storage unit. A flash bang provided cover while the lock was disengaged. Jake stood back, watching the smoke clear as the blue door rolled up.

"All clear," Alpha team announced.

Jake watched Richter holster his weapon, before they entered the crowded storage unit with the rest of the team. Boxes lined the walls, a few pieces of modest wooden furniture piled in the center. Besides agents and officers, the space was devoid of life, or any signs of it. The inside of the unit looked exactly as Jake left it when he and Dana stowed Claire's belongings there months ago.

"He's not here," Jake said.

Richter scratched his 5 o'clock shadow. "Maybe we shouldn't have warned him."

Jake shook his head. "A standoff wouldn't have served anyone. Better to play it safe. Besides, it doesn't look like anyone's been here."

"Now what?" Richter asked.

Jake nodded to the nearest camera mounted on a light pole. "Let's check with the office. Maybe we can access the security footage."

Richter nodded. "On it."

Jake sighed, reaching for his phone to let Dana know the results.

95

DANA SAT IN HER LEATHER ARMCHAIR IN HER HOME OFFICE, DOUBLE checking the camera aimed at Claire was recording. She gave the hypnotherapist a nod, and they got started.

Claire lay stretched out on Dana's worn leather sofa, her socked feet crossed at the ankles. She looked impossibly small laying there, eyes closed, hands folded over her stomach, clutching her eyeglasses. It always struck Dana how young the twenty-five-year-old looked when she wasn't hiding behind her signature cat eye frames. And now, laying still and alone on the couch made her look as fragile as a child.

"Let's begin," the therapist said, instructing Claire to follow her deep breathing technique, before slowly counting her into a hypnotic state.

"10."

"9."

"8."

"7."

"6."

"5."

"4."

"3."

"2."

"1."

"Claire, are you still with me?"

"Yes," she replied, her voice relaxed and dreamlike.

"Good. We're going to take a journey together. You won't be alone, and no one can hurt you. Okay?"

"Okay."

"I want you to imagine a long white hallway lined with doors. Can you picture it?"

"Yes."

"Behind each door is a memory. We're going to open the doors I ask you about together. Will you do that with me?"

"Yes."

"Good. I want you to go to the first door and think back to the first time Meredith Kincaid came to visit you at Passages. Can you picture it?"

"Yes," she said again.

"Good, let's enter that room together. Tell me when you're inside."

"I'm there."

"Good, Claire. Tell me, who else is in the room with you and Meredith?"

"Dr. Dvita."

"Anyone else?"

"No."

"What are you discussing?"

"My progress at Passages."

"What about your progress?"

"Dr. Dvita says I've come far. He's proud of my progress. Says I'm ready for more."

"More? Can you elaborate?"

"More responsibility. Like Meredith."

"What kind of responsibility does Meredith have?"

Claire's eyes dart back and forth beneath her closed eyelids like the question makes her uncomfortable. Finally, she answers. "Meredith is an instrument. But she doesn't want to be."

Claire's fingers begin to twitch, her fingers balling into fists around her glasses.

"What's happening now, Claire?" the therapist asked.

"Meredith is leaving. Dr. Dvita is mad. He ends our session."

"Okay. Good work, Claire. Let's move on. Take me back to the hall. Are you there?"

"Yes."

"Good. Now, open the next door. Inside is your second meeting with Meredith. Tell me who's there."

"Me, Meredith, and Dr. Dvita."

"Anyone else?"

"No."

"What do you discuss?"

"The same thing. This time Meredith agrees with Dr. Dvita."

"Agrees with him about what?"

"That I'm ready."

"Ready for what?"

Claire twitched violently, her hands losing their grip on her glasses. As they fell to the floor, another voice spoke. It came from Claire, but it wasn't her. It was dark and sinister, just like the smirk on her face. It was the same voice Dana heard when Dvita put Claire under.

"I can't tell you that," the voice warned.

"Why not?"

"That's not part of the game."

"I wasn't aware we were playing a game. What are the rules?"

"Ask her," the voice said.

"Who?"

"Claire."

Dana shivered at hearing her friend's name spoken by the other worldly voice.

"We're not here to talk about Claire. We're talking about Meredith."

The voice tsked with disapproval. "Meredith wouldn't play this game."

"Why not?"

"She's afraid."

"Afraid of what?"

"Her destiny."

"What's her destiny?"

Claire twitched again, her head thrashing back and forth warring with whatever was possessing her, because Dana was more convinced than ever that she was under the spell of some sort of poltergeist.

"Stay with me, Claire," the therapist instructed. "You're safe. Breathe."

But Claire was panting, gasping for air.

"We need to stop," Dana demanded. "Bring her out of it."

The therapist held her hand up to silence Dana.

"Claire, you're safe. Go back into the hallway and count with me. When you get to one, you're going to wake up. But I want you to keep your eyes closed and tell me the last thing you see."

"Five."

Inhale

"Four."

Exhale

"Three."

Inhale

"Two."

Exhale

"One."

Claire stilled, her entire body slack for a moment. Then, she spoke; in her voice this time. "Seven must sleep for all to rise."

Dana stifled her gasp. She moved to Claire's side, picking up her glasses and placing them back in her pale hands. She squeezed Claire's arm, wanting her to know she was safe, but the touch jarred her awake. Eyes wild, she sat up, looking around the room in terror. "What happened?"

"You were under hypnosis," Dana said. "Do you remember?"

She pulled her knees to her chest and slowly nodded. "Did I help?"

The therapist asked, "What's the last thing you saw in the hallway, Claire?"

For a moment she frowned, then said, "I saw my face staring back at me."

Dana squeezed her hand. "You showed us another piece of the puzzle."

The hypnosis may not have explained Meredith's involvement, but it validated her fears about Claire. This was more than depression or PTSD. This was something sinister, and she'd bet money Dr. Dvita was behind it. She just had to prove it.

Her phone buzzed in her pocket. *Jake.* "Did you find Max?" she asked.

"No."

Her eyes met Claire's for a moment before she walked out of the room. "Jake, I think you need to come home."

96

DANA STOOD IN THE DOORWAY TO HER OFFICE, WATCHING JAKE'S JAW muscles wage war with the cinnamon gum he'd been punishing since returning with Richter.

Things had gone from bad to worse when Jake had to deliver the news to Claire in person that Max wasn't at her storage unit, nor was there any trace of him on the facility's surveillance. She was already a mess having watched her hypnosis video. Finding out Max was still missing was the final straw.

She'd dissolved into inconsolable tears leaving Dana to wonder if maybe Jake had been right, and this was all too much for Claire. The shell of a girl Dana helped to bed in her guest room said it was.

Dana had already gotten an earful of Jake's opinion on how she'd handled things, in particular letting Claire watch her hypnosis video. Now that Jake was witnessing it for himself, she could imagine he would be even more adamant it was a mistake.

As that haunting demonic voice filled her office, Dana couldn't say she blamed him.

Richter was the first to speak when the video was over. "Well, it's not exactly a smoking gun," he said as he got to his feet.

"I disagree," Dana argued. "At best it proves Dvita is playing some twisted game, at worst it shows he's abusing his license."

Richter shook his head. "His medical license isn't in question here."

"Well maybe it should be," Dana demanded.

"Look, I don't disagree with you, but it won't help our case. The DA will laugh me out of the room if we try using this," he said, pointing to the video. "Plus, it will discredit any evidence we've obtained from Claire."

"Then why did we bother putting her through the hypnosis?" Dana asked.

"If she gave us something solid, connecting him to the murders we could've used it, but convulsing, speaking in tongues, I'm afraid all that does is prove Claire's not exactly a credible witness."

"Seven must sleep for all to rise," Dana repeated. "Claire gave us proof Dvita is trying to brainwash his patients into playing some twisted version of the Seven Sleepers ritual."

"It supports your theory, but it's not enough," Richter argued.

"If we don't do something Dvita will be released tomorrow. We can't just let him carry on killing people because he's deluded himself into thinking they'll all be resurrected. There has to be something we can do."

Richter sighed and pushed past Dana to grab his coat. "Sometimes the best thing we can do is wait."

"You can't be serious," Dana demanded, charging after him. "We should at least put his patients in protective custody and add extra security to Meredith."

"I'd love to do that, Dr. Gray, but we don't have one shred of evidence—" he held up a hand when she started to object. "Actual, factual, hard evidence—linking Dr. Dvita to any of the Reaper murders. Get me that and I'll be the first one in line to nail the bastard."

"It's him, Richter. I know Dvita is behind this."

"Maybe he is. If that's the case, we're on to him, and he'll slip up sooner or later. They all do. And we'll be there to stop him when he does." With that, he shrugged on his jacket and headed out her front door.

"Where are you going?" she asked, following him out onto her porch.

"Back to the lab to meet up with my team, see if they've found anything new to add to the profile. I'll keep you in the loop. You do the same."

She stood there, watching his taillights fade into the distance before going back inside. Jake was right where she'd left him. He sat at her desk, staring at her laptop screen. It was frozen on a still of Claire, her features paralyzed with fear.

"Richter's gone," she said, walking over to join him at the desk.

"I heard," Jake replied, getting to his feet the moment she sat down. "I'm going to go check on Claire."

"I just checked on her."

"Well, I'm going to check again."

"Jake, I know you didn't want her to watch the video, but she begged me. She didn't want to be in the dark anymore."

"You think that's why I'm pissed?" He huffed a laugh. "That's not what this is about."

"Okay, then what?" She stood up, too. "Jake, just talk to me."

But he shook his head and walked out of the room.

97

DANA STOOD IN HER OFFICE, BLINKING AT THE EMPTY SPACE WHERE JAKE
had just stood.

She'd been expecting a fight.

Not getting one hurt worse.

She was used to butting heads with him, but this was different. It
was like he was giving up, and that wasn't like him. It was clear he
needed space, but there wasn't time. This case was more important
than either of them, and they were running out of time.

The sun had set; it was reaping hour.

Dana found Jake on the porch. He was drinking out of a coffee
mug—like she didn't know it was filled with bourbon. She'd seen the
bottle he stashed above the fridge. And how it held less and less each
day. She took the mug, downed a sip to confirm her suspicions, then
poured the rest over the porch railing.

Jake muttered a swear. "That's Blanton's Special Release!"

"And?"

"And it costs too much to dump into your shrubs."

"Well, the time for brooding into your bourbon is over. We have a
killer loose in D.C., and it doesn't seem like anyone else is doing
anything to find him, so I need your help."

"Dana, can we not do this now?"

"This is precisely the time to do this. You're pissed so just tell me why so I can fix it and we can move on."

"Move on?" he scoffed bitterly. "Trust me there is nothing more I'd rather do."

"Jake, what's going on? Why won't you just talk to me?"

"Because, you're just going to say something to convince me you're right, because you're always right."

"About what?"

"Everything. Nothing." He sighed heavily and raked a hand down his face. She could see the fatigue lining his eyes when he finally looked at her. "You pushed her too far today, Dana."

"You were there when I asked Claire to help. She wanted to. She's stronger than you give her credit for, you know."

Jake's anger sparked quickly as he stood, pointing back toward the house. "Maybe she's strong, but what we made her do in there ... that is not helping things."

"Neither is ignoring the fact that she's troubled. More troubled than either of us have the capacity for in the middle of all of this."

"So what, you want to lock her up at St. Elizabeth's with Meredith?"

The sharpness in Jake's voice stung, but Dana resisted her urge to bite back. He lashed out when he was hurt. The last thing she wanted was to hurt him further. "No," she said calmly. "But we have to be realistic. I'm working with the BAU, and you have family obligations once your suspension is up. Claire needs a professional who can help her make sense of whatever she's battling. You saw how her session ended. She saw herself in the hallway. That means she blames herself for whatever demons she has locked away."

"People lock things away in their subconscious for a reason, Dana."

"Yes. And you and I both know that doesn't do any good." She crossed the space between them and touched his chin, begging him to hear her. "Demons rule in darkness. They need to be dragged out into the light and dealt with if we're ever to find peace."

When he didn't answer she said, "It's what I want, Jake. For all of us. A chance for peace in this life."

Jake laughed. "Anything else? Why not end war and hunger while we're at it?"

It was a good sign that Jake's sarcastic humor returned, but Dana was too tired to continue dancing around their issues. "I'm serious, Jake. We don't know who this Reaper is, but Claire's a target, you're suspended, I'm working with the BAU ... I don't know the right move, but I know we stand a better chance if we face it together."

He shook his head. "You said it. I'm suspended. I hate it, but my hands are tied."

"That's never stopped us before," she pressed.

A hint of interest sparked beneath the calm blue waters of his gaze. "What do you have in mind?"

98

"I'VE GOT TO ADMIT," JAKE SAID AS THE ELEVATOR BEGAN TO MAKE ITS decent. "I've actually missed this place."

"Me too," Claire agreed.

"I'm just glad Richter agreed to let you come," Dana added as they descended to sub-level three.

"Mitigating factors," Jake said, repeating Richter's term for extending the parameters of his house arrest. "Though, I think he would've agreed to anything to get you off the phone."

"Persistence pays off, right, Dr. Gray?" Claire added, her mood lighter than Jake had seen in days.

Dana grinned. "That's right."

"More like pesky," Jake teased.

Elbowing him, Dana said, "I prefer the term persuasive."

The ding announced their arrival and the heavy stainless-steel doors rolled open. The potent smell of old books assaulted Jake as he followed the women into the climate-controlled interior.

It was almost as cold as the frigid spring night in the underground section of the Smithsonian, but Dana had been right about one thing. This was the safest place for them to be tonight.

Even with Dvita locked up, threats remained. If someone else was

killed with a scythe tonight, they'd know they had the wrong guy. If
not, they'd make the most of their time digging into every known
legend of scythes, Reapers, and the Seven Sleepers; which is what led
them here. Every case he and Dana had worked had started here, in
her subterranean lair of all things supernatural below the
Smithsonian.

"Work it with me," Dana had whispered on her porch. *"Like we used
to. In the beginning."*

Maybe she was right. Maybe the answers they were looking for
lay here, hidden in one of these centuries' old books, just waiting to
be dusted off to spill their secrets.

Claire had jumped at the distraction. And Dana had agreed to
Jake's terms. *"We stick together. You, me, and Claire, to the end."*

There had been a short argument about him being needed elsewhere, to look for his father, but with Jake's suspension in place, it
was a moot point and Dana reluctantly agreed.

"So," Jake said, taking in the grand splendor of the towering
stacks. "Where do we start?"

Dana grinned, leading them over to the row labeled, Christian
Artifacts. "At the beginning."

99

A VIBRATION AT JAKE'S HIP DRAGGED HIM FROM HIS DREAMS. HE SAT UP, momentarily jarred by the glass encased skull in front of him. The sound of Dana stirring next to him brought him back to his senses. He gently shifted her weight off his shoulder and stood from the too small couch in her office beneath the Smithsonian.

His back popped loudly as he stretched and took in his surroundings. Dana slept, glasses askew, legs tucked under her, book still open in her lap. Claire dozed curled up like a cat in the wingback chair in the corner. The table between them was littered with books, scrolls and manuscripts. The disturbing details they'd researched last night came rushing back with razor clarity.

It started with Papyrus 18—a third century Greek copy of the Book of Revelation; where the Grim Reaper's story originated, then morphed into studies of each culture's harbinger of death; their morbid research culminating with the disturbing tale of the Seven Sleepers and religious persecution.

Jake was surprised he'd slept at all thanks to the subject matter surrounding them. Then again, the Army had taught him how to sleep anywhere.

Despite the subject matter, Jake found himself feeling nostalgic. It felt like old times pulling an all-nighter alongside Dana and Claire. Even the faint scent of left-over Thai takeout made him sentimental.

Leave it to Dana and Claire to deliver a slice of normalcy amidst the chaos of the past few days. It made him hopeful that things could be righted, put back on course. Perhaps all he needed to do to right their course was stop trying to steer and give in to the current.

He gazed at Dana, realizing how easy it would be to get swept away by her.

Navigating relationships wasn't something Jake was good at. In the few he'd managed, he was the alpha. But Dana was his equal in every way. Dedication, determination, strength, loyalty; he admired it all. And her brilliant mind ... it was a thing of beauty that never ceased to leave him in awe.

Last night she'd walked the stacks, locating untitled books like she was visiting old friends. With the simple stroke of its spine, each book gave up its secrets to Dana, enabling her to rattle off facts about Reapers, religion, possessions, and rituals that helped shape the profile of a killer.

Claire also chimed in with facts about Reapers, but there was no emotion behind her words. She simply regurgitated facts, like a walking Wikipedia. With Dana, it was different.

Where most saw nothing but death and evil in her work, she found understanding, existence, humanity. On that level, even the most ancient occult beliefs could translate to the world today and beyond.

It was like witnessing magic. And if Jake was honest, it's why he'd fallen for Dana in the first place. She was a star in the night sky, lighting the way through the darkness, and Jake had existed in darkness for far too long.

It assuaged any doubts he had about where he belonged.

Together they'd compiled a mountain of evidence supporting Dana's theory. The D.C. Reaper was systematically butchering chosen victims to recreate the legend of the Seven Sleepers and gain the gift of immortality through resurrection. What they'd yet to prove was the who and why?

Whoever it was, Jake now believed like Dana, the killings wouldn't stop until all seven were dead.

A second buzz from his pocket had Jake pulling out his phone. One missed call. One voice mail. Both from the same number. 202. It was a D.C. area code. He was about to listen to the message when another phone began ringing.

The sound stirred both women awake. Claire, jolted upright, startled. Dana was slower to rouse. "Is that my phone?" she asked, adjusting her glasses.

Jake uncovered it from beneath the mess of papers and books on the table. Handing it to her, they paused, both reading the caller ID at the same time. *Hartwell.*

"Hello?" Dana answered breathlessly, placing the call on speaker.

"Sorry to call so early ..."

"Is there another body?"

"No. Nothing from the Reaper."

Dana's gaze met Jake's. "Then it proves we have the right guy. Dvita is the D.C. Reaper."

She could hear the frustration in Hartwell's exhale. "Not finding a body isn't enough to prove guilt."

"So, what are you saying?"

"Dvita's walking in a few hours. We'll put a tail on him, but there's not much else we can do. Just wanted to give you a heads up."

Jake spoke up. "What about the jump drive?"

"His attorney's turning it over as soon as he's released. BAU should have it by noon."

"Okay. I'll meet you at the lab," Dana said. "I need to see what's on that drive."

Dana hung up and looked at the time. "If we leave now, I'll have enough time to shower and make us something to eat before meeting up with the BAU team."

"Let's go," Jake said, jacket already in hand.

100

JAKE WAS ON THE PHONE WHEN DANA FINISHED SHOWERING. SHE COULD hear his voice drifting down the hallway from her office. His tone was somber, professional. It was the voice he used with the Bureau. Much different than the voice he reserved for her and Claire. A trace of a smile played on her lips realizing she knew the difference.

She dressed and poked her head into her office. No longer on the phone, Jake was sitting at her desk, staring at her laptop, the weight of the world on his shoulders.

"Everything okay?" she asked.

Jake looked up, momentarily caught off guard. "Yeah. More than okay, actually. Just got off a call with my attorney. My suspension's been lifted."

"Jake! That's great news. Now you're free to follow up on your father. Were you able to trace an address from the phone number?"

His lips turned down. "Working on it."

"You will," she said, smiling encouragement. "Come on. Claire's insisted on making pancakes. That'll cheer you up."

"I'll be there in a minute," he said.

She paused. "You could come with me today. I can ask about

Claire, too. I know Richter would be happy to have the help now that you've been cleared."

"I think it's best if I stay here with Claire. Keep her away from all the pain the investigation's sure to bring up." Jake looked past Dana to where Claire flitted around the kitchen gathering ingredients for pancakes. "She seems more herself today."

"She does," Dana agreed, following his gaze. "You're probably right. Staying here is best for her. But for what it's worth, I enjoyed last night. It felt good to be working together again." She gave a shy shrug. "Well, I better go help Claire before she dismantles my kitchen. Come join us when you're ready."

———

JAKE WATCHED DANA WALK AWAY. He could see her in the kitchen with Claire. She moved through a splash of sunlight gathering mixing bowls and sugar, an easy smile gracing her face. It was hard to tear his eyes away. Claire seemed to feel the same, watching Dana with as much reverence as Jake.

A moment later the rich aroma of coffee mingled with the scent of butter melting on the skillet. It was enough to tempt him away from his work. But he couldn't put this off any longer.

Attention back on Dana's laptop, he stared at the address he'd typed in the search bar. Hitting enter, he watched the map populate the location. Zooming in, he switched to street view and took in the stone splendor of 18 Rue de l'Abreuvoir. The pale limestone building resembled a flatiron, soaring seven stories into the gray Parisian sky. The slate black roof, pitched and peaked, and was adorned with dormer windows and ornate iron work.

Jake toggled the view to take in every angle of the cobbled streets surrounding the Montmartre apartment until he could almost imagine the phone ringing inside.

He hadn't been completely truthful when he'd told Dana he was working on tracing the phone number she'd traded favors for. Tracing the address was easy. What he was working on, was what to do with it.

He'd been cleared of all charges and with his suspension over, there was nothing stopping him from pursuing this lead. Nothing but his own conflictions.

Clicking on another open tab, Jake reviewed the airline ticket in his cart. D.C. to Paris. Leaving tonight. His chest tightened as he let the mouse hover over the purchase button.

A conversation from last night drifted back to him.

"We have the how," Dana said, *after adding another page to the report supporting her Reaper theory. "What we need now is the why and who."*

"Why's not important. Find out who and we can put an end to this," he replied.

"The why is just as important, Jake. Occult killings like this will never cease without truly uncovering the heart of the issue. We need to know where they went wrong in order to stop this from occurring again."

"Maybe, or maybe we just have to cut the head off the snake."

Dana shook her head. "That only solves a small percentage of the issue. You taught me that. Whoever the Reaper is, they're following the teaching of others, who were following the teachings of those who came before them. It's an endless cycle. The BAU profile indicates the Unsub is a highly intelligent, skilled professional who works alone. With an all-encompassing scope like that, there's a real danger of these types of murders increasing in our society."

Jake scoffed. "Highly intelligent, skilled professional who works alone, huh? You could be describing me."

"Or me," she countered. "We all gaze into the abyss, Jake. It's when it gazes back that we see what we're made of."

He'd wanted to say something, but the way Dana's dark eyes drank him in left him at a loss for words. She'd stared into his darkness, yet here she was, still offering to be the light. He knew it wasn't because she herself hadn't experienced the depths of unimaginable pain and horror. On the contrary, she'd been surrounded by it from childhood. The difference was, Dana had found a way to embrace it, and she somehow made him believe that with her by his side, he had the strength to do the same.

"Jake, get in here," Claire called, abruptly dragging Jake from his thoughts. "You have five minutes or I'm eating all the pancakes."

Drawing his attention back to the laptop, he closed the window on the plane ticket, and then the map. Standing, he walked to the kitchen, his decision made. Choosing to stay where he was needed, or rather where he belonged.

101

THE SMELL OF STALE COFFEE AND FAILING DEODORANT GREETED DANA when she stepped into the FBI lab turned BAU command center. Hartwell and Richter were already there, bent over a laptop watching something.

"Are those Dvita's recordings?" Dana asked, joining them.

"Yeah, lot of good they're doing us," Hartwell grumbled.

"What do you mean?" she asked.

"The faces of his patients are blurred out, and he used a voice distortion, so we have no way of knowing who's who," Richter explained.

"How are the sessions labeled?" Dana asked.

"That's even harder to crack," Hartwell said, pausing the video and backing out to the drive.

Dana saw what he meant. There were hundreds of files, each named with a sequence of numbers.

"We've ruled out time, dates, social security numbers, and bank accounts," Agent Walsh interjected.

"That's why he offered it up so freely," Hartwell muttered. "Bastard knew he was handing us a needle in a haystack."

"Then maybe we stop looking for the needle," Dana said, excitement coursing through her.

"Huh?" Hartwell grunted.

Richter scratched his head. "I don't follow, Dr. Gray."

"Hartwell's right. Dvita gave this to us knowing we'd spend all our time trying to crack his code. But the answers we're looking for are still here, in the footage."

"There's days' worth of recordings here," Hartwell argued. "We'll never get through it all."

"We don't have to." Dana turned to Walsh. "Can you search for keywords in these recordings?"

"Yeah, I can write a program for that right now if you've got the words."

Dana grinned. "Lead the way."

It took Walsh less than twenty minutes to write the program, then five more to extract all the keywords from the report Dana had compiled at the Smithsonian last night. It spanned the entirety of her library's collection on Grim Reaper history from inception to modern personification, referencing any culture or religion where the legend of the Seven Sleepers coincided.

Dana had Walsh extract the non-essential interrogative and demonstrative words, organizing what was left by repetition. Dana helped eliminate anything unnecessary, narrowing the target further. Walsh plugged those words into the program, then began uploading the video files.

"Alright, we're up and running," Walsh announced as lines of code began filling the screen.

"How long is this going to take?" Hartwell asked.

"As long as it takes," Walsh replied.

"Great," Hartwell grumbled on his way to refill his coffee.

"The words we're searching for aren't in the average vocabulary," Dana said. "In theory, the program should pick them up, and narrow our search field significantly."

"I've had enough of theories, Dr. Gray," Hartwell said. "I've got dead bodies and a murderer at large in my city. We need cold hard evidence or heads are gonna roll. Literally, people!"

102

No sooner had Hartwell stormed out of the room, than Walsh's program began to bear fruit. An hour later, seven words were highlighted on her screen.

Infection, possession, vigilante, resurrections, reborn, sleepers, purge.

Dana couldn't ignore the chill in her spine. It felt like more than a coincidence that the pingback had only located seven words.

"What've we got?" Richter asked, looking over Walsh's shoulder.

"Lucky number seven, sir."

"How many videos did it locate?"

"Twenty-six."

"Now that's a number we can deal with," Richter said. "Let's go, team. All hands on deck. Queue up the videos, Walsh. Everyone take two, tag and highlight anything relevant to the case so we can add it to the board. We've got a killer to catch."

Dana wasn't sure how long they'd been at it. Time held no meaning in the windowless room she'd locked herself in with Hartwell and the BAU team. She'd seen all the videos, some multiple times. Even with the voice distortion, Dana got chills each time one of the patients would slip into an alternate personality. She'd recognize that other-worldly voice anywhere. It was the same one she'd heard from Claire each time she'd watched her under hypnosis.

She heard it again now, speaking through at least five other people. Thanks to the code names chosen by each Passages patient, Dana had been able to help identify almost all of them since Dvita called them by that name in each session.

The smart board now held a new list.

Taft tapes = Congressman Norton Hayes. The first Reaper victim.

Lincoln tapes = Cash Holloway. The second Reaper victim.

Betty tapes = Kylie Marx. The third Reaper victim.

Nancy tapes = Claire Townsend.

Laura tapes = Meredith Kincaid.

"That's only five," Hartwell said, stating the obvious. "I thought you said there would be seven victims if the Reaper is trying to recreate this Seven Sleepers resurrection theory."

"We have to assume Dvita is the seventh and final victim," Dana replied.

"Okay, then who's number six?" Hartwell asked.

Dana rocked back on her heels, staring at the board. "I don't know."

"What about the Max kid who's still missing?" Richter asked. "What's his role in this?"

Another unanswered question. Dana hoped they'd have learned more from the tapes. But all they proved was that there was something truly disturbing going on at Passages.

"Well, it's not a smoking gun," Richter said, echoing her thoughts. "But these tapes cast reasonable doubt that Dvita is implanting subliminal murderous intent to his patients."

"So what? You want to get him on malpractice?" Hartwell grumbled.

"It's enough for a warrant," Richter said. "Who knows. We might get lucky."

"And find a shed full of scythes and black robes?" Hartwell scoffed. "Good luck."

"Stranger things have happened," Richter argued. "Got Ted Bundy on a traffic stop. David Burkowitz with a parking ticket."

Hartwell sighed in resignation. "Call for your warrant. But we keep working this case. Revisit crime scenes, reexamine evidence. And I want eyes on all the tapes. Not just the ones Dr Gray identified. This guy gets off on manipulating minds. He thinks he's smarter than us, but he's not. To beat him, we just have to think like him. Outside the box."

103

I WILL TAKE PLEASURE IN THIS KILL MOST OF ALL. SURPRISING HIM AT HIS own game was my own clever invention. He thinks he found me. He has no idea.

I let him think it was his plan all along. Let him think he was in control. After all, he's a controlling man. But I'm the one in charge here. I've had years with nothing to do but plot. And now it's finally here.

His death will only be one part of what I have in store for him.

For what he did, he will pay tenfold.

I will resurrect him just to kill him again and again. Only then may he taste the torturous existence I've been confined to.

The blade is an extension of me now as I carry out my vengeance.

104

For the second time in as many days, Dana found herself riding shotgun in an FBI vehicle with Agent Richter. They pulled into position on Dvita's street to wait for the rest of the team to get to their marks. This time, it wasn't just the tactical team on location. A slew of unmarked vans followed them; the search and seizure team ready to bag and tag everything the warrant allowed.

Richter checked his weapon, vest and then radio to confirm that the final team was on location. That's when the call came in. Richter answered. "What is it, Walsh?"

"You're never going to believe this, sir. I figured out the code."

"What code?"

"The numbers on each recording file. It's the date of each murder, multiplied by seven."

Dana's breath caught, floored by how devious Dvita's mind was.

"We knew he was organized," Richter said. "This helps our case. It shows this was premeditated."

"Can you use the code to predict the next murder?" Dana asked.

"Way ahead of ya," Walsh said. "Thing is, I think he messed up."

"What do you mean?"

"Meredith Kincaid. The date you tried to visit her, multiplied by seven. Her tapes are labeled with that number. According to our parameters, she should've been the fourth victim. Meredith's supposed to be dead."

Dana swallowed the bile trying to rise in her throat. "He tried to kill her that day."

"That's our smoking gun!" Richter said. "Good work, Walsh. We'll take it from here."

Richter ended the call and immediately called Hartwell to relay the new information. Dana could practically hear him grinning on the line. "Guess my pep talk worked. Let's go nail the bastard."

Dana remained outside Dvita's home while the agents served the warrant, precise and professional, just like the last time they were here. Only this time things were different. Quiet.

Every window of the brick two-story colonial home was dark. She watched the agents enter the home, a path of light following them from room to room until they reached his home office.

That's when she heard the call come through the radio Richter had given her. "Boss, you've gotta see this."

Unable to quell her curiosity, Dana left the vehicle and joined the rest of the team inside.

Dvita sat at his desk, head slumped back against his chair revealing the gaping wound in his neck, a bloody scythe resting on his lap. Hartwell swore, donning his gloves to check for the pulse he knew wasn't there. "Body's still warm. I want all units patrolling the area. Perp can't have gotten far."

Dana stared at Dvita's lifeless eyes. They were wide open, glossy with the far-off look left behind when life fades away.

"So much for questioning our prime suspect," Richter said.

"Good riddance," Hartwell crowed in a voice much too jovial for a crime scene.

"The man didn't slit his own throat with a scythe," Richter argued. "This wasn't a suicide."

"I know that, but I heard those tapes. He took advantage of his patients. I'm not gonna lose any sleep over one less predator in the world."

"Looks like we got it wrong," Richter admitted.

Dana was still reeling. "I was so sure it was him."

Richter put a hand on her shoulder. "I've been there. Best thing you can do is shake it off and go back to the drawing board. I'm going to call this in to BAU, see if Walsh can use the new development to tell us anything."

105

A NUMBNESS SETTLED OVER DANA AS SHE STARED AT THE EMPTY BOARD in front of her. She was back at the FBI lab, helping the BAU create a new profile on the D.C. Reaper.

Behind her was the old board. The one with Dvita at the center. She knew if she turned around, she'd see a large X over his photograph. But it hurt too much to look at. Not because she mourned him, but because she mourned the loss of her confidence.

She'd never been so wrong before.

"Scene's been wiped clean," Richter was saying. "What does that tell us?"

"No fingerprints?" Officer Lennox asked. "That doesn't make sense. Dvita saw patients there. It should be littered with prints."

"Exactly," Richter replied. "Something our Unsub knew and took the time to eliminate. What else does that tell us?"

Agent Garcia spoke up. "No DNA or prints at the scene suggests good hygiene. Our Unsub is organized, intelligent. Only leaves evidence he wants us to find."

"Good," Richter said. "What else?"

Annoyance flashed through Dana as she was reminded of her university lecture days. She hated how calm everyone was. This was a murder investigation, not a classroom. Where was the sense of urgency? They had five dead bodies and if they didn't figure out who was behind the murders, two more were inevitable.

"What about the orderly, Max Durnin?" Dana interjected. "Of the three passages patients we identified he's the only one without an alibi during Dvita's murder."

Richter shook his head. "That's a leap, Dr. Gray. For all we know Max Durnin isn't even alive. Besides this exercise requires us to ignore our previous suspect list until we've come up with an accurate profile. We have to start from scratch if we're to remain unbiased."

"But we're not starting from scratch," she argued. "We know this is the same killer. We don't have time to throw away all the research we've already collected."

"Then what would you suggest?"

"We need to go back through our original profile. See where we went wrong. Look for the subtle differences."

"This kill deviates from the original pattern," Lennox offered. "All the others were outdoors, mostly in isolated areas. This one was in Dvita's home. More brazen and staged differently, too. Like the Unsub is gaining confidence."

"Or just becoming more unpredictable," Walsh said.

"Or it's been multiple Unsubs all along," Dana added.

Richter disagreed. "This is what happens once the established pattern is broken," he explained. "It doesn't necessarily mean more than one killer. Now that the Unsub has deviated from his MO, he's more dangerous than ever. We have to assume the murders will escalate."

"Which is why we need to put the remaining patients in protective custody," Dana implored.

"I agree with Dr. Gray," Hartwell said.

Dana turned to find him standing near the doorway and wondered how long he'd been there.

"We have a mountain of evidence from Dvita's and not enough time to go through it. Without any tangible leads, a safe house is our best option."

"It's certainly something to consider, but there's more we can do here to dial in our profile."

"We're out of time." Hartwell walked into the center of the room. "I've already contacted the US Marshals. They're setting it up as we speak."

"Who's on the protective custody list?" Dana asked.

Hartwell handed her a folder. The first page inside held a list of names. Richter read it over her shoulder, his mouth pressing into a thin line. "For all we know we could be locking the Unsub up with these people."

"Or this will lure him out," Hartwell added. "Either way, we'll be there to catch the son of a bitch and end this once and for all."

The mood in the room was tense as Hartwell gave marching orders to Richter and his team. It was obvious Richter still believed there was more profiling to be done, but Hartwell's move had set a new plan in motion. One Dana wasn't looking forward to sharing with Jake and Claire.

106

"WHAT ABOUT MAX?" CLAIRE ASKED WHEN DANA FINISHED EXPLAINING Hartwell's plan.

Dana glanced at Jake. She'd called him on her way home to give him a heads up about Dvita and Max. Since Max's whereabouts were unknown and he was currently listed as a potential suspect, his name wasn't on the protection list. A detail Claire hadn't missed.

"Max is still missing," Dana said. "We have no way to contact him to let him know about the safe house."

"That's not fair. He needs protection, too," Claire argued. "He's not answering any of my texts or phone calls. I'm really worried about him."

"The FBI is still searching for Max," Jake assured her.

Claire fidgeted with her sleeves, pulling them over her fists. Jake noticed it was something she did when she was nervous. "This is a trap, isn't it?" she asked.

"What makes you say that?" Dana asked.

"I'm not stupid," Claire snapped. "It's only Passages patients that are getting picked off. And since our identities are supposed to be confidential it means the killer is an insider. So, locking us all up together will make the killer surface. It's a good plan."

Again, Dana looked at Jake, at a loss for how to respond.

"You realize that paints you as a suspect, too?" Dana added.

"I know," Claire said, directing her defiance at Dana. "I'm not afraid to do whatever it takes to prove I'm not."

"Alright," Jake intervened. "Right now, the best thing we can do is follow protocol and get you to the safe house. Go pack."

Claire reluctantly left the room, heading to her bedroom to pack. When she was out of sight, Jake led Dana to the office. "What the hell was that?"

"What do you mean?"

"You've got to lay off the accusations with Claire."

"I didn't accuse her of anything."

"You didn't have to, Dana. Your face is an open book."

"Jake, you didn't see the tapes. Dvita brought something out in Claire, something dark and lingering. The voice that was speaking through her ... through all of them, he planted it there."

"What, like some kind of demonic spirit? This isn't *The Exorcist*, Dana."

"You spent all night researching this very thing in the Smithsonian with me. There are centuries of accounts. We can't rule it out."

Jake scoffed. "Great, let's call Richter and tell him the Reaper is a demon and all we have to do to stop it is shut the portal to hell."

"Jake, I'm serious."

"I know you are. That's what's scaring me."

"You have to admit something is off with Claire. It has been ever since she showed up here in a trance. She's been having mood swings and sneaking around. She knows all of the victims. She's been in contact with Max. And today she didn't even blink when I told her Dvita was dead. It's like she knew."

"That's enough!" Jake snapped. "Dvita was her therapist, not her best friend. And this morning you were convinced he was the Reaper. Claire is the victim here. She's lost her friends, her doctor, any sense of normalcy. The last thing she needs is to feel like she's losing us."

"I know that, Jake. It's the last thing I want. But we can't let our emotions cloud our judgment. We have to face reality."

Jake exhaled trying to rein in his anger. "The reality is we don't have any proof. Until then we do our jobs. Right now, that means getting Claire into protective custody." Dana opened her mouth to argue but Jake cut her off. "I want in on the protection detail. Who's point?"

"Good luck. Hartwell's running the show."

"You let me deal with Hartwell."

107

I MUST KILL. I MUST.

I can feel them closing in. This isn't how it was supposed to be. But I can't stop now.

I adapt.

I learn.

I have to play my part.

Just a little bit longer. Then we'll be reunited. And this will all be worth it.

I will do it for her. For her, I do everything.

108

DANA WATCHED THE SUN-WORN LACE CURTAINS FLUTTER IN THE OPEN window above Jake's head. The moonlight sallowed their color to a shade between eggshell and fresh butter. The radio on Jake's hip crackled to life and Hartwell's voice filled the small attic. "All units relay your position."

Jake barked back his code, then gave Dana an insufferable wink.

As promised, he'd talked his way onto the protection detail, demoting Dana to glorified babysitter. She wasn't even in the main part of the house with Claire and the other patients. She'd been sequestered to the attic with Jake, where his sharpshooting skills would be put to the test if the Reaper showed up. Assuming the murderous maniac wasn't already inside.

She'd be lying if she said it wasn't comforting having Jake on the case. The problem was, the safe house attic wasn't big enough for both their egos, especially now that hers was bruised.

It hurt how easily he'd dismissed her theory. Dana didn't want Claire to be involved in this anymore than he did. But Dana was trying to be rational. She'd convinced herself Dvita was the Reaper and because of it, had been blinded to any other option.

She wouldn't let that happen again. Not if it meant more people would pay the ultimate price.

"You mind toning it down over there," Jake taunted. "I can hear the gears turning in that mind of yours. It's hard to concentrate."

Dana glared at him, annoyed by the amusement on his face.

"Just admit you're glad I'm here," he teased.

"Yes, I'm overjoyed to be freezing to death in a dusty, cobweb filled attic in the middle of nowhere with you."

"I know you've been to more remote places than a farm in Green-belt, Maryland." He smirked, shrugging out of his FBI field jacket. "And if you're cold, just say so," he said, draping the jacket over her shoulders.

It was still warm and smelled intoxicatingly like him, which shamefully subdued her annoyance.

"Better?" he asked.

Begrudgingly, she nodded.

"It's really remote out here."

"It's a safe house, Gray. Keyword is safe."

"I know," she muttered, "but if the plan is to draw the Reaper out maybe we should've picked a place closer to the city."

"It's only a thirty-minute drive," Jake replied. "Besides, hosting a shootout in the city seems a tad irresponsible. Out here there's plenty of room for us to hide."

He was right. The property was crawling with SWAT, BAU, US Marshals, and Metro officers. If the Reaper showed up, escape wouldn't be an option.

Jake went back to his rifle, kneeling to adjust the scope another millimeter or so. The McMillan TAC-338A was an impressive piece of machinery. When they arrived, Dana had watched in awe as he assembled the thirteen-pound sniper rifle like it was as simple as putting batteries in a flashlight.

"Do you think you'll have to use it?" she asked quietly.

Jake answered without looking at her. "Anyone already thinking about pulling the trigger has no business behind this kind of weapon."

"Right," Dana said, biting her lip, sorry she'd asked.

Jake finished his tinkering and sat up with a heavy exhale. "Didn't mean to sound harsh. It's just been a while since I've used something of this caliber. Brings back memories."

"Ghazni?"

He nodded.

"Is it easier?" she asked. "Taking a life from so far away?"

Jake leaned back against the wall, his shoulder brushing against hers. "No. Double tap to the chest or picking 'em off from 700 yards, it all weighs the same on your soul." He turned to look at her, his blue eyes aglow in the moonlight. "But I don't have to tell you that."

Her chest tightened the way it always did when she thought about that day on the hill, when she'd taken the shot. The decision had been life or death. Jake or Meredith. She hated that it had been frighteningly easy. Hated that faced with the same dilemma, she wouldn't change a thing. Dana reached out and grabbed one of Jake's scarred hands, squeezing it. "I don't regret it. You know that, right?"

"I shouldn't have brought it up."

Dana squeezed her conviction into his hand. "We need to be able to talk about these things if we're ever going to move forward. Our cases, our losses, war ..."

Jake exhaled, looking away again. "Being home is its own kind of war."

"It doesn't have to be."

He looked at her. The confliction dancing in his eyes hollowed her insides. "Jake, I don't want to be another battle you have to face."

"You're not."

"Then why does it feel that way?"

"Because it's impossible to be in two places at once."

"Then don't. I know your family needs you."

His eyes darkened as he turned toward her, pinning her face between his hands. "That's what I've been trying to tell you, Dana. *You're* my family."

Dana's pulse quickened, every part of her tightening as she focused on Jake's lips, inches from her own. She'd never wanted to kiss him more. Breathless, she grabbed his collar, ready to pull him toward her when something flashed in the distance.

"Jake..." she whispered, trying to warn him, but his radio beat her to it.

"All units be advised. Tango approaching."

109

Jake silenced his radio and switched over to his earpiece, gaze already searching through his scope. He spotted the target instantly. Adult male, black sweatshirt, hood up, silver scythe glistening in the moonlight. "Tango sighted. Awaiting command," Jake relayed.

"Hold fire," Hartwell replied.

"Is it him?" Dana whispered. "Is it Max?"

"Can't tell," Jake whispered back, "But he's approaching a sea of officers and agents with a weapon. If he doesn't stop, this doesn't end well."

"Jake, we have to take him alive, or we'll never know the truth!"

"That's the goal," he said, not taking his eyes off the target.

He could hear Hartwell on the bullhorn speaking to the approaching assailant. "This is the police. Drop your weapon and put your hands behind your head."

The hooded figure did no such thing. He kept moving, one foot after the other, never breaking stride. He moved as if in a trance, slow and disjointed. Images from too many zombie movies flipped through Jake's mind. He locked them away, focusing on the target in his sights. His shadow elongating in the moonlight cut an eerie picture.

"Grab my range finder," Jake instructed. "See if you can get a better look."

Dana moved to the space next to him in the window, range finder in her hands. Out of reflex he pushed her head down. This wasn't a warzone, but he still felt more comfortable with her head out of the line of any stray bullets should this thing go south, which it very well might.

Jake could feel the tension crackling in the air. It always felt this way. The calm before the storm. His instincts could usually tell him which way things would fall. Right now, his gut told him catastrophe was coming.

"I can't see his face," Dana said. "The hood's in the way."

Hartwell's orders rang out again, but they fell on deaf ears. The hooded figure just kept approaching. He was eighty yards from the house now.

A stiff breeze picked up, the old lace curtains billowing above Jake. For a second the hooded figure paused. He turned, looking up, in Jake's direction. The wind blew again, and the hood slipped back just far enough that the moonlight illuminated the face beneath it.

"It's Max," Jake confirmed into his mic. "I repeat, Tango identified. Max Durnin."

"Hold fire," Hartwell barked over the mic, before continuing his negotiations on the bull horn. "We have you surrounded. Put down your weapon and surrender."

The wind howled as if it too was afraid of what walked in its midst. Jake took the range finder from Dana. He needed to readjust his shot. Distance, temperature, wind speed, velocity; he had it all lined up. Through the magnified lens he got a closer look at Max. His face was pale in the moonlight, which only made the bloody slit at his throat bolder. Jake's gaze moved to the scythe. He could see evidence of blood on the blade. Had this kid tried to slit his own throat? It would explain the slow, staggering gait. Whatever was going on, they needed to stop Max before he got any closer.

"I have a clean shot," Jake said into his com.

"Hold fire," Hartwell ordered.

Max was a hundred yards from the farmhouse and his lumbering gait showed no signs of stopping. Jake didn't want Dana here to witness this. Or Claire. Neither of them needed the burden of witnessing another death. "Dana, go downstairs and find Claire. She doesn't need to see this."

Dana hesitated. "Richter told me to stay with you."

"And I'm telling you to go downstairs. I don't know all these players. If this thing goes wrong, I don't know who's trigger happy. I'm not taking any chances that you two get caught in the crossfire. Do you have your gun?"

She nodded.

"Get Claire, find a bathroom, lock the door. And if you need to, defend yourself."

He watched her determination outweigh her fear. She nodded then disappeared down the stairs.

With his distractions eliminated, Jake adjusted his sight one last time. A sniper's job was to follow orders, not make the call. It was the thing he hated most about his time in the Army. But he wasn't in the Army anymore. This time fate was his to control.

Jake was trained to take the kill shot, severing the brainstem from the spinal cord. But that wasn't his goal tonight. He adjusted his sight, making sure if he took the shot, it would eliminate the threat without eliminating life.

Max had no chance of escape. The farmhouse was surrounded by cops and federal agents. The real risk in this situation was itchy trigger fingers and friendly fire.

Seventy yards.

Sixty.

"I have the shot," Jake repeated.

"Hold fire."

Fifty yards.

"Any closer and I lose long range," Jake said.

"Hold—"

A shot rang out, stealing the rest of Hartwell's words. Then two, then three.

Jake watched it all play out in slow motion.

Someone's nervous trigger finger unleashed a staccato of gunfire.

That was all it took. Max lurched forward when the first bullet struck him in the shoulder. The next two were in the chest. After that Jake lost track as the sound of gunfire ripped through the night air. All he could do from his perch was watch Max's body collapse to the ground.

110

DANA CLUNG TO CLAIRE, PULLING HER TIGHT AGAINST HER CHEST. THE girl's hands were clamped over her ears as she screamed, unable to block out the sound of gunfire.

She'd known it was Max. She'd known the moment she'd seen Dana come down the stairs, her face filled with fear. She hadn't asked Dana to confirm it, following her to the bathroom silently.

They locked themselves inside, standing in the bathtub.

Dana did her best to hold onto the girl who was breaking apart in her arms. "It's okay. It's okay." Dana repeated the phrase over and over, unsure who she was trying to convince. "It's okay. It's over now."

YELLOW POLICE TAPE guttered in the wind, marking the perimeter of last night's deadly shooting. Agents and officers turned in their discharged weapons and began the daunting procedure of filling out weapon discharge forms. Ambulances stood stoically silent, their medics inside the farmhouse offering counseling to those still reeling from shock.

Claire refused treatment, though she was the one perhaps most in need. Especially after learning about Max's self-inflicted injuries prior to the shooting.

Once the gunfire had ceased, Claire bolted from the bathroom. Dana and the other officers had done everything they could to restrain her, but hanging onto the wiry girl was difficult. Dana's arms bore scratches and bruises as proof. In the end, it was only Jake who could subdue her.

Dana watched him whisper something in her ear, then she collapsed into his arms, folding in on herself like a paper doll as she dissolved into hysterical wailing. Claire remained in the spot where she'd collapsed just outside the front door of the farmhouse. Dana remained there, too. Kneeling by her side despite the ache in her knees.

She's lost track of how long they'd been there. Long enough for the stars in night sky to dissolve into the twilight glow of dawn. She shivered, feeling every creak in the old wooden floorboards of the farmhouse porch as first responders, officers, and agents bustled by. Despite the foil blanket the EMTs had draped around her and Claire, she couldn't escape the chill that settled in her bones.

But Dana silently vowed to stay where she was for as long as it took. She owed Claire that much for ever doubting her. First Dvita, then Claire. Dana had been wrong again. It made her question everything. Most of all, her ability to continue helping the FBI.

Jake sauntered over, hiding his exhaustion behind his Fed persona. It only slipped when he reached Dana and Claire. "We can head home now," he said quietly, reaching down to help them up. Dana took his hand, her own feeling small and cold beneath Jake's rough calloused warmth. Claire, however, remained crumbled on the floor, her legs tucked under her at awkward angles, like a newborn fawn unfamiliar with the lanky appendages.

Stooping, Jake scooped Claire into his arms. She looked hollow, brittle almost—like the stiff breeze swelling across the farmland would tear her apart as though she were made of ash. Dana understood the feeling. Losing someone so suddenly and brutally was a burden the soul wasn't equipped for. And Claire had been through it more than enough times.

Again, guilt lanced through Dana. Of course Claire was different now. It would be impossible not to be after all she'd witnessed in the past year. Dana herself had to admit that the past few years of terrifying FBI cases had changed her, too. And possibly, not for the better.

Yes, she was stronger now, and liberated by the truths she'd uncovered about her past. But it had come at a price. She'd shot someone, been shot, taken lives ... it was a different burden than what she'd carried before, but a heavy one all the same.

Her mind suddenly went to Lennox, the young cop who'd fired the first shot tonight. "What's going to happen to Lennox?" she asked Jake once he'd tucked Claire into the safety of his backseat.

Jake didn't answer until they were through the police blockade swarming with press. He finally said, "He'll face Metro's firearms discharge review board; beyond that, I don't know."

Dana glanced back to check on Claire. She was lying on her side, facing them, eyes closed, finally getting some much-needed sleep. Dana turned up the radio, letting the melancholy sound of R.E.M.'s *Everybody Hurts* drown out her words as she spoke quietly to Jake. "I couldn't see anything from the bathroom. Was the gunfire warranted?"

Jake exhaled slowly, his jaw muscles ticking. Dana watched him glance in the review at Claire before answering. "From where I was, no."

"I could hear Hartwell. He gave Max plenty of time to surrender."

"I know," Jake said. "But suicide by cop is an efficient and selfish method too many criminals choose."

Another question rested at the tip of her tongue. She wanted to know what Jake had said to Claire in the aftermath to calm her down, but she decided to wait until they were alone. Instead, she asked, "What happens now?"

"Now we all get some sleep."

Dana continued to gaze at him, until he gave her a real answer.

He sighed, rubbing the fatigue from his face at a stoplight. "Hartwell and Richter will finish up the investigation. Once all the evidence has been examined and cataloged, and the review board rules on the discharged weapons, they can close the case."

"How long will that take?"

Jake shrugged. "There's a lot of paperwork, and the media isn't going to let this go quietly." Jake glanced at Claire in the review again, his jaw still ticking with agitation.

"What are you thinking?" Dana asked, seeing the concern on his face.

"Maybe it wouldn't be such a bad idea to get out of town for a bit."

"Is that allowed?" Dana asked.

Jake cut a glare at her, keeping his voice low. "She's not a suspect."

"I know that," Dana whispered. "I'm the first to admit I was wrong. This case ..." she shook her head. "It was different from the others. And I can't shake this feeling that it's unresolved somehow." Sighing, she added. "I don't know. Maybe you're right. A change of scenery would help clear our heads."

"We have been staring at the same four walls for a while now. I know I could use some fresh air."

"What were you thinking?" she asked.

"The cabin is great this time of year."

A mix of emotions crashed over Dana at the mention of Jake's cabin. They'd been through so much there; good, and bad. But it was a flush of warm memories that filled her cheeks when she responded. "The cabin sounds perfect."

Jake reached over and took her hand from her lap. He threaded his fingers through hers, settling them on the console between them. "I was hoping you'd say that."

His grin melted the last bit of cold still clinging to her bones, and she couldn't help but smile back. "There's something I need to take care of first."

111

RELIEF SWEPT THROUGH DANA THE MOMENT SHE SPOTTED MEREDITH. Mere stood on the opposite side of the hospital door, grinning at Dana as they both waited for the metallic buzz to come, unlocking the door. The moment it happened, Dana rushed into the room, wrapping Meredith in a fierce embrace.

"I'm so glad you're okay," Dana whispered, holding her friend tight.

"Me?" Meredith leaned back so she could look at Dana. "You're the one I was worried about."

Dana waved her off. "I'm fine."

Meredith shook her head. "No, you're not. And that's okay. Working these cases can't be easy."

Dana sighed. "At least this one is over."

"And thanks to you, I'm still alive," Meredith said, tears welling in her eyes. "I truly can't thank you enough."

"You just keep getting better. That's all the thanks I need."

"I am," Meredith said, "Getting better, I mean. I owe that opportunity to you, too." She took Dana's hands. "Thank you for never giving up on me."

Dana grinned, noting the tiny ladybug charm dangling from

Meredith's wrist. It was identical to the one Dana wore on her charm bracelet. One that not too long ago had made her think she'd lost her best friend forever. Time was a funny thing.

"I still can't believe Dvita wasn't the D.C. Reaper."

"I know, me too," Dana said. "So much of this case still doesn't add up."

"I'm sorry I didn't tell you more the first time you came asking about Claire."

"Yeah, why didn't you?"

Meredith shrugged. "I've already caused you enough pain for one lifetime. I didn't want to accuse Claire when I had no proof of what was really going on. Besides, look where I am. How much weight do my accusations really hold?"

"Mere, you're my friend. You'll always be my friend. I would've believed you."

Meredith squeezed Dana's hand, grinning through tears. "You don't know how much that means to me."

Dana pulled her into a fierce hug, and it took both of them a moment to collect themselves.

"I still can't believe it was Max," Meredith said, dabbing her eyes with a tissue. "I always thought he was just a pawn in whatever Dvita and Claire were playing at. There was definitely a power struggle in their dynamic."

"I never got a chance to meet him, but I agree. I was so sure Dvita was behind it all."

"But it's over now, right?" Meredith asked.

Dana nodded. "Seems to be. There's a few loose ends Hartwell and the FBI have to tie up before they can officially close the case. Jake and I are going to take Claire and get out of town. Go to the cabin. Get some peace while the dust settles."

"That's a good idea," Meredith said. "I'm still so grateful you figured out I was a target. How did you know?"

Dana shrugged. "When I saw your room number written in Dvita's planner, I knew. Something just felt wrong in my gut. Jake always tells me to follow my instincts, so I did."

"Then I guess I owe Jake a thank you, too. You two make a good team."

Dana bit her lip. "Maybe more than that."

"What do you mean?" Meredith asked.

"Jake said he wants more."

Meredith's big blue eyes widened. "More, more? As in a relationship?"

Dana nodded through the heat burning in her cheeks.

"Is that what you want?" Meredith asked.

Dana covered her face with her hands to hide her burning cheeks but couldn't resist nodding. "Yes, I think so."

Admitting it out loud for the first time overwhelmed Dana with emotion.

Meredith squealed and pulled Dana over to the bed. Both girls pulled their knees up, grinning at each other like they used to in college when gossiping over boys. Meredith took Dana's hands and said, "Tell me everything."

112

THE COUNTRYSIDE BLURRED BY AS DANA'S OLD '83 CLASSIC RANGE
Rover chewed up the rural dirt roads. The cabin couldn't arrive soon
enough. Jake had bitten his tongue twice since they left the paved
roads of civilization behind.

"Tell me again why we decided to take your car?" he complained,
his teeth rattling with each bump the timeworn suspension failed to
absorb.

"It's a classic," Dana said, grinning as she shifted gears in her
ancient rust box.

Jake struggled against the fraying tan seatbelt that seemed to be
getting tighter by the moment. "Yes, and it would be better off in a
museum than on the road."

Claire's monotone voice drifted from the back seat. "She'll never
get rid of it. It was her father's."

Jake's eyebrows rose. "Is that true?"

"Yes," Dana replied with a sudden vulnerability that made Jake
regret his words.

This sentimental side of Dana was unexpected. The entire time
he'd known her, Jake had only seen one framed photo of her parents,
which she kept on her desk at the Smithsonian. Next to it was the

retired green pager. It too had belonged to her father. Another fact Jake had only learned after his relentless teasing.

Frowning, he made a mental note to ease up on his sarcastic nature. It was a trait he'd sharpened to perfection in the Army and often slipped out without regard. He knew Dana had thick skin and was tough enough to handle some ribbing, but she'd had to endure an entire lifetime of mockery. Jake didn't want to be the source of more.

Especially when it was merely a defense mechanism to deflect the inadequacy he often felt in her presence. Dana was by far one of the most incredible people he'd ever encountered. He was beyond grateful that they were ... well, whatever they were to each other.

He'd made it clear that he wanted more and was working on making his peace with not getting it. He would find a way to be satisfied with having Dana in his life in whatever capacity she offered.

"I'm glad we're doing this," Jake said, changing the subject.

"Me too," Dana agreed.

"You're going to love the cabin, Claire," he said, turning to face her. "First order of business, s'mores. I'll gather wood. You and Dana work on unpacking the provisions."

Claire gave him a morose nod. Considering the circumstances, it was the best he could hope for. She'd been more aloof than ever after yesterday's events, but Jake hoped some fresh air and nature would help. It always did wonders for him.

Jake turned to Dana. "You never told me; how did it go with Meredith yesterday?"

Dana kept her eyes on the road. "It went well."

"That's all I get?"

"Jake, I know how you feel about her. You're just asking to be polite."

He smirked. "Since when do I do anything to be polite?"

Even with her gazing ahead, Jake could still see Dana's signature eyeroll.

"Come on," he said. "I wouldn't ask if I didn't want to know."

Dana sighed. "Mere's doing well. She's really making progress. This last visit ... it was like old times."

"I'm glad."

Dana gave him a patronizing glance. "No, you're not."

"I am. If you're happy, I'm happy, bottom line."

The smile Dana let slip satisfied Jake's soul. He grinned back, just as the cabin came into view.

113

Sparks leapt from the flames, dancing into the gray evening sky like fireflies. Dana had always loved getting lost in the mesmerizing magic of watching fire. Her wood-burning fireplace was one of the reasons she'd chosen her home. But there was something even more wonderful about sitting next to a campfire. Especially given the company.

Full of copious amounts of hot cocoa and s'mores, Claire had retired inside for a nap before the planned *Ghostbusters* movie marathon.

Jake and Dana remained by the fire, adding bourbon to their hot cocoa, and clinking their tin mugs together in silent celebration. They had survived another case.

The scars from this one would linger, of that Dana had no doubt. But the important thing was they'd made it to the other side. Together.

They sat by the fire in satisfying silence watching the logs glow into ash. Dana snuggled deeper into her jacket as the temperature began to drop. It was remarkably colder under the thick canopy of trees than it had been in town where they'd stopped for groceries.

"Looks like I need to replenish the firewood," Jake said, standing from his Adirondack chair to grab his axe.

Dana joined him. "I'm glad we came to the cabin," she said. "I think it'll help Claire."

"I hope so," Jake replied as they walked into the woods. "I think she really loved Max. Losing someone like that ... she's going to need our help to get through it."

Dana nodded, her mind still churning with details of the case. It was always hard to set an investigation aside when it was over, but this one felt different. She still couldn't shake the feeling that they'd missed something.

"I can hear you thinking over there," Jake said as he swung his axe at a downed tree.

"I know I should let it go, but it just doesn't fit."

"What part?"

"All of it. Starting with Max and Dvita. They couldn't be more different. Age, race, height, build. They'd never be mistaken for each other. But the witness accounts don't fit their descriptions. The only matching details were a hooded figure fleeing the scenes."

Jake swung the axe again. "Witnesses get it wrong sometimes. Especially in heavily publicized cases like this one. They're influenced by the media. Say they saw something vague to feel like they're part of the investigation."

"It's not just that," Dana argued. "Each crime scene seemed different. Other than the scythe, there wasn't a clear signature. The first two murders were brutal, more physical than the others. The third was more skilled, with just a single death blow. The fourth was a miss if we're to believe Meredith was the target. The fifth completely deviated from the MO with Dvita and the sixth death was suicide by cop if we're to believe that was Max's goal."

Jake stopped chopping wood. "You still think there was more than one Unsub?"

"I think it's possible. The Alchemist did, too."

"Did you ever discuss that with Richter?"

"Yes, but I was so fixated on Dvita I didn't allow myself to fully explore any other alternatives. I don't know. I guess it could've been Dvita and Max ..."

Jake shrugged. "Anything's possible."

Dana stood silently stewing on her thoughts, unable to set them down despite wanting to. "You know, if Lennox hadn't shot Max, we'd be looking for a seventh victim right now." Dana couldn't push past the obvious. "I think they were saving Claire for last. I mean think about it. She and Max were supposedly in love, but Dvita always had this possessive vibe about him when it came to Claire. What if this was all just some big game between them and Claire was the prize?"

Seeing her distress, Jake walked over and put an arm around Dana's shoulders. "Claire's safe. She's here, with us. We may never fully understand this one, but the important thing is, it's over. Let's just enjoy this reprieve while we can. We've earned it. In fact," he reached into her back pocket and grabbed her cell phone. "Let's turn this off so we can do what we came out here to do."

"Hey!" she yelled, trying to take it back but Jake just raised the phone up higher, out of her reach.

Once he'd powered it off, he handed it back. "Already turned mine off," he said when she started to argue. "We came here to unplug and get some peace, right?"

Dana nodded, stowing her phone back in her pocket before picking up the bundle of kindling she'd been collecting. Jake went back to the log he'd cleared. Together they returned to the campfire with their bounty.

"There's one more question I've been wanting to ask," Dana said as she stacked the wood once Jake split it into manageable pieces. "What did you say to Claire at the farmhouse when she was trying to get to Max?"

"I told her she'd see him again."

Dana paused, her eyes meeting Jake's. "As in an afterlife?"

Jake smirked. "I'm not getting into a religious debate with you, Doc."

"That's not what this is."

Finally, he put the axe down and looked at Dana. "Yes, I meant heaven, the place we go when we die. I know you don't believe in that—"

"Claire doesn't either," Dana interrupted.

"Maybe you don't know her as well as you think," Jake offered.

"What does that mean?"

"Just that she might surprise you if you stopped trying to anticipate and analyze her every reaction."

"I don't do that," she argued, though the defensiveness in her voice betrayed her.

Jake laughed. "Whatever you need to tell yourself, Doc."

Shock left Dana momentarily slack jawed, but her surprise was quickly replaced with indignation. "Is that seriously how you see me?"

"Listen, your mind is an incredible thing. But you overthink everything."

Her hands flew to her hips. "Like what?"

"Like us, for one."

Dana had walked into that trap and was at a loss for words, but Jake wasn't done. He stalked toward her until she was pinned between him and the wood pile. Grinning, he brushed a stray curl from her face. "And more importantly, Claire doesn't have a problem with us being together."

Dana needed to close her mouth before something flew in it, but she was dumbfounded. She tried to step back and break the connection. She couldn't think clearly with Jake's hands on her shoulders, but he refused to let go. "You asked her?"

"No, but she's not blind. She knows both of us too well to not have a sense of what's going on. She said she's happy for us."

"Really? When?"

Jake shrugged. "After what happened to Max. You were with Meredith and Claire was oscillating between despair and despondency. In one of her more lucid moments, we had a bit of a heart to heart, talked about feelings and life being fleeting and all that." He shrugged. "She gave me the green light. Said life's too short not to follow your heart."

"Why didn't you tell me?"

He huffed a laugh, his beautiful mouth quirking up at the corners. "We had a lot going on. Besides I was starting to get the feeling you weren't interested."

It was Dana's turn to grin. "Does the Bureau know how bad your instincts are?"

"What does that mean?"

"It means you're an idiot," Dana said, grabbing Jake's collar and pressing her lips to his.

When they came up for air, Jake's eyes glowed like twin blue flames ready to devour her. "Are you sure?" Fear. Anticipation. Desire. They wrapped each word he whispered, his heart hammering against her chest.

She grinned, reaching up to place her palm over his heart. "I want the same thing you do, Jake."

His hand covered hers as he let his forehead press against hers, his eyes closing as though he were in pain, but when Jake opened them, she'd never seen him look so elated. His breathing was shallow and fast as he shook his head, a grin fighting through a turmoil of emotions to grace his lips. She watched his throat roll before he spoke. "You don't know how long I've waited to hear that."

Then his lips crashed into hers and her feet left the ground.

114

To Jake, it felt like the movie would never end. He didn't know how he'd made it through the first *Ghostbusters* film. But surviving the second one might actually kill him. He wanted the river of ectoplasm to just swallow the city and be done with it already.

He couldn't help it. With Dana sitting on the same couch, he'd reverted into a damn teenager trying to reel in his emotions. The problem wasn't that Dana was on the couch, it was that Claire sat between them. Knees drawn up to her chin, merrily munching popcorn, oblivious to the ridiculous smile Jake couldn't scrub off his face if his life depended on it.

Dana, however, had not missed his schoolboy smile or the uncomfortable way he shifted every time she leaned her head back against his arm. He'd stretched it along the back of the couch unable to stop himself from touching her. But the feel of her silken hair slipping through his fingers was torture. And she knew it.

From the sultry smile tugging at her lips, he could tell she was enjoying it.

Just you wait, Gray.

Jake was already plotting all the slow and torturous ways he and Dana would spend tonight if this cursed movie ever ended.

When Dana kissed him and said the words he'd been waiting to hear he'd died right there on the spot. The man he was now was different, changed, reborn. He'd emerged into a world full of new possibilities. It was equal parts thrilling and terrifying. But the fact that it was all happening here, at the cabin, meant even more.

Many a sleepless night brought Jake back here to the memories of all their false starts and near misses. But this was a second chance to get things right. A fresh start.

When he closed his eyes and let himself imagine him and Dana finding their way to each other, it was always in this place. It was their hallowed ground. Where they'd stood and fought for each other, time and time again.

Finally, the war was over. *Now if only the damn movie would end!*

115

Mercifully, the movie ended, and Claire called it a night.

Dana began collecting the dishes, but Jake intervened, tossing them unceremoniously into the trash before sweeping Dana off her feet.

"Jake!" Dana laughed, doing her best to keep her voice down as Jake carried her to his bedroom. "We can't do this here."

"Nope, I waited through not one, but two terrible movies. You said this is what you want and there's no take backs."

Hand to her chest, she pretended to be offended. "*Ghostbusters* is *not* terrible."

"It is when it's standing between you and the woman of your dreams."

Dana practically swooned. *Lord help her.* She was no match for Jake Shepard when he turned on the charm. "I'm the woman of your dreams?"

"And beyond," he crooned, wrapping his arms around her waist, and pulling her in for a kiss, which quickly escalated until she pulled away, panting for air. "Wait," she breathed against his neck as he pinned her to the wall, her legs hitched around his waist.

She could see it took herculean effort, but Jake stopped, dropping his forehead against her shoulder as he tried to regain control. "Having regrets already?" he asked.

She knew he was being sarcastic, but she knew him well enough to realize there was always a bit of truth in his jabs.

Dana grabbed Jake's face with both hands, relishing the feel of stubble against her palms. "Jake, I have no regrets when it comes to you."

His stormy gaze bore into hers. "But?"

"But maybe we should take it slow?"

A broad smile spread across his face. "Dana, I don't think it's possible for two people to move any slower than we have."

She laughed. "Okay, you're right. But what about Claire?"

Jake nuzzled her neck. "I thought we cleared that up."

"We did, but she's in the next room. Don't you think we should tell her first?"

Jake suddenly shifted positions, hauling Dana over his shoulder like a fireman. "Let's go wake her up and tell her right now!"

"Jake!" Dana smacked his ass, trying to contain her laughter. "Put me down, I'm serious."

Relenting, he dropped her carefully onto the bed and took a seat next to her. Jake threaded his fingers through hers and sweetly kissed Dana's hand. "Tell me how you want to handle it."

Dana bit her lip, fighting the tornado of butterflies in her stomach. "Let's tell her tomorrow morning."

"Okay. What does that mean for tonight?" he asked.

Dana unleashed a grin that made her face hurt. "It means, take me to bed or lose me forever."

Jake's eyes glowed with desire. "Did you just quote my favorite movie?"

Dana nodded, unable to stop smiling.

"Just when I didn't think I could love you more," Jake whispered, scooping Dana into his arms.

116

Dana's pale skin glowed blue in the slash of moonlight spilling in through the bedroom window. Jake stripped away her top, his fingers trembling with restraint. He'd waited too long to rush. She stepped closer, out of the moonlight, to slip her hands beneath his shirt. Jake yanked it over his head, eager to feel her touch.

She grinned, standing on her toes to kiss him. It was deep, passionate, and nearly his undoing. Taking control, Jake walked Dana backward until her back was pressed against the wall. Bathed in moonlight once more, Jake kissed a slow path from her jaw to the hollow at her throat. When he reached the silver scar at her collarbone he paused, flicking his eyes up to ask permission. Dana tilted her head back further in invitation.

Jake slowly pressed his lips to the delicate flesh of her scar tissue where the bullet had entered. His bullet. He hadn't known it then, but that horrible moment years ago was when it happened. When he fell for her. The brilliant, fearless doctor had stolen his heart.

He still hated the memory. Hated that he'd ever caused her pain. All he wanted now was to kiss every inch of her, to erase every scar and painful memory and replace it with this. Them. Passion.

The ache building inside him was exquisite as he kissed his way down her arm, stopping to press his lips to the tender flesh of another scar on her palm. He looked her in the eye as he did so, knowing she was remembering it, too. The night she'd cut herself in his kitchen and finally let him in. That night she'd peeled away another layer of his armor.

A tear rolled down Dana's cheek and Jake wiped it away, pulling her closer. She whispered his name like a prayer, and his lips swallowed the word with fervor. Jake carried her to the bed. Lying back, he settled her on top of him, letting her take control.

Dana ran her hands over his chest, making his eyelids heavy. But he wanted to see, wanted to burn every second of this into his memory. She traced his scars, a patchwork of pain that covered most of his chest and back. But she didn't shy away. She never had.

It was in this very room where she'd reached out and touched him for the first time. Jake remembered the moment with searing clarity. It was the first time he hadn't wanted to cringe away from the guilt and pain that flooded him each time someone bore witness to his scars; his violent past. But Dana's touch was liberating. He'd never wanted her more than that night.

It had killed Jake to walk away from her then. Bliss overwhelmed him now, knowing he'd never have to walk away again.

Dana leaned forward to kiss him; her gorgeous brown hair draped around them like a veil shutting out the rest of the world. Jake could stay here forever, in this undiluted sanctuary, worshiping at her altar until the end of time.

When her nimble fingers fumbled with his belt, he shifted, pulling Dana beneath him. She lay on the bed, grinning up at him with unrestrained desire.

Unspoken emotion swelled within him as he thought of all they'd endured—the pain, loss, heartache—it somehow all felt worth it in this moment. Grinning back at her, he picked up where she'd left off on his belt, but a flash of light stopped him.

Dana paused too, both of them staring at each other in confusion as the light grew brighter, until the source bore into the room with blinding ferocity—*headlights*.

"Who knows we're here?" Dana asked, sitting up and covering herself with the sheets.

"No one," Jake said, quickly climbing out of bed, Dana right behind him.

They both dressed quickly to the sound of car doors closing outside the cabin.

"Get your gun," Jake said, grabbing his own from the nightstand. "Wake Claire."

117

DANA TRIED TO REMAIN CALM AS SHE MOVED DOWN THE HALL, BUT SHE was distracted by the sound of Jake's booted footsteps moving in the opposite direction. The cabin was small enough that she could see straight through to the kitchen, where Jake now stood. In the darkness, Dana could just make out his silhouette as he used the nose of his gun to move the curtains and peer out the small window toward the front porch.

Her heart pounded. *What's going on? Who's here?*

The loud knock on the front door forced Dana to refocus. Feeling the weight of her gun in her hands, she took a deep breath and pushed open the door to Claire's room without knocking.

A burst of cold air and an empty bed greeted her. Dana stood in the doorway, staring at the open window, curtains fluttering inward. Claire was gone.

Dana ran to the window. Peering out she saw the black and white squad car. The sight made her heart drop.

Cops appearing at your door in the middle of the night ... it was the modern equivalent of the Grim Reaper.

Male voices drifted down the hall, pulling Dana back to reality.

She darted out of the room, racing toward Jake. "She's gone!" she shouted. "Claire's gone!"

Jake turned toward her, revealing their unexpected guest. Hartwell stood in the doorway; his face hardened. "We need to go, now!"

"What?" Dana blinked in shock. Had he not heard her? "Claire isn't in her room. We need to find her."

"That's why I'm here," Hartwell growled. "Claire is dangerous. I need to get you two out of here right now."

Dana shook her head, unable to comprehend what was happening. "We're not leaving without Claire."

Jake spoke calmly. "Hartwell's discovered new evidence in the Reaper case. They found letters from Max and Claire in a stolen news van Max was hiding out in."

Dana looked at him, the fog in her mind starting to clear. "It's not over?"

"Not by a long shot," Hartwell muttered. "Claire's been behind it the whole time."

Dana shook her head. "No, that's impossible."

"I assure you it's not!" Hartwell yelled. "And if you picked up your damn phones you'd understand, but there's no time now. You're just lucky Meredith knew where this place was. Now come on, let's get the hell out of here while we can!" Hartwell marched onto the porch and down the steps. The lure of Meredith making Dana follow.

"Meredith's here?" Jake asked, following Dana outside.

"That must be how Hartwell found us," she replied. "I told her we were coming up here."

Jake switched on his phone; the unmistakable ping of missed calls and messages began coming through. She was sure hers was the same, but she'd left it in the bedroom.

The cold night air bit her skin making her shiver as she took in the eerie scene. Her mind was still trying to catch up. Hartwell was halfway back to his car when Dana spoke up. "We're not leaving without Claire."

Hartwell whirled around, impatience filling his voice. "What don't you understand?" he shouted. "Claire is the Reaper!"

"That's not possible!" Dana yelled back.

Hartwell turned toward his cruiser and motioned to whoever was inside. Officer Lennox got out and opened the back door, helping a woman from the backseat.

Dana gasped. "Mere?"

"I'm sorry, Dana. It's true. You need to listen to them and come with us, please! It's not safe! Claire's been behind this the whole time!"

Tears welled in Dana's eyes. "You're lying!"

Meredith shook her head, eyes pleading. "I wish I were."

"We don't have time for this!" Hartwell yelled. "We're leaving, now, even if that means I have to haul you both out of here in cuffs."

Dana watched him start toward them, but a flash of silver caught her eye. By the time she realized what it was, it was too late. The axe swung in a vicious arc, landing a sickening blow to Hartwell's back. He went down, but rolled, drawing his weapon. Dana and Jake did the same, but the axe moved faster, already arcing for Hartwell's chest.

A spray of bloody foam spurted into the air like pink mist dancing in the beam of the headlights. The axe remained lodged in the sucking chest wound, as Hartwell lay still on the ground. If he wasn't dead already, he would be shortly from the whistling gurgle that indicated blood rushing into his punctured lung.

Dana was frozen, Jake just as still by her side as they watched the hooded figure standing over Hartwell tilt back their head to bask in the moonlight. Dana knew what she was seeing but every fiber of her being fought to deny the truth. Even when the hood fell back, even when the wind blew the dark black hair away from the face in front of her to reveal cat eye glasses and that familiar smile.

"No," Dana whispered. She said it again and again because this wasn't Claire in front of her. This was someone else—*something else*—wearing her skin, using her voice. It had to be. Claire would never do this.

Jake's voice pulled Dana from her shock. "Claire, put your hands up!"

But she did no such thing. She knelt next to Hartwell's body, giggling when she came up with his gun aimed directly at them.

Meredith screamed and Lennox began shouting orders along with Jake. Too many voices filled the air, demanding Claire's surrender. Jake's gun was trained on her, but Dana began to lower hers.

"Dana ..." Jake warned, his voice drawn across gravel. "Don't."

But she'd already made up her mind. If she could get through to Claire, she could end this without further bloodshed, and Dana had to be the one to do it.

Slowly, she set her gun on the porch rail and put her hands up, cautiously walking down the stairs. "Claire, I know this isn't your fault. I know you would never do this if you didn't have to. This wasn't of your own free will. We can figure it out. Just talk to me. You know I'll understand."

JAKE'S HEART was pounding so wildly he couldn't make out what Dana was saying, only that she was in his way now, blocking his shot as she moved closer and closer to Claire. Glancing around him he evaluated his surroundings, searching for anything to help him end this. That's when he noticed Lennox, standing uselessly by Meredith's side, weaponless.

Rage flooded his veins when he realized why. The rookie cop had handed over his service weapon after the shooting. *He shouldn't even be here!* Hartwell should've known better than to bring someone who couldn't back him up. But a glance in the fallen cop's direction showed he'd paid the ultimate price for his poor decision.

Jake refused to let his and Dana's fate be the same.

Think, Jake! Think!

But he was out of time. He saw it all happen in his mind moments before it played out in real time, powerless to stop it. While trying to talk Claire down, Dana had gotten too close. Claire seized her chance, lunging forward with Hartwell's weapon. Dana tried to duck but Claire was fast. Fueled by the adrenalin from her kill she whipped Hartwell's Glock 19 into the side of Dana's head. In her stunned state, Dana was easily overpowered.

Now Claire held all the cards, and she knew it.

Grinning maniacally, Claire's eyes darted wildly from side to side, and she pressed the gun to Dana's head. Jake froze, helplessly watching as Dana's tear-filled eyes begged him with silent desperation not to shoot.

"Claire!" Jake yelled into the night. "Don't do this."

"It's already done," she sang, her voice strange and ethereal. "Seven must sleep for all to rise." She repeated the phrase over and over, breaking Jake's heart with each word. The Claire he knew was gone, replaced by some sort of psychotic fiend that couldn't be reasoned with. The girl he knew was lost. And if Jake didn't do something soon, he'd lose Dana, too.

Dana was still conscious, but even in the moonlight, Jake could see the blood slicking her hair. A splotch smeared across her cheek as Claire stroked the barrel of the gun from Dana's temple to her chin, whispering something he couldn't make out in another language.

"Vita est morte est vita."

Dana shook her head. "Claire, please listen to me. This isn't you. I know you didn't do this on purpose. Let me help you."

Claire laughed. "I don't need your help. I did what had to be done. Seven must sleep for all to rise."

She moved toward the police car, dragging Dana with her. Jake's gun traced their movement, his finger never leaving the trigger as he struggled for breath. He couldn't think straight. Not with Claire in his sights. It was Claire, but it wasn't. He knew that, but the internal struggle fought against every instinct telling him to take the shot.

It was Dana who stopped him. "Don't," she mouthed. "Don't."

"Claire, don't do this," Jake warned. "I don't want to shoot."

Dana shook her head wildly. "She's not going to hurt me, Jake. Right, Claire? Tell him you won't hurt me. I know you're still in there, Claire. Just tell me what you need."

"The keys," she sneered, edging even closer to the cruiser.

"Here!" Lennox shouted, catching Claire's attention as he dangled the keys. He and Meredith had been inching closer to the porch.

They now stood only a few feet from Jake. "I have the keys," Lennox said. "Just take them and go."

"Throw them here," Claire demanded.

Lennox looked to Jake. He nodded and Lennox tossed the keys toward Claire and Dana. They landed near Dana's feet. Now was Jake's chance. Claire was bending for the keys. Dana just needed to lean the opposite way and he'd have a clear shot. He locked eyes with Dana jerking his chin to the left, but she met his gaze with forlorn defiance, and shook her head.

"Move," he mouthed, willing her to listen just this once so they could end this.

But she stood still, her eyes never leaving Jake's as she mouthed two words that shattered his heart. "I'm sorry."

Her words spurned Jake into action. This was not how their story ended. Jake lunged, grabbing Dana's discarded weapon, and calling Lennox's name as he leapt down the steps and tossed him the gun. Lennox caught it, but the gun-shy officer was too slow. He took aim, but Claire's finger was already on the trigger.

A deafening pop tore through the night and Lennox dropped to the ground.

118

MEREDITH SHRIEKED. HELPLESS WITH HER HANDS CUFFED BEHIND HER, she could do nothing but watch the young police officer to her right take a bullet to the chest. He hit the ground, his final sound a sickening wheeze as he fell face down into the wet leaves.

Blood seeped through the back of his pale blue uniform shirt like a gruesome ink blot. He hadn't been wearing a vest. From the amount of blood, it would take a miracle to save him.

Shouting drew Meredith's attention back to the scene. Claire was at the car now, Dana a living shield blocking Jake's shot. Meredith stood there trembling as she listened to Jake begging for Dana's life.

"Drop the gun, Claire!" Jake screamed. "Do not make me shoot you!"

"Jake, don't do it!" Dana pleaded. "She won't hurt me. Tell him, Claire. Just let us help you." Dana caught Meredith's eye and changed tactics. "Mere, tell her. We can help her like we helped you."

"Th-that's right," Meredith stammered. "Dana will help you."

Claire laughed. "She didn't help you, Meredith. You live in a cage. That will never be me. And you shouldn't even be here. I sent someone to take care of you." Claire cackled. "Your death would've been a mercy killing. But somehow you always survive. But maybe not this time. Not when I take Dana from you. Your little good luck charm."

Jake nodded to Meredith like he wanted her to keep talking, but she was out of words. What Claire said rang true. What kind of a life did Meredith have? Nothing could make up for what she'd done, the lives she'd taken. She'd always be locked away at St. Elizabeth's or someplace worse.

She looked at Claire, frightened when she recognized her own reflection in the wild-eyed girl. Meredith had once been her, determined and deranged. Driven by the infallible belief she was serving a higher power. She knew the seduction of that pull, just like she knew Jake and Dana would never be able to reach the girl they'd once believed her to be.

They were out of time.

Claire reached for the door, releasing her hold on Dana.

Dana tried to stand her ground, tried to shield Claire from the shot Jake would surely take, but Claire kicked her out of the way.

For one silent heartbeat, Claire stood at the open door of the police cruiser, Dana crumpled at her feet, gun pointed at Jake. In the next, an explosion of gunfire ripped through the night.

Meredith didn't feel the pain at first; only Jake's arms around her as she fell, the shocked look of horror on his face as he called her name. But she barely heard it as the bed of damp leaves rose up to cradle her head.

Her chest felt warm as she stared at the leaves, at ease knowing she'd done the right thing. Dana had saved Meredith time and time again. This time, she got to repay the favor by saving the man that meant everything to Dana.

It was the right choice. The only choice.

Dana and Jake could have a life.

Meredith's was over a long time ago.

She let her eyes close, clinging to the peaceful redemption of paying one more debt before leaving the world behind.

119

GUN FIRE AND SQUEALING TIRES ERUPTED ALL AROUND DANA BUT SHE only heard the sound of her own screaming as she lay on the ground watching Meredith's eyes close. She wanted to crawl to her, but each time she moved the world swayed with dizzying ferocity.

Dana forced herself to her knees only to retch violently. She tasted bile as her vision tunneled in and out. Bright orbs of light dancing to and fro, making the gruesome scene in front of her even more surreal.

Then Jake was there, his arms around her, pulling her into his lap. He had his phone to his ear, barking orders. "I repeat, two officers down. Three injured. Where are my buses?"

He rattled off codes and terms she didn't understand, all the while holding her in his arms. She looked up at his tear-streaked face, wondering if she was crying, too.

How could she not be?

All around her, bodies lay fallen and motionless.

Even Claire's.

Dana forced herself to look at the body of the girl she'd once loved. It was hunched against a bloodstained airbag of the police cruiser nearby. Dana gazed at her through the spiderweb of glass where a single bullet hole punctured the windshield.

Claire looked like a broken doll. But as Dana stared at her and felt nothing, she feared she was the one who'd truly been broken.

That's when she heard a snap, followed by the sorrowful whine of wood giving way. She looked up to see the tree Claire had crashed the cruiser into lumbering toward them in slow motion. She raised her arm, pointing toward it, begging Jake to look. He did. But she was too late. All she could do was close her eyes.

120

JAKE'S HEAD POUNDED FROM THE RELENTLESS WHIRL OF AMBULANCE lights, painting the forest red and white. Only two remained. The one carrying Lennox had sped off immediately, hoping to get the critically wounded officer the lifesaving care he needed.

Another had rushed off with Claire, shortly after. The single shot Jake fired had hit its mark, wounding Claire without hitting any vital organs, just as he'd intended. However, the impact she'd sustained after she lost control of the car and slammed into a tree left her with a shattered pelvis and legs. The medics had assured him she would live, but she would probably never walk again, thanks to the massive tree that had crushed the front end of the squad car.

Jake and Dana had barely escaped the tree's wrath themselves. If Dana hadn't called it to Jake's attention, they would've been crushed. Thankfully, he'd pulled them away just in time.

The two ambulances that remained held Meredith and Hartwell. Only Hartwell's flashed lights of urgency and hope. Meredith's bus was as silent and still as the cloth draped body inside.

Jake still couldn't believe what she'd done—sacrificing herself to save him. He'd never liked her, never been willing to look past what she'd done that day on the hill, especially because of all the pain

C. J. CROSS

she'd caused Dana. But how could he hate her now? She'd traded her life for his. Yet somehow Dana was still the one hurt in the end.

Jake had held Dana upright while they loaded Meredith's lifeless body into the ambulance. She hadn't even cried. She just stood there, numb and broken—a mirror image of the torment Jake felt. It was only sheer instinct that kept him going. The Army had instilled that in him. The ability to put one foot in front of the other no matter what, compartmentalizing the chaos around him to deal with later.

With Hartwell finally stabilized, the EMTs announced they were leaving. Leaving Dana where she sat on the porch, Jake jogged over to squeeze the officer's hand as they loaded him.

"You're gonna pull through," Jake said.

"Damn right," Hartwell wheezed, still trying to bark orders to the officers on scene. He'd been wearing his vest when he was attacked. It was likely the only reason he was still alive. It had deflected the first blow and protected his vital organs enough on the second strike that he'd only sustained a punctured lung and a chest wound.

Jake thumped on the back of the bus, sending his prayers for a safe and swift journey to the hospital. He watched the taillights fade into the gray morning as the vehicle lumbered down the dirt road away from the cabin.

He and Hartwell had a tumultuous past, but in the end, Jake owed Hartwell his life. If he hadn't gone the extra mile to race out here and warn them, it might very well be Jake and Dana in the back of the silent ambulance.

Inhaling deeply, Jake steeled himself to face the rest of the police swarming his property. He knew the drill. They'd need statements from him and Dana, though she was in no condition to give one. She had a lump the size of a baseball on her head and a concussion to go with it. Not to mention vertigo from the gun being fired so close to her ear.

The laceration where Claire had struck her with the Glock 19 was superficial at least and had already been stitched up. Though it was the wounds Jake couldn't see that worried him most.

Dana lost Meredith and Claire today. Her world had been rocked and might never be the same.

374

Jake returned to her side, sitting next to her on the porch steps. She let him put his arm around her and didn't resist when he gently pulled her head to rest on his shoulder. But she didn't say anything. She hadn't since the felled tree silenced the forest.

His phone rang for the hundredth time. Jake saw Richter's name on his caller ID and knew he needed to answer. Kissing the top of Dana's head, he stood to answer the call.

"Shepard."

"Jake, I know you're in the thick of it up there, but there's been a new development in the Reaper case."

"You're kidding me," Jake muttered. *Would this never end?*

"I wish I were. Hartwell filled you in on the notes we found in Max Durnin's stolen news van?"

"Briefly."

"Well, it got me thinking. I went back to Dvita's house, and we found the mother lode."

"I don't understand," Jake said. "Hartwell came here telling us Claire was the Reaper."

"Not just Claire. All of them. You have to see it to believe it. How soon can you get back to the city? We need Dr. Gray's expertise."

Jake glanced back at Dana. "Richter, she's in no shape to assist with an investigation right now. She just watched her best friend die, while her colleague held her at gunpoint."

"I know, and I wouldn't ask if it wasn't dire," Richter explained. "I'll send you some photos so you can see what I mean."

Jake exhaled, scrubbing a hand over his face. "Alright, but I'm not making any promises. Right now, I'm focused on wrapping up this crime scene and getting Dana home."

"No," Richter said. "That's what I'm trying to tell you. You can't bring her home."

"What? Why not?"

"Jake, just look at the photos."

121

"ARE YOU SURE?" JAKE ASKED AGAIN. "WE DON'T HAVE TO DO THIS IF you're not ready."

Dana kept her eyes trained on the road ahead. "When are you ever ready to find out how deeply you've been betrayed?"

Jake pulled up in front of Dvita's house, finding a spot on the street among the other police and federal vehicles. He shut off the engine and turned to her. "Look at me."

She did.

"It hasn't even been twenty-four hours. Whatever BAU found inside, it'll still be there tomorrow. We can go home, get some rest, and come back with clear eyes."

"I can't go home."

"My home," he corrected, reaching over the console to take her hand. "It's yours for however long you need."

She pulled out of his grasp and opened the car door, muttering, "I just want to get this over with."

Jake followed Dana into Dvita's house. It was swarming with agents, officers, and forensics. Richter greeted them at the entrance to the large home office. "This way," he said, ushering them toward the

GIRL BETRAYED

wall of built-in shelves lined with an inordinate amount of leather-bound books. It reminded Jake of a law library.

Richter walked ahead of them, removing a book, and pushing a button behind it. Jake heard a click and watched the bookshelf creak open, revealing a hidden room behind it.

"Christ," Jake muttered. The room was straight out of a horror movie. The walls lined with pages of love letters, newspaper clippings, drawings of the Grim Reaper, Latin phrases, and photographs, all of the same woman. The only thing missing was the anarchy symbol and a sacrificial altar to the devil.

Jake had seen some strange things in his day, but this might top it all.

"Who is she?" Dana asked, pointing to the dark haired girl in all the photographs.

"Annabelle Sorkin. She drowned ten years ago while sailing on the Chester River. It was ruled an accident, but her family maintains it was a suicide. She was undergoing hypnotherapy for depression at the time."

"Let me guess," Jake said. "Dvita was her therapist."

"Bingo."

Dana moved past Jake to the shrine built around the photograph of the beautiful raven-haired woman. "She looks just like Claire," Dana whispered more to herself than anyone, but Jake heard and had to agree. The similarities were eerily alike.

He watched as Dana scanned the lines of poetry that were written sporadically around the room in large red letters. It looked like a child had taken a crayon and scrawled the eerie words there.

Dana read a line out loud. "My darling—my life and my bride, in her sepulchre there by the sea—in her tomb by the sounding sea." She turned to face Richter. "This is Edgar Allen Poe's poem. Annabel Lee."

"Correct," Richter said, sharing a look with Dana that told Jake they both understood something he didn't.

"What am I not getting?" Jake asked.

"Poe's poem about lost love is widely regarded as the anthem of necromancy." Dana moved around the room to read another line of

377

poetry. "And so, all the night-tide, I lie down by the side of my darling." She looked at the bewildered room of agents. "Lying down beside the dead body in the tomb hints at necrophilia."

"Christ," Jake muttered again.

"Exactly," Richter said. "And look at this."

He led Dana back to the small desk in the corner that acted as an altar of sorts. Annabelle Sorkin's framed photo sat atop, surrounded by a mound of melted candles. Richter pulled open a drawer that had been hidden by the wax. Inside were a collection of bones.

"These are human remains," Dana said. She looked at Richter. "Annabelle Sorkin's?"

"That's what we believe."

Dana's eyes lit with the excitement of a theory. "He was trying to bring her back! That's what the Reaper murders were. He needed seven sacrifices. Seven must sleep for all to rise. Dvita was trying to raise the dead and bring her back. He was in love with her."

"It seems so." Richter said, walking to another small table in the room. "We found several diaries where he details the intimate relationship between them."

Jake felt his stomach turn. "The girl in the photograph looks like she's barely nineteen. Dvita was in his seventies. Whatever sick twisted game he played with the vulnerable girl backfired and she killed herself, leaving him remorse stricken and what, deranged enough to think he could bring her back by hypnotizing his patients into a murder pact?"

"Precisely," Richter said. "He details it all right here," he said, pointing to what looked like a scrapbook with written pages pasted into it. "Right down to how he chose which patients to target."

Dana flipped through the book, her gloved fingers shaking as she read the words Dvita had stolen from his patient's tragic pasts.

Norton Hayes – My son was stillborn. That's when it all started. The darkness. The addiction.

Kylie Marx - Losing my father nearly killed me. I did everything I could to numb the pain.

Cash Holloway – My girlfriend died in a car accident. I was driving.

My parents pulled me out of school after that, but that just made my depression worse.

Max Durnin – My mother died giving birth to me. I never met her, but I feel the void where she's supposed to be. It's like an anchor and I don't know how to swim.

Meredith Kincaid – I don't deserve forgiveness for all I've done. And those who give it to me make my guilt even heavier.

When Dana got to the page about Claire, she fought against the bile burning her throat.

Claire Townsend – I miss her every day. I'm the only one who knew her. I'm the only one who cares that she died. When I lost her, I lost a part of myself. But I won't rest until I'm reunited with her.

Tears stung Dana's eyes as she realized the pain Claire had been hiding all this time. She knew watching Sadie die had scarred Claire, but she hadn't understood the depth until now.

"They all had the same vulnerabilities. Childhood traumas, deep loss and depression that made them loners, prone to addiction and influence."

"He preyed on these people," Dana said, her voice tight.

"He did," Richter said. "We believe through hypnosis, he was able to convince them of his cause, that sacrificing themselves was the right thing to do, because they'd all come back in the end, renewed, reborn with a clean slate."

"Why did it keep happening after he was dead?" Jake asked.

"Because the damage was done," Dana said, without tearing her eyes from the book. "Dvita had already poisoned their minds to do his bidding." She looked at Richter. "It's why the profile never fit. There were multiple Unsubs."

He nodded. "Turns out you were right. We now believe Dvita killed Hayes. Kylie Marx killed Cash Holloway. Max killed Kylie, then Dvita, then himself; suicide by cop, which he confesses to Claire in the letter we found in his car."

"What about Claire?" Jake asked. "What was her role in all of this?"

"This is where it gets interesting," Richter said. "According to

Max's letter, it sounded like Claire was orchestrating the whole thing."

"That doesn't make any sense," Jake argued. "Dvita is obviously the master mind. Look at this place. Claire's the only one who didn't kill anyone in this Reaper scenario."

"That's not true," Dana said, staring at him. "She thought she killed Hartwell. He was the seventh. And she ordered the assassination on Mere at the hospital."

"That makes no sense," Jake said. "Why wouldn't Dvita plan to be the last one standing so he could bring back Annabelle?"

"I think that was his plan, but Max and Claire had other plans." Richter handed Dana his phone. On it was a photograph of a scythe with the same Latin inscription on the blade as all the others. It was in a small nondescript room surrounded by boxes, but Dana recognized it immediately. "That's my attic."

"We found the seventh and final scythe there."

Jake swore. "That's how she did it!"

"Did what?" Dana asked.

"The night she snuck out to meet Kylie and Max, she said she snuck out the window, but I knew she was lying because I had security cameras set up. The window never opened, but Claire came and went somehow. Is there access to the attic from your guest room?"

Dana nodded. "Through the closet."

"We believe she was saving the final scythe for you, Dr. Gray," Richter said, handing a copy of another letter to Dana. "This was found in Max Durnin's stolen vehicle as well. We believe Claire wrote this one. We just need Dr. Gray to identify the handwriting."

Dana read a few lines before her hands began shaking too badly to continue. "It's her handwriting," Dana whispered, a choked sob slipping free.

Jake intervened, taking the letter from her. "That's enough."

"I'm sorry," Richter said as Jake escorted Dana out of the house of horrors.

122

THE SUN WAS SETTING AS DANA WALKED OUT OF THE PRECINCT ON Indiana Avenue. She was surprised to see Jake standing on the curb, his silhouette cutting a sharp line against the burnt orange backdrop of D.C. at sunset. His interview had been over hours ago. The fact that he was still wearing the FBI sweats he'd changed into after surrendering his clothes as evidence told her he hadn't gone home yet. "I told you not to wait," she said as he opened the car door for her.

"You did," he answered. "I waited anyway."

"Jake, I don't have the energy for this."

"Neither do I," he replied. "Let's go home, shower, sleep for three days, eat our weight in take out. Any order you want."

He tried to pull her into his arms, but her resistance made him hesitate. Taking a step back, Jake rubbed his jaw. "Dana, I don't know the right way through this, but I know it'll be a helluva lot easier if we try to figure it out together."

"I can't," she whispered. "This is killing me."

"Do you think this doesn't kill me, too?" he asked, his voice cracking with emotion. "I loved Claire. I covered for her. I believed her. She betrayed me, too."

"I know," Dana sobbed. "But when I look at you ... I see her. And I just can't right now."

She turned to walk away but Jake reached for her, grabbing her hand. "Dana, I know you think you need to do this alone, but trust me, I've been there. It doesn't make it any easier."

Dana swallowed her tears. "You're probably right. But I need to try." Then she turned her back and walked away.

DANA WENT BACK to her home alone. The crime scene tape greeted her, but mercifully all the agents had left. The inside was eerily quiet, so she turned on music while she showered. Anything to drown the silence.

Finally clean, she went to the kitchen and made herself a cup of tea before forcing herself to sit down and face the letter she hadn't been able to finish reading at Dvita's.

SHE'S LIKE US MAX, she'll welcome it. She craves the darkness like we do. She's taught me everything I know. Death is the most beautiful gift I can give Dana. Then she'll be with us forever. Just stick with the plan. You take out Dvita. I wish I could be with you to see his eyes when the light fades. I wish I could be the one to give him what he deserves. But we all have our part to play. I'll take care of Dana. I'm saving her for last.

DANA CLOSED HER EYES, forcing back the sting of tears.

How had Claire gotten it so wrong? If she thought Dana welcomed death, her protégé hadn't known her at all.

Dana had spent her life surrounded by darkness, that much was true. But it hadn't been by choice. The manner in which she'd lost her parents had catapulted her into that world. Once there she found purpose in shedding light on the misunderstood. Bringing understanding to the many misjudged and condemned occult rituals.

She thought Claire wanted that, too. But perhaps having been touched by too much death, Claire had been dragged too far into the darkness to cling to the light. Whether she was a victim of circumstance or fate, it was clear, the girl Dana had once considered family was gone.

I was so wrong.

Dana's stomach twisted against the bitter taste of regret and betrayal.

The best way out is always through. Dana didn't know why the Robert Frost quote came to her now, but she couldn't help thinking how misleading it was.

She'd studied Frost's theory on human suffering extensively. His words on finding light among the darkness had always been a source of encouragement. An anthem of resilience in the face of adversity. But now they only made her want to scream.

Light was no match for the darkness she'd seen. And what was the point of being resilient? Death and darkness would always win.

Another of Frost's quotes floated to the forefront of her mind. *In three words I can sum up everything I've learned about life: it goes on.*

Dana fell to her knees, wishing she could defy those three horrid little words. Because right now, her world had stopped spinning. She'd done her best to be strong, to face her fears, to pursue the truth above all else. But this time, the truth hadn't set her free. It broke her heart.

123

JAKE SAT IN HIS SUV WATCHING THE QUIET STREET. DESPITE THE police tape still clinging to her front porch, things had returned to normal in Dana's neighborhood.

He'd been parked outside since she got home. He could respect that she needed time to process everything. *Hell, who wouldn't?* But as for being alone, he disagreed. If she needed to keep him at arm's length for now, he could deal with that, but it didn't mean he'd stop looking out for her.

Sipping his coffee, Jake rolled his window down drinking in the cool night air. He could hear the faint sound of jazz coming from Dana's place. Duke Ellington from the sound of it. Gazing at Dana's he couldn't help noticing every light that blazed brightly back at him.

Loud music, bright lights ... she was trying to drown out the terrifying silence that came after tragedy. Danger waited in that silence, ready to pounce and drag victims under the weight of 'what ifs' and 'should haves.' Jake knew it all too well.

He also knew the instinct to face the silence alone was a foolish one.

So, whether Dana liked it or not, he would be out here, keeping watch over her until the lights went out.

Though it wasn't his only reason for being there. He logged onto his laptop, pulling up the video footage he'd asked Richter for the moment he'd seen the photo of the scythe stashed in Dana's attic.

Something had been nagging him since he saw it. He knew how Claire had gotten in and out now, but he wanted to see the footage to confirm another theory.

Jake opened the files downloaded from the doorbell cam. It came from a house across the street from Dana's. The one he was parked in front of now. Thanks to the wide manicured median of hedges and crepe myrtles that divided the street, the camera angle perfectly captured the entire front of Dana's home, including the roofline. It's why Richter's team had requested it when they found the scythe.

The inexpensive doorbell cams were designed to catch package pirates, but Jake had seen them aid in many an investigation. Including this one.

Jake queued up the video with the date Claire had snuck out to meet Max. The news vans and reporters milled outside on the street, partially blocking the view of Dana's front porch, but the roof was fully visible. Focusing on the dormer windows, he watched intently until finally, he saw a pale face peeking out. Claire's face.

A moment later, dressed in black, she opened the window, slipped out and disappeared beyond the roofline where she could've easily climbed down into the backyard thanks to the gentle slope of the Craftsman-style roof.

Now that he knew what to look for, Jake closed out the video and opened a new one with an earlier date. The date this all started.

Holding his breath, he watched a dark figure walk up the steps to Dana's front door and let themselves in with a key. Jake fast forwarded until he appeared on the tape, smashing out the sidelight to enter Dana's burglarized home, weapon drawn.

His eyes flicked to the dormer windows again, praying he was wrong. But sure enough, the same slight figure slipped out the window and along the roofline before disappearing from view. Just as Claire had done in the video before.

It had been her all along.

She'd been the one who broke into Dana's home. She stashed the

C. J. CROSS

scythe in the attic, then changed clothes and wandered Dana's neighborhood until the cops picked her up and delivered her right to Dana's doorstep, none of them the wiser.

Jake swore. Hating that he hadn't seen it sooner.

Claire had been deceiving them all along.

Somehow the knowledge of that betrayal cut him deeper than everything else she'd done.

He didn't know what to believe—had Claire been brainwashed, possessed, or just plain deranged? None of those scenarios made him feel any better. No explanation would.

It would be easier to blame a supernatural source of evil for the Reaper murders and Claire's part in them. But Jake had seen too many times the wickedness mere mortals were capable of.

He would have to tell Dana about this. But not tonight. Maybe not even the next. As Jake watched her lights flick out, he told himself she would be okay. She was the strongest person he'd ever met. She'd get through this. He'd be there to make sure of it.

Starting the engine, he pulled away from Dana's house, driving toward his own, heart heavy with the truth.

124

Shirtless, Jake answered his door, gun in hand. At 3AM, he didn't know who he'd been expecting when his doorbell rang, but it wasn't Dana Gray, duffle bag in hand, tears in her eyes. He took one look at her and pulled her inside.

"I'm sorry I woke you," she sobbed into his chest.

"You didn't."

"You were right. I don't want to be alone."

Jake wrapped his arms tightly around her. "Tell me what you want."

"I want to forget." She looked up at him with those pleading brown eyes. "Can you make me forget?"

Words were no longer necessary. Jake picked her up and carried her to his bedroom.

In the new morning light Jake stretched his taut muscles like a cat in a pool of sunshine. A smug smile carved his lips even in sleep as the memories from his night with Dana began to resurface in the stolen moments between dreams and waking. Each perfect memory knitting itself to the next to block out the pain. Against all odds, they had found salvation in each other; love amongst tragedy. Life amongst death.

Jake rolled over in bed, reaching out for Dana already craving more. When his hand met cold sheets, he awoke. Even before he was fully alert, he knew the truth. His feet had yet to touch the floor, and already he knew there would be no coffee brewing in the kitchen. No duffle bag in the living room. No Dana.

She was gone.

Grabbing only his phone and gun, he went looking anyway.

125

THE LIGHTS OF THE CITY HAD LONG FADED IN HER REARVIEW, BUT DANA could still feel the tether pulling her back no matter how many miles she put between her and D.C.

After six missed calls and a slew of text messages, Dana finally answered Jake's call. It was the last message that had pierced her heart. Four little words she couldn't ignore.

Jake: Tell me you're ok.

Dana answered the next call. "I'm okay, Jake."

"Where are you?"

"I'm sorry. I-I just needed to get out of the city."

"Don't apologize. Just tell me where you are, and I'll come."

"I don't want you to."

"Dana ..."

"No, I mean it. I need time or space to figure this out."

"I get that, but I thought we decided we'd figure it out together."

She was silent for so long Jake thought he lost her.

"Dana?"

"I'm here."

"Gray, talk to me."

"I can't trust myself."

"I know it sucks that you were right about Dvita. You were right about Claire. But you were right about us, too, Dana. That should count for something."

The agony in Jake's voice was killing her, but she pushed through her strangling emotions because he deserved the truth. "Jake, you're one of the things I need to figure out. And I can't do it in D.C. I see her everywhere. On the news, in my house, in you. I just need a change of scenery for now."

"Okay. I get that. Just please tell me where you are."

"Halfway to New Orleans." His silence made her keep talking. "I have an eight week grant I've been putting off. I accepted it last night."

Jake's silence told her he was digesting the painful notion that she'd known she was leaving before spending the night with him.

"I just ... I think burying myself in work is the best thing I can do right now," she said. "And I think you should go to Paris."

"How did you know about Paris?" Jake asked.

"You never erased your search history on my laptop."

"I wanted to tell you ..."

"I know. Now you have the time to pursue it. Your family needs you to."

"I thought I made that clear, Dana. *You're* my family."

Tears blurred her vision as she drove, and she quickly wiped them away. "I wish I could believe that."

"It's true."

"Maybe it is. But maybe that's not enough. Please don't come here."

Then she hung up.

EPILOGUE

THE SOUND OF THE TAPE RECORDER MADE CLAIRE GRIN.

"I remember you," she said fondly to the device. It was how it all started. A simple recording of a hypnotherapy session.

"Please state your name for the record," her court appointed attorney said without meeting her eyes.

This was the second time Claire sat across from the woman. The first time Claire had been in a hospital. She hadn't been able to speak yet thanks to all the drugs they'd pumped her full of to stave off the pain.

Now she wasn't so lucky. Hands restrained to her sides in what could only be described as a strait jacket, she was painkiller free and confined to her wheelchair.

A bit overkill since she wasn't exactly a flight risk.

Several surgeries had saved her life, but not her legs. She stared at the bandaged stumps where her knees had once been. She was losing the battle with the phantom pains the doctors told her didn't warrant medication.

She surveyed her surroundings. This was her first visit to one of the private rooms at the pretrial detention center reserved for attorney-client meetings.

The fluorescent lights buzzed overhead, doing nothing for the attorney's pasty complexion. Claire knew hers didn't look much better. Her pallor was as gray as the bare concrete floors and cinderblock walls in the windowless room.

"Please state your name," her attorney repeated.

"Claire Townsend."

"Can you tell me about your involvement in the Reaper killings?"

Claire cocked her head to the side, a feline grin splitting her face. "Are you sure you want to know?"

"Six people died," the attorney said. "Max Durnin, Meredith Kincaid, Kylie Marx, Cash Holloway, Congressman Norton Hayes, and Dr. Roman Dvita. Two more were injured. Officers, Hartwell, and Lennox."

"Yes," Claire said dryly. "Is there a question?"

"My question is, what can you tell me about these murders?"

"I can tell you this story would've ended differently if seven people died."

"How so?"

Claire smirked. "It's a long story."

"Then you better start from the beginning."

"Are you sure you want to hear it?"

"Miss Townsend, my job is to establish if you're mentally fit to stand trial. So yes, I'm here to listen to whatever you think the truth is."

A giggle escaped Claire as she leaned closer to her attorney. "Do you want to know a secret?"

"Why not," the woman said, folding her hands atop the case folder on the scarred Formica table.

"I knew it would end this way."

"Because that's how Dr. Dvita planned it?"

"Dvita!" A wry laugh escaped Claire. "He had no clue."

"He was the brainchild of this Seven Sleepers suicide pact, was he not?"

Claire shrugged. "Was he?"

"You tell me? The general consensus is that he hypnotized you and the others to commit murder. Were you under his spell?"

"I don't know. You have all the facts in front of you. What do you think?"

"My opinions are irrelevant. I'm here to find out what you think, Miss Townsend."

"The truth?" Claire purred.

"Preferably."

Claire sucked her teeth. "I don't know if you can handle it."

"Try me," the woman said, her tone beyond bored.

It tickled Claire to think the woman across from her thought she understood. She hadn't a clue. None of them did. But she would. They all would.

"Do you trust me?" Claire asked.

The woman huffed her annoyance.

"That's a no." Claire smirked. "Good. Smart. But I don't need your trust."

"You're the one who needs to earn trust here, Miss Townsend. That starts by you telling the truth."

"Truth is subjective," Claire replied. "I'd rather tell you a story."

"I'm listening."

"It starts with my sister." Claire could see the instant confusion as her attorney began flipping through the file in front of her. "Oh, you won't find her there. No one knows about her. My parents made sure of that. They gave her up. Let a new family adopt her. They wanted us to forget. But I never did."

The woman stopped flipping pages and looked at Claire. "Who is your sister?"

"Her name was Annabelle."

The woman blanched.

"She fell in love with the wrong man. But we made a plan to pay him back for all the wrong he'd done, me and Annabelle." Claire closed her eyes wistfully for a moment. When she opened them, she could see the fear in her attorney's eyes.

"Are you talking about Annabelle Sorkin?"

Claire nodded. "Do you want to meet her?"

"Your sister?" the woman asked cautiously.

Claire nodded. "She's here right now. She can tell you everything we planned."

"How?"

"It's simple. She's waiting just on the other side. All you have to do is let her in. Count with me."

Claire met the woman's gaze and began counting down, her voice a whisper, "Ten."

"Nine."

"Eight."

"Seven."

ALSO BY C. J. CROSS

DANA GRAY MYSTERIES

Girl Left Behind

Girl on the Hill

Girl in the Grave

Girl Betrayed (Coming soon!)

Stay up to date with C.J. Cross's new releases and download her **free** Dana Gray Prequel, *Girl Awakened* by heading to the link:

ALSO BY WITHOUT WARRANT

More Thriller Series from Without Warrant Authors:

Dana Gray Mysteries by C.J. Cross

Girl Left Behind

Girl on the Hill

Girl in the Grave

Girl Betrayed (Coming Soon!)

The Kenzie Gilmore Series by Biba Pearce

Afterburn

Dead Heat

Heatwave

Burnout

Deep Heat

Fever Pitch

Storm Surge

Night Watch (Coming Soon!)

Willow Grace FBI Thrillers

by Without Warrant and C. C. West

Shadow of Grace

Condition of Grace

Hunt for Grace

Time for Grace

Piece of Grace (Coming Soon!)

Gia Santella Crime Thriller Series

by Kristi Belcamino

Vendetta

Vigilante

Vengeance

Black Widow

Day of the Dead

Border Line

Night Fall

Stone Cold

Cold as Death

Cold Blooded

Dark Shadows

Dark Vengeance

Dark Justice

Deadly Justice

Deadly Lies

Vigilante Crime Series by Kristi Belcamino

Blood & Roses

Blood & Fire

Blood & Bone

Blood & Tears

Queen of Spades Thrillers by Kristi Belcamino

Queen of Spades

The One-Eyed Jack

The Suicide King

The Ace of Clubs

The Joker

The Wild Card

High Stakes

Poker Face

Join Without Warrant's private reader group on Facebook!

ABOUT THE AUTHOR

CJ Cross grew up in a snowy little Northeast town, cutting her teeth on true crime novels to stave her love of all things mysterious. The writing bug bit her early and she found her way into the publishing world, writing 50+ books under various top secret pen names over the years.

Now relocated to a place where she can safely trade in her snowshoes for flip flops, she's found a reason to dust off her old Criminal Justice degree and she's turned an old passion into a new flame, writing compelling thrillers novels.

When she's not writing you can usually find her drinking bourbon with fellow authors or spoiling her rescue pup.

Sign up for C.J.'s newsletter and download her free **Dana Gray** Prequel, *Girl Awakened*:

Made in the USA
Middletown, DE
24 June 2024

56276898R00229